D0981956

THE MAJORITY RULES

THE MAJORITY RULES

THE HONORABLE
EUGENE SULLIVAN

A TOM DOHERTY ASSOCIATES BOOK
New York

This is a work of fiction. All the characters and events portrayed in this novel are either fictitious or are used fictitiously.

THE MAJORITY RULES

This book is printed on acid-free paper.

A Forge Book
Published by Tom Doherty Associates, LLC
175 Fifth Avenue
New York, NY 10010

www.tor.com

Forge® is a registered trademark of Tom Doherty Associates, LLC.

ISBN 0-765-31141-0
EAN 978-0765-31141-2

First Edition: January 2005

Printed in the United States of America

0 9 8 7 6 5 4 3 2 1

FOR LIS—FOREVER

ACKNOWLEDGMENTS

Publishing a novel is like climbing three world-class mountains. Few can do it without help.

The first mountain was writing the novel. Historian, author, and Vietnam brother, Dr. Tom Carhart, helped me get started. Able advice on the criminal process and technical devices came from Dave Binney, a former Deputy Director of the FBI. David Groff gave the book structure when he edited the novel midcourse. Finally, my editor at Forge, Brian Thomsen, with his comments and vision, put the novel over the top. Thank you Tom, Dave, David, and Brian.

The second mountain was finding an excellent agent who believed in the book and in me. Frank Weimann of the Literary Group, thank you, my friend.

The third mountain was finding a publisher. Here it was luck that my manuscript landed on the desk of Forge's creative and forward-thinking editor Brian Thomsen. Thanks again, Brian, for your thoughtful advice.

To the other people I worked with at Forge: Natasha Panza, Nicole Kalian, and of course, the boss—Tom Doherty, sincere thanks for your professionalism.

Through the whole journey was my family. Lis my wife, Kim and Gene, my children. I never would have made the climbs without you.

"Gloucester, 'tis true that we are in great danger.
The greater therefore should our courage be."

Shakespeare, *Henry V,* part IV.

PROLOGUE

ON THE LAST DAY OF HIS LIFE, FEDERAL JUDGE MAX ROGERS went to a party. The party was an evening reception at one of the three United States Senate office buildings in Washington, D.C.

Few people knew it, but the most exclusive "party place" in Washington was the House and Senate office complex on Capitol Hill. At the end of the day when Congress adjourned during a session, the parties and receptions in this set of buildings were just starting. On any given night during the working week, at least a half-dozen receptions or buffet dinners were held by corporations, associations, or special-interest groups inside the committee rooms or meeting rooms within this huge office complex of six buildings connected by subterranean pedestrian tunnels. Lobbyists, lawyers, and high-ranking members of all three branches of the federal government attended these parties.

These Senate and House parties fuel many stories, including the "urban legend" of a bachelor Senate staffer who allegedly never paid for an evening meal on a working day for over three months running. At the close of business each day, the staffer would just check the sheet of events sponsored by special-interest groups or corporations, and then zero in on a reception or party. No one would ever check a senior staffer of an important senator for an invitation. Whatever group hosting the event was more than happy to give him a name tag and let him graze on the usually excellent buffet supplied by one of the best and most expensive caterers in town, the U.S. Congressional Catering Service.

Tonight, just as Congress had returned from its Labor Day break, there was a big reception in the historic Senate Caucus Room, high-ceilinged and hung with massive crystal chandeliers, adorned with gold moldings and many large mirrors on the walls which visually aggrandized its already massive size. The most famous room in the Russell Senate Office Building, it still echoed with Senator Sam Ervin preaching the Constitution during the Watergate hearings of the early seventies, Senator Joe McCarthy ranting against Communists in the Pentagon during the Army Hearings of the 1950s, and Senator Harry Truman maligning the waste of government contractors during the early days of World War II.

A group of gun-control organizations was sponsoring tonight's affair, their key objective this year the congressional passage of an omnibus crime bill that would require, among other things, mandatory trigger locks on all handguns sold in this country. The reception was for the senators and the staff of the Senate Judiciary Committee, but other people of influence in Washington had been invited. Lavish spreads of regional foods subtly emphasized to the senators that gun control was a nationwide movement. The Midwestern delegations had ordered huge barbecue spreads spilling off red-and-white checkered tablecloths in one corner of the Caucus Room. In a second corner sat a New England raw bar of oysters, shrimp, and lobster salad. The West Coast table overflowed with California wine and cheese and Columbia River salmon, while the aroma from the New Orleans Cajun food representing the South wafted over the entire room. All food stations included fully stocked bars.

By six o'clock, the room was crowded and abuzz with cocktail chatter and last-minute lobbying ploys. Laughter, sprinkled with suppressed shouts, flowed freely and raised the decibel level of the Caucus Room. The room was getting warmer as more people crowded in.

Judge Maxwell Rogers, looking distinguished in a navy pin-striped suit, dark regimental-striped silk tie, heavily starched white shirt, and gold cuff links, broke off from one group of attendees and checked his watch. He looked absentmindedly around, then headed for the nearest bar, his empty wineglass in hand. He was a slender, handsome man of medium height. His neatly trimmed mustache and his carefully combed hair were black, both obviously dyed, and his tanned face and etched features almost made him look like a movie star from some earlier era. Any stranger would have guessed him to be quite a bit younger than sixty-two. His penetrating blue eyes exuded intelligence and, with his horn-rimmed glasses balanced on the bridge of his nose, he had the cerebral air of an Oxford don.

As he waited at the bar, someone tapped him on the shoulder. Startled, he turned and confronted a young man whose eyes were a startling, gentle green.

"Pardon me, Senator Dalton, but I have a question for you."

Rogers felt himself blushing at this unexpected compliment. Calvert Dalton was not only known to be an attractive man, but usually he was the only senator who made the Best Dressed lists in magazines. It pleased Rogers to be mistaken for Senator Dalton. The young man who asked the question was in his late twenties, well dressed.

"No, no, I'm not Senator Dalton . . ."

Rogers was struck with the young man's looks.

"Oh, I'm sorry." The green-eyed man grinned shyly. "You look a lot like him, you know."

The older man smiled, nodded, and turned back to the bar. The drink line was stopped dead. Waiting in line could be exasperating, so he turned back to face the younger man. "How about you? Are you part of this gun-control event?"

"Yes, actually I'm a research assistant at the Washington office of Concerned Citizens for Handgun Control," the young man rattled off. "Our group, CCHC, is one of the sponsors of this reception. My name is Ben. What's yours, if it's not Calvert Dalton?" He smiled.

Ben extended his arm, and the two shook hands. "I'm Max," Rogers answered. "So what does a research assistant do?"

Ben smiled again, then shrugged. "Well, I'd like to say I write high-level position papers that are immediately published in national magazines. But really, I just do Internet research for the senior people in our organization and do gofer jobs like make coffee if I'm the first one in, which I am supposed to be."

Maxwell smiled at Ben's candor. The two men quickly fell into typical Washington talk—the long hours, the D.C. work ethic, Ben's desire to go to law school. When they both had their drinks, they moved over to sit at a small table that magically opened up next to the bar.

"Ben, before you get so committed to law school, be sure you really want to be a lawyer. It may not be the right thing for you. I mean, there are plenty of other options besides law out there."

"Well, I know that, but just being in Washington, it seems that everyone with any kind of power, why, they're all lawyers . . ."

Maxwell Rogers could only smile at Ben's boyish naiveté. "I know, I know, but good law schools are hard to get into and the work is tough. And to boot, most lawyers work truly ungodly hours on boring, tedious problems of other people."

Ben seemed a little hurt. "Well, I know you don't know much about me, but I'm smart enough to get in and handle a good law school. And I'm not afraid of hard work to get somewhere."

Maxwell quickly realized that he had hit a tender spot. "No, no I wasn't thinking of you or your ability. You obviously are a smart, articulate young man with a bright future in any field you choose. What I meant was that the law can be a hard, lonely profession. I was thinking about your long-range plans. Wife and kids, living in the suburbs? That sort of thing."

Ben laughed easily, and Maxwell felt oddly relieved. "Oh, I see, I see where you are going: What do I want in life outside of work? Well, frankly I don't think I'll ever get married! At least not unless I have a true change of heart."

Something leaped in Maxwell's chest. "What do you mean, Ben? Don't you have a girlfriend?"

Ben lowered his head, breaking eye contact, and looked at the floor, speaking softly. "No, no girlfriend. I do have friends who are women. I never have been involved in that way. I mean . . ." Then Ben looked straight in Maxwell's eyes and smiled sweetly. Maxwell looked confused. Ben leaned forward and whispered in his ear, "Let's go have a drink at the Adonis Club."

Maxwell pulled back in surprise and studied the younger man. Ben had just given him the answer to his question with a most unusual and stunning invitation. "I'm not sure about that place, Ben. I've heard of it, but I've never been there."

"It's a cool place to get a drink. We should cut out of this place and go there. This place is too crowded." Ben grinned, his eyes hotter and more intense now. "Besides I think we have a lot to discuss. But first," Ben said teasingly, "why don't you tell me your full name, or is it really Senator Dalton?"

Judge Maxwell Rogers heard a distant warning deep in his head as he lied, "I'm Maxwell Newman. I'm a lawyer with a small D.C. firm."

The practiced lie he told easily. Whenever he wanted to protect his privacy, Rogers always kept his first name, but used the name Newman as an inside joke he enjoyed: He felt like a new man when he assumed an anonymous identity for his private life.

Maxwell knew Ben was suggesting a dangerous adventure. The judge had heard of the widely renowned Adonis Club, a favored hangout on Capitol Hill for gay men out for a little private fun. It was located inside a cavernous building in a neighborhood of warehouses, rundown public housing, and vacant lots off South Capitol Street. You could get decent food and drink there twenty-four hours a day, and male strippers performed wearing nothing but socks. Ben had only suggested having a drink at the bar, but Maxwell also knew the real reason the club was popular was that it offered a steam room and a sauna as well as private dressing rooms you could rent by the hour. He also remembered someone saying that the rooms had small beds in them. Maxwell's mind raced at that thought. Maybe he would end up taking a steam with Ben. Sharing one of those small dressing rooms with this beautiful stranger was a delicious notion.

No, it was dangerous.

He recalled a newspaper article, just a few years ago, about a few off-duty D.C. police officers who would stake out the Adonis Club parking lot. These rogue cops would write down the license numbers of men using the club, then get computer access to the Division of Motor Vehicle records to learn the identities, addresses, and marital status of the club patrons. If they were married, the cops would phone them a few days later to extort money from them. In a town like Washington where personal morality was honored in the breach, most wives and employers would be interested in knowing about visits to the Adonis Club. Although he was no longer married, Maxwell dreaded like death the possibility of scandal.

"Come on, Maxwell, let me buy you a *real* drink, not this watered-down government shit. Adonis is cool, and we'll have a great time. Let's go."

Maxwell looked at Ben and saw he was smiling at him, jumpy and urgent as a puppy. He didn't know Ben, but already the roar of the room had vanished and he was caught in the warm pull of the young man's charm. Life is short and lonely, and sometimes it's worth taking a chance. Ben was handsome, well dressed, very pleasant—and young. And it had been so long now. Besides, being with Ben could be a welcome relief from the terrible stress he just had been through, making a tough decision last week to report a very strange pattern of cases at his court. For Maxwell, that day last week had been an unusually anxious day of indecision for him, a judge known for being decisive. Reporting suspected wrongdoing by a member of the bar of his court—a well-known attorney—was very tough for him.

He usually tried to close his eyes to unpleasant things. Life for Maxwell was hard enough dealing with his own inner demons.

Dismissing the disturbing thoughts of last week, Maxwell smiled and nodded to Ben. "Well, why not? One should seize the moment in life to have a little fun. But Ben, let's not drive there. Bad neighborhood. Better to take a cab, okay?"

"Sure. The club is only ten minutes away. Come on, we can catch a cab right outside."

Ben and Maxwell threaded their way among the sweaty lawmakers and the lobbyists seeking so urgently to seduce them. Soon they were out of the hot, crowded Senate Caucus Room and into the cool, quiet white marble foyer of the Russell Senate Office Building, then down the steps to Constitution Avenue. Getting a cab in the late rush-hour flow of traffic would be easy. Across the street when they got into the taxi, the stately, brightly lit dome of the Capitol stood serenely overlooking Washington.

On the following evening, a warm Thursday in September, Federal Judge Maxwell P. Rogers was just the slightest bit anxious as he edged ahead through the remnants of rush-hour traffic on the Fourteenth Street Bridge. Off to his right was the Jefferson Memorial, beyond it the Potomac River. He was invisible to other drivers behind the tinted windows of his black Lexus 400 sedan. *Damn D.C. traffic, almost as bad as New York,* he thought. To combat his building impatience, he slipped one of his favorite CDs into the player. Instantly, the twelve speakers of the Bose sound system filled the tan leather interior with the soft strains of Puccini's *Turandot.* How appropriate, he thought, to be listening to the only opera Puccini had written that revolved around a lover withholding his identity from his mate.

He and Ben had had an outrageously wild time last night at the Adonis Club. They had drinks at the main club bar, but later drifted off to the more private sections of the club and wound up naked in a steam bath together. Ben's hard body was beautiful, his touch reassuringly gentle. At Ben's suggestion, they had agreed to meet in a small public park in Virginia just across the Fourteenth Street Bridge near the huge north parking lot of the Pentagon. The LBJ Park was, Ben assured him, a well-known safe place where gay couples in the D.C. area often met.

In the park there were small cleared areas within the dense vegetation—little "nests" in the thick bushes under overhanging tree branches. Cradled in the soft leaves in these nests, a couple was able to find temporary privacy in a public area. Maxwell had worried aloud that they would be sitting ducks for a morals arrest by the U.S. Park police, which had jurisdiction of the park. However,

Ben reassured him, saying that, of course, the police knew what was happening, but in the relaxed atmosphere of the new twenty-first century, the love nests in LBJ Park and their transitory occupants were quietly tolerated. Just so they didn't, as Lady Asquith had so famously said in Victorian England, "do anything in the streets that might frighten the horses."

Maxwell was both frightened and excited about the possibility of making love in the open air. Sexual desire had always pained him. His one marriage had ended childless after only three years of little more than misery. Like so many men, he had married the wrong person. In his last year at Northwestern Law and with only a few unsatisfactory sexual experiences in college, he was extremely naive when he met Peggy, a smart and pretty blond Northwestern undergrad. It had not taken Peggy long to realize that Rogers was a very good catch. He was third in his class, extremely bright, with plenty of family money, and he already had a job offer from the top law firm in Chicago. Before he knew it, her period was late and then they were married—before graduation. That late period had been a false alarm, maybe a complete pretense. Their marriage soon soured. He realized that his wife didn't love him and wanted no employment except that of being a full-time wealthy lawyer's wife.

Perhaps he had married not just the wrong person, but the wrong gender. Maxwell never really had much of a passionate sex life with his wife. Sex with Peggy became no more than a sweaty exercise. Soon he just stopped trying and his wife became a little more than a roommate—a mean, nasty, increasingly demanding roommate. Finally he had moved out. When he got the divorce papers in the mail, he felt more relief than anything else. She had cost him a certain amount each month for several years until she remarried, but he was earning plenty at the firm and, moreover, had a very nice annual income from a generous family trust.

After the divorce, he buried himself in work at the law firm work and closed off all social life. His first seven years as an associate in the firm had been a blur, and when he became a partner, he labored even harder, working sixty, seventy hours each week, almost every Saturday, and many Sundays. Outside of the office, he had no life.

But then on a Caribbean vacation he had taken on a whim to escape another cold Chicago February, late one night in a little bar in Martinique, he had met a beautiful, truly beautiful prostitute, brown-skinned with flashing eyes and teeth and witty and wise, very experienced no doubt from plying the tourist trade. Now at last he knew sex could be wonderful, glorious, exciting with the right person as a partner. What a shame it had taken him so long to realize that he could find true fulfillment only with a man.

He was sixty-two now, and over thirty years of bachelor life working hard, first for his Chicago law firm, and now in the federal government, he had been lonely but furiously protective of his private life. There had been openly gay lawyers at his firm, but he kept his secret from them; it seemed unprofessional for a partner to do otherwise.

On anonymous trips to Provincetown or San Francisco, he had paid for nights with strangers—discreet, handsome, well-paid young men. Since he had been in Washington in government, he had been even more private and secretive. A double life was the price he would pay for the balance he needed . . . and now especially after the mental anguish of reporting the strange pattern he had seen in some cases at his court, he wanted the respite from stress a young man like Ben could provide.

After crossing the Fourteenth Street Bridge, he turned right at the third exit, which led to the Pentagon's North Parking area and the LBJ Park. He slowed his car and avoided looking at the Pentagon looming large on his left, separated from him by an enormous, almost empty parking lot. Ahead, he saw the short-term parking area for the LBJ Park on his right, less than half full now, holding perhaps ten or twelve cars. He passed most of them, and nosed into an open space at the end of the lot, near a Park Service tool shed with a white van parked in front of it. Fifty feet and several cars farther down toward the middle of the lot was Ben, wearing a black T-shirt, blue jeans, and a New York Yankees baseball cap. He was leaning against his beat-up red Toyota, with what looked like a gym workout bag at his feet.

Maxwell uneasily glanced at his watch. It was just after seven. The September sun had not yet set, but it painted the leaves of the tree branches off to his right in beautiful shifting shades of orange. As Maxwell turned off the ignition, Ben stood up and took a few steps toward him. He looked so hard and lean. Given the nature and the jeopardy associated with the homosexual liaison in which he was about to engage, Maxwell was nervous, almost paranoid about being compromised and having his identity revealed in some sort of police gay bust. He certainly didn't want to take any chances today, so he pulled his wallet, his money clip, and his leather judicial-identification case out of his pockets and tucked them under the front seat. Now he had no ID and his pockets were empty except for two foil-encased condoms.

As he stepped out of the car, he slipped his keys into a magnetic case and discreetly put the case under the left front fender. Then he stepped around the front of the car, smiling, and walked toward Ben. Their handshake was firm and warm. They walked down the sidewalk of the parking lot toward the bridge, which they would take over the waterway to enter LBJ Park.

"How are you, Ben?"

"I'm fine, Max, and I have some goodies for us to relax with."

"Oh?"

"I have a nice, chilled bottle of white Bordeaux wine, some pate, some fresh French bread, and a soft blanket. And I have another surprise for you, but that will come later." He smiled devilishly and Maxwell felt almost as young as Ben himself.

He started nervously checking the other cars in the small lot. They appeared to be empty. The only exception was a big white van back near his car. Leaning against the van at the front was a bulky white man with a shiny, shaved head, wearing the dark green uniform of a National Park Service employee. Maxwell couldn't help but notice a long white scar that ran from the corner of the man's right eye straight down his cheek to his jawline. Another uniformed man, a large black man with neat cornrows, was at the back of the van, pulling out a wheeled gardening cart of some sort. They didn't seem to notice Maxwell and Ben. The judge stopped checking around and turned his full attention to Ben.

"So what's this 'other' surprise?"

They had just started over the wooden pedestrian bridge, a long arch that spanned the channel of water perhaps a hundred feet wide.

"Well, I have some magazines and toys for you to see."

Maxwell inhaled deeply. "Really? Sounds exciting."

They started down a wide dirt path into the wooded area to the left. "Once we get past this first row of trees," Ben told him, "we'll go down this footpath near the edge of the water. You see up ahead, those thick, low-hanging branches, and the bushes? In there are the love nests." He scrambled ahead. "Right up here looks like a good one."

Maxwell glanced around nervously as Ben went ten or fifteen feet into the bushes and down toward the now-invisible water edge. There was not a sign of anyone else around and now Ben had disappeared. A moment later, Ben came out of the bushes, holding back a large branch with one arm and beckoning with the other. Past Ben, Maxwell could see a bed of brown leaves, and beyond that, through the dense bushes the reflection of the water. He shuffled down the steep slope, and as he got to Ben, he noticed Ben had taken off his baseball cap and hung it on the uphill side of the branch, so that anyone approaching would see it. Maxwell stopped again, and pointed at the cap.

"What's that for?"

"It's a signal so that anyone who comes along will know that this nest is occupied, and they won't disturb us. It's the custom here. Privacy is respected." He grinned, jumpy with excitement. "Relax, everything is cool."

Maxwell smiled and brushed past Ben. Then the branch was released, and they were gone from sight.

Ten minutes later, Maxwell was lying flat on his stomach on the blanket, naked. His hands were behind his back, tied together, as were his ankles. A ball gag in his mouth had kept him from crying out while Ben had taken him slowly but roughly from behind. Now, a sweaty Ben collapsed on Maxwell's back, then rolled off and whispered in his ear. "Okay, you fucking old queen, party's over. It's time for you to go."

Ben turned him over and pulled a length of rope from the backpack. Maxwell's eyebrows shot up in horror. He tried and failed to cry out.

A grim-faced Ben wrapped the rope around Maxwell's neck and pulled it tight. Maxwell's air disappeared.

"Sorry, Maxwell, this is just business."

Ben put his knee firmly in the middle of Maxwell's chest for leverage and pinned his body as he tightened the rope. Maxwell's eyes grew wider as he vainly struggled for air, his thoughts racing from fear to horror to regret, and the awful realization that he had been set up, and why.

Those were his last thoughts:—He had been betrayed.

. . .

A short time later, Ben came out of the vegetation, grabbed his baseball cap, and waved. Fifty feet up the footpath two gardeners were trimming the weeds at the edge of the path. Both stood up and looked around. There was no one else in sight. The man with the shaved head scrambled down the slope and brushed past Ben through the thick overhanging branches into the love nest. Ben walked up the slope to the path and faced the big man with the cornrows.

"You're supposed to have my money and my ticket, right?" Ben asked. "Oh yeah, I did it just like they said to," he quickly added as he saw the man's face tighten with displeasure.

"Did he touch the magazines?"

"Yeah, and he got all excited looking at the pictures. Then he let me tie him up, and I did him. Now, *where's my stuff?*"

Cornrows nodded and put his strong hand on Ben's shoulder to steady him. "Easy now. Let's slow down. Let me hear confirmation from my man."

Both of them turned and looked down the slope toward the love nest. Soon the shaved-headed man emerged, brushing through the branches and up the hill. "Is the job done?" Cornrows asked him.

"Bloody well done, it is. Give him the money."

Cornrows turned and walked to the garden cart, raised the lid, and reached in, pulling out an expensive black leather briefcase. He opened it, showing the contents to Ben.

"Okay, before I give you this briefcase, I want to confirm what's inside. Here is twenty thousand dollars in hundred dollar bills, a one-way ticket to San Francisco tomorrow, and a little reward the boss said to give you for a job well done."

Ben peered into the briefcase and broke into a huge smile as he fingered the plastic baggie with dark crystals inside. "Whoa, Mexican black tar, my favorite. I don't get this very often. Party time tonight." He frowned. "I'll have to do it all tonight. Can't take a chance on the airport security jokers and their drug dogs tomorrow. God damn! Thanks. Now, you guys are gonna clean up the mess down there, right?"

"We gotta do things in order. First, count the money."

Ben riffled through the bills, counting aloud through the ten packs of hundred-dollar bills, twenty in each. "Okay, I'm satisfied that I've got twenty thousand here. Now, you guys are going to clean up, right? No clues?"

"Don't worry, we're professionals. The old dude will fit nicely into the big cart. By the time you get on that plane tomorrow, this old boy will be inside the cart holding onto five hundred pounds of cement in two hundred feet of water out in the Chesapeake Bay."

Ben grinned again, bouncing on the balls of his feet. "Magnifico! Okay, if you can clean up without me, I'm out of here. I've got some bags to pack, and this fucking uptight town will never see my ass again. Adios!"

As Ben ran off, the two men, Cornrows and the Brit, went down to the body and made a final check of the scene . . . but they did not clean up the scene. Instead, they left the body and other evidence of Ben's presence in place, then climbed back up the trail until they reached a point from which they could see Ben's Toyota pull out of the parking lot across the short span of water. Once the young assassin was gone, they unhurriedly wheeled the cart over the bridge to the parking lot. Then, still wearing their gardening gloves, they approached Maxwell's car.

Cornrows got the key from beneath the front fender where he had seen Maxwell hide it, then opened the car. He checked around inside and quickly found under the front seat the dead man's wallet, the judge's ID credentials, and the money clip. He threw them in a paper bag, then relocked Maxwell's car and replaced the key in its hiding place.

Cornrows pushed the garden cart down to the National Park Service shed at the end of the parking lot. He quickly picked the lock, opened the shed door, pushed the cart and tools back into it, then closed, chained, and locked it. He climbed into the white van.

As the van left the parking lot, Cornrows couldn't keep from commenting to the Brit, who was driving, "You know, the U.S. government has got four heavy mowers in that shed, lots of other stuff—there's gotta be several thousand dollars' worth of equipment in there, and they secure all that shit with a two-dollar lock. The government is so fucking stupid."

As they crossed the Potomac on the Fourteenth Street Bridge, the Brit spoke. "Listen, Number Two, good job. You handled things spot-on with that little wanker."

The firm that employed these two men had a rule: No names should ever be exchanged by operatives on a mission. Each team member was to be called by a number. The senior member was named Number One.

Cornrows smiled. "Thanks. Things were going okay, but I realized I had to slow down that little motherfucker. He was way too hyper. He was burning to split and shoot up that heroin we gave him. Got to do things by proper procedure."

"Right, well, we're half finished," the Brit said. "It was a clean watchover. No witnesses, the event was sealed, and the site left proper. Now that the goods have been delivered, we just remain chilled and watch the endgame play out at the home site."

Cornrows nodded. "Roger that, brother. We are definitely in the final lap and headed for the barn." He glanced over at his partner. This man, the Brit, was an expert and efficient driver, changing lanes smoothly and quickly in the busy D.C. traffic. He was grasping the steering wheel in the standard military-taught antiterrorist driving position, palms inward, gripping the wheel at four and eight o'clock.

This guy's background was obviously military, probably either British Special Air Service or Royal Marines. Cornrows had spent some time at Hereford, the home of the SAS, on a joint exercise when he was with the U.S. Delta Force, and he held SAS members in high regard—they were cool under pressure, tough, and very, very good in wet operations. The Brit started rolling up his sleeves. Cornrows spotted a small black tattoo on his inner right forearm, an upward-pointing sword with wings extending to either side from the blade just below the hilt, a written scroll etched farther down the blade. Cornrows recognized it as the badge of the widely renowned British Special Air Service Regiment—the SAS. His guess on the military background had been right.

"'Who dares wins.' I guess you Hereford boys don't worry about showing your colors, do you?"

The Brit laughed. "You are wrong there, mate. We weren't allowed giveaway tattoos like this when I was on active service, especially not while I was under, in Ireland. No, I got this put on during a three-day drunk after I retired. Ten years ago now."

The two operatives had the military in common. They never exchanged names.

The van edged through the dying traffic of the downtown D.C. workday and turned onto Twentieth Street in the Adams Morgan residential area, then made a right onto Raymond Street; just blocks away from the usual evening traffic jam on Connecticut Avenue. Cornrows alighted at the corner and walked forward half a block, expertly surveying the area while the van followed slowly. Two orange traffic cones in the street, and two D.C. police emergency NO PARKING hoods placed over the two parking meters, had reserved them a large parking space immediately across from Ben's apartment. Cornrows picked up the cones and removed the parking meter hoods as the van pulled into the space. Then he opened the rear door and climbed in.

. . .

The Brit had already moved into the van's rear and was powering up the thermal-imaging device, mounted and stabilized on a tripod. The Brit directed its lens through a small opening in the one-way mirrored window on the left side of the van. Cornrows moved past him toward the front of the van, flipped some switches on a panel of the large radio receiver, and put on a pair of headphones. He was listening to audio bugs they had put into Ben's apartment earlier that day.

The Brit sat on a stool behind the infrared device and stared through it. It was a Palm Heat 380 model that someone had stolen from the FBI, and it worked like magic. Directed at one of Ben's curtained windows, the device clearly revealed Ben's thermal image to the Brit as Ben moved around in his tiny studio apartment. Meanwhile, Cornrows, listening to the audio surveillance devices, learned that Ben was on the phone to a friend; he was lying about his destination the next day, saying he was off to Miami for a few days. Ben made several more short calls, then sat down on a chair, opened the bag of heroin, and began to prepare to shoot up his unexpected bonus.

Cornrows heard Ben whistling as he injected his arm, then sat back and began to moan in ecstasy. But soon, the moans turned to groans, and Ben's entire body began to convulse. Within a few minutes, he was in full seizure as he slipped to the floor. Cornrows turned to the Brit. "Sounds like our boy couldn't handle one hundred percent pure shit. I get noises like he is in seizure now. What's it look like?"

"He's flopping like a mackerel on the floor, he is. Slowing down now. Easy . . . easy . . . there we are. Quiet now. Any noise?"

"Nope, looks like he's gone. Nothing on audio."

"Right. Saves us havin' to go in and help him take it, doesn't it? We might have left bruises on the fucker, and that would have defeated the purpose of this exercise. Well, he's saved us some work by whackin' himself. What do you say we give him a couple of minutes? We don't want to give the bugger false hopes of a rescue, now, do we?"

Cornrows laughed quietly. "No, that would be cruel. How about we both smoke a butt, then we go in?"

"Right, I could use a fag about now, and that should give him just enough time to completely check out."

As they slipped into the apartment, the table light revealed Ben flat on his back, motionless, the inside of his elbow still stabbed by the syringe, his mouth splayed open in ecstasy or pain. Both men wore surgical gloves. Cornrows quickly checked for Ben's pulse. His voice was a harsh whisper. "Nope. Okay, I put the wallet, money clip, and ID stuff over on the table here. Next, we get the bugs. And then we've got to find the cash, the plane ticket, and the briefcase. Where the fuck are they?"

"The briefcase is over here. The money is still in the briefcase with the ticket. I guess all he took out was the bloody heroin. Bloke knew what was important, didn't he?"

"Okay, Number One—you were the one who put the listening devices in, so you take them out. I'll do a sweep to double-check."

Soon the Brit was inside the bathroom, pulling the last bug off the top of the door frame. "Got it. Right on for final check: briefcase, money, ticket, two bugs, kitchen table setup. Check all. That's it, isn't it?"

"Roger that. Let's move, we're history."

A few blocks away, the van pulled over, and Cornrows stepped into a pay-phone booth and dialed 911. It rang only once before he heard a female voice. "What is your life-threatening emergency?"

Cornrows took a deep breath. "Listen, I was just shootin' up with a guy at 2012 Raymond Street in Adams Morgan, and he went down. I think he fucking OD'd. Before that, he was braggin' about killin' some old queen in a Virginia park by the Potomac somewhere." Cornrows was good at sounding scared.

"Sir, what is your name?"

Click.

Back in the van, Cornrows pulled out a cell phone, dialed a beeper number, and punched in 555.

A man with a mane of white hair felt a vibration on his hip, inclined the face of his beeper so he could see it, and read its message: "555." He smiled as he deleted the message. He then replaced the beeper on his belt and ordered another scotch neat at the Jockey Club bar.

Cornrows pulled into an Exxon station. While he filled the tank, the Brit walked over to the pay phone and used a phone card to call London. After two rings, a crisp female British voice answered. "Ram Security."

"This is the blue sales team. Both sales have been completed according to projection. No deviations from the sales plan. Local tax returns have been properly reported. That is all."

"Right. Report back to headquarters for usual sales debrief."

The white van had been gone for more than an hour when a police cruiser finally arrived at 2012 Raymond Street. The first patrolman on the scene found an open door and saw Ben's body on the floor. He checked to make sure he was dead, called the Violent Crimes Unit of the D.C. Metropolitan Police Department, and began to seal off the apartment with yellow tape as a crime scene. His partner began to canvass the other apartments in the building, looking for witnesses or someone who had heard any unusual noises. It was after midnight when two detectives from the Violent Crimes Unit arrived.

Like 85 percent of the population of the District of Columbia, both were African-Americans. The senior of the two was Detective Sergeant Turner. He had twenty-five years on the job. His younger partner, Detective Rashid, was a rookie in the VCU, only three years out of the D.C. Police Academy. As they entered the apartment, both snapped on latex surgical gloves. While the younger detective started to examine the body of the dead man, the detective sergeant carefully took out his reading glasses and put them on, then joined his partner.

The syringe still inserted in the dead man's arm immediately told them that he had probably overdosed. They bagged and tagged the syringe, then searched his pockets and found a wallet. The driver's license inside the wallet and a phone call tentatively identified the deceased as Benjamin Alfred Warren, a young man with arrest records in D.C. and Virginia.

Then, they began to look around the apartment. On the kitchen table, Sergeant Turner found another wallet—an expensive eelskin billfold—together with a money clip that clasped a wad of bills, and a black leather credential case, a gold eagle seal stamped on the outside. The senior detective ignored the wallet and the money clip and immediately picked up the credential case and flipped it open. His eyebrows shot up, then slowly came back down.

"Holy shit!"

"What is it?" asked the rookie detective.

"Damn! Look, this is the ID of a federal judge. And not just any judge. This belongs to Maxwell Rogers."

The senior detective gently laid the ID back on the table. He knew Judge Rogers. Years ago he had worked a case with him. Rogers had come to the U.S. Attorney's Office in D.C. from a rich Chicago law firm and was very tough on criminals. He also treated the police with respect. Turner liked him and wasn't alone in his view of Rogers. Lots of guys on the job respected him and were glad when he went to the bench. Rogers was a good "law and order" judge. "I'm worried now," Turner said softly to Rashid.

"Why? It's a judge's wallet and ID. Maybe this guy just mugged him. Evidence of a robbery."

"Negative. Remember the call to nine-one-one said that the piece of shit over there, before he OD'd, had just wasted someone in a park over in Virginia." Turner grimaced. "Seeing a judge's ID without a judge makes me real nervous. I'm gonna call the U.S. Marshal's Service to check on Judge Rogers."

The U.S. Marshal's Service was the law enforcement agency responsible for the protection and safety of all federal judges; they had the emergency telephone numbers and the manpower required to contact any federal judge immediately. Turner got through to D.C. Command Center of the U.S. Marshal's Service on his cell phone and told the duty marshal the circumstances. The marshal informed him they would try to contact Judge Rogers and report back to him.

The marshals went to work, but soon they told Turner that repeated phone calls and a physical visit to the judge's apartment in the Watergate Apartment complex failed to locate him. Meanwhile, the detective sergeant had called the U.S. Park police and the Arlington police. Turner relayed the information to them and asked for their assistance in searching for a body in all local Virginia parks along or near the Potomac River.

Early the next morning, Turner received a call from the U.S. Park police telling him that Judge Rogers's car had been found in a parking lot in a park near the Pentagon. The park police soon called back to tell him they had located a body in the nearby LBJ Park, under the low-hanging branches along the navigation channel off the Potomac River. A picture ID confirmed that the body was that of Judge Maxwell Rogers.

Because the victim was a federal judge, the U.S. Park police notified the FBI, which quickly established a high-priority investigation. As Turner arranged to meet with Special Agent Berger, the FBI's lead agent assigned the case, a FBI forensics team was called in to recover the body and conduct a crime-scene search. By late morning, bags of debris recovered as evidence from the nest in the park were being sifted and combed, and fingerprints were being taken off the bondage magazines found at the scene. Tests were also being run on the used condom found in the victim's rectum, as well as DNA tests on the semen it contained. The victim's clothing was sent off to the FBI lab for fabric analysis. The clothing of the OD on Raymond Street and items from his apartment were also sent to the FBI lab for trace element comparative purposes.

Turner and Rashid didn't get much sleep that night, and by noon, they were conferring with Dave Berger, the lead agent from the FBI. They all tentatively agreed that the chief judge at the U.S. Court of Appeals for the D.C. Circuit should be personally informed of the death of one of his judges. Since it had become a joint investigation, the FBI case agent—after checking with his supervisor—gave the green light to the three of them making the visit to the chief judge that afternoon. A call to the chief judge's chambers set up a one-thirty P.M. appointment for that day.

At the end of the preliminary criminal investigation, all evidence recovered at both crime scenes pointed to the conclusion that the death of Maxwell Rogers was a robbery-murder. Judge Rogers had been robbed and strangled in a park next to the Potomac River by

Benjamin Alfred Warren, a twice-convicted felon, now dead of an accidental overdose. Within twenty-four hours, the expedited lab and DNA results came back to confirm this theory. High officials in the D.C. Police, the FBI, the Department of Justice, and the White House were briefed. A small team of officials from the FBI, the U.S. Justice Department, and the D.C. Police made a discreet visit to the chief justice of the U.S. Supreme Court to tell him the results of the investigation. After a few days, it was determined that the D.C. Police would take the lead and issue a form P.D. 252, which would summarize the entire joint investigation and also officially close the case out as a solved crime.

When it was Senior Detective Turner's turn to sign the P.D. 252 as the primary D.C. investigator, he was a bit uneasy about one crucial detail—the purity of the heroin in Ben's body. The lab reports showed that it was almost 100 percent pure, and the detective had only seen heroin that pure on a few rare occasions, such as when the U.S. Customs at Dulles Airport caught mules from South America flying in uncut heroin concealed in plastic bags they had swallowed. Turner had never seen it uncut and pure like this on the street. He had checked with friends in the Dangerous Drug Section, and no one there could remember a recent possession bust that involved heroin this pure. He also checked with the D.C. Crime Reporting Unit that tracks all drug overdoses in D.C.-Baltimore area hospitals, and was told that there were no recent heroin overdoses that involved a purity anywhere near this. But the pressure was on to close this case ASAP, and his supervisor told him not to highlight any comments about the purity of the heroin in his section of the report—just sign the damn form 252 and close this politically sensitive case.

So the detective sergeant signed. Nevertheless he still wondered how a street punk like this guy Ben Warren could have scored on heroin that pure. It was a mystery. It just didn't make sense to him as a cop. Why wouldn't any dealer cut the stuff with baking soda and make more money? Besides, if horse that pure was on the street, why weren't there any more drug deaths turning up? Turner didn't like this at all.

CHAPTER 1

THE *WASHINGTON POST* THAT MORNING HAD A SHORT ARTICLE in the Metro section about the civil sexual harassment trial in progress at the federal courthouse in Washington. A young former FBI agent, Kathleen Falco, was suing the Federal Bureau of Investigation for her alleged wrongful discharge following her refusal to accept a transfer to the FBI field office in Fargo, North Dakota. The ACLU Washington representative was quoted in the article as saying that Ms. Falco's case was illustrative of the widespread sexual harassment still present in the law enforcement agencies like the FBI. The ACLU spokesperson had expressed disappointment in Ms. Falco's attorney, Tim Quinn, and his refusal to allow the ACLU to join the case and make it into a class action. The paper also noted that Quinn had refused comment while the case was pending.

Quinn frowned as he read the article. Damn it! Was the fucking ACLU trying to get a mistrial in his case with that statement about "widespread sexual harassment"? Tim hoped that the judge would let the case continue. The jury had been warned not to read the papers during the projected three-day trial. No doubt Judge Lashly would poll the jury about reading the *Washington Post* before the morning session started.

On the ACLU request, Tim had refused to let his case be used for anyone's agenda. This was a simple case of an employee being abused by her boss.

His client, after graduating from the FBI Academy, had been posted to the Washington Field Office. There, at the WFO, she had the bad luck to be assigned to a middle-aged and oversexed squad supervisor. He groped her on several occasions. Moreover he made numerous lewd comments and suggestions to her in his campaign to get her to date him. When she had rebuffed all his advances, he arranged for her to be transferred to North Dakota. She had refused the transfer and the Bureau had terminated her employment. A secretary from Tim Quinn's law firm who was Falco's neighbor had suggested that she see Quinn.

Quinn liked and believed her from the start. The pretty young agent had been the victim of a one-way office romance that eventually ended her dream of being an FBI special agent. Tim had filed this suit after his attempt to use the FBI's administrative process to reverse the termination had failed. Now they were in the second day of a jury trial to prove that the FBI had wrongly fired Ms. Falco.

At the beginning of the suit, Tim had a slim chance of winning. The only real evidence of the harassment was his client's testimony. Discovery had been a disaster; the squad supervisor, Lester McKnight, had denied any misconduct and no one else came forward to substantiate his client's claims. The typical "Curtain of Blue" had descended on Quinn's attempt to back up his client's story—law enforcement officers do not rat out a fellow officer. Then a week before trial, Tim was called at his home by a convincing, but anonymous female voice and told that Special Agent William Sharkey had seen several of the incidents of harassment. The next day Tim put Sharkey on his witness list. Discovery was closed and it was too late to depose him, so Tim had no idea what he would say at trial. Flying blind was not Tim's style, but Sharkey was the only chance he had to find evidence to back up his client's version of her termination.

Later that morning, the courtroom was half filled when Kathleen Falco finished her testimony and left the stand. When Ms. Falco was seated at the counsel's table next to him, Tim Quinn told the court bailiff, "The plaintiff calls William Sharkey."

Moments later a balding man slowly walked toward the front of the courtroom. Tim guessed his age as fifty and noticed the squinty eyes with hooded lids that made it seem that he was almost asleep. However when he passed Tim on the way to the witness stand, Tim saw that the sleepy-looking eyes were alert and burning with anger. Clearly Agent Sharkey didn't want to be here.

After the witness was sworn, Tim asked a few preliminary questions that established that Sharkey had worked in the same section of the FBI as Ms. Falco and her supervisor, Mr. McKnight.

"Mr. Sharkey, did you ever see Ms. Falco and Mr. McKnight together?"

"Yes."

Then came the "make or break" question.

"Did you ever see Mr. McKnight touch Ms. Falco?"

As Tim waited, he had no idea what the answer would be. Even though Tim knew this was a hostile witness, Sharkey's FBI personal data sheet, which had been furnished to him by the government, was encouraging to Tim. The biographical data—which included his work assignments and his FBI commendations—all indicated to Tim that Sharkey was an honest FBI professional. So

Tim was expecting the truth—even if it may be a tough truth for Sharkey and the FBI. And it was.

"Yes."

The low raspy answer seemed to come reluctantly from deep inside Sharkey.

Tim leaned toward Sharkey and asked a follow-up.

"Please describe for the court where Mr. McKnight touched Ms. Falco."

Sharkey's face was in a tight frown as he uttered the words, "He touched her on her buttocks once and another time he put his hand inside her blouse."

A hush seized the courtroom. At the defendant's table, McKnight, who was sitting next to the assistant U.S. attorney, slumped in his chair . . . all color seem drained from that vain, smug face of the FBI supervisor.

The members of the jury were now on full alert as Tim elicited the facts and circumstances of the two incidents from a grim-faced Special Agent Sharkey. When Tim had finished his direct examination of the witness, the government attorney wisely declined to question Sharkey further. There is a saying among trial attorneys: "If you find yourself in a deep hole, don't reach for the shovel and continue to dig."

Mercifully for the government, Judge Lashly called the trial into recess for an early lunch. Once the jury had filed out, the judge called both attorneys up for a side bar. Quinn and Wilson approached the bench and stood looking up at the judge. The judge put his hand over the bench microphone, leaned forward, and spoke in a whisper. These words would never appear in the court transcript.

"Mr. Wilson, I assume you were looking at the jury during Agent Sharkey's testimony."

"Yes, Your Honor." Wilson's face was in a tight frown.

"Do I have to say it, Mr. Wilson? . . . Do I really have to suggest settlement?" The judge locked his eyes on Wilson, the government's lawyer and the defender of the FBI and Mr. McKnight.

"No, Your Honor. I'll call the chief of the civil division right away and have discussions with Mr. Quinn ASAP."

"Do you have anything to say, Mr. Quinn?"

"All we were looking for is a rehire, a decent job assignment, and some damages to pay for the forced unemployment, Your Honor."

The judge gave a brief nod and said, "Seems reasonable to me, very reasonable, Mr. Wilson. And I suggest you repeat those words verbatim to your boss. I'll delay the jury's return until three so you boys will have some time to hammer out something and get this clunker off my docket. Now step back."

The settlement was reached by three: Ms. Falco was rehired, $95,000 in damages were agreed to by the parties, and after a month of paid leave Ms. Falco was going to continue her career as a special agent in the L.A. Field Office.

When a satisfied Tim Quinn went home that evening, he felt he had used up his luck for the week. He was wrong.

CHAPTER 2

AT TEN O'CLOCK SHARP THE NEXT MORNING AND WITHOUT an appointment, Chief Judge Harold Winston of the U.S. Court of Appeals for the D.C. Circuit strode into Tim Quinn's office at his law firm in Georgetown. Tim had been Winston's personal attorney for over ten years, ever since he had handled Winston's divorce. The two had hit it off from the start and soon Quinn was doing all Winston's legal work. Winston was very wealthy and had a lot of real estate holdings in Georgia and investment properties in the Caribbean. These investments generated a fair amount of legal work. But there was more than an attorney-client bond here. They were friends. And perhaps a hint of a father-son relationship, even though the age difference was only a decade or so.

Tim noticed that the judge looked tired and older than he had ever seen him before.

"How are you doing, Chief?"

"I had a rough day yesterday. Max Rogers was a good friend and this was so unexpected. A random robbery and murder. The police say the young man who killed Max OD'd on heroin right after the robbery. Terrible, just terrible."

Tim didn't say anything, he just let Winston sit down in a wing chair. Tim sat opposite him in a matching chair.

"What's on your mind, Harry?" asked Tim in a soft tone.

Winston straightened up in his chair and looked into Tim's eyes.

"Max is gone, but life goes on. Tim, I want you to take his place. I want you as a judge on my court."

Tim was literally speechless. He was being offered a federal judgeship. He never saw this coming.

Once he got over the shock, there were questions that went blazing through Quinn's mind: *How much do I want to be a judge?* Tim Quinn asked himself. *Is the political campaign to become a federal judge worth risking my marriage? The respect of my children? Can I survive a tough look at my life by the FBI?*

Outwardly Tim remained shocked. "Chief Judge, I don't know what to say," he managed, practically stammering. "I'm flattered you would think of me. But surely there are more qualified people that the president would choose to replace Judge Rogers."

Chief Judge Winston seemed to shed his gloom and a slight grin creased his face. Winston clearly shifted to a salesman mode. A salesman who wanted to close a deal.

"Why, Tim boy, you are far too modest!" The chief judge was a Southern gentleman who had transplanted to Washington, D.C. decades ago but still spoke with a friendly, slow Georgia drawl. "Ever since I hired you to handle my divorce from Camellia and to act as my personal attorney, I thought that you'd make a fine judge someday." He paused for effect, studying Tim's face.

"My boy, that someday is now. You'd be a great judge. Hell, with your pedigree and professional biography, you ought to be running for president. In my view, you'd be a very strong contender, *very strong* especially with your high-powered law firm behind you."

Tim didn't respond and the chief judge looked both disappointed and anxious.

Winston leaned forward and dropped his voice in a conspiratorial tone. "I can see your hesitancy. Well, Tim, what if I let you in on a little secret?"

After a short pause, he continued in a low voice. "You see . . . the president and I have a little arrangement. On cases he really needs badly for the administration, he calls me and I deliver. He's done it only three times: the campaign finance case, the Philippine treaty case, and the transfer of jurisdiction case for that Iranian terrorist last year. And I got the decisions for him all three times. Why do you think I was chosen by the White House to swear in the attorney general and the secretary of defense? Normally a Supreme Court justice does those sorts of ceremonies. Hell, I get invites to state dinners at the White House all the time. The president owes me and he will give me who I want on my court."

Tim was stunned to hear this. It was no secret in the D.C. bar that some judges would side with an administration of their particular party, but to hear that the White House—Christ the president himself—would ask for and actually get certain decisions from the chief judge of a powerful federal court was almost beyond belief for Tim, even though he had been around the political circus of Washington for over two decades.

"Another thing, Tim boy, this president may have a slot or two to fill on the Supreme Court before his term ends. I'm too old to be considered, but you—why you could wind up on the Big Court. I would do that for you. You would make a better Supreme Court justice than some of the pansies and moral cowards now on it. Come on, Tim. Take the ride of your life. I'll make it happen. Trust me."

Tim's mind raced. The Supreme Court. God, that would be great. So often Tim was almost sickened when he read about a recent decision. On many of the cases, true justice was clearly not being done, with the predictable, agenda-driven votes of most all justices and the one or two equally predictable "swing votes." If he got there, he would be a true independent, applying the law from a clean slate, an open view that may force the others to follow. He could really make a difference. What a dream come true!

Then Tim found his voice and said, "Harry, I am really touched. Deeply touched. You are quite a friend. Give me some time to think it over and to talk with Katy. Okay?"

"Sure, this is a big shift in your life. Take some time and think about it. But not too long."

The judge ended his request with a wink and a big smile.

"I will think on it, Chief Judge, I will. And I'll call you tomorrow," Tim said.

"You do that, Tim boy. Let me know. Remember you're my man. I need you."

The chief judge then rose, shook Tim's hand with an extra squeeze, and was gone, leaving Tim alone in his office with his prospects—and his risks.

Timothy R. Quinn certainly knew where he was in life and was thankful for his position. He was a certified winner on the fast track of the Washington, D.C. legal world, a senior partner in the law firm of Wellington & Stone, LLP, a firm that was foremost among those that handled corporate America's legal problems. He had spent twenty-five years here. The firm's client list included *Fortune* 500 companies and the firm represented at least ten countries in their dealings with the U.S. government. For the last few years, Wellington & Stone had been recognized by *Legal* magazine as the top lobbying firm in the nation, and as the firm had done well, Tim Quinn had done well too. His partnership draw last year was well over three million. He had a large corner office on the ninth floor, the top floor of his firm's office building with a view of the rooftops of historic Georgetown below him.

Tim stretched in the leather high-back chair behind his antique Chippendale desk and gazed contemplatively through the glass walls of his office, beyond the small corner balcony.

His view was absolutely magnificent. If he looked to the right, he could see the traffic on Key Bridge and the twin curved buildings that were the headquarters of Gannett News and *USA Today.* Through the left outside wall, he saw the Potomac River and the oak-crested ridge in Virginia that ran south all the way down to the Custis-Lee Mansion whose white pillars broke the treeline above Arlington Cemetery. Winston had visited him at the end of the day, and now every few minutes, an airliner following the path of the river in its final glide to Reagan National Airport would fill his window, bringing people into the city to do business for themselves, their companies, or the nation. And Tim Quinn could survey it all.

Just past his fifty-fifth birthday, Tim was an erect six feet tall with short graying hair. Once a letterman on the West Point lacrosse and hockey teams, he tried to stay in shape with a half-hour swim at the University Club pool most workday mornings, a form of exercise he found easier on the leg that had gotten shot up in Vietnam. His military education and his two tours of combat duty in Vietnam, now more than thirty years in the past, still played a central role in how he perceived and conducted himself. He was proud that his demeanor with people was noted for calm and steadiness, especially during the hectic pace of a major felony trial in federal court. No courtroom battle, however, could compare to the intensity he experienced too many times in combat when, for example, Viet Cong 60mm mortar rounds crunched into his platoon's night-ambush position, killing three of his men. Tim felt this sense of proportion about life gave him an inner strength not taught in law school.

Suddenly Tim grimaced at the beautiful river view he had from his office windows and swiveled his chair inward. He focused on himself and his past. He was aware his character had flaws. No one was perfect. Famous people had famous failings—General MacArthur was a world-class egotist. President Kennedy and other presidents going back to Thomas Jefferson had a hidden lust for forbidden women—but everyone had frailties. Tim had parts of his past that he was not proud of. He forced himself to measure the risk he would run if he mounted a campaign to succeed Federal Judge Rogers. He shuddered, suddenly chilled with a concrete fear: If he engaged in a high-profile effort to become a member of one of the premier federal courts in the country, a particular secret in his past might surface. Nowadays, the past of any presidential nominee for a high-ranking position had to sparkle like fresh snow. Nannies whose taxes or Social Security weren't paid properly, puffs of marijuana years in the past, youthful alcohol problems—all had torpedoed presidential nominees in recent years.

The FBI background check for a federal judgeship had become very thorough and was itself a dangerous threat to Tim's secret. If you added to that threat a hardball, partisan Senate investigation of any nominee, along with the relentless inquiry into a nominee's past by a media that equated gossip with politics, the whole world might discover what Tim fervently wanted no one to know—not his wife, not his children, not his colleagues: That he had committed adultery.

It had been a few years ago, but Tim's reputation as a straight arrow would make it very relevant to his sitting as a federal judge in Washington. In light of his present chairmanship of the Ethics Committee of the D.C. bar, his enemies would gleefully label him as a hypocrite if his affair became public. Then there was that highly publicized op-ed piece about politicians' lack of sexual restraint in the *Washington Post* that Tim wrote during the Clinton scandal years. What made Tim even more vulnerable was that the woman he had bedded was still in town and probably hated him. For all he knew she may have told other people about the affair or could in the future, perhaps during the FBI background check.

Still, he found himself aching for the job and, more importantly, a real shot at the Supreme Court. Winston with his White House "arrangement" could make it all happen. Tim had always wanted to be a judge. His very first law job was with a judge; for a year, he had been a law clerk for a federal appeals court judge in New York City. It was quite a normal dream, really. A federal judgeship was the fantasy of almost every trial lawyer. A lifetime job with value and prestige, a federal judgeship was the closest thing America had to European nobility: People stood when a judge entered a courtroom, called the judge "Your Honor," and used the word "Honorable" before the judge's name. Judges, with the power and position they held, were the closest things to American royalty.

The title "Honorable" came with the judgeship. It became yours forever as a federal judge. Tim believed he was an honorable man and could be a worthy judge. But it was a dangerous dream to pursue, given his past.

He turned back to his corner windows and stared at the streets of Georgetown beneath his balcony. After several minutes, Tim finally came to a tentative decision. He couldn't pass up this opportunity, a judgeship and a shot at the Supremes. He had never been one to shirk risk—a man never got anywhere if he spent all his energy calculating and debating the odds. Tim never would have succeeded in West Point, Vietnam, law school, the spy business, or even trial work if he hadn't just plunged in. He really wanted to try for the Judge Rogers vacancy, but he needed to talk to his best friend. So he would cancel his appointments today and go home and tell his wife, Katy, about the possibility of a judgeship—and the Supreme Court. He knew she would listen lovingly and give him her honest views. The secret of his adultery and all his Catholic guilt about it—he would thrust those in a back compartment of his mind where he rarely visited. He was blessed with an ability to compartmentalize. That was how Katy thought Tim had been able to shake the ghosts of Vietnam. And she was right.

Tim and Katy had a long talk that day. The judgeship question was still up in the air when they went to a dinner that night at the residence of the Greek ambassador on Massachusetts Avenue, in honor of two justices of the Greek Supreme Court attending a judicial conference. Tim and Katy Quinn were among the guests because one of Tim's clients at the firm was a Greek shipping company and, as a result of his dealings with the embassy on a regular basis, Tim had become a close friend of the ambassador. With the two judicial VIPs visiting from Athens, the Quinns had been a natural choice as guests for the farewell dinner.

There were only ten guests at the huge dining table so the dinner could be classified as intimate by Washington standards. When the dinner conversation hit the controversial topic of Greece's adoption of an American-type jury system for civil lawsuits, Tim jumped in with his opinion, which was directly opposite that of the two visiting justices. At one point, he expected a kick from Katy under the table because of his passionate domination of the topic. But when he glanced at her during the lively debate, she winked and smiled.

The party broke up early. The justices were flying back to Athens the first thing in the morning. The Greek ambassador showed unusual courtesy by walking Tim and Katy to the door of the embassy's beautiful old mansion. "Tim and Katy, so good of you to come," he declared at the threshold. "Our guests were very interested in your views on the jury system. You have given them much to think about. Thanks for making the evening an entertaining one. Those two judges are used to 'yes men' back in Athens; I think they enjoyed the debate."

As Tim and Katy walked to their Land Rover parked in the long driveway of the ambassador's residence, Katy was suspiciously quiet. And Tim wondered again if he had done something wrong—been too brassy with the Greek Supreme Court justices or stared too long at the deep cleavage of the Greek actress who was among the dinner guests. But as soon as Tim opened the door for her, Katy stood, looked into Tim's eyes, and said, "You were brilliant tonight, honey. I know I've had my reservations about it, but I think you should go after that judgeship. You have passion about the law. Tonight I could see the glow in your eyes." She grinned and shivered a little in the September air. "Go for it! You'll be a great judge. And who knows? Perhaps as Harry Winston says, you can get to the Supreme Court if the president is reelected."

The relief Tim felt was tremendous. This was the go ahead he wanted from her. Still standing before the open door, he pressed her into his arms and held her tightly.

"Baby, you know I'm very happy at the firm," he said as they drove across the Potomac toward home. "And do you realize how much cash flow we will lose, if I get the judgeship?"

"Tim Quinn, you never took any job based on money in your whole life. Besides, the kids are grown and out of the nest and we have plenty of money in your retirement funds from the firm. Thank God it's in bonds, not stocks. And besides, you said that a U.S. Court of Appeals judge makes almost a hundred and sixty thousand a year. As a lifetime salary, that's a very reasonable sum for anybody. We'll be just fine."

Tim smiled. Katy was giving her full support to him, letting him do what he really wanted to do. Their marriage was a true partnership. Katy had always been totally committed to Tim's career and likewise he had tried his best to give her the things that mattered to her.

As they drove home, Tim outlined to Katy the campaign he would have to wage to become a federal judge. Katy said she would line up support from some congressional wives she knew. It was fun having Katy on his campaign team.

Later that night, after they made love, Katy cried softly. Tim asked, "What's wrong, baby?"

"Nothing, I'm just so happy."

Tim couldn't get to sleep for a long time.

The next morning Tim called the chief judge and said yes.

CHAPTER 3

BY THE NEXT MORNING, TIM QUINN WAS HAVING SECOND thoughts. He started to worry again about the risk to his marriage he was taking by campaigning for the judgeship—so he decided to get advice from Chief Judge Harry Winston. Tim called Winston. A little on edge, he kept his voice steady. "Chief Judge? Tim Quinn here—"

"Tim! Glad to hear from you! What can I do for my favorite judicial candidate?"

"Do you have time to see me for a few minutes?"

"For you I have all the time in the world."

They agreed to meet at a Starbucks on Fifth Street near the court. This was a critical encounter for Tim. He had to tell the chief judge something before he committed himself fully to the campaign for the judgeship.

Soon the two men were settled comfortably with their coffee in a back booth, far from the front window and the customers whose ears might have picked up their conversation.

The chief judge smiled and looked around as he stirred his latte. "Very smart, Tim. You are operating like a real Washington pro. It's an excellent idea not to be seen around the courthouse. Good to have distance between us now. I can be more effective for you that way."

The chief judge proceeded to fill in Tim on what had transpired since Judge Rogers's death. Just this morning the White House had unofficially notified him that the administration was going to move quickly to fill the vacancy. As a matter of fact, the Office of Legal Policy in the Justice Department had already started to put together a short list of candidates to fill the seat. He outlined the steps Tim needed to take now to get on that list.

Tim held up his hand. "Wait a minute, Harry. I haven't even told my firm and gotten their blessing."

"Well, Tim boy, you better get moving! You have got to get your name on that Justice Department list going to the White House ASAP."

Tim took a deep breath. "Harry, I don't want to try for something I can't win. Tell me again my chances. Can I really get it?" Even as he spoke these words of doubt, Tim was mentally calculating how much support he could muster over at Justice to get on the list.

Winston grinned and threw up his hands in mock frustration. "Come on, Tim, you're a winner. All you've got to do is get into this race. You've got a great track record in government service and in private practice. You're a decorated veteran, and you're with a very well-connected firm that can push for you in Justice, in the White House, and on the Hill. Moreover, your ace in the hole is me." The chief judge smiled wickedly. "As I told you before, I'm going to push for you from the deep inside, very deep inside. The president owes me big time and I'm calling in the chit for you, boy. Take it."

"Okay, Okay, Harry. I'll talk to the firm today. But . . ."

The "but" hung out there for five long seconds, as Tim mentally replayed the dilemma that had plagued him for the last few days. The chief judge was silent. It was as if he could see the turmoil in Tim's eyes and was transfixed by it. He started to lean forward to get closer to Tim.

Tim hit him with the burden he had been carrying alone. "Harry, there may be a problem."

The chief judge's eyes rolled up and he leaned even closer. "What problem?" he asked softly.

Tim straightened his back. He wanted to read the chief judge's body reactions as well as his response in words so he kept his eyes steady and dead on the judge. "A few years ago, there was a woman."

Winston didn't say a word while Tim related the story of his adultery—an encounter, really, not more than that, but with a woman who may not be exactly happy he didn't turn his transgression into a continuing romance. The chief judge kept his face devoid of expression; the only reaction Tim saw was when he said the woman's name—a prominent prosecutor at Justice—then the judge's eyebrows went up briefly. Perhaps he knew her? "So," Tim finished, "during the FBI background check or later in the nomination process, I'm worried that the secret could come out. And then—"

He watched Winston's face, wondering if he had just lost the chief judge's support.

Winston leaned back in his seat and slowly nodded. "Tim, you have some fences to mend with this woman. This is not a deal killer, but you have got to talk with her right now to see if she will say anything. Remember the Anita Hill thing? Does anyone else know? Katy?"

"No, I don't think so. And Katy, I never . . . I just couldn't tell her. She wouldn't ever understand." Tim felt his hands shaking as he thought of Katy.

The two men talked for another half hour, laying out various scenarios for what could happen in the nomination process thanks to this potentially exposed Achilles heel. Winston was understanding and acted like a true friend, which relieved Tim and made him feel even closer to the genial, worldly-wise Southerner. The advice he gave was solid: Tim's immediate priority was to find out if this secret was going to stay buried. The two parted. The judge went back to the courthouse and Tim caught a cab back to his office to make an important phone call, a call that would be the start or the finish of his judicial campaign.

As soon as he was in his office, Tim pulled out a U.S. government phone book from his desk. He looked in the section showing the Justice Department, Criminal Division listings, and found the Public Integrity Section. Ms. Victoria Hauser was listed as the section chief. With a deep breath, he punched in the numbers.

An officious voice answered the phone after only one ring. "Public Integrity Section, how may I help you?"

"This is Tim Quinn from Wellington and Stone. Could I speak to Ms. Victoria Hauser, please?"

The Public Integrity Section of the Criminal Division in the Justice Department is the key unit that handles corruption of public officials. The phone book listed twenty-odd lawyers who worked in her unit. Vicky Hauser held a very important position in Justice.

"One moment, sir."

After a brief pause, there was a distinctly chilly voice on the phone. "This is Ms. Hauser."

"Uh, Vicky, this is Tim Quinn. How are you?"

"I'm fine. How can I help you?" Her voice was more than professional; it was all frost.

"Vicky, I need to talk to you. Would you meet me after work at the Dubliner?"

"Would . . . would this proposed meeting be for official business, or is it strictly social?"

"Vicky, well ah . . . no. It's about business, no, I just need to talk to you. Something important has come up." Tim felt more and more flustered. "Please."

"Well, why don't you just come to my office rather than propose a meeting in a bar?"

It had been years since they had last been together. Their reunion had been a mistake, and her anger had not abated with time. "Look Vicky . . . I really need to talk to you. It's important. I can meet you anywhere you want. Five o'clock? You name the place."

She sighed slightly. "All right, the Dubliner will do. I'll meet you there, but today's a very busy day. It will probably be five-thirty or a quarter to six before I can get over there."

"That will be fine. Thank you for agreeing to meet with me."

There was a momentary silence. Tim waited. Then a softer voice answered. "All right, Tim, I'll see you at the Dubliner."

Tim stared out his window at the Potomac River. This was going to be an interesting meeting. He called Katy and told her that he had a meeting with the chief judge to discuss plans for the judgeship campaign. No mention of the chief judge's advice to meet with the woman he was worried about. Katy was pleased and as encouraging as always. Tim said he would be home late, business meeting after work. He felt crummy when he hung up.

Later that day, Tim met with the three members of his firm's executive committee—the partners who were elected to run the policies and operation of Wellington & Stone. The meeting couldn't have gone better; they were behind his judgeship bid. Solid. It would be good for the firm to have a federal judge as an alumnus. At 5:30 P.M., Tim left for the Dubliner.

. . .

As with his rendezvous with the chief judge, this was another meeting Tim wanted no one to overhear. He sat at a corner table in the rear of the bar area, the back of his chair touching the wall. From this position, he could see every patron as they walked into the Dubliner, perhaps the best-known Irish pub in town, only four blocks from the Justice Department. Tim glanced at his watch. It was nearly six. Tim didn't know if Vicky Hauser would show. One of the top prosecutors in the U.S. Justice Department in Washington, D.C., and now assigned in the Public Integrity Section of the Criminal Division, targeting corruption in public office, she had made her mark not only with a well-publicized corruption case of a federal judge in Louisville, but more recently by putting away a member of Congress for taking bribes from Japanese car makers. Once she got attached to a case, she was an absolute bulldog who would never let go until her target had been convicted.

While being a bulldog may have been an apt metaphor for her prosecutorial zeal, it was far from a meaningful physical description. Vicky Hauser was certainly a striking woman, a tall, leggy, well-endowed blonde whose professional manner could never quite obscure her allure. She was strong and independent, and had never been married, although she had lived with a man on a few occasions.

And one of those men was Tim.

As he carefully nursed his second Jack Daniels on ice, his mind floated back to the relationship he had shared with Vicky Hauser in law school. Tim was considerably older than her. They had met when both of them served on the *Columbia Law Review*. At the beginning of her second year and Tim's third and last, they were matched on a blind date.

He had been simply stunned that first night, one of those love-at-first-sight things. After dinner and several drinks, they had gone back to her place. There, with music and slow dancing, things progressed quickly. During a heated session of kissing and touching, she suddenly stopped him, stood up, and pulled off her creamy sweater, exposing full breasts in the white half-cups of her demi-bra. Her tiny waist and narrow back accentuated their size all the more. She reached behind her back and unhooked her bra, and Tim was lost.

Within two weeks, she had moved in with him in his Columbia University student apartment in Morningside Heights. The romance had lasted almost three years. After graduation Tim stayed on in New York and clerked for Judge Breedlove, a federal judge in Manhattan. After the clerkship, Tim moved to Washington to take a job with the Wellington & Stone law firm, but Vicky stayed in New York. In her final year at Columbia, she had decided to go to a big Wall Street firm, this despite his pleas that she join him in Washington. That first year apart, they wrote and talked on the phone, with occasional visits to one city or the other on weekends, but the fires were ebbing. The final split was over careers. Early in their relationship, they had talked about marriage on a "what if" basis, but Vicky's firm Wall Street decision had extinguished the last spark. Within two years of breaking up with Vicky, Tim had married Katy, a Danish exchange student he had met at a Georgetown party.

He had never looked back.

As he glanced at the doorway of the Dubliner wondering whether Vicky would be a no-show, he thought back to the last time he saw Vicky. It was six years ago when he was at an American Bar Association convention in New Orleans and staying in the same small hotel in the French Quarter. On the first day there he found that Vicky was not only staying at the same hotel, but was attending the same criminal law section meetings with him. At their first meeting, she had been frosty and reserved, but on the second night of the convention, they had shared dinner with a half-dozen other conferees in the restaurant of their small hotel. Instead of going out for another night on Bourbon Street with the group, however, Tim and Vicky had stayed in the cozy bar adjoining the restaurant. Tim told her about his marriage and family. They had a long talk about life and the unexpected places it had taken them, drank quite a bit more, and then danced on the small dance floor in the bar area. And as they moved around the floor, Tim felt those familiar curves pressing against him. The renewed memories stirred him into insistent desire. Before he knew it, he was in her hotel room. The nightcap she promised was never served because as soon as they were in the sitting room of her small suite, they were hugging and kissing with all the urgency of their dating years. They were pulling off each other's clothes as they moved purposely toward the bed in the next room, kissing passionately, her arms clutching him and her hips pressing rhythmically against his groin.

The next morning, he woke in strained sunlight. Vicky's head lay on his shoulder, her blond hair spread out over his chest. He looked at his watch, saw that it was two minutes to nine, and bolted upright into a sitting position. Vicky, displaced, opened her eyes and looked up at him.

"Vick, it's nine o'clock! We have to get up! Our committee is going to meet again at nine-thirty!"

Vicky yawned and stretched, extending her arms above her shoulders, her breasts rising, pink nipples tight and hard. Then she sat up and reached across the bed for him. "We work too hard. Come on, Tim, let's play! Little Timmy looks like he's up and ready to play again."

Tim backed away, his head pounding with guilt and passion. He was married to Katy, but Vicky was so beautiful, even in the morning. If he let her get her hands on him, naked and hungry, he wasn't sure he would even make the flight at four that afternoon. "No, no, Vicky, don't do this to me. Come on, we've got to show up at the committee! I'm presenting this morning, and I'm supposed to launch the first proposal."

"So? Come on, you can launch little Timmy right here! Play hooky with me. We'll have fun! Come on, don't go, we can order breakfast in bed." She was seductive, but there was a need in her voice.

"No, Vicky, no! I've got to get back to my room and shave and change. And I was supposed to call my wife at eight," he added, his voice faltering as he realized the mistake of using his wife as an excuse.

Vicky rolled over and buried her head in the pillow. "All right, you coward, go to your fucking meeting!"

He picked his clothes up off the floor and pulled them on. "Vick, you don't understand, I've really got to . . ."

But she didn't respond. He had his pants and shoes on and was pulling his suit coat on, his shirttail still half out, his tie loose and draped around his neck as he opened the door and stepped into the corridor.

Half an hour later, Vicky was forced to sit next to Tim in the only vacant chair at the section meeting. She was as beautiful and composed as ever, but cold and silent. She would not even look at him. That afternoon, they flew back to Washington at different ends of the same plane. He had never called her after their return.

Now, six years later, he wondered if not calling Vicky—not talking it out back in D.C.—was one of the major mistakes in his life. As he sat waiting for her in the Dubliner, he realized that he shouldn't be surprised if she stood him up. It would serve him right.

At six-thirty, he drained his glass and stood up, reaching down to gather up his raincoat and briefcase. She obviously wasn't coming.

He didn't blame her. Tim threw some dollars on the table and looked toward the door when someone touched his shoulder. He turned and looked into those familiar green eyes. Then her lips parted and he felt his heart race.

"Hello, Tim."

"Hello, Vicky. Here, sit down, I think this is still my table. Thanks for coming."

"I almost didn't. But here I am."

Vicky sat down as he waved to the waiter. He took a chance that she still liked white wine, and shouted his order over the din.

"One white wine, one Jack Daniels, on the rocks!"

Ten feet away, the waiter nodded and started back toward the bar. Tim sat down and faced Vicky. She looked a little older, or at least wiser, around the eyes, but she was undoubtedly the same woman he had romanced as a young man and desired so much that night in New Orleans. In spite of himself, he was grinning with relief and pleasure. "Okay, Vicky, again I appreciate you coming. Now let me tell you why—"

She held up a hand. She was smiling, but it was a chilly smile.

"No, Tim, before you start, let's get something straight between us. This is a not a social meeting. I am here because whatever you are going to say sounded serious. Up front, I want you to know that I am seriously involved with a man I may marry, and so I have no social or sexual interest in you whatsoever."

The waiter delivered her wine and his Jack Daniels. Tim looked her straight in the eyes. "I'm glad, Vicky, you deserve a good man."

"Well, he is a good man. He's a lawyer at Justice, Antitrust Division, and he would never treat me the way you did in New Orleans."

"New Orleans is what I want to talk about, Vicky. I'm very sorry, I should never have tried to recapture what we had in law school, even for a night—"

She turned to face him. "No, you shouldn't have done that, Tim. God, you slept with me and the next morning turned into the typical guilty married man with absolutely no regard for my feelings."

"Vicky, I was a shit and I am so sorry I hurt you."

"I'm sure you are! What did you care? You never called me once after the trip! Not once! No! You went silently back to your wife, as if nothing happened. For a man, the whole thing is different. But I'm a woman, a single woman, and I felt used. I felt like a slut, a one-night stand."

Vicky hid her face with her hand. Tim briefly thought that she was crying and he took the white handkerchief out of the breast pocket of his suit and almost handed it to her. But she soon looked up and her eyes were dry and steely.

"Vicky, I was afraid to call. I didn't want to start something that might get out of control. I'm really sorry, I just can't tell you how much this has bothered me, and I do hope . . . Vicky, please forgive me."

Vicky pulled herself upright, composed and businesslike. "Tim, I'll never forgive you. So don't waste your time. Now why am I here?"

Tim looked at her helplessly. What could he say? The objective of this meeting seemed impossible, the fences beyond repair. He knew he had hurt her; only now did he realize how much. Christ, how was he supposed to ask her to keep quiet and possibly lie for him in the exhaustive background check for the judgeship?

Vicky gazed hard at him. "Out with it."

Tim plunged in. He was *almost* completely truthful with her. He told her a lot. He laid out how possibly he was in a good position to take Rogers's place on the United States Court of Appeals. He even told her he had a shot at the Supreme Court. He did leave out the relationship and favors done between Winston and the president. Christ, he couldn't tell a federal prosecutor that the chief judge was throwing cases for the president. Nixon was completely wrong when he said, "If the president does it, it's not a crime." What Winston and the president were doing—fixing cases—could well be a federal crime, obstruction of justice. Tim naturally kept that from Vicky and was feeling uncomfortable even knowing about it.

Then Tim delicately went to the heart of the meeting and told her of how the New Orleans tryst with her could sink his chances for the judgeship. She listened attentively. Finally, Tim asked her directly, "Vicky, will this get out in the background check?"

She examined his face. His heart almost stopped as he waited for her response.

"Only *if you* tell someone," Vicky said with a grim smile.

Tim was shocked. Did he mishear or was Vicky giving him what he wanted? "I don't understand, Vicky. I know how much I hurt you. Why would you help me?"

"I didn't say I would help you. But I certainty won't hurt you on New Orleans. Whether you get the judgeship won't depend on what happened between us there."

Then Vicky abruptly got up, threw the rest of her wine in his face, and left the bar.

Tim was stunned. God damn! He wiped his face with the same handkerchief he almost offered to her.

On the way home, Tim called Chief Judge Winston from his car with his cell phone and told him that he thought Vicky Hauser would remain quiet.

"Ah, that's good, you're smooth with the ladies, my boy," Winston said. "Sounds like you did a nice job with her."

Tim didn't say anything in response. He just briefly thanked

Winston for his advice and hung up. Tim mouthed a silent thank-you to Vicky as he drove. He would always be grateful to her for the gift of compassion she showed him today. He still didn't understand the "why," but he knew that, even though she was still angry with him, she wouldn't hurt his chance at the judgeship. He could always trust her word. And he knew he could never thank her outright for this. Some gifts can never be mentioned.

At nine A.M. ten days later, Tim ignored the panorama outside his windows and reached for the telephone. With Vicky willing to keep their liaison private, with his firm behind him, and with the support of his wife and children, he had begun his campaign to be a judge. He would conduct a strong campaign, even though he knew that, if Winston did actually help with the president, then the nomination for the judgeship was his since the ultimate decision-maker was the president. However Tim had been in Washington long enough to know no deal is done until it is signed, sealed, and delivered so he intended to campaign hard.

Tim had not previously devoted much time or effort to advancing his own political fortunes in this most political of all cities, but Chief Judge Winston had energized him to help control his own destiny. Tim was proud of how much he'd accomplished at the firm, often under the most difficult of circumstances, thanks to the focus and dedication he could bring to any task he undertook. Success usually flowed from this type of total effort. He guided his life by the motto of Hannibal: "I will find a way, or make one." He had always wanted to be a judge; he would make it happen.

His network of influential friends swung into action on his behalf. Still, most of the work was still up to him personally, and the political skills he knew he had to muster. That meant lobbying on his own behalf with people like Mark Daly, the chief of staff for the powerful Senator Edwin Aaronson, the number-two Republican on the Senate Judiciary Committee and a key player in the appointment process of federal judgeships.

Tim's friendship with Mark Daly had begun fifteen years ago at a reception at the National Archives, where Tim learned that Mark had served with the 82nd Airborne. As fellow paratroopers, they hit it off right away, and their bond grew over the years. Tim had also been a key sponsor of a fund-raiser that had brought in a sum in the high six figures for the senator's last reelection campaign, so he had some political chits that he would not mention, but that he knew would be counted in any request for a favor. He had discussed the judgeship possibility with Mark yesterday, and Mark had asked for a copy of all the background papers Tim had given to the Justice Department.

Following Winston's advice, Tim had immediately started his campaign for the judgeship through contacts at the Justice Department. Tim had told a friend, Ronald Branson, who was the current president of the D.C. bar, that he wanted the judgeship and asked for help with Justice. Branson, in turn, had sent a letter recommending Tim to the Office of Legal Policy at the Justice Department, which screened candidates for federal judgeships. Last week, that office had notified Tim that he was a leading active candidate and requested a package of information on him, including his resume, a list and summary of court cases in which he was the primary counsel, and three character references.

After a review process in Justice, a short list of candidates was sent to the Presidential Personnel Office at the White House. Tim had learned that his name was on that short list. In the coming weeks, the decision-makers in the White House would select the name of one person from the list to send to the Senate for confirmation pursuant to the Advice and Consent clause of the Constitution. Tim was calling Mark in an effort to get Senator Aaronson to influence one of the key decision-makers in the White House, Attorney General Taggert.

Mark had gotten the package of Tim's bio and endorsement materials. "Does your firm support you on this?" he asked.

"Oh, yeah, they're behind me one hundred percent. Listen, buddy, I want to meet you so we can discuss strategy to get Taggert in my camp. Have you got time for lunch with me today?"

"Well, the Senate is in session, but they'll break at one. Let's make it one forty-five over at the Monocle Restaurant."

"Okay, I'll see you there. And Mark, I really appreciate this. Thanks."

"Tim, I'm glad to help, the senator and I think you will be a great addition to the D.C. Circuit. I just can't understand why you would give up the big bucks to become a judge."

"Mark, I'll explain it over lunch."

He put down the phone and pulled a legal pad out of his desk drawer. Through his sources in this administration, he knew about an ad hoc group called the "Judicial Selection Committee" that met almost weekly. Tim thought it would help him now to outline the players of this committee. He wrote "WH" at the top, indicating the White House, and then drew a large circle, representing the table around which the committee members would meet. Then he began to populate the table.

The first seat belonged to the counsel to the president, Bill Monroe, and this guy was going to be a problem. He and Tim had crossed swords many years ago when Monroe was a junior staffer on Capitol Hill and Tim had been the attorney for a witness at a hearing during a congressional investigation. Monroe had leaked an embarrassing half-truth about Tim's witness to the press, then denied it. But Tim had proof of the unauthorized leak and formally reported it to the committee chairman, who dressed down

Monroe. Monroe might want payback. He didn't know what to do on this. Maybe he should do nothing.

Next on the pad was the director of presidential personnel, Milton deBlatin III, an officious ass who thought himself the most important person in Washington after the president, or perhaps before him. Tim did not know him personally, but he did know that deBlatin had his own candidate, a college friend from Harvard, and that was trouble. Tim would not waste any time on this guy; he would just have to neutralize him by getting him outvoted.

Several people at Tim's firm knew another player at the table, the special assistant to the president for political affairs, Duke Albrecht. Jay Wellington, the managing partner at Tim's law firm, said that he would make a special full-court press on Duke, and he was confident he could deliver his vote for Tim.

Okay, Tim thought, that covered three seats. He could count on Monroe as one vote against him, probably on deBlatin as another vote against him, and maybe Albrecht would be one vote for him. The situation wouldn't be very hopeful if only those three picked the nominee for the judgeship, but there were two other seats at the table: the attorney general, and the chief of staff of the White House. Tim had to be very careful in approaching these two because they were vital to his cause.

In spite of his rank, the attorney general, Donald R. Taggert, had only one vote at the meeting that would select federal judges. However, as attorney general of the United States he was someone to listen to on judge selection. With Taggert, Tim felt blessed to know Mark as well as he did, for Mark's boss, Senator Aaronson, was a senator from Nebraska and had been primarily responsible for getting his fellow Nebraskan Taggert selected as attorney general. Help from Aaronson, of which Tim now felt confident, could all but guarantee Taggert's vote for Tim.

The last circle drawn on the legal pad was that of the chief of staff of the White House, Susan Wentworth. The first woman to fill this post, she was extraordinarily efficient and effective in running the White House operations. She was probably the most powerful vote at the table, and her vote was a "must have" for Tim's candidacy.

Long ago, Tim and Wentworth had both been trial attorneys at Justice together, but they were only distant acquaintances. But Tim knew that Susan Wentworth had been a senior partner at a big Wall Street law firm before she took the White House job, and would probably return there after her tour with the president ended. And while he would not feel comfortable calling her up at this stage of his campaign, he did know two of her former partners very well. He had telephoned them two days ago and was scheduled to fly up to New York tomorrow morning to have lunch with them at the Tavern on the Green. He was sure they would help get Wentworth on his side.

Tim put the yellow pad away and went back to the telephone—this time to call the deputy chairman of the Republican National Committee, George Labowski. Tim composed his thoughts as George's private line phone at the RNC rang. Tim had done a lot of fund-raising for the Republican Party, and he was now going to call in his chit.

Labowski greeted him like an old friend. "Tim! I talked about you with the chairman, and he's willing to weigh in however way you want. What can we do?"

"I need a push from the RNC with Susan Wentworth at the White House. I'm meeting with two of Susan's old law partners in New York tomorrow," he told Labowski. "I think they will also call her, but there's nothing like a strong word from the RNC telling Wentworth I'm a good guy for the judgeship."

George laughed. "Very clever, Tim. Well, you've helped us a lot and we owe you. So don't worry, the call will be made, and we know what to say."

After the call, Tim leaned back in his chair and pondered his next step. He needed to put pressure on each of the five members of the Judicial Selection Committee in the White House. Gentle pressure, to be sure, but effective pressure: He wanted to win. A final endgame touch was needed for his White House strategy.

But nothing came to him. A knock on his half-open door startled him and he turned to see Tom Reardon, one of the senior partners of the firm, looking at him quizzically.

"Am I disturbing you?"

"No, no, come on in, buddy. I'm just working the phones and doing some thinking on the judgeship."

Reardon plopped down on the sofa. "Well, old friend, I was just talking with Wellington about you, and he and I have come up with a little plan to help you out at the White House."

"Great! What's the plan?"

"Well, Wellington thinks that, with a little luck and a few phone calls, we could get the senior Democrat and the senior Republican on the Judiciary Committee to sign a joint letter to the president supporting your nomination."

"Jesus, Tom, that would be dynamite! A joint letter from Senator Gavin and Senator Williams to the president—nothing like pressure from the top down! Do you guys really think you could pull that off?"

"I don't know—is this the best law firm in Washington, D.C., or not?"

Both men smiled and then laughed hard.

"I've got an appointment tomorrow morning at eleven o'clock with Senator Gavin," Reardon continued, "and once I get his John

Hancock on it, I'll head on over to Williams's office and leave it with Amy, his chief of staff. She's expecting it and already got the senator to agree to do it, so get cracking!"

Tim was stunned. "My God almighty! You guys are really something!"

"Yeah, I know, I know. So write me up a draft of a letter telling me how great you are, pronto, because I know that, with your modesty, I'm going to have to pump it up a bit with some superlatives when you're finished."

Tim smiled. The "Quinn for Judge" train was definitely gathering momentum.

CHAPTER 4

TIM QUINN WAS STANDING OUTSIDE THE LARGE TOWNHOUSE of weathered red brick, balanced by neat white trim, with a black door and shutters and wrought-iron bars on first-floor windows, on N Street in the heart of Georgetown, the elegant realm of the government's powerful. This was the home of Chief Judge Harold S. Winston. Tim was waiting for Jay Wellington, the senior partner of his law firm. Today Harry was going to do Tim a big favor. Winston was putting on one of his famous "power lunches" for Tim, in the hope of influencing key players to favor Tim in the judicial-vacancy selection process.

Winston, the man who was so central to the realization of Tim's ambitions, was a small man, not quite five and a half feet tall, but what he lacked in height he made up in stature. He was a wiry, still-fit man who had wrestled in college and still cared a great deal about his looks, from the cut of his thin gray hair to his expensively tailored suits. He was a focused, dapper man who laughed easily in social settings and was genuinely enjoyable company. His

Southern charm and ready wit made him the magnetic center of any gathering.

Long since separated from his wife—but officially divorced only recently, thanks to Tim's efforts—Winston had carefully avoided any lasting commitment to another woman, but Tim knew he had long been an insatiable womanizer and worried that Mrs. Winston might have used it against him in a divorce trial. He was rich, powerful, and highly eligible—why *wouldn't* gorgeous young women flock to him? From what Harry had told him, Winston never had a relationship lasting enough to cause enduring harm to the woman. In fact, the young female Capitol power-seekers he associated with would remember a liaison with him as a thrilling romantic sleigh ride. His Southern charm worked just as easily on men as it did on women, and many casual acquaintances found him nothing short of charming, warm, and most impressive.

Winston had graduated from prestigious Hobbes College in Greenfield, Georgia, and won a coveted Rhodes scholarship. After two years at Oxford, he went on to Yale Law School, where he graduated near the top of his class, serving as an editor of the *Yale Law Journal* in his senior year. Then he clerked for a year for a top federal appeals court judge in Atlanta, which was sixty-odd miles north of his family home in Macon, Georgia. Although he and his wife never had any children, he supported her generously after their marriage fragmented. She still lived in the Winston family mansion in Macon, where—from what Harry sadly intimated—she lived a lonely, alcoholic life.

Winston put on three or four of these extravagant Sunday lunches at his beautiful home each year. He had suggested having this lunch to show political Washington that Quinn was his candidate. The guests at the lunch would be selected key players from the White House, the Senate Judiciary Committee, and the Justice Department. After the lunch, key policy makers would have the clear indication that Quinn was Winston's pick without Winston ever having to utter the words. Tim had to smile when he thought of the great indirect political influence the chief judge of the Court of Appeals had. It wasn't surprising, since he headed a powerful court, a court often called upon to approve or disapprove the programs that implemented the president's governmental policy. By going along with Winston's choice on Judge Rogers's replacement, the present administration could avoid antagonizing him. Moreover the special relationship with the president that Harry had confided in him could make the judgeship a done deal—if Harry actually did call in a marker with the president.

To further move Tim's cause along, the chief judge had also invited a gossip columnist from the *Washington Post.* Some mention in the local press of Quinn, a known candidate for the judgeship, appearing at a party thrown by the chief judge, could not only help Quinn's candidacy but probably would also discourage the interest of others in the position. The chief judge had a gift for influencing power in Washington. Winston had asked Quinn and Jay Wellington, the managing partner of Wellington & Stone, who was performing the unofficial role of campaign manager for Quinn, to come to the lunch an hour or so early, in order to brief Winston on the status of Quinn's quest.

"Parking is always a bitch in Georgetown!" Jay Wellington said as he came up to Tim.

"Did you learn this before or after you moved our firm here?" Tim asked, smiling.

Wellington just shook his head and shrugged. They went up the front steps and rang the doorbell. They saw Winston's sleek form take shape through the glass and wrought-iron front door.

He wore a wide smile as he greeted them. "Tim, Jay, welcome to my humble home. Come on, let's go into my library. I hear that someone brewed some very good coffee in there."

The library's floor-to-ceiling built-in mahogany bookshelves were full to overflowing. Sunlight streamed through the French doors that opened onto the brick-walled patio behind the house. The three men settled into overstuffed green leather chairs that formed a crescent around the marble fireplace.

"Chief Judge, we are deeply indebted to you for your support of Tim's efforts to win a seat on your court," Wellington promptly began. "We've already garnered strong support for Tim from both parties on the Senate Judiciary Committee—"

"Which is pretty damn terrific," Winston interjected.

"The only sticking place we can see now," Wellington went on, "is on the Judicial Selection Committee in the White House, and we're working on that. It's looking good. We think we have two solid votes—Attorney General Taggert, and Albrecht, the special assistant for political affairs. We're fairly hopeful about the White House chief of staff, Susan Wentworth. But Tim and I are less certain about Bill Monroe, the counsel to the president." He glanced at Tim. "We're also pretty certain we won't get the vote of deBlatin, the director of presidential personnel, he seems to be pushing his own candidate, one of his old Harvard buddies."

"Hmmm," breathed the chief judge. "Well, among the guests that RSVPed for today, I know Monroe said he would come, plus three senators from the Judiciary Committee, old friends of mine. Wentworth, it seems, is out of town." He raised his eyebrows. "Curiously, I invited deBlatin, but he begged off with a lame excuse about working today, a Sunday. But I agree with you on that one. I think you can write off deBlatin." Winston smiled and winked at Tim. "Hell, you might not even need deBlatin. He does what the president says." Wellington seemed puzzled at this remark and Tim kept silent, thinking that Winston may have already called in a favor with the president himself. Tim then outlined his plan to get the White House chief of staff on his side.

After they chatted a while, Winston got up and suggested perhaps Jay should be out back in the garden where the buffet lunch was being served and that Tim stand by him at the front door as he greeted his guests. Soon they started arriving. Tim was fascinated at the warm Southern reception Winston gave each guest.

"Hell-ooooo, Betty Lou, I am so delighted you are here, I am simply charmed by your presence," Winston drawled. It was practically a parody of the Southern gentleman, but it worked wonders. Betty Lou, a reporter with the *Washington Post,* was giggling.

"Hello, Chief Judge, I am happy to be here. This is Joe Riley," she said, gesturing at a disheveled-looking man bedecked in cameras. "He's a photographer with the Style section."

Winston beamed a broad smile, pumped the photographer's hand, and said, "Welcome, Joe. I'm Harry Winston. The name is the same as the New York jeweler. He has the gems and I have the girls!"

With that, the chief judge hugged Betty Lou and kissed her cheek.

Betty Lou blushed with the show of affection but managed to say, "We plan to do a little piece on your party, if you don't mind."

"Why, Betty Lou, of course, if you so desire," Winston said, chuckling. "But please understand that I invited you first as a friend and not as a reporter for the *Washington Post*!" He lowered his voice. "Later on, let's chat a bit, I may have a White House leak on a judicial nomination I know you would just love. Excuse me, won't you. That's Senator Williams at the bottom of the steps."

Tim greeted the reporter from the *Post* and watched her and the photographer as they strolled through the house, examining the rich collection of English antiques, and out into the backyard. They positioned themselves strategically by the outdoor bar.

Winston never missed a beat as he reached the front door, which the butler had opened.

"Senator Williams, I am so pleased that you have seen fit to spend some time in my humble home at this small gathering. I am honored. By the way this is Tim Quinn, one of Washington's legal stars."

The senator eyed him and smiled. He knew exactly who Tim was and why they all were here. "Pleased to meet you, Tim. I must say, Harry, it's always a pleasure to come to one of your power lunches. I should add what you call your 'humble home' is far from that. You remember my wife, Ruth, don't you?"

"How could I forget such a lovely woman, senator, and may I say, Missus Williams, you are every bit as beautiful as ever. Please, just go right on through to the backyard. With this beautiful weather, I decided to set up lunch there."

After most of the invitees arrived, Tim and Winston moved to the back garden where the guests filled their plates from the bountifully laden tables. They were served glasses of Krug champagne or other drinks by waiters moving about with silver trays in the sun-splashed, walled-in lawn and garden. Some people began to sit down in the wrought-iron chairs that surrounded small white linen-draped tables, others stood under trees talking and laughing freely.

White House Counsel Bill Monroe was one of the last to arrive. Winston put his arm around Monroe's shoulder when he greeted him and introduced him to Tim. Winston raised his hand and an attentive waiter appeared. "Bill, try one of these Georgia Bloody Marys, I only recommend them for the stronger men who come to my brunches, for they contain a little extra bite of horseradish and Kettel One vodka."

"Thank you, Chief." Monroe took a big swallow of the drink, gasped, and smiled. "Wow, that does have quite a kick to it."

"Yes, that's something, isn't it? Listen, Tim and I have to talk to the reporter for the *Washington Post,* so why don't you talk to our mutual friend, Jay Wellington." Winston signaled to Wellington who quickly came over. "Jay, you take good care of the president's number-one lawyer, hear? I've got some things I have to do . . ."

Wellington and Monroe shook hands warmly.

Winston and Tim disappeared inside the house. After the introduction by Winston, Tim dutifully chatted with Betty Lou and got his picture taken, but he kept wondering what Monroe and Wellington were talking about. After finishing the hasty interview with the *Washington Post* reporter, he joined a small cluster of guests, but couldn't stay focused even on small talk. When he looked over his shoulder and saw the two men emerging into the garden, he felt nothing but relief. Monroe stood at the edge of the gathering, eyeing Tim. Wellington came over to the knot of guests and tapped Tim on the arm; Tim looked around, pretending to be surprised.

"Excuse me, Tim, Bill Monroe, the White House counsel, wants to have a word with you. Don't worry, we just spoke and he's in a friendly and forgiving mood. I read him as sniffing the political wind and seeing that you are a winner for the president. But be careful."

Tim took a deep breath and went over to talk to Monroe, who had moved to a corner of the garden near the rose trellis, a spot where the two men could talk with no one near them.

"It has been a long time, Tim. Good to see you again," Monroe began. "I was just telling Jay Wellington that I am very impressed with your strong bipartisan support. And it seems like the chief judge has endorsed you to boot. But I do have a couple of questions for you on your judicial philosophy. I know this is a bit unusual, and I don't want to put you on the spot, but it would be helpful to talk off the record."

"Shoot. Glad to help straighten out any questions you have."

"What I'm going to ask you is strictly off the record. I understand that you are a practicing Catholic, so tell me your views on abortion."

"As a Catholic," Tim started, then paused noticeably. How to phrase this. "I am personally opposed to abortion. But as a judge, I will do my duty and enforce the laws of the land. If abortion is legal, then I will enforce the law as written."

"Hmmm. . . . How about capital punishment?"

"I am for capital punishment, and, although I doubt its deterrent effect, I would have no trouble affirming a death sentence if one came my way since it is a legal punishment."

"Okay," the White House counsel said. "Thank you for your candor. And good luck in your efforts. I've got to get back to the White House now, but I'm glad we had this chance to chat. I'll say my good-bye to the chief judge."

As soon as Monroe left Tim, Wellington came over.

"So what happened?"

"Well, Jay, he asked me for my positions on abortion and capital punishment."

"Shit! He's not supposed to ask those litmus test questions and he knows it. So what did you say?"

"He did say it was 'off the record' before he asked."

"Yeah, right! What did you say?"

"I told him I was opposed to abortion but would uphold the law of the land, and that I was in favor of capital punishment."

Jay closed his eyes and groaned.

"Damn, Tim! Don't you know he's a knee-jerk liberal in favor of abortion and against capital punishment? He's one of the few bleeding hearts on the president's team."

"Yeah, so I've heard, but so what? I've told him where I stand, and if I don't get the job because of that, you'll have to keep putting up with me at Wellington and Stone."

Wellington shook his head and grimaced. The two men turned and looked toward Winston across the yard. He and Monroe seemed to be in an intense conversation.

Then Monroe shook the chief judge's hand and left. Winston walked over and joined Wellington and Tim.

"Too bad the counsel didn't stay for lunch. How did it go with him?"

"I was asked how *hard* my support was for Tim," Winston calmly replied.

Tim and Jay said nothing and waited to see if Winston would share his answer with them.

"I told him to tell the president that I was rock solid," Winston dryly went on. "And I would be very disappointed if Quinn didn't make it."

Wellington and Tim broke into smiles. Then Winston abruptly said to Jay Wellington, "Jay, do you mind if I have a word in private with Tim?"

"Certainly, Chief Judge." And Wellington left to go to the bar nearby.

Winston moved close to Tim and whispered, "I did it. I called in the chit with the president for you. I told him to tell the president that I wanted you nominated and that I wanted him to put his full weight behind it for a quick confirmation. Monroe knows my relationship with his boss. And he knows the favors I've done for this administration. Hell, he's the one that called me for the president on that Iranian terrorist case. Tim boy, unless the White House wants to lose my friendly court, you are soon to be nominated."

Tim broke into a wide smile. He was astonished with the directness of the words to the president's counsel from the chief judge. Tim was also a little frightened that the chief judge had tied his nomination to past and perhaps future decisions from the court.

But exhilaration won over caution. And Tim almost burst with glee inside.

Then in an instant, the chief judge's smile suddenly changed to a stern face and the laughing eyes went dark.

"By the way, don't *ever* tell anyone what I just did, not even your wife," Winston added firmly.

This switch shocked Tim. "Don't worry, Chief Judge, it won't pass any further."

Tim paused and added, "Harry, I'll never forget this. I can't thank you enough."

Winston changed like a chameleon back to the familiar, smiling, Southern good old boy. "That's quite all right, Tim boy. What are favors if you can't use them? Well now, let's go socialize with our guests."

Winston motioned Wellington over to join them and they all took a fresh wineglass from a passing waiter.

Winston clinked glasses with Wellington and Tim and said, "Here's to the next judge on my court, God and the Senate willing."

Then they strolled over and joined two other judges from Winston's court and a few other D.C. lawyers in a group by the water fountain. A well-regarded defense lawyer was talking as Winston approached from behind, and one of the judges interrupted him to welcome the chief judge.

"Hold on, Jim, hold on, Chief Judge Winston is joining us."

The attorney turned, smiling, and opened his arms to wave Winston into the circle as the group parted and made room for him.

"Chief Judge! We were just talking about Judge Rogers's tragedy and the rising numbers of these homosexual robberies, and the predator nature of some of these criminals who seem to target older people."

Tim grimaced. The Rogers death kept bothering him. It seemed out of place even to talk about at lunch in a Georgetown back garden.

Winston's low voice resonated solemnly. "Yes, it was a tragedy. Of course, we must do something to control our streets, particularly in the nation's capital. Not more but better police may be the answer. And not just in the city proper, but in our parks." He sighed sadly.

As the others reflectively nodded and mouthed support for the chief judge's sentiments, Tim saw him look warily around, then nod to himself as he gazed at the *Post* reporter and her photographer some distance away. Just then one of the lawyers started discussing the lack of detail about Rogers's murder that appeared in the media. In a self assured-voice the lawyer was saying, ". . . and you know the press just drools at the opportunity to embarrass judges, so I was simply flabbergasted that none of that lurid stuff about the way his body was found ever got into the papers. You'd think it would have ended up on *A Current Affair*."

Another chimed in. "And really, from what I saw in the *Post*, and then a little piece in the back of the "A" section in the *New York Times*, you really had to think about it to realize that his murder was related to a homosexual encounter. It might have been just a robbery until you put two and two together . . ."

"You mean about the love nest under the trees?"

"Yeah, and you might notice, the Washington *Times* only had his name in the obituaries, no news article at all, and that article in the *Post* was very restrained . . ."

Winston was looking abstractedly out at his party. A district court judge from Virginia blurted his view. "But, don't you see, that's all because of the chief judge here—he just called his friends in the media, and almost nothing came out."

One of the lawyers who had had a little too much to drink

laughed as he put his arm around Winston's shoulder in a too-friendly manner, bringing him back into the group. "Now, Your Honor, I call that first-class Washington, D.C., spin control."

Winston shrugged frostily and the lawyer's arm dropped as he sheepishly backed off before the chief judge's icy stare.

The lawyer looked like a dog hit with a slipper. "Your Honor, I . . . I only meant that in . . . that spin thing was intended as a compliment, not . . ."

Winston straightened his suit jacket. "I despise that term, 'spin control.' All I did was make a few phone calls to some long-standing media friends in my official capacity of chief judge. Sir, I do not do public relations work. Judge Rogers was a fine and respected judge. No one should be allowed to besmirch his name. He was my very close friend."

Tim was taking the whole exchange in about the control of the media. Chief Judge Winston had just risen another few notches in Tim's estimation. The chief judge was a powerful and skilled ally.

Two days later, Tim saw a small but prominent article in the Style section of the *Washington Post* about the "power lunch" that Chief Judge Winston had hosted. The piece featured a photo of Winston, Tim Quinn, and Senator Williams, the chairman of the Senate Judiciary Committee, talking together in a friendly manner in front of Winston's garden fountain. In a city of where images counted heavily, Tim knew that his judgeship was progressing smoothly due to the awesome power of Chief Judge Winston.

CHAPTER 5

TIM HUNG UP THE PHONE, FURIOUS AND FRUSTRATED. THE situation was maddening. Thanks to what the Senate staffer had just whispered to him on the phone, the judicial nomination he had worked so hard to achieve—calling in all his favors, successfully lobbying friends and friends of friends, and ultimately winning over the White House and the president—was now in serious jeopardy.

And he was the only one who knew it.

For anyone who didn't know what he knew, the prospects for his nomination looked great. Word of his nomination by the president had been met with approval, even applause, which was rare in a hyper-politicized Washington. His Senate Judiciary Committee hearing was on track, set for the next week. As an added bonus, C-SPAN had already committed to live full coverage nationwide, which meant that the committee most likely would not want to postpone it. It had been a dream scenario for a nominated judicial candidate—until now.

The senate judiciary staffer had just leaked to Tim that one of the junior Republicans on the committee—a born-again Christian—was going make a grandstand play about the morality of public officials. To make his point, the senator had decided to ask specific questions during Tim's hearing about the candidate's drug use and incidents of marital infidelity, in order to show his constituencies the kind of questions that should be used to qualify a judicial nominee. "Mr. Quinn, it's nothing personal," the staffer had told him. "Senator Jackson just wants to trumpet his high sense of moral values on C-SPAN, for everyone back home. I'm sure it's not a problem for you, but I just wanted to make sure you were . . . alerted."

Tim kept his voice casual and thanked the staffer, then hung up angry. The general counsel of the Judiciary Committee had given him an unofficial clean bill of health—nothing even remotely derogatory had surfaced during the FBI and the separate Senate background checks. Nevertheless, Tim knew he was in trouble. He didn't want to face *any* questions about his sex life, especially under oath. Depending on the questions by this publicity hound of a senator, Tim could be facing possible perjury charges if he lied about his private life. And he might have to—with his wife and children sitting right behind him at the hearing.

Tim absolutely had to head off this line of questioning—if he could. And he had to keep a low profile doing it, so he didn't raise any suspicions about himself. Which meant he had to ask for a big favor from an old friend, the chief of staff of the number-two ranking Republican on the committee.

Tim watched Senator Aaronson's chief of staff Mark Daly walk through two massive brass-and-glass doors of the University Club. They shook hands, and walked down the mahogany-paneled, richly carpeted hallway. Mark had never been inside this club and was appropriately awed. As they began to ascend the wide, red-carpeted stairs, Tim, feigning a light mood, began to chat about the history of the club. At the midway landing of the stairs sat a white bust of Caesar. It was Augustus, arguably the greatest of the Caesars.

"For the life of me, Mark, I've never been able to figure out why this bust is here. They say that old Augustus here found Rome brick and left it marble. But so what? Personally, I think that the only reason it's here is because the founder of the club, President Taft, loved Caesar Augustus and wanted something to fill out this niche here at the landing on the stairs, and it has been here ever since. I've always found it a little bit odd—the man who effectively killed off the Roman republic and established an empire, front and center in a D.C. club. Shouldn't it be Lincoln or Washington? But Caesar Augustus?"

Upstairs, in the General Pershing Bar and Grill, which featured an enormous portrait of the World War I general in full uniform, they took a table by the window looking out over Sixteenth Street and ordered lunch. Partly to warm Mark up, and partly because he dreaded bringing up the reason for the lunch, Tim started to tell the Senate staffer about one of the oddities of the club, the FBI listening post on the third floor, a relic of the Cold War. The University Club was situated right next door to the old Soviet embassy, and, as Tim explained, the U.S. government was most interested in the club's location.

"You see, one of the worst-kept secrets in Washington was the University Club's accession to an FBI request allowing them to install in the club a listening post for the Russian embassy next door. The post is no longer in use, but the deserted site is one floor above us. Why don't we pop up there and see it?"

Mark was game and interested to see the FBI room so Tim told their waiter that they would be gone for a few minutes. Then they went down to the reception desk of the club and got the key for the FBI room and took the elevator to the third-floor corner suite. After opening the door, Tim flipped on the overhead lights. In what had once been a two-room suite for club members who needed to stay overnight, black curtains covered the windows and the room was bare of furniture. Decaying wires stretched across the walls and the ceiling.

Tim told Mark how the FBI tore down the wall between the sitting room and the bedroom to accommodate their equipment, all to monitor the embassy phone calls and photograph everyone who came and went.

"How did they monitor the phone calls?"

"Oh, they had phone taps in tunnels under the street, and the wires from these taps led to this room. This was the command center for monitoring the Soviet embassy. The FBI also had listening devices up on the roof and outside the windows, and I think they had a secondary listening post across the street, too." Tim gestured into a corner. "Over against this wall, they had receivers and other machines stacked up in racks and on metal shelves. They had all this old-style electronic equipment with cathode tubes and very rudimentary verbal pickup capability. All that's left now is that shelving over there, plus a few electrical junction boxes, and some of the wiring from the phone taps. And look, here's the old safe they left behind, the one in which they used to store the daily tapes until they sent them to FBI headquarters for analysis. Pretty interesting, huh?"

Mark ate this information up, as Tim knew he would, until he shepherded the staffer back down to the dining room. As they started to eat, they exchanged the requisite family updates. Mark's wife was still teaching; their only child, a son, was at Michigan State. Tim in turn filled in Mark about his daughter Anne, a photo editor in New York, and his son Paul, an attorney with a Chicago law firm. Inwardly nervous, Tim knew he had to lead naturally into his real motive; he had to make it appear that this was no big thing—disguise that his request was of critical importance to him. "Mark, let me just say that I cannot tell you how grateful I am that you got your boss on board my campaign. He's been crucial. Without him, I don't think that I would have received the nomination."

Daly grinned. "Well, from what I heard on the grapevine, you're being too modest. I heard you mobilized some major juice. Now you've got the whole judiciary committee primed to confirm you next week. It'll be the smoothest approval for a judgeship in years."

"Well, I could use some more help," Tim said.

Keeping his voice casual—and never revealing his source—Tim launched into the problem of Senator Jackson and his proposed questions on drugs and sex. These kinds of questions were completely without justification, he declared. "Mark, I think that just asking them is embarrassing, after the kind of thorough background check I've undergone." Tim paused, shook his head slowly, and glanced down. Then he looked directly into his friend's eyes and delivered the decisive point of the meeting. "Just asking them—well, I resent the implications. I don't think this is a good precedent for the Senate, either."

Mark was shocked to learn about Jackson's planned line of questioning. "This is the first I've learned about this, Tim," he said. And yes, he would talk to his boss and put some real pressure on the junior senator. He was sure his boss could turn Jackson around and control the questioning during the hearing, at least from the Republican side. "And you're right—the practice of allowing improper questions, without foundation, was no way to treat a quality Republican judicial candidate like you."

Tim could barely hide the relief in his face. Still he had learned long ago that in D.C., promises mean nothing until the deed is delivered. So he would wait and see if Mark could deliver. The business part of the lunch was now done. The talk turned back to lighter subjects.

It had been a long week before the Senate hearing.

At the hearing, Tim was relieved that Mark Daly and Daly's boss, Senator Aaronson, had delivered the promised hassle-free questioning during the confirmation hearing. Not one question from the junior senator. No questions at all on the subjects of drugs, morals, or his personal life. Tim's nomination went to the Senate floor by a 12-0 committee vote. Once the nomination was called on the floor, Tim was easily approved by a voice vote. Now he became Judge-designate Quinn. All that was left to becoming a federal Judge for life was the official swearing-in ceremony.

The preparation for the ceremony put Tim downtown the afternoon after the Senate confirmation. He needed a judicial robe for the ceremony. The clerk of the U.S. Court of Appeals had directed him to the only store in D.C. that sold robes to judges. The clerk had even made the appointment for Tim, since the store had limited hours and was open mainly by appointment.

Tim Quinn was a little early for his appointment when he locked his silver Land Rover and looked around at what he thought looked like a pretty rough neighborhood. Could this be the right address? He pulled out the piece of paper and checked it again. Yes, this was the address the clerk of court had given him. He set his jaw and crossed the street, avoiding several little piles of trash and broken bottles, and started checking the street numbers. He had walked nearly a full block before he came to the right number. The sign above the door told him it was a police uniform and supply shop, and he knocked on the door. A loud buzzer let him in. He closed the door behind him. It was dark inside, and he heard the greeting from somewhere to his right before he saw any movement.

"May I help you, sir?"

A tall, thin man came out from behind the counter, his friendly smile the first reassuring sign Tim had encountered in the last fifteen minutes. "Uh, I'm not sure I'm in the right place . . . do you sell judicial robes here?"

"Yes, of course, Your Honor, you've found the right place." The man's smile softened into apology. "I know the neighborhood is not like it used to be, but we've been doing judicial robes for judges in the District since 1936."

"Oh, okay . . . but, how did you know I was a judge?"

The man winked at him. "Well, we only serve police and judges here, and who else would be asking for a judicial robe? Besides all I have this afternoon are two appointments, both for judges."

Both men laughed.

"I'm Quinn. I'm a little early for my appointment—and please don't call me a judge. I'm not sworn in yet and I don't want to jinx it." Tim looked over the man's shoulder, trying to see what was in the room behind him. "Do you happen to carry the old-fashioned type of robe? Perhaps the type of robe that Supreme Court Justice Oliver Wendell Holmes would have worn—you know, with double bell sleeves, buttons instead of a zipper or Velcro, cut deep in the front to show shirt and tie?"

The man nodded. "Yes, I'm familiar with that style. Some other judges have asked for that in order to show their shirt and tie. Now, if you will follow me to the rear of the store . . ."

The tailor led Tim through the narrow aisles lined with police uniforms and accessories. At the rear, the tailor showed Tim some swatches of material from a book. He picked a midweight wool blend. The tailor pointed to a small platform before a three-sided mirror. “Now, sir, please take your jacket off and step up here. You can try this robe on for the sizing.”

“Oh, don’t you want me to wear my suit coat when you measure me for the robe?”

“No, no,” the tailor said. Tim discerned amusement at his naiveté. “It would be much too hot in the courtroom. Judges usually wear their robes without suit coats underneath.”

Tim stepped up onto the small platform facing the mirrors.

“Okay, on the length, most judges usually wear their robes cut at about midshin so they won’t trip going up steps. How’s this suit you?”

“Looks good. But my shirt and tie will show, won’t they?”

“Yes, yes, I know, the ‘Holmes style’—plenty of shirt and tie showing.”

“Good. How about replacing the zipper? Can you do that?”

“Sir, you really are traditional,” the man said, with a little admiration. “Okay, we can do that, but it will take an extra day to replace the zipper and put in buttons. Your robe should be ready . . . let’s see, this is Tuesday . . . we can have it by noon on Friday. Is that okay?”

“Perfect. My swearing in is next Monday, so you’ll have to make sure I can get it by Friday. Here’s my credit card. I believe the clerk of court said the robes run in the three hundred dollar range.”

“Yours will be three fifty-seven with the tax. Let me get your receipt.”

Just then the buzzer went off. The tailor went forward to the front door to let in someone that Tim immediately recognized: Judge Franklin, the second-ranking judge on Tim’s new court.

“Judge Quinn!” Franklin said genially. “I’m glad I caught you. Chief Judge Winston had asked me to come over and oversee the fitting of your robe—as a courtesy. He’d be here himself, but he just couldn’t make it.”

"That's very touching." Tim really was moved. "But I feel guilty to have dragged you down here."

"No problem. Besides, I needed a new lightweight robe anyway." Franklin went on to give the tailor specifications for a silk-blend robe which, according to the tailor would cost over one thousand dollars. Franklin told the tailor to order the robe and to send it and the bill to the clerk of the U.S. Court of Appeals. On the way out of the store, Franklin confided that if Tim had simply borrowed a robe for the ceremony, he could have saved some money.

"Once you're on board and sworn-in, you'll see the chief judge is very generous to his judges. If he approves, we can usually get the court to pay for almost everything related to our judicial duties."

Tim went directly home after the tailor shop. He got out of his car inside the garage of his Alexandria townhouse and went up the stairs to the kitchen on the first floor. The house was silent. He hung his keys on the brass hook, then turned into the hallway, and hollered up the stairs. "Katy?"

Her answer was filtered through the intervening doorways and down the stairs. "I'm up in the bedroom, honey. I'll be right there."

Her hurried footsteps grew closer, and then he saw her dark tweed skirt preceding her down the stairs. She descended slowly, carefully. As she got closer, he could see the familiar slight shaking of her head. Katy had been diagnosed with Parkinson's disease nearly three years ago, but with the medication she was doing just great. He reached out as she came near and took her into his arms. He wrapped his arms around her tiny waist and clasped her to his chest, then leaned back and lifted her off the ground. "Oh, Katy, I love you so much!"

"I love you too, honey, but put me down!"

"I heard some big news today."

"*More* big news?"

"Guess who's going to swear me in?"

"What do you mean?"

"You know—the person who will give me the oath of office at my swearing in, or my 'investiture' as it's officially called."

"I . . . I don't know, who? The president? Oh, my God! The *president*!"

"No, no. But you're close. It's going to be the chief justice of the U.S. Supreme Court. That's who will swear me in."

Katy cocked her head. "Oh, are all new federal judges sworn in by the chief justice?"

"No, not at all, This is very unusual. Chief Judge Winston mentioned the possibility to me a few days ago, and then he called me this morning and told me it was all arranged. Rehnquist has agreed to swear me in. The swearing-in part will have to be at the beginning of the investiture ceremony because Rehnquist has to leave right after he swears me in. He has another engagement. So as soon as he leaves, our ceremony will continue. The speeches and all."

Katy pondered this. "Sounds like Chief Judge Winston is pretty powerful politically."

"He is a heavy hitter about this town."

"Just please don't feel you owe him any favors."

"No, of course not," Tim said. "The court isn't built to work that way."

Tim closed his eyes and hugged her tight again. "Honey, who'd have ever guessed we'd end up like this? When we got married, I was just a young lawyer with no money, and you were this Danish woman who had to leave home and family to marry me. And when little Paul got so sick with the stomach problem—"

"And then after his operation the insurance wouldn't cover his hospital expenses, and then a month later, he had to go back in and have more surgery . . ."

Tim squeezed her tight. He felt tears welling. “Yeah, we almost lost him . . . he was so tiny . . .”

Katy said, “And without telling me you went out and sold the MG and cashed in your life-insurance policy.”

“Riding the bus was okay.”

“No, Tim, you always faced up to our problems and found solutions, one way or another. That was one of the things that really attracted me to you. You have always been my rock.”

Tim looked deep into his wife’s blue eyes. What a risk to his marriage he took running for a judgeship. Thank God that nightmare was past. He was confirmed now. And his marriage was safe. He smiled at her. “I just don’t think I’ve ever been any happier in my whole life than I am right now.”

On the day of his investiture, Tim escorted Katy and his two children through the packed ceremonial courtroom of the U.S. Court of Appeals for the D.C. Circuit, leading them to the reserved seats, where they were seated by the law clerks that were acting as ushers. Tim then went with the clerk of court out the back of the courtroom and into Chief Judge Winston’s chambers.

“The chief justice is getting out of his limo right now!” the clerk exclaimed.

Winston nodded and smiled wryly. “Now let’s calm down, Bill,” he said in his deepest Georgia accent. “Just go out there and meet him at the elevators and then escort him back here. I told him he could use my chambers to robe for the ceremony. Besides, I want to introduce our new judge to him.”

“Yes, Your Honor.”

“Mr. Chief Justice!” Winston boomed as the chief justice quietly walked into Winston’s chambers, followed by his administrative assistant and a plainclothes bodyguard from the U.S. Supreme

Court police force. The administrative assistant withdrew the chief justice's robe from a garment bag and laid it across the back of a chair. Winston warmly greeted the chief justice and introduced Tim to him with glowing praise.

"Oh, I enjoy coming down here, Harry, and it's a pleasure for me to get out of the Supreme Court for such an important ceremony. I think I saw half the D.C. bar when I came down the corridor." Rehnquist smiled genially. "And Tim, I've been aware of your excellent legal career over the years and I know you are going to make a fine judge on this court."

Tim grinned happily and started to speak, but Winston intervened. "Well, Mister Chief Justice, we better start getting robed up, because we should start the ceremony soon. I promised to have you out of here in twenty minutes, because I know you have a reception across town, so we have to make haste for your benefit."

Tim was escorted to the courtroom and the chief justice and the other judges of the court moved into the judges' entrance area of the courtroom, a small space behind the tall maroon curtains immediately behind the bench. No one in the packed, noisy courtroom could see the judges there. All ten active judges and the three senior judges greeted the chief justice and chatted with him for a few moments before Chief Judge Winston gave a signal to the judges and to the clerk of the court that the ceremony should start.

The judges all moved into their positions behind the curtains for their respective judge's chairs, with the chief justice taking the center position behind the curtain. As the clerk struck the gavel three times and called on all present to rise, everyone in the courtroom immediately stopped talking and quickly rose to their feet. The chief justice and all the judges parted the curtains in front of them and moved forward to stand behind their chairs while the clerk's voice boomed out:

"Oyez! Oyez! The chief justice of the United States and the

judges of the U.S. Court of Appeals for the District of Columbia Circuit are now in session. All who have business before this honorable court draw near and be heard. God save the United States and this honorable court."

When the clerk had finished reciting the official opening of the court, the chief justice and the judges moved around their chairs and sat down, leaving only one chair empty, the one on the far right as one looked at the bench. This was the chair where the most junior judge would sit. The seat of the soon-to-be Judge Quinn.

Chief Justice Rehnquist leaned into the microphone. His low baritone voice reverberated through the high-ceilinged, quiet ceremonial courtroom. "Please be seated. I am most pleased to be presiding at this special session of the United States Court of Appeals for the District of Columbia Circuit. We have a most enjoyable task before us today, and that is the investiture of the newest member of this bench. Timothy J. Quinn will shortly become a member of this court. I must apologize ahead of time that I must leave immediately following my swearing in of Mr. Quinn. But my brother, Chief Judge Winston, will continue the ceremony after I leave. At this time, I call upon Mr. Quinn to approach the podium. I would also ask that his wife and his daughter and son accompany him."

Tim stood and proceeded to the podium. Katy Quinn and her children made their way down from the front row of the public seating, came through the gate of the bar rail, and joined him. Then the chief justice, in his distinctive black robe with four gold stripes on each sleeve, got up and moved around behind the other seated judges. The chief justice came down the stairs into the courtroom well and moved to the podium, where he faced the Quinns. Katy was at Tim's left side. She held the Bible out for him with her right hand. Tim solemnly lay the palm of his left hand on it and raised his right hand. The chief justice also raised his right hand

and read from a small card he had removed from a pocket in his robe.

"Timothy J. Quinn, please repeat after me. I, state your name, do solemnly swear that I will administer justice without respect to persons, and will do equal right to the poor and to the rich. . . ."

Katy steadied the Bible under the pressure of Tim's hand. His voice was loud and clear. "I, Timothy J. Quinn, do solemnly swear that I will administer justice . . ."

As he spoke the serious words, Tim felt Katy's hand begin to shake beneath the Bible. Tears welled up in her eyes. He knew she didn't want to shake in front of everybody. They had come so far to reach this moment. Without missing a beat, Tim moved his left hand down the side of the Bible and grabbed Katy's hand, steadying it. Out of the corner of his eye, Tim could see that his daughter, Anne, aware of her mother's tremors had reached over to hold Katy's other hand. God, he was so proud of Anne at that moment.

Tim's son, Paul, next to Anne, put his arm around his sister as Tim boomed out the last phrase of his oath of office: ". . . and that I will well and faithfully discharge the duties of the office on which I am about to enter. So help me God."

There was a brief moment of silence as the chief justice raised his eyes and looked at Tim and extended his hand. "Congratulations, Judge Quinn, and welcome to the bench."

Katy swayed, as if she would faint, and grabbed Tim's arm as the packed courtroom burst into applause. He put his arm firmly around her shoulders, and she lifted her face to him and closed her eyes. Tim was swept away by the sweetest public kiss of his life. As they broke apart, he could only hear Rehnquist's voice through a fog.

"Judge Quinn, you may now be robed by your son, Paul, and your daughter, Anne, and join your colleagues on the bench."

Paul and Anne, having been coached by the clerk and their father earlier that day, brought the robe forward and opened it for their father as the official photographer blazed away. After they helped him into the robe, Tim carefully secured the many small buttons down the front. As he completed the job, he winked at Katy, then hugged his son and daughter. Katy joined them in the middle, and the Quinns rejoiced in a big, but brief, family hug. When they broke, Katy, Anne, and Paul all had tears in their eyes. Tim fought a mist in his eyes as he stood there looking at the three loves of his life. He was starting to lose the fight when he was startled by the commanding voice of the chief judge who had moved to the center seat vacated by the chief justice. "Will everyone please rise as the chief marshal escorts the chief justice from the courtroom."

The courtroom obediently got to its feet. But Chief Justice Rehnquist kept the courtroom waiting as he shook the hands of Katy, Anne, and Paul. He turned toward the bar rail separating the well of the court from the public seating area. Tim nervously watched the still-robed chief justice, escorted by the marshal, stride through the gate of the bar rail and down the center aisle to the main door at the back of the courtroom. Then he heard Winston's voice again.

"Please be seated, and at this time, I will ask our newest judge, Judge Quinn, to join us on the bench and make a few remarks to this session of the court."

Tim took a deep breath and walked around the bench and up the stairs. He took the empty seat on the end and spoke.

"Thank you, Chief Judge, for your gracious welcoming ceremony. You have made both me and my family feel very welcome in this court. I am especially honored that you were able to arrange for the chief justice of the United States to administer the oath of office. I am very pleased by that special touch added to the ceremony. To my family, I want to let you know how much I appreciate the many years of hard work, sacrifice, and patience with which you have paved my road to success. Without your support, I simply could never have reached this high position. To my friends at Wellington and Stone, thank you for many wonderful years of friendship and loyal support. But now that I'm on the bench—no more Mister Nice Guy."

Loud laughter rang through the courtroom.

"To my friends in the intelligence community, thank you for opening a whole new world to me. I will never forget your impressive degree of competence and the selfless service to country I have seen you display on a daily basis. To my fellow members of the D.C. bar, thank you for the constant courtesies and favors you have shown me over the years—but now that I am 'the judge' don't expect me to reciprocate any longer."

Another wave of laughter cascaded through the hall.

"Chief Judge, I don't want to keep these wonderful people who have done me the honor of coming to my investiture away from the wonderful buffet I know awaits them in the foyer, so I will end my comments here. But I want to again thank you personally for a wonderful ceremony. You really do know how to make a new member of your bench feel welcome."

The chief judge leaned forward, looked down the bench at Quinn, and grinned as if he had just been present at the birth of his baby. "Thank you, Judge Quinn, for your generous remarks. I will concur on your first and most prudent judicial recommendation and adjourn this special session."

He banged the gavel once.

"This court is adjourned, and all present are invited to the reception in the foyer."

After an hour of standing at the reception, Katy told Tim that she was tired, so Tim told her to go with the children down to the car and he would be there in ten minutes. Tim wanted to say good-bye to the chief judge. The crowd had thinned dramatically, and Tim found Winston quickly.

"Thanks again for that ceremony, Harry, and I really appreciate what you have done. I know it is most unusual to have the chief justice of the United States swear in a judge. How did you ever arrange that?"

Winston smiled slyly. "Well, Tim, let's just say I called in a chit," the chief judge said with a wink.

"Well, Chief, I certainly appreciate it. I'll always have photos of the chief justice swearing me in as evidence of your power. I'm also very touched by your kindness and your grace with my wife and my children." Tim felt himself getting more fervent than he meant to. "You are truly a special friend, and I will never forget what you have done for me. I know you are responsible for me getting on the bench, capped by this delightful ceremony. I can't thank you enough."

Winston beamed as if he had just scored a hole in one. "Well, Tim, you just enjoy this day, because tomorrow I'm going to put you to work."

CHAPTER

STILL ELATED THE DAY AFTER HIS SWEARING IN, TIM QUINN realized he was actually whistling as he walked down the hallway toward his chambers. Then he entered the reception area of his chambers and saw the enormous towers of boxes lining one wall six feet high, and the tune died on his lips. He stood dumbfounded.

"Is all this *mine?*" he asked.

Loretta D'Antonio, his secretary at Wellington and Stone, was already busy unpacking boxes and making neat towers of papers and books, and she looked up at him and smiled wearily. "Lawyers accumulate a lot of paper over a lifetime, Judge."

A plump Italian-American from New Jersey, Loretta was married to a high school teacher in suburban Virginia and had worked for Tim nearly ten years. Smart, loyal, and possessing a sixth sense that let her see through pretense, she was a perfect filter of information for Tim, who tended to believe what people told him. She often put her interpretation on the messages she relayed to him. Firm yet polite and sincere, she somehow managed to make everyone feel special. She was a first-class mediator with the outside world. Officially Loretta was still employed by Wellington & Stone, but she and Tim had discussed her joining him at the court. The lower government salary was a barrier, however. Tim had been wondering if he could pay her the salary difference out of his own pocket—would that be legitimate? He wasn't sure. With her continued status so uncertain, it was a bittersweet pleasure for him to see Loretta here in his new offices.

Tim took off his suit coat and pitched in, under Loretta's directions. He was soon caught up in the rhythm, ripping open the taped boxes and sorting through papers, trying to understand Loretta's system, then transferring books and files to bookshelves and filing cabinets.

By late in the morning, they had moved on to the heavy work, rearranging some of the furniture in the chambers to make it more functional. It had all belonged to Judge Rogers, who had been so grotesquely murdered. Some of the furniture was beautiful old mahogany, including a huge, ornate desk with plenty of drawers. Tim could imagine how much pleasure Judge Rogers would have gotten from this cozy room.

"It looks like an organized hurricane in here," a voice drawled behind them in the doorway.

Tim bolted upright.

"Tim, good morning, and to your assistant, good morning, ma'am," said a smiling Chief Judge Winston.

Loretta half bowed at him. "Good morning, Chief Judge."

"And what is your name, ma'am?"

"Sir, I'm Loretta, Judge Quinn's secretary from Wellington and Stone."

"I thought I recognized your beautiful voice. We have spoken many times when I have called Tim."

Loretta was blushing as the chief judge turned to Tim. "Well,

Judge Quinn, there are a few matters I would like to discuss with you in private."

"Please come on in, Chief Judge. Would you like some coffee?"

"No, just a few minutes of your time, if you don't mind."

Tim let Winston lead the way into his inner office. He then followed, and turned silently to close the door. As he did so, he saw Loretta staring after them intently. He looked at her, nodded and winked to signal that everything was under control, then closed the door behind them.

"Please, Harry, sit down. I hope you'll excuse the mess, I'm just getting settled in here." Tim had to clear stacks of papers from two chairs so they could sit down amid the piles of boxes.

"Well, Tim, I just wanted to see if you needed anything." His voice got serious, almost with commanding authority. "And to remind you that, even though you are the most junior judge on the court, you are the equal of all other judges and you will be treated that way. Your vote always counts."

Winston went on to explain in detail the workings of the court's random rotation system, how cases are assigned, and how judges sit in panels of three to hear appeals. He gave Tim a paperback copy of the *Court Rules* and a slim bound history of the court. "Don't forget, Tim, that you always have one-third of the power on any panel." He smiled, now good-humored as ever. "I trust you'll use it wisely."

"I will and let me say again that I'll never forget your invaluable help in getting me here. I owe you big time, Harry."

"Forget about that. You got here on your own abilities, and you don't owe me anything."

Then Winston uttered a most curious thing that puzzled Tim.

"Tim, there are some cases that we, as a court, have to make go a certain way—there will be things outside the record that dictate this—you must trust me in those times."

Tim's instincts and sense of gratitude prevented him from

asking for an explanation of this statement. All he did was mutter, "Sure, Chief."

Winston's face showed a satisfied smile, almost as if this was the main point of his visit.

"Good. Good. Well now, on you getting settled in, I want to make sure you're as comfortable as possible."

Then the chief judge got up and wandered around the room inspecting the familiar furniture, rubbing his hands over some of it with apparent affection. He looked lost in thought. Judge Rogers had been a close friend of Winston's, Tim thought. It probably was painful to return to these rooms.

"I apologize that you still have this old furniture that was used by Judge Rogers; I will see to it that this is all cleaned out and replaced with new furniture in a style of your own choice."

"No, thanks anyway," Tim said quickly. "I actually like this stuff a lot. Judge Rogers had very nice taste. The court doesn't need to spend any money on new furniture. Maybe I'll need some new filing cabinets, but that's about it." Tim got up and moved to the chief judge. "But as long as you are here, I would like to talk to you about a hiring problem I have."

"Why sure, Tim, what is it?"

"Well, you just met Loretta, my secretary from my law firm. She's worked for me for ten years, and we really have become a good team. Bottom line, I want to bring her over here to work with me, but I'm only allowed to offer her a GS-nine salary here, and that would mean a big pay cut for her."

Winston replied with a wave of his hand. "Don't you worry about that. As the chief judge, I'm authorized two GS-twelve slots for my secretaries, and I only use one of them. So why don't I just hire Loretta as if she were working for me, and detail her to your chambers to work for you? I do believe a GS-twelve makes over sixty thousand per year. How does that sound to you?"

Tim sighed, relieved. "That sounds great."

Winston clapped his hands and headed toward the door. "Well, that was an easy problem to solve. Come to me anytime. You are in the court family now, and the family helps each other out." He eyed the inner office again. "I understand that you want to keep this early American style of Max's, but we need to brighten this place up. Paint, new carpets. We'll get a first-class interior decorator to come in here and make this set of chambers truly reflect your own personality."

"Well . . . thank you, Harry—" Tim was taken aback. "I thought, I mean, I was told by the clerk that with the tight budget, there just isn't money for that."

Winston chuckled, the generous-host laugh of his Georgetown power lunch. "Now, now, don't you worry about that." He smiled conspiratorially. "That's what I tell the clerk to say for general public consumption. But for new judges, we are authorized to spend a certain amount of money to redecorate your chambers. So you can shine it up just the way you like it. I'll give the clerk of the court a call about this."

"Well, Harry, I don't want anybody to get in trouble for bending the rules."

"Oh, come on." Winston frowned at him. "It's authorized by the Administrative Office of the U.S. Courts. Besides, if there is a little overrun, I have some discretionary funds. Now separate subject. It's a tradition for the chief judge to buy lunch for a new judge on his first day at court. Are you free for lunch?"

"Well, sure."

"Good. I'll get us a good table at La Colline, and why don't you drop by my office at twelve? I always make my lunch dates at twelve noon—that way I don't have to worry about forgetting the time."

"You are too kind, Chief. I'll see you at twelve."

Tim walked the chief judge to the outer door of his chambers. Winston bowed and winked to Loretta as he passed the desk in the outer office and disappeared through the hallway door. Loretta stared at Tim quizzically. "What was that all about?"

"The chief judge just solved our salary problem."

Loretta was happy and agreed immediately to be his judicial secretary. "Great!" Tim said. "Katy will be happy to hear that you are still going to be taking care of me."

When Winston led Tim through the large glass doors of La Colline, the maître d' practically fell all over himself to greet the chief judge. As he escorted his guests across the large dining room, Tim had to hurry at first to keep up, but the procession was slowed as many diners waved and called out to Winston, some of them half standing to reach clumsily across tables for handshakes. The stir caused three men at a table off to the left to turn and look at them. Tim recognized two of his partners from Wellington & Stone with someone he didn't know, probably a new client. He smiled and nodded to them. They raised their glasses to him, but it was clear to Tim that he was only an accessory to the heavy hitter walking in front of him.

Soon they were seated at a table in the back, beneath a large, gilt-framed painting of a Paris street scene. The waiter arrived and Winston asked for the wine list. While they waited for him to return, Winston turned to Quinn. "What are you drinking, Tim?"

"I think I'll just have iced tea."

Winston frowned. "That's unacceptable, Judge Quinn. This is a special occasion and we're drinking champagne."

Soon the waiter returned and Winston quickly scanned the wine list and said, "Waiter, we'll start with a bottle of Roederer Cristal."

"Excellent choice, sir. Should I bring that now, or with your meal?"

"Right now, sir! My mouth is so dry I feel like I'm spitting cotton!"

Winston smiled widely and turned to Tim, who was pondering whether the bottle of champagne cost $250 or $300.

The meal was a delight. Excellent French dishes were washed down by a second bottle of champagne. Winston regaled Tim with stories, some of them no doubt inflated or embellished, about his youth in Georgia and his days at Yale Law. He was an amazingly good, even spellbinding storyteller, and Tim found himself divided between rapt attention and sometimes uncontrollable laughter. Then, as coffee was brought, Winston turned serious.

"Tim, I will try to be delicate, but we all have human demands, and please don't take offense, because I am not trying to pry into your private business." Winston fingered his champagne flute almost shyly. "But, I know that, in leaving Wellington and Stone, you must be taking a huge pay cut, and I know that sending your two children to those private prep schools and, later on, to Ivy League colleges, must have given you some punishing tuition bills."

Tim started to respond that things really weren't so bad, but Winston held up his hand. "Now, Tim, what I'm trying to say is, now that you are a member of my court, I can arrange for you to earn an extra twenty thousand dollars a year from teaching, which is the maximum outside income a federal judge can earn according to the law." He swallowed the rest of his champagne. "This involves your agreeing to teach a seminar each semester at Jefferson Law School right here in town, and it's not a difficult task. For instance, of the other eight judges on our court, I have been able to place two of them, Franklin and Janoff, on the faculty at Jefferson Law. I arranged that, because I knew they needed the extra money, and I would be happy to arrange the same thing for you if you want."

Tim sat there puzzled, a little woozy from the champagne. This was too generous. Winston went on, as if Tim's silence were reflexive reluctance, not surprise. "There's not a lot of heavy lifting involved, if you get my point. As a matter of fact, I shouldn't say this, but I happen to know that Judge Franklin and Judge Janoff often have their law clerks fill in for them teaching the seminars. They're like ghost professors, coming to the first class of the semester then disappearing."

Tim thought he saw Winston wink as he delivered those last words. Tim blinked hard. He hadn't had this much to drink at lunch for a while, but the champagne sure was good. He tried to clear his head . . . wasn't he supposed to answer something? Oh yeah.

"Well, Chief, that's very generous of you, but let me also be very candid. I am grateful for your offer, but I don't need the money. I made some good investments when I was at Wellington and Stone, and I'm in fairly good shape financially."

Tim thought he saw a shadow of disappointment pass across Winston's face. But if it was there it was now gone, perhaps imagined for all Tim knew, and Winston was smiling again.

"Well, Tim, I am delighted to hear that. Now, let me pick up the check, and we'd better get back to work."

Tim felt he had somehow offended Winston and blurted out an impulsive invitation. "Chief, this has been a wonderful time, and I must tell you that, while I can't match your grace in storytelling, I can certainly reciprocate and extend the hospitality of my home and the excellent Danish cooking of my wife." The words had come out in a rush. "What I'm trying to say is, please, would you and a companion or friend, if you like, come to our home in Alexandria next Friday evening for dinner?"

The chief broke into a huge smile. "Why, that's very kind of you. I would be delighted to meet your lovely wife again, and this time on her own territory, where she can feel more relaxed." Then he winked again. "And if it's all right with you, I would like to bring along a young lady friend that I have been squiring around town recently."

"Great," said Tim.

Soon he was back at his chambers. His first day couldn't have gone better, he thought at the end of the day.

There was one nagging thing: Maybe this is not a healthy court, if the president can ask for and receive results on certain cases? Maybe that's what the chief judge meant when he told Tim earlier that some cases have "to go a certain way" and that I should "trust" him in those times.

This was a disturbing thought for his first day, so Tim put it in his mental rearview mirror and out of his mind.

CHAPTER 7

OVER THE NEXT WEEK, TIM TURNED HIS FULL ATTENTION TO his first big problem as a new judge: the hiring of three good law clerks. At the rapid pace in which cases appear and are decided in a U.S. Court of Appeals, it was essential that he have bright, hard-working law clerks available to help him process the high volume of paperwork. Now he was sitting across from one of the law-clerk candidates.

Quinn had become a judge at a particularly bad time to hire law clerks—April, very late in the recruiting year. Virtually all the top candidates graduating from the best law schools were already committed to either clerkships or elite law firms. Yet for many first-year associates at big firms, a late opportunity to get hired as a clerk at the prestigious U.S. Court of Appeals for the D.C Circuit offered a major boost to their careers. The law firms who had hired them were eager to have one of their associates garner that experience at the federal appeals court in their jurisdiction. It could be an invaluable advantage for both the law firm and the young lawyer.

Through two friends who were the deans at Columbia and Georgetown law schools, Tim identified two recent graduates now at large D.C. firms who might be eager to serve one-year clerkships in his chambers. Now, as Dorothy Taylor, a poised young black woman candidate, took her seat, Tim settled himself in his old wooden Boston rocker marked by the now-faded golden West Point crest at the top of the chair. Katy had given it to him some years ago, when his back had begun to bother him. Slow rocking had given him many hours of relief when nothing else, not even a heating pad, would dull the pain. Over time, the rocker became his favorite chair.

"Well, Ms. Taylor, thanks for coming over on such short notice," Tim began. "I've read your resume, and I'm very impressed. I see that you were on the law review at Georgetown, that you have graduated quite high in your class . . . what was your ranking?"

"Your Honor, I was fourth."

"Yes, yes. I also see that you wrote an interesting article on overseas investments in the *Georgetown Tax Review Journal*. Tell me, what was that about?"

Dorothy took a deep breath and collected herself. "Well, Your Honor, it was a narrow comparison of parts of the corporate tax systems in the United States, Great Britain, Germany, and France. Now, as you probably know, those three European countries all take different approaches to the taxation of corporate profits, and naturally, they all think they have the best system." She stopped to breathe again, then resumed. "And of course, everyone subject to the U.S. tax code suffers the so-called 'double taxation' penalty, which means that corporate profits are taxed once to the corporation, and then again a second time the same profits are taxed after they have been distributed to the shareholders, but this time as individual income . . ."

Tim could see that her nervousness was making her try to show off her knowledge of tax law, a place he didn't want to go, so he gently cut her off.

"I see. That's interesting, and so is the recommendation I got from the managing partner at your firm." He smiled at her reassuringly. "Now I understand that you've been there for only eight or nine months. How would you feel about taking a break from that firm and clerking in my chambers for a year?"

Dorothy smiled back. "Your Honor, I think I'd like that very much. Clearly, it's a great opportunity. And my firm is fully behind this . . . that is, if you select me."

"Good. Now before we go any further, let me tell you a little bit about what the duties of a law clerk would be in my chambers."

"Yes, Judge, I'd like that."

"First, your primary duty would be to prepare what we call 'bench memos,' which really means a summary of the facts and the law for each case before the oral argument takes place. Now this bench memo is important to me because it's a key part of my own preparation for the oral argument. You'd prepare this bench memo by analyzing the record and the two briefs filed by the opposing parties, and then summarizing the positions of the parties and your recommendation on what my decision should be for each case." Tim realized he was going into too much detail so he cut it short. "So you see, a law clerk in this court occupies a very important and responsible position, one that often has a very strong influence on this court's decisions. How do you feel about that?"

Dorothy leaned forward, her gaze intent on his. "Your Honor, that sounds like both a challenging and a fulfilling job. Should you choose me to fill that role, I promise you that I'll work very hard."

"Well, Ms. Taylor, everything I've received about you from your law school and from your law firm seems to indicate that you are a smart and hard worker." Quinn paused and thought. Not only were her credentials stellar, but he liked how she had maintained eye contact with him so steadily. And she knew how to listen—a rare skill. He made his decision right then. "Would you like to be my law clerk for the next year?"

Dorothy looked elated. "Judge, yes, yes. I accept. Thank you. When do you want me to start?"

"Well, how long will it take you to wrap up work on your cases at the law firm?"

"I think that I can be ready a week from this Monday."

"That would be fine with me. I'll tell my secretary, Loretta, to give you the necessary employment forms. But now that you are my law clerk, let me give you my three rules for my clerks. I learned them long ago when I clerked myself."

Dorothy nodded, ready to take mental notes.

"Rule number one: *Whatever* is said in chambers *stays* in chambers. That means you are under judicial privilege now and forever. If I ever hear outside these chambers something I have said about one of the cases or one of the other judges, I had better not find out that it came from you. Is that clear?"

"Yes, Judge, it's quite clear. There will be no leaks from me."

"Rule number two: You will *always* refer to any judge, state or federal, by their titles. That means all judges are addressed as either Your Honor, Judge, or sir or ma'am. You'll give respect to the office, even if you don't respect the person holding that office. This applies whether you are talking to them face to face or on the phone. Any questions on that?"

"No, Your Honor."

"Good answer. You're a quick learner."

Both of them laughed.

"Rule number three, and this will really be general advice about how I want our chambers to operate. It's something I learned from reading about the origins of the common law. These exact words have been stated over and over again since the 1600's by the master of Jesus College at Cambridge University in England. He said them to the newest don who had just been hired to teach there, and by tradition, it is repeated to all the new professors since then. The master always told the new professor, 'Don't try to be clever, we're all clever here. Just be kind, a little kind.' To me, this means that all the people who work in my chambers should really function as a family, and I don't want people to be competitive inside this family. I want us all to do our jobs, but I also want us to help each other, and as much as possible, to have fun in the process."

Dorothy seemed impressed, maybe even relieved. Tim could tell she was mulling over the "just be kind" quotation, an injunction far different than what law students and attorneys usually heard. "Yes, Your Honor."

"Okay, that's it. Welcome aboard."

The next clerkship candidate was a political referral from the White House counsel's office. Tim was a little uneasy when the chief judge suggested he call Bill Monroe, the president's lawyer, and see if he had any lawyers from his office who wanted to clerk for him. Tim thought that his clerks should be nonpolitical and he knew that most of the young lawyers hired by the White House were from the conservative Federalist Society, but he didn't want to rebuff a suggestion from Winston, a man he owed so much. So he called Monroe who was very pleased to send over a recent hire. "You'll like him, Judge. He's a ball of fire and a quick study, an honors graduate of Duke Law."

And Tim did like the energetic, sincere young man. He was a true conservative, but that was okay. Tim was the judge and would make the decisions in his chambers, not the clerks. Some weak judges let their law clerks heavily influence them and literally make the decisions. There was an old Washington anecdote with a fair amount of truth to it—that one of the liberal justices on the Supreme Court once said to his clerks when he was in ill health, "If I die, don't tell the chief justice, just prop me up behind my desk and keep voting for me."

Tim hired the Duke grad, just as he did his first clerk, at the end of the interview. The chambers had to be up and running at full capacity if Tim was to join the court as a judge at top speed.

By the next Friday, Tim had hired all three of his clerks, whose credentials and characters had impressed not only him but also Chief Judge Winston—who was particularly pleased that the young White House lawyer had been hired.

Winston was coming to dinner at the Quinns that night with his lady companion, so Tim left the courthouse early. As he climbed the stairs from his garage to the first floor of his town house, he saw Katy's dress blur by. He sniffed the kitchen air. "Oh, baby, Danish-style pork roast! Thank you for marrying me!"

Katy reappeared briefly to peck his cheek, then bustled back into the kitchen. Tim followed her.

"I hope your chief judge and his date like pork roast as much as you do," she called behind her. "What can you tell me about Caroline Foster, the woman friend he's bringing?"

"I don't know too much, honey. She works as an investment advisor—I think that's what the chief said. The rumor mill has it that she's kind of young. She's half the chief's age. And . . ." Tim paused.

His wife stopped stirring the gravy. "And what?"

"Well, one of the partners at my firm told me that she may have a drug problem."

"*Really*. It looks like it is going to be an interesting evening!"

Tim went upstairs to shave and shower. He was zipping up his slacks when, out the window, he saw a long black limo slowly pull into his driveway. Tim grabbed his blazer and pulled it on as he hurried down the two sets of stairs and out the front door. The limo was stopped and the driver had come around the front of the car to open the right rear passenger door. Harry Winston emerged, smiling and laughing as he extended his hand. Tim was stunned. Assuming Harry didn't own his own limo, he must have hired a car and driver for the occasion.

"Hello, Tim, it's great to see you, and I want you to meet my friend, Caroline."

Tim looked into the limo and saw a striking blond woman slide across the seat. Caroline wore a low-cut black velvet dress and, as she leaned forward to emerge, Tim could see the bare, sumptuous curves of almost all of her breasts. He averted his eyes and stuttered his greetings as she exited the limo. "Hi, I'm Tim."

Caroline adjusted her dress as she stood, smiled warmly, and extended her hand. "Good evening. I'm Caroline." She proffered her hand and Tim shook it.

Winston turned to the driver. "Now, I want you back here no later than eight o'clock, parked in this driveway right here, you understand me?"

That was too early. "Chief—" Tim began.

"Be right with you, Tim."

Tim leaned forward and whispered to the chief judge in a low voice. "Uh, Chief, dinner probably won't be served until nine, and your driver certainly won't be needed before ten."

The chief judge spoke directly into Tim's ear. "Tim, I'm paying good money for this colored boy tonight, and I'm not going to tell him he's free until ten, because I know these people. He'd probably go out and drink, and then I would be driven home by a *drunk nigra*. No, I'm not going to take that chance. No, sir. Now, let's go inside. I want to meet your lovely wife again."

Tim was stunned. He felt his face go red. The chief turned to the driver and waved his hand. "Get on, boy! I'll see you at eight, and if I'm not here, why then, you just sit in the car and wait for me."

Tim didn't think he had heard anyone referred to as a "colored boy," let alone a "nigra," even in the movies, since, what, the sixties? And he was surprised by the cold way the judge treated the driver. Even calling him "boy."

I thought I knew this man.

But even as his Yankee blood rose in his neck, Tim forced himself to grant Winston some concessions: He had grown up in the Deep South, and what was racist and wrong everywhere today had been norms during his Georgia childhood. No, he told himself, be charitable. We are all flawed, and this is a man who has risen to a very high position in life. I'm sure that as a federal judge, he is fair and honorable.

Katy warmed quickly to Winston's Southern charm. Once again, his insider stories about Washington were really spellbinding, and he usually had clever twists at the end that were either sidesplitting or politically fascinating. "Will Rogers was right," the chief told them as they all moved into the dining room. "He didn't make up jokes—he just looked at the actions of the government bureaucrats in D.C. and reported them."

Tim had carefully nursed his one Jack Daniels before dinner, adding ice and water whenever he refreshed his guests' drinks. The chief had two Wild Turkeys, and Katy her usual glass of white wine, but Caroline had drained three scotches over ice, and had also disappeared into the bathroom three times for perhaps five to ten minutes on each visit. She was getting loud and laughing more than necessary. Well, Tim thought as they sat down, nothing bad could happen here.

They seated themselves at the long mahogany table, Tim and Katy at the ends, Harry and Caroline opposite each other at the middle. Tim opened and poured the wine as Katy brought plates loaded with food in from the kitchen. As they ate, Winston was ever the gracious guest. "This roast is certainly delicious, Katy. I must say, it's a rare pleasure for a bachelor like me to eat in someone's home, not a restaurant. I don't remember when I have had a better meal."

"Why thank you."

"And the wine, Tim, this is a wonderful Bordeaux. May I see the bottle?"

Tim handed the bottle across the table.

"My, my. Chateau Haut Brion, 1992. No wonder my taste buds are so happy. Caroline, isn't this wine wonderful?"

"Yeah, Harry, it's fine. Excuse me, I gotta pee."

Caroline stood unsteadily, regained her balance, and then walked down the hall. She startled the group into silence, but as soon as the bathroom door closed behind her, Harry jumped in. "Well, you folks understand, Caroline is a little bit earthy and she's young, and I hope you will excuse her occasional roughness . . ."

"Harry, she's just being honest," Katy said. "She's fine."

Harry then launched into a story about the Southern belles who would visit the college boys at Hobbes in the late fifties, how silly the girls could get after a little Wild Turkey. He was telling them about a wild beauty named Jeanette who rode a motorcycle up the stairs of his fraternity house, when Caroline slipped back into her chair, her eyes glassy. Harry let his story falter.

After a beat or two, Katy stood up. "We've got coffee and key lime pie, so how many for pie, and how many for coffee?"

Everyone wanted pie and coffee. Tim helped Katy ferry the goods in from the kitchen and as they reassembled themselves at the table, Tim noticed Winston's neckwear. "I see you're wearing your Yale tie this evening, Chief Judge."

Winston leaned forward and smiled. "That's a good guess, but this happens to be a tie from Hobbes. It's just coincidental that the school colors for Yale and Hobbes are the same, blue and white. Now, being a Hobbes man from Georgia up at Yale Law School in Connecticut, I'll tell you, that was quite a change, and it took some adjustment, not just for me, but for the Yankees as well. You see, as a young man, I spoke with what must have been a true deep Georgia drawl, and in class at Yale, when I stood up and spoke, I got a bunch of blank stares. It seems that none of those Yankees could understand a word I was saying. And besides, it was hard for me to understand all those fast-talking northern boys myself. That first semester up at Yale, I felt like I was living on the first floor of the Tower of Babel."

Everyone laughed, but Tim could sense some residual resentment in Winston's words. The northerners had thought he was a hick.

"I don't know why Yale and Hobbes both use blue and white," Winston went on, "unless maybe it's to show you up front that you are going to feel blue after they bleed you white for alumni donations once you graduate and start making some serious money." He smiled widely. "I must admit, sometimes I feel like they ought to change the name Hobbes to Winston College, the amount of money they squeeze out of me."

"A good idea, Harry."

"But being a big contributor has its perks," the chief judge said. "I was glad to be able to help Judge Janoff's son get into Hobbes. I believe in helping my friends." Winston winked. Tim caught his meaning and winked back.

Caroline bent forward over her dessert, leaned on her right elbow, and extended her coffee cup in her right hand. "You know, the main thing I remember about my college . . ."

The coffee cup fell from her hand and spilled its contents over the middle of the table. As the brown stain spread through the white tablecloth, Caroline remained frozen, her mouth open, staring down at it in surprise. Katy jumped to her feet with a napkin and hurried to Caroline's side. "You poor dear, here, let me . . ."

As she reached in front of Caroline with the napkin and started to blot the stain, she also put her hand on Caroline's shoulder. But Caroline shrank from her touch, slumping and turning in her chair to look up at Katy with vacant eyes.

"Caroline, are you all right?"

Caroline shook her head, then leaned back in her chair. "Yeah, I'm all right, I'm sorry . . . I'm so tired, I'm sorry . . ."

Winston was already on his feet and coming around to Caroline. He grabbed her upper arms and pulled her to her feet. She blinked hard, looking as if she was unsure of where she was or what was happening. Winston turned to Katy and Tim. "Tim, I believe Caroline and I are going to depart now. It has been a long day for all of us, and Caroline and I are quite tired. We have had a wonderful evening. Katy, thank you so very much for the wonderful meal and your splendid hospitality."

Winston had to support a wobbly Caroline to the door. Tim hurried ahead and opened it, then saw the driver jump out of the car and open the passenger door on the limo. As Harry and Caroline felt their way down the steps, Tim stayed in the doorway so as not to overhear their muffled words. After Harry loaded Caroline into one side, he walked quickly around the back. Harry smiled and waved to Tim again, then got in and closed the door. As the limo pulled out into the street, Tim turned to Katy, who had joined him. "Well that was a quick end to the evening, wasn't it?"

"Yes, poor Caroline. I hope it's not the flu or something."

Tim turned and raised his eyebrows. "You really think she has the flu?"

"I don't know. She seemed ill. She was pale and clammy when I touched her arm."

"Well, I think the rumors on Caroline are dead-on right. I think she was high on coke or something and got sick when she mixed them with alcohol. When I was a prosecutor in the Justice Department, I saw a lot of druggies, and believe me, she is one."

"Really? How can you tell? Why wasn't it just alcohol?"

"Katy, she had all the signs. I mean, for starters, she went to the bathroom a lot and stayed in there a long time. And every time she came out, she was quiet and glassy-eyed. And after she dropped her coffee cup in the middle of a sentence, she just zoned out."

Katy looked upset. "Well, you may be right on the drugs. But how does the chief judge end up with a girl like that? I mean, he must be close to seventy, and she was what, late twenties? I almost felt like he was dating one of Anne's college friends, except they have a lot more class than she does. Are they living together?"

"All I know is the word around the courthouse is that Winston lives alone, but he does take Caroline to a lot of social functions, and that's been going on for more than a year now."

"Well, she wasn't exactly what you'd call 'high class,' was she? Come on, help me with the dishes."

As they were cleaning up, Tim mentally started replaying the evening. "Wait'll I tell you about the limo driver."

"Why? What happened?"

Tim related the limo incident to Katy, including Harry's words. "And get this, Winston not only referred to the driver as a 'colored boy' and a 'nigra,' and he even said 'get on, *boy*' to his face."

Katy just couldn't swallow it. "No! Come on, Tim, today no federal judge is going to call someone a 'colored boy' or a 'nigra.' That's preposterous!"

"Honey, I'm telling you, I heard it."

"He sounds like some plantation owner from the last century.

And he brought that young girl into our house, where she may well have been doing drugs in our bathroom! How could he get away with all that? Because he's rich?"

"Katy, money is too easy an answer. Winston is rich but that doesn't explain it all. Washington has special rules. Come on, baby, let's go to bed. It's been a long day."

CHAPTER 8

"LORETTA, DO YOU KNOW IF ANY OF THE CLERKS ARE STILL around?" Tim asked late Tuesday afternoon just a few days before he would be hearing his first case. "I've got a bench memo I'd like Dorothy to write by tomorrow afternoon."

"Well, Judge, I'll call her, but you'll spoil her fun if you make her stay late tonight. Tuesday is the evening all of the clerks go out to the Dubliner Pub for happy hour after work. You know, to gossip about all the judges."

The Dubliner. That was the place where Vicky Hauser had thrown her wine in Tim's face a few months before. Had Tim inadvertently given the clerks something to gossip about? He was shaken by the possibility. He got up from his desk chair and walked to the window behind his desk with his back to Loretta. She was very good at reading his feelings on his face. *Christ, I have to watch my step,* he thought. *I am a married man and the court has a big-time rumor system.*

"Oh, and Judge Bowen asked if she could ride with you over to the reception at Wellington and Stone tonight," Loretta added. Tim's old firm was hosting a belated farewell reception for him. It would be very well attended by members of the D.C. bar as well as most of the members of his court. The chief judge was out of town and had sent his regrets.

"No problem. Tell her I'll leave at four-thirty sharp."

After Loretta left to call Judge Bowen and Dorothy, Tim tried to dismiss the Dubliner from his thoughts. That episode with Vicky was definitely in the rearview mirror of his life. If anyone who knew him had seen the wine-throwing scene, well, there was nothing he could do about it now. What was beyond his control should be beyond his worry.

He was happy to give a ride to Rosemary Bowen. He knew only the bare facts of her. He did know that she had never married and was in her early sixties, small and frail looking. She had been raised in Philadelphia and graduated from Bryn Mawr College and the University of Pennsylvania Law School; she had been a tax lawyer before being appointed to the federal bench. She frequently missed court these days; it was an open secret in the courthouse that she had just started undergoing chemotherapy for uterine cancer. Her prospects for recovery were said to be good.

Although Tim had also studied the bios of the other judges and met them briefly at his swearing-in ceremony, he really only knew Winston. He wanted and needed to get to know them well; it was important for an appeals court to have collegiality. He had heard rumors that this court could get quite contentious, and he didn't want to be part of that. He wanted to fit in and get along.

True court insiders, including some of the appellate attorneys at his old firm, had told Tim that his colleagues could be classified into two distinct groups. The larger faction was called the "Independents." Five of the ten judges on the court, their votes did not fall into predictable patterns, and they voted independently of each other, so that you never knew how they were going to come down on a given case. The second group was referred to as the "Chief Judge's team." Only about three judges were on this so-called team; they tended to vote right down the line with the chief judge on most cases. As the brand-new judge, Tim figured that he might possibly be classified as an unknown. But people were probably betting that he would join the chief judge's crew when he started voting on cases, especially since it seemed to be common knowledge that Winston and Tim were old friends. . . . But Tim had resolved that he would not be beholden to Winston, that he would vote according to the merit of a case as he saw it, and not be unduly swayed by any other judge's views.

Thanks to the bumper-to-bumper traffic on M Street headed toward Georgetown, Tim had plenty of time to get to know Rosemary Bowen. She was very pleasant and chatty. Tim learned that she commuted to the court from Leesburg, Virginia, where she lived with her two tabby cats in an old Victorian mansion that she was renovating. Tim liked her right away; she was candid, unpretentious, and sincere. He could detect, however, that she lacked the passion about being a judge that Tim and Winston had. To her, the judgeship was just a job, and she couldn't wait to retire. She did adore the chief judge: "He has such a brilliant mind," she told Tim. She was glad that Tim had been selected for the court because the chief had confided to her that Quinn was his choice. "He's a dear friend of mine, you know," she said as they drove into the parking garage. "In fact, he recently helped me get a loan from a banking friend in Georgia to do an addition on my house." Interesting, Tim thought. Harry Winston really seemed to take good care of his judges.

The reception was well underway by the time Tim and Rosemary arrived. His old law partner, Jay Wellington, had promised Tim that there would be no speeches, just an informal reception for invited members of the D.C. bar to meet the new judge who was the firm's former partner. Tim got a Jack Daniels from the bar and looked around for Wellington. When Tim finally spotted him, Wellington was part of a throng of admirers circling one of the superstars of the Washington legal establishment, Leo Draco.

Leo Draco was tall and thin, with cool blue eyes that exuded intelligence. His most striking physical feature was his hair. It was snow-white and thick, combed straight back and kept moist-looking with gel. Tim had known him casually for a long time and was familiar with his pedigree: Harvard undergrad, Yale Law, a former White House deputy counsel in the Ford Administration. Draco had also been the deputy solicitor general of the United States and had argued in excess of thirty cases before the Supreme Court, winning all but four cases. He was a past president of the D.C. bar and was considered a legend in appellate courts. Draco was a real tiger in the courtroom. Some people likened him to a combined Alan Dershowitz/Ken Starr on steroids. A very savvy, very successful lawyer who headed his own small firm that specialized in appellate practice. Tim was pleased that the reception had brought out this type of big hitters in the Washington legal world.

Tim went over to say hi to Wellington and Draco, and the knot of lawyers parted to welcome him. "Judge Quinn!" Draco exclaimed. "I must offer you my sincerest congratulations on your ascension to the court. From all I hear, you're the perfect man for the job."

"Uh, thank you, Leo, glad you dropped by," Tim said. Knowing that Leo Draco was a frequent advocate before his court, he felt uncomfortable engaging him in extended conversation so he excused himself quickly and pulled Jay Wellington aside. "Miss me at the firm?" he asked.

"Yeah. The theft of office supplies has been dramatically down since you left."

Tim broke into a smile and hugged Jay. Then the two old friends started circulating, greeting the guests just they had done for years while they were building their firm. It was a great party and Tim liked visiting with old friends.

Tim was sitting at a table in a small cafeteria-style sandwich shop near the court having a late lunch when someone tapped him on the shoulder. "May I join you?" drawled a familiar voice. He turned around and saw a smiling Chief Judge Winston. Winston sat across from him with his tray of food. He, like Tim, was having the specialty of the house—a tender New York-style beef brisket on a kaiser roll. "Loretta told me where you were," he said. After querying Tim about the reception the previous Tuesday and expressing effusive regrets about having had to visit old business acquaintances in Georgia, he asked, "Have you had a chance to look at the cases we'll be hearing tomorrow?"

"Why, yes, Chief, I have bench memos on them, and I've just finished making my final review."

"Fine, fine. Tim, on that last case we're hearing tomorrow, I believe it's called the Ryco case—a construction-contract lawsuit between the prime contractor and the sub. It's about a big government building here in D.C. The federal government stands as a guarantor for the prime if it loses."

"Yes, I just finished going over it."

"Well, I don't mean to put any pressure on you before we hear the case, but I thought it might be helpful for you, since you're a new judge and all, to tell you how I feel about that one. You know, sort of show you how things are done around here?" Winston took a sip of his iced tea. "Bottom line, I think the prime should lose, and that the subcontractor, Ryco Construction Company, should win. Would you agree?"

Tim felt a sudden tightness in his chest. He didn't want to appear ungrateful or contrary to the chief judge, but he felt like Winston was stepping way out of bounds here—prejudging a case before oral argument and in a direct way gently lobbying him for his vote. On the other hand, he didn't want to alienate Winston after he'd been so generous to him.

"Well, uh . . . I really appreciate your sharing your view on this case with me. And you may be right. I . . . I'll tell you the truth, going through the briefs and the exhibits in the record . . ." Tim finally got his thoughts to cohere. "Well, to be frank, I thought the case should go the other way. I thought it was pretty clear that the prime contractor did make full disclosures to the subcontractor about the soil samples and that Ryco should be liable for its own cost overruns. I mean . . ." He was faltering again. "However since you see it going the other way, maybe I should go back and take a closer look at this case. You're right, I am brand new, and maybe I missed something."

Tim looked up at Winston and thought he caught a frown. But then it was gone and replaced by his usual smile. "Well, good, Tim. It's not a big thing; another look at the case might be prudent. I've already spoken to Judge Franklin, and he agrees with my view that the prime contractor is in the wrong here. So I guess as a practical matter with our two votes, the case really has been decided, but it sure would be nice to have a unanimous decision. Besides, I would hate to see you waste one of your first votes in a losing cause. As a new judge, I think you should just follow my lead on some cases. Well then, why don't you see what you can do about joining us on this one?"

Before Tim could collect himself to make a response, Winston adroitly changed the topic to how the president was handling the terrorism threat and homeland security. The rest of the meal and the walk back to the court passed with casual conversation between two old friends.

Yet Tim remained disturbed. Sure he was new, but he knew that judges on a U.S. Court of Appeals are not supposed to discuss or lobby other judges about a particular case before the oral argument on that case. And here Winston was, nakedly trying to influence him and tell him how to vote—was this really the way things worked? Or was the chief judge just trying to help him get started properly on his first few cases?

Back in his chambers, Tim walked over to one of his large windows and looked down onto Constitution Avenue. He slipped into his problem-solving mode, a conscious method of analysis he had long ago developed in himself, back as a cadet at West Point and then later as an intelligence officer and lawyer. When he was confronted with a challenging and unexpected situation, he tried to take the time to stop, define the problem, and develop options.

After five minutes of hard thinking, Tim went to his Rolodex and found the phone number of Judge Warren Breedlove of the U.S. Court of Appeals for the Second Circuit in New York City. Breedlove had been on the Second Circuit for nearly thirty years, and had taken "senior" status, which means semiretired, in the mid 1990s. As a senior judge, he had a reduced caseload and sat only occasionally. Many years ago, Tim had taken the white-collar crime seminar Judge Breedlove had taught at Columbia Law School. Tim had clerked for him for one year after he graduated. Breedlove had been his mentor ever since.

When Tim got Judge Breedlove on the line, he briefly told him what transpired at the surprise lunch. Breedlove sighed. "Tim, I'm very surprised about Chief Judge Winston. I've never heard of anything like this before. Occasionally, one judge may discuss a case in general with another judge before oral argument. But for a chief judge to try to pressure another judge for a vote . . ."

"Warren, listen, maybe I misread the situation. The chief is an old friend, and quite frankly, he helped me get on the bench. Maybe he was just trying to give some guidance to the new kid on the block. I could be wrong about his intentions. Please don't tell anybody about this."

"No one will learn of this from me. Tim, why don't you just see how things go? A 'wait and see' policy is a good compass for a new judge. Just remember that your job demands that you be your own man."

The next morning for his first day on the bench sitting to hear cases, Tim felt well prepared. The first oral argument started after the clerk banged his gavel and the judges filed into the courtroom through their door behind the bench and took their seats. Sitting on the three-judge panel that day, to hear the four cases scheduled for appellate oral argument, were Chief Judge Winston, Judge Franklin, and Judge Quinn.

On another floor in the courthouse, three other of Tim's new colleagues formed another panel and were also hearing cases. The other four judges on the court were not hearing cases that day but would sit on other panels later that week. The identity of judges sitting on these panels was kept secret until the day of oral argument; an attorney scheduled to argue that week would not know who would hear his case until the morning of the oral argument. Judges themselves were usually told one or two months in advance what cases they would sit on. Cases were assigned at random by a computer program administered by the clerk of court and set up to rotate them equally among the judges. For most cases heard at this level, this was the final chance at justice. Even though the U.S. Supreme Court was technically the ultimate court of appeals in the U.S. judicial system, of the eight thousand or so cases heard at the court of appeals level, fewer than eighty would be granted certiorari (the legal term for review) by the U.S. Supreme Court.

The process here was simple. The two lawyers on each side would be given twenty minutes to make their presentations to the judges on the panel. At the end of the four oral arguments, the judges would confer in private in the judges' conference room and discuss the cases. They would decide at that time who will prevail and why. The voting would be straightforward. It only took two votes to win a case. The decision in every case is decided by a majority.

The first case on Quinn's first day on the bench appeared to be an easy one: a criminal case involving a search warrant, with the defendant arguing that it had been wrongly obtained in his criminal case. The three judges asked few questions to the attorneys. Even the most casual onlooker from the gallery would quickly have realized that this case was so open and shut that the conviction on appeal would most likely be affirmed by all three judges. A three to zero majority opinion.

The second and third cases of the day were civil cases, mandatory reviews of decisions made by federal regulatory agencies that had been appealed to Tim's court. To the courtroom spectators—a mix of lawyers, students, and members of the public—these oral arguments were tedious and technical. But even on these routine cases, Tim's excitement was almost electric. This was a major day in his life, sitting high up behind that grand, dark, mahogany bench and actually deciding cases for parties arguing their cases before him. But his enjoyment that day was diluted by his uneasy anticipation of the day's last case, the civil lawsuit of *Ryco Construction Company v. Standard Buildings, Inc.* This was the case that Winston obviously wanted Ryco to win.

Tim still thought that Ryco should lose.

Ryco had been the concrete subcontractor for Standard, the prime contractor for a huge government office complex on the D.C. waterfront. When Ryco's foundations failed to settle properly, Standard forced Ryco to tear up the initial foundations and repour them.

Ryco lost over two million dollars on the project and had brought this lawsuit to recover its losses. Standard won in a judge-alone trial in the court below, the trial judge holding that even though Standard had given accurate soil samples to Ryco showing the unusually porous nature of the soil at the construction site, Ryco negligently failed to look at the samples before bidding and starting work. As a direct result of this negligence, Ryco had installed faulty foundations that had to be redone at a considerable expense to Ryco. The concrete subcontractor had appealed. Even after he reviewed the case a second time at the urging of the chief judge, Tim thought this was a slam-dunk win for Standard. Why should the prime contractor, Standard, have to pay for Ryco's obvious mistake?

Leo Draco was the lawyer for the appellant Ryco Construction Company. Tim was impressed with the brilliant argument Draco made on such a weak case. He had seized on a technicality—that Standard had used a noncertified soil engineer to do the testing, so Ryco couldn't be faulted for not using the soil results. Draco had even found an obscure supreme court case that vaguely supported this legal point.

Draco skillfully answered Tim's questions when he pointed out that noncertified engineer or not, Ryco was still negligent in ignoring the soil tests. Tim, in grilling Draco, received no help from either Winston or Franklin. Not a question from either. They remained silent the entire hearing. Most unusual for an appellate argument on such a high-stakes case.

Notwithstanding the amazing display of appellate advocacy that Leo Draco put on, Judge Quinn thought that there was not sufficient precedent for his court to overturn the decision of the trial judge. The judge in the court below had determined with his factual finding that Ryco was negligent in not relying on the soil samples furnished by Standard Buildings, Inc. In addition, the court below had specifically found that Ryco was further negligent in failing to conduct independent soil samples. Moreover, Tim thought that his questions to Draco during the oral argument had seriously undermined Ryco's case.

At the end of the Ryco argument, the three judges left the bench and adjourned to a large conference room. All clerks and other court administrative staff were excluded; it is an inflexible judicial rule that only the judges who heard the oral argument are present in the conference. No tape recordings or other records are kept of the content of the conferences other than the handwritten notes of the judges. These were the central precepts of the secret deliberative process of any appellate court. It allows judges to discuss the cases frankly knowing their words would never be revealed. It was an unwritten but inviolate rule that the sanctity of these privileged judicial discussions was always preserved.

The first case of the day, the criminal case, was quickly affirmed by a unanimous decision of the three judges. Likewise the three judges rapidly reached agreement on the next two civil cases heard that day. When the panel got to Ryco, the chief judge initiated the discussion. "Now on the Ryco case, I think we will all agree to the basic principle that a contract imposes due diligence of both parties."

Tim nodded agreement on this point.

"However, I believe that Standard Buildings, Inc., the prime contractor on this government-insured contract, really should lose because, as Leo Draco argued, there was an unqualified and faulty soil sample furnished to Ryco."

Tim's head popped up in surprise. This was inaccurate.

"Oh, Chief," Tim interrupted, "the soil sample wasn't faulty. Draco was just using a technical point based on the fact that the soil engineer wasn't certified by the D.C. government. The soil sample was okay, and besides, Ryco was found negligent by the judge below in not conducting its own samples."

"Tim, the law is based on technicalities and I vote for Ryco. Hell, the U.S. government is the insurer on this anyway, so it's no big deal," Winston retorted.

Tim fought back on the fact and pointed out that the record in the court below clearly showed that Ryco had been negligent in failing to analyze the required soil samples before bidding. Therefore Ryco should be liable for its cost overruns. "The law is clear on these points," he concluded. He turned to Judge Franklin, who had obviously become the swing vote. Surely Franklin would follow Tim's strong lead.

"Seems to me that the prime contractor had a duty to give fully certified samples. I vote with the chief judge," Franklin said.

Tim argued for a few minutes more about the bad precedent this case would set, but when he saw that the chief was getting annoyed with him and that Franklin was unmoved, he switched his vote and joined the other two judges—Ryco won 3–0. He had gamely argued his position, but lost. So why not go along with the majority?

The other two judges left the conference room together, chatting about their plans to play golf the next weekend. Alone, Tim slowly gathered his papers and reflected. Did he give in because he deferred to the chief judge's good judgment or because he didn't want to spoil his relationship with the man who might put him on the Supreme Court? Tim was a little ashamed that he didn't stick to his position and write a dissent. That would have been the courageous thing to do. His first day at court and he had given into the "go along and get along" trap. Not a good start to a judicial career.

CHAPTER 9

THREE DAYS AFTER THE RYCO CASE, TIM LOOKED UP FROM his desk to find Judge Carl Franklin peering into his office. Franklin walked over to a framed photo on the wall next to Tim's sofa. "Great photo. What is this?"

"Why, that's a satellite shot of South Boston, where I grew up."

"I see. What does it say below? I don't have my reading glasses."

Tim explained that it was a farewell gift from the director of the National Reconnaissance Office, where Tim had worked as the general counsel during the Reagan Administration. The NRO was the super-secret agency that operated the spy satellites for the military, the CIA, and the National Security Agency.

"Interesting. How long were you there?"

"Almost five years. Coffee, Carl?"

Carl sat down in one of two wing chairs facing each other across a small coffee table. "No, no, I just was passing by, and I thought I would chat about tomorrow's hearing. Now, you and I and Arnie Janoff will be sitting on Panel B, and since I am the most senior of the three of us, I'll be the presiding judge. Do you have any questions on the cases?"

"No, I don't I think so. They all seem very straightforward."

"Good, good." Carl frowned. "There is one case that has been bothering me, and that's the criminal case about the search, *United States v. Meyers.* Can you believe this man's home was ransacked by the FBI?" Judge Franklin gestured in the air with both hands. "The man was convicted only after the government had stomped all over his Fourth Amendment rights. In my view, this case clearly should be reversed—don't you think?"

Tim felt a nervous quiver in his stomach. "Well . . . I really . . ."

"Man, in this country, you'd think a person should at least feel safe inside his own home!" Franklin had leaned forward and pounded his fist into his other hand.

Tim was instantly wary. "Well, honestly, the brief of the government was excellent and the search warrant, well, it looked good to me. It seemed to me that the record clearly supported the warrant . . ."

Tim stopped himself. He was getting into the weeds of a discussion that he didn't want to have. He leaned back in his chair and tried to disengage. "Carl, why don't we wait until tomorrow to talk about this? I feel a little uncomfortable discussing cases before oral argument. Tell you what—since you feel strongly on it, I'll look at the case again and then we just wait and see how the oral argument goes tomorrow."

Franklin didn't want to let go of the case; he continued to ramble about the FBI and the too-easily-trampled Fourth Amendment. "I have to admit I'm a little surprised at your reaction," he went on. "I asked Harry to take a look and he agreed that the search warrant would never stand up. He and I play golf together, you know."

Franklin, obviously a golf nut, abruptly launched into a monologue about which of the Washington area's golf courses was the best. Tim mentioned he belonged to the Army-Navy Country Club and the two of them agreed that they would play there sometime that summer. Franklin then brought up his job teaching at Jefferson Law School. He told Tim that he and Judge Janoff were adjunct professors there. "The money's a nice little bump to our salary. You know, I think you should teach there, Tim." He glanced up at the satellite photo from the NRO director. "You have a lot of trial and government experience to share with the students. You would be great."

Tim was a little surprised at how shallow and scattered Franklin seemed. Whatever had gotten him into the court hadn't been brains. Tim knew that Franklin had gone to a small, unaccredited law school in California, passed the D.C. bar exam on his fourth try, and had worked for twenty years with a national civil rights organization. According to attorneys' gossip, Franklin's had been a politically motivated judicial appointment offered as a bone to civil rights interests. He was noted neither for his legal expertise nor his mental horsepower.

At last, Franklin stood up. "Well, I'll see you tomorrow for court. On the *Meyers* case, I just thought I would try to save you some time and effort on this case by giving you a whiff of which way the wind was blowing. Judge Janoff, the third judge on our panel, is with me on this." He waved good-bye at Tim in a friendly way and left.

Tim went over to his conference table and opened the *United States v. Meyers* case file. He flipped through the file and studied the bench memo again. It was another case where Leo Draco was handling the appeal. Tim wondered how the great Draco would try to put his magic spin on what Tim viewed as a for-sure loser. Tim stared at the file for a while and replayed the Franklin visit. Was another judge trying to get his vote locked up before the oral argument? What is going on in this court? Judge Breedlove definitely would not approve of this practice of lining up votes on a panel before the oral argument.

That night at dinner, Tim told Katy of the curious Judge Franklin visit that day.

"Well, so you have a difference of views with Franklin," Katy said. "There will be three judges on your panel—maybe the other judge will go your way?"

Tim said there was no chance in this case, because the third judge sitting with him was Arnie Janoff, who was well known for having a reflexive aversion to anything he could interpret as governmental abuse of individual rights. "On a case like this, it's a sure bet that Janoff will never vote for the government. Besides, Franklin told me that Janoff was with him on this," Tim told her as they started to clear the dinner table.

"Janoff. I know that I met him at the court reception," Katy said. "Sort of short, scruffy, and looks anorexic—is that him?"

"That's him! With his wire-rimmed glasses and long, graying, sandy hair kept in a short ponytail, most people referred to Janoff as the "hippie judge." Then Tim went on to tell Katy that, outside of the chief judge, Janoff was considered to have the best legal mind on the court. However his mind was very closed—his rebellious, antiwar youth and twenty years of being in the D.C. Public Defenders Office seemed to have made Janoff an "agenda judge," who could be counted on to be antigovernment and sympathetic to criminal defendants. Another experience had further hardened his hatred of big government: His wife died three years ago of a rare type of breast cancer, and the bureaucrats in the FDA had refused to approve use of the only experimental drug that could have saved her. After that Janoff moved into deep hatred of the federal government. To some, Janoff 's opinion of the federal government was understandable, but government attorneys roundly criticized him for letting it enter the courtroom, where each case should be judged on its own merit.

Katy frowned. "Watch yourself tomorrow on that case," she told him. "Don't lose your Irish temper."

The gavel banged loud and everyone in the courtroom rose. The three judges filed in and stood behind their seats while the clerk droned through the opening ritual words: "All rise. The United States Court of Appeals for the District of Columbia Circuit is now open and in session. All those having business before this honorable court draw near. God save the United States and this honorable court."

The judges sat down in their black leather high-backed chairs. Judge Franklin, sitting in the center seat as the presiding judge, spoke: "Please be seated. The court calls the first case of the day, *United States v. Daniel Meyers*. Mr. Draco, as the attorney for the appellant, you may proceed."

"Thank you, Your Honor, may it please the court. My client, Mr. Meyers, was convicted on twelve counts of fraud against the government. All twelve of these convictions are based on evidence obtained through an illegal search of his home by federal law-enforcement agents. The search warrant that allegedly justified the search was not based upon sufficient probable cause, as the Constitution requires."

Tim interrupted Draco. "Counsel, how can you say that? The record clearly shows the warrant was based upon an affidavit by an undercover FBI agent who described how he personally saw the computer records of Mr. Meyers's company in the home. In fact, he was even involved in the fraudulent alteration of those very records. Given that, how can you say that there was 'not sufficient probable cause' here?"

Like the seasoned advocate he was, Draco listened carefully to Tim's question and opened his mouth to respond—but before he could, Tim heard the high, whining voice of Judge Janoff. "Well, Mr. Draco, isn't it a fact that, because four hours had elapsed between the departure of the FBI agent and the execution of the search warrant, the statement of the FBI agent became 'stale' as a matter of law?"

Janoff had cut off Draco's answer to Tim, a clear violation of courtroom protocol. Draco wisely and confidently grabbed the life preserver Judge Janoff had thrown him. "Yes, Your Honor, the evidence was stale. Who knows who might have entered Mr. Meyers's home during that long period and either altered the records, or even planted fake records that were then seized, all just to incriminate my client? Could the FBI, eager as they were to convict my client, have gone in and altered the records or planted new ones? The record is replete with instances of FBI harassment of my client and his family over many months. For instance . . ." Draco skillfully continued on.

Tim was stunned. Here was a judge on his own court helping a lawyer answer the question Tim had asked him. Moreover, Janoff was pointing the lawyer to the only slim legal theory that could save Draco's client, Meyers, from the eight-year sentence he had received in the court below. And richly deserved in Tim's view.

Tim was quiet, but silently fuming during the rest of Draco's argument. When the assistant U.S. attorney representing the government on this appeal rose to make her argument, Tim had only one question, which he asked immediately after she introduced herself at the podium.

"Counsel, there has been some mention made of stale information used by the FBI to obtain this warrant. Can you point us to the place in the record of the court below where, I believe, an FBI agent testified that the Meyers house was under constant surveillance during this period, and that no one entered or left the house during this period?"

"Yes, Your Honor. I'm glad you brought that up, because I had intended to highlight that point myself. The record clearly shows such testimony, at pages one hundred and forty-seven through one hundred fifty-four. Therein, two FBI agents testified under oath that no one had entered or had left the Meyers house during that key four-hour period. Also, Your Honor, I would like to point out that the U.S. Supreme Court, in the case of *United States v. Penrod,* a case we cite in our brief, has said that a search warrant can be based on information as much as twelve hours old, and such information is not 'stale,' so long as the status quo of the site has been preserved."

"Thank you, counsel. I have no further questions."

Tim remained silent while the other two judges quizzed the assistant U.S. attorney on the reliability of the FBI agents and the patterns of harassment alleged by Meyers during his trial in the court below. In Tim's mind, the points he had made with his questions were sufficient to win the case and there was no need for him to ask any more questions.

The *Meyers* case ended and the oral arguments of the other three cases of the day passed without event. At the end of the fourth case, the three judges moved directly into the adjoining conference room where, alone, they would discuss and decide the cases of the day. As soon as he entered, Tim slammed his folders on the table, tore off his robe, and threw it on one of the chairs.

Carl quickly said, "Well, that was a good day. We had some interesting cases, I think. Let's start with the *Meyers* case, and Tim, why don't you lead off?" Carl had obviously sensed an explosive situation and was trying to restore calm.

Tim could hear the distant warning bells going off inside him and knew he was letting his anger show. But he didn't care; he was steamed and wanted to get something straight at the start of the conference. "Well, before we go any further, and now that we're out of the courtroom and in private, I've got to say something," Tim said in a low voice. He turned to Janoff and pointed at him. "Arnie, I may be the new boy on the block and not know much, but I do know that one judge should not interrupt another judge while he is questioning counsel. Don't ever do that again."

Janoff was physically taken aback by Tim's words and nervously looked to Franklin for help. "Why are you looking at me when you say that, Tim? I never interrupted you! Carl, tell him I didn't."

Tim felt his face redden with anger. "That's bullshit! Right out of the gate, in the *Meyers* case, you never let Draco answer my question, you just jumped in before he had even opened his mouth, and you threw him the biggest life preserver I ever saw! Now, not only did you interrupt my line of questioning, but you answered my question for him!"

Carl extended his arms before him, palms to the other two judges in a calming gesture. "Now, Tim, let's be collegial, and why don't we all just calm down."

"Don't give me that 'collegial' crap! If you want to be collegial, join a bowling team!"

"Okay, Tim, okay, it won't happen again. Right, Arnie?" Franklin nodded to Janoff reassuringly.

"Okay. Sorry, Tim. I won't do that again. I just couldn't help jumping in—I got so worked up over those lying FBI agents, that's all," Janoff offered.

Tim rolled his eyes. "Christ, Arnie, how can you say they're lying? It's sworn testimony on the record, and we're supposed to accept that as true on appeal."

Carl sternly said, "Okay, gentlemen, let's move on and decide this case. Now, let's start with a preliminary vote. This is on the *Meyers* case. Arnie, how do you vote?" Carl obviously wanted to get the *Meyers* case over quickly and was rushing a vote.

"I vote to reverse. I think this was stale information and that made the search warrant illegal. And I would further hold that the *Penrod* case is not applicable here."

"Okay. Tim, what's your vote?"

"I vote to affirm. I think the search warrant was solid and valid, and that the *Penrod* case is not only applicable but it is Supreme Court law controlling this court on the issue of stale information."

Carl Franklin was trying to keep playing his role as presiding judge. "Thank you. Well, I haven't read *Penrod*, but I, uh, well, Arnie, I think you're right. This case should be reversed. We can't have the FBI harassing citizens and invading people's homes like the Gestapo, can we? I vote to reverse. That's two to one. The case is reversed."

Tim was almost numb when he heard this. But he was not really surprised after having heard their questions during the oral argument. Arnie was showing himself to be the predictable antigovernment zealot, and Carl seemed to be nothing more than just a slacker and mental dwarf. Remembering Franklin's visit to his chambers yesterday, Tim suspected this case was decided before it was heard in court by two judges with closed minds.

"I will write a strong dissent!" Tim shut his case file and slammed the folder on the table.

The sharp slap of the heavy file on the conference table made both Carl and Arnie flinch, but Tim's threat didn't seem to faze them. Two votes decided a case. What mattered was the decision and the result—that Draco's client, Meyers, would soon be free.

That, in Tim's view, was a judicial mistake . . . or worse.

The rest of the conference proceeded without incident. Tim's anger subsided and he became all brusque business. He coldly joined in the discussions on the three cases and the voting was unanimous on all three. At the end of the meeting, Franklin immediately left, leaving Tim and Janoff alone in the conference room. Arnie seemed nervous, dropping one of his files in his haste to pack up his stack of papers and files for the four cases. Tim couldn't be sure, but he thought he saw Janoff 's hands shaking. "Good-bye," Janoff said in a weak voice without looking at Tim.

Tim just stared at him and Janoff scurried out of the room. Tim faintly smiled at the notion that the little "hippie judge" might be frightened by his new colleague's outburst and didn't want to be in the room alone with a "Vietnam vet psycho."

Back in his chambers, Tim tried to distract himself by reading bench memos for future oral arguments. But he just couldn't stop thinking about the *Meyers* case. He paused for a moment, then, on an impulse, decided to call an old friend he hadn't seen since his investiture. He and Sam Goldstein had been young lawyers working together in the intelligence community fifteen years earlier. Sam was now an U.S. District Court judge in the same building, downstairs. The U.S. Courthouse in Washington, D.C., was home to both the U.S. Court of Appeals, on the top floors, with most of the U.S. District courtrooms on the bottom four floors. The floor placement was very logical: the Court of Appeals was above the District Court, from which appeals floated up, both literally and figuratively. Goldstein had just finished a jury trial and was in his office; Tim went up to see him.

"Tim, what's up, buddy?"

Tim let out his feelings of anger and confusion. He started with the case he had just sat on with Franklin and Janoff. The reversing of the rock-solid Meyers conviction. Judge Janoff, who thought all FBI agents were liars and consistently ruled against the government. And how he caved in on the Ryco case. He also mentioned the attempts to get his vote before the oral argument on both the *Meyers* and *Ryco* cases.

Tim was surprised and irritated when Sam began to smile. "Did I say something funny?"

"No, Tim, it's really not funny. Let me tell you some of the rumors about your court that have been going around the courthouse. First of all, it is said that your court is a big friend of this administration on politically sensitive cases."

Tim kept his mouth shut on that point, thinking of the favors to the president that Winston had confided to him.

Goldstein continued, "Next, with regards to Draco. I know he's brilliant and has a solid-gold reputation, and all that, but still . . . he wins, or his firm wins, an amazing percentage of its appeal cases. He has built up quite an appeals specialty practice, and the big corporations and the big-dollar defendants go to him when they lose down here, because he wins on appeal almost all the time.

"Hell, there was one case of mine that was completely airtight, but your chief judge and that dumb-as-a-board Franklin bought a slick argument of Draco's and reversed me in a two-one decision. I was hoping the Supreme Court would take that case, so I'd be vindicated, but they never did. No, my friend, these past several years, your court has delivered some very strange opinions, a lot with Draco as appellate counsel."

Tim nodded and listened intently. Of course, he knew personally of Draco's skill, but here was a U.S. District Court judge adding a sinister tinge to it. "What else have you heard, Sam?"

Goldstein fidgeted in his chair. "Well, word is that two or three of the judges are very deferential to your chief judge."

"I've heard that too."

"There are three judges who tend to go along with the chief judge most of the time. It is sort of a predictable bloc. They usually vote the way he votes, period. And one of them is that guy Franklin."

"Who are the other judges?" Tim asked quickly.

"Bowen and Janoff."

"Do you think anything fishy is going on with this alliance?"

Goldstein rubbed his chin with his hand. "Let me tell you something about being an old judge. You hang around on the bench as long as I have, you see a lot of strange things, and sometimes, you just don't understand them. But you also get a sixth sense. My intuition tells me something funny is going on, but I wouldn't go so far as to suspect that any judge on your court is fixing cases for anybody—although I have heard some speculation or gossip to that effect."

Now Tim was even more disturbed. "Is that what you think it is, gossip?"

Sam shrugged. "Who knows? That might be all there is to it. Somebody is sore at losing a case and starts some courthouse gossip. But I don't think you should get started in your new court with the wrong idea. Give the other judges the benefit of the doubt. Watch what's going on and see. Maybe within a few months or maybe next year, you may look back on this in a much different light."

"Thank you, Sam. That's very good advice, and I'll take it."

Tim didn't tell Judge Goldstein about the special "arrangement" between the chief judge and the president. Hell, that probably got Tim on the federal bench. Besides, there seemed to be enough suspicion about his court flying around the courthouse. Even though he trusted Goldstein, he didn't want to feed the gossip fire in the District Court. The fire seemed to be burning well enough on its own.

CHAPTER 10

A WEEK AFTER THE TALK WITH JUDGE GOLDSTEIN, LORETTA was in Tim's office having trouble putting a file in one of the drawers of the old desk that Tim had inherited from Judge Rogers. She pulled too hard on the stuck drawer and the entire drawer fell on the carpet and turned upside down.

Tim was across the room working at his stand-up desk when he heard the crash. Then Loretta called him, looking worried.

"Judge, look at this—a sealed envelope."

Tim came over, picked up the drawer, and laid it on the top of the desk.

There was a manila envelope securely taped to the underside. Tim picked the tape away from one corner, then pulled the envelope loose. He turned it over, opened it, and shook the contents out on the desktop. There were four pieces of paper. Tim picked them up and brought them over to the conference table, where he spread them out. Tim began examining them, but after a few seconds, Loretta could no longer restrain her curiosity. "Judge, what could this mean? Do you think this is related to Judge Rogers's murder?"

"Well the envelope and tape look rather new so Judge Rogers probably put it there, but no, Loretta, I don't think it's related to his murder. That's a closed case. It was some druggie who robbed him and killed him and then overdosed himself."

"Okay. But what are these papers?"

"It looks like the first three pages are from the Official Annual Report of the cases decided by this court. They've been carefully torn out, probably with a ruler—see the little rough edge? They are cases from this court, because the citations show it, see?"

Loretta leaned forward and noted the "D.C. Cir." and the year of the decision at the end of the citation of each case. "Why is it marked like that?"

"I don't know. Some of the cases are highlighted in yellow, and some have sets of initials behind them. And look, even though the initials are different, all the highlighted cases have a handwritten 'D' in front of them. This must be some research that Judge Rogers was working on. I wonder what that 'D' means."

"Does it mean Defendant?"

"No, I don't think so, because there are defendants in every case."

Tim picked up the fourth piece of paper, a yellow legal sheet containing handwriting. He looked at the writing for a few seconds, then turned to Loretta.

"Loretta, why don't you go out front to cover the phones; I want to study this a bit."

Loretta withdrew to the outer office, and Tim sat down at his conference table with the four pieces of paper. He laid the yellow sheet down next to the others and studied it. This was the most intriguing of the pages. He stared at the four handwritten lines it contained:

✓ *1. Check Fin. Disclosure forms*
✓ *2. Call Yale*
✓ *3. Talk to the C.J.?*
4. Call FBI

This yellow page must be connected to that list of cases, he thought. But how? What's the connection? The first line, "Check Fin. Disclosure forms"—that had to refer to the standard financial disclosure form submitted yearly by every federal judge. Tim had just filed his form with the clerk of court when he came on the bench, publicly listing all his assets, loans, and income sources.

There was a check beside this notation, which must mean that Rogers had done this task. Why? Maybe Rogers had forgotten to list stock he owned, say IBM, and then had sat on a case that indirectly involved IBM, making his participation in these highlighted cases a conflict of interest that he should have reported. But that seemed awfully far-fetched. How could there be so many cases with a conflict of interest?

The next line on the page was equally puzzling: "Call Yale." He knew Rogers had not gone to Yale, either as an undergraduate or as a law student. Even though the line also had a check mark, he still didn't know what the reference meant. The only Yalie on the court was Winston.

Rogers had also checked off "Talk to the C.J.?" Maybe "C.J." meant the Chief Judge. But talk to him about what? But the line below it really worried Tim. "Call FBI" was unchecked. Was Rogers killed before he could call the FBI?

Tim laid the papers on his desk. They could be evidence in a murder. Shit, he thought, another problem on the court: resolving the mystery of a package apparently left by a dead judge. Should he show it to the chief judge?

A warning bell went off inside him. He could not ignore the fact that this manila envelope had been taped to the bottom of a desk drawer of a judge who had been murdered. This was very suspicious, closed case or not. Tim decided not to do or say anything until after he had taken the time to read the highlighted cases on the list and try to find a logical explanation for the envelope, its contents, and its strange location.

He took the four sheets and walked through the door to his outer office. "Loretta, make me a copy of these four pages so I can take them home to study them. Then put the originals in an envelope and lock it in our safe."

Tim also put the taped manila envelope in a separate large envelope and told Loretta to keep that with the envelope containing the originals. Tim knew that any evidence should be safeguarded. Perhaps there were some fingerprints on the manila envelope or the tape? Besides his and Loretta's, Tim thought.

"And, Loretta, please, don't tell anyone about what we found."

Tim slept badly that night, his sobering talk with Goldstein echoing in his head and combining with images of Draco and the mystery papers he'd found in Judge Rogers's desk, which he had pored over that evening. He gave up on sleep at five A.M. and got up, eager to get to the office. He needed access to some law books to do the proper legal research on Rogers's papers.

Tim's car was in the shop for a tune-up so he boarded the subway. Coming up the escalator out of the cool Metro cavern at the Judiciary Square station, he was blasted with a wave of humid heat. The brief Washington spring was already giving way to the scorchers of summer. He quickly walked across the John Marshall Plaza to the main entrance of the Federal Courthouse, opposite the soaring structure of the new Canadian Embassy. Amphitheaters of government still impressed him, not only with their solidity but their apparent probity. Even though he knew better, as he walked up the short flight of stairs to the courthouse security checkpoint, he still asked himself how justice could ever go astray in a building as rock-solid as this.

He nodded to the U.S. marshals on duty as he walked around the metal detectors, a courtesy extended to all federal judges. The marshals all knew who he was, since they had been required to study photos of all the judges in the building, and the chief U.S. marshal quizzed them on the pictures until they could recognize them all.

Knots of people clogged the hallway of the Federal Courthouse. It was motions day in the U.S. District Court, one of the busiest days of the week. Instead of using the private judges' elevator in the rear of the courthouse, Tim got on one of the public elevators with a lawyer who was obviously shepherding a family up to a hearing in one of the many trial courtrooms upstairs. The lawyer was briefing the family in hushed tones on how to act and what to expect in court as the elevator ascended. The family looked fearful and awed, and Tim wondered what case had brought them to this place and how they and their family member—defendant? plaintiff?—would fare as justice was done. The group got off on the third floor, leaving Tim alone for his ride up to the fifth floor. Up here, at the Court of Appeals level, life was calmer, quieter, especially when it was not court week, the five days each month when his court heard oral arguments.

At the end of the marble hallway was a guard's desk, where a lone U.S. marshal sat, screening the entrance to the judicial corridor where the judges' chambers were located. The only people he allowed to pass his checkpoint were judges, their secretaries and clerks, or people with appointments he would individually clear. In these difficult times, the extra layer of security made Tim feel more secure—even as he realized that the real threat to justice might lie within these hallways, not without.

Quinn was still bothered by the Rogers papers. After that talk with Goldstein, Tim was worried something was going on at his court. So he decided he had to act. Was there a connection between Draco's successes and those papers of Judge Rogers? And if so, what was it? Last night when he retrieved the hidden papers from his briefcase, he could see their significance far more clearly than when he first looked at them. The letters in the margin, meaningless to him at first, he now realized were the initials of other judges who sat on his court. These initials next to the cases highlighted in yellow must be those of the same judges Goldstein told him voted as a bloc: Winston, Janoff, Bowen, and Franklin. Now he suspected that the "D" in the margin probably meant the Draco law firm. To confirm this suspicion, Quinn would carve out some time today to look in more detail at the cases Judge Rogers highlighted on those four pages. When he entered his chambers, he told Loretta to hold all calls until lunch. He was going to be doing some research and wanted no distraction. He waved off Loretta's suggestion that he get his law clerks to help him.

Alone in his office, Tim spread the papers on his conference table. Each case had been appealed and decided by his court over the last two years. He went into his adjacent small library, found the volumes of *Federal Reporter 3rd* containing the case decisions, took the pile of law books back into his office, and set them on the conference table.

The first case he looked at was *United States v. Plumm Media Inc.*, a civil case that involved the application of a FCC regulation. He saw right away from the case heading that, as he suspected, Draco represented the appellant, Plumm Media Inc. In addition, he confirmed that the initials of the three judges who heard the case matched the initials written in the margin. He read the case carefully and was not surprised to confirm his suspicions that the case had been reversed when it should not have been. The chief judge and Franklin, both of whom sat on the *Plumm* case, voted to reverse, and the third judge had written a strong dissent which, to Tim, seemed to correctly state the law. The *Plumm* case was definitely decided wrong, Tim concluded.

Tim then looked quickly at the headings of the other eight cases. He noted that the initials of the judges in each case were the same as those written in the margin. In addition, Draco or his firm represented one of the parties in all these cases. There was no further room for doubt that the "D" in the margin of the Rogers list meant that it was a case handled by Draco's law firm.

At this point, Tim wondered if those nine cases were the only ones that Draco and his firm had handled over the last two years. He went over to his computer and typed in a West Law search for a list of cases where the Draco law firm had appeared before his court over the last two years. Seconds later, a list of fifteen cases appeared. Tim was not surprised that nine of these were already listed and highlighted on the Judge Rogers list. But now Tim had more cases to read.

Three hours later, after he had scrutinized all fifteen cases and taken copious notes, Tim concluded that there were some important distinctions between the nine cases listed by Rogers and the others. First, the highlighted cases all involved big money, while the other six nonhighlighted cases were either criminal, low-paying court-appointed cases involving indigent clients, or else they were minor civil cases that did not involve large sums of money. Draco's firm won only one of these "low-paying" six cases and lost the other five, a predictable outcome of those types of cases on appeal.

Tim then focused on his analysis of the nine highlighted cases. Draco's firm won seven of those cases, an extraordinarily high winning percentage on appeal. Tim knew of Draco's reputation as a skillful advocate, but in his experience, few lawyers were so good that they could win sure losers.

To his growing unease, he saw that the highlighted initials were, in every instance, those of four judges: Chief Judge Winston, Judge Franklin, Judge Bowen, and Judge Janoff. Two or three of those judges always made up the majority in every one of the "big money" cases that were won by Draco's law firm.

The amount of money involved in these seven winning cases was amazing. In some of the cases, the figure was so large that Tim had trouble computing or even guessing it. Several cases, however, were straightforward. For instance, in one Environmental Protection Agency enforcement case involving a negligent toxic dump of chemicals, Draco's client, a plastic container manufacturing company, was able to avoid fines totaling four million dollars, thanks to a reversal. That was clear enough. But after that, things got murky. One case reversed the Department of Justice Antitrust Division's voiding of a merger. How do you put a price on that? Another involved the granting of a cable television license. Tim wasn't exactly sure, but he estimated that the antitrust and the cable television license cases easily involved tens of millions of dollars.

Tim sat back and crossed his arms. He thought silently for a few minutes, focusing on the one central question: Had these seven "big money" cases really been properly decided? It was difficult for him to judge whether or not the outcomes of these cases fell within the acceptable bounds of judicial action. If they didn't, that alone might indicate there was some improper influence on the decision-making process.

But *why?* If there was some sort of common scheme among these four judges, to what purpose were they doing this? The first thought was the obvious one—money.

Twenty minutes later, Tim crossed the plaza of Union Station to arrive at the adjacent Thurgood Marshall Judicial Office Building. In the atrium, after he showed the guards his federal judge ID, he was quickly directed to the third floor Public Information Office, where the financial disclosure forms of all federal judges were filed. When he asked to see and was given copies of the forms of all the judges on the court for the past three years, he did not disclose that he was a judge. These forms were public documents and could be viewed by anyone.

The forms of Janoff and Franklin indicated that they were teaching at Jefferson Law School and getting the maximum they could under the judicial regulations, just over twenty thousand dollars. Tim thought that amount was very high for teaching one seminar per semester. The financial picture of Franklin was unsurprisingly modest, since he had had a career in low-paying public interest jobs. Janoff's form showed a recent upswing in recent years, probably due to the insurance proceeds from his wife's death.

Winston's form was very predictable to Tim, considering he had been Winston's lawyer for the last decade. Winston was rich and had extensive land and stock holdings. The only slight surprise was that Winston had listed that he was a trustee of Jefferson Law School and Hobbes College. Judges could be trustees of nonprofit institutions, but that was reportable information. That probably explained Franklin and Janoff teaching at Jefferson and the admission of Janoff 's son into Hobbes.

Judge Rosemary Bowen's form showed she was house and land poor, with two heavy mortgages on the Leesburg home and the adjoining farmlands. The largest of her loans was from a bank in Gardenia, Georgia, which Tim was familiar with; the small bank had handled a lot of Winston's financial dealings over the years.

After Tim returned the disclosure files to the clerk, he started back to the courthouse. The trip to the administrative office had been worthwhile. All three judges seemed to be financially beholden to the chief judge. Yet nothing was wrong with these publicly disclosed connections. It could just be the chief doing proper favors for his friends.

Or was it more?

Back in his chambers, Tim returned to his notes on his seven "big money" cases. In four of them, he decided he could see absolutely no justification for Draco's side to have won. They were dead-on losers. In the other three cases, the decision was closer, although Tim still thought Draco should have lost. But then he thought: What if I am letting myself become biased against Draco?

He rubbed his face, then got up and stretched. God, he was tired. He went over to his credenza and poured himself a cup of coffee from the thermos Loretta always kept filled there. Looking out over the Mall, he asked himself if he was objective enough to think this out clearly. Then suddenly he knew what to do. He went back to his desk and punched in familiar numbers.

"Good afternoon, Judge Breedlove's chambers," said a pleasant female voice.

Breedlove was soon on the line. Tim got right to the point. He gave Breedlove the citations of the three cases he wasn't sure about and asked his old friend to read the three cases, then call him back with his opinion on whether they were rightly or wrongly decided. "Warren, I can't explain why right now—I don't want to influence you, okay?" he asked.

Breedlove agreed to do it. He was a true friend, one who would do a favor without asking any questions.

An hour later, Tim grabbed his unlisted direct line on the first ring. It was Breedlove.

"Tim, what's going on? In my view, all those cases have been decided the wrong way."

"Really? You're sure?" Tim felt himself tense.

"Yes. I've been a federal appellate judge for over thirty years, and it's my opinion that if I, or any of the judges that I respect who sit with me on the Second Circuit, had sat on those panels, the cases would have been decided in the exact opposite way. What's this all about?"

Tim took a deep breath. He had been holding onto this by himself too long. "Warren, I think the cases may be connected to a scheme to fix cases on this court." He told Breedlove that the three cases he had read were from a list of seven, with the other four wrongly decided on the face of it. "I just needed your reaction to the other three."

"My reaction is that the decisions stink. What are you going to do with the list?" Judge Breedlove asked.

"Well, it is not just the list." Tim briefed Breedlove on Draco and the two-majority decision that always came from the same four judges—the "go-to majority" which might be more than just a like-minded or persuadable cohort.

"Tim, you're in a bind. If you're right, there's some kind of case-fixing scheme going on. But this is all speculation, based on the reactions of two judges—you and me—reading cases long ago decided by other judges. This whole thing could have some innocent explanation which would involve no illegal activity whatsoever. Moreover, I don't know Draco, but I do know a little bit about Winston."

"You do?"

"Sure. I've known Winston for years. We've served on judicial committees together, and I've been involved with him in various bar activities, and I'll tell you this: The man is a control freak. He uses his Southern charm, high-powered intellect, and old-fashioned hard work to steamroll people."

"Yeah, I'm learning that. Harry's definition of an agreeable person seems to be one who agrees with him." Tim sighed. "Warren,

I feel I now have an ethics dilemma. I know too much. And I don't know what to do with what I know."

"Maybe you should do nothing," Breedlove said. "You've got no conclusive evidence that anything illegal is going on. If you run to the FBI now with a theory that some cases are wrongly decided and ask them to look into it—well, for one thing, that kind of contact with the FBI won't be a secret for long in a place like Washington. Instantly you would be the most hated judge on your court."

"Warren, I—"

"You'll be a rat . . . Is this really a risk you want to take? You're a new judge. There are times you may have to close one eye to some things. Do you really want to know the answer to your suspicions? Can you stand the heat of what it takes to get to the truth of what may be going on?"

"I—I feel like I must do something, but right now, I just don't know what that is."

"Tim, all you have is a list of cases that we both agree were decided wrong. You don't know anything more. There is nothing to suggest that any of your judges are being influenced to decide the cases this way or that way. And if that's indeed what's happening, it's going to be hard to discover, and harder yet to prove. In fact, remember that case several years ago in California, where some federal judge out in California was taking bribes to reduce sentences after trial . . ."

"Yeah, I remember that, what was his name? Gibson?" Tim asked.

"That's it! Judge Gibson. Well, none of the other judges on his court blew the whistle on him, even though, I'm told, it was an open secret on his court that he was on the take."

Quinn remembered the case. It had required an undercover FBI operation to nail the judge, instigated by a complaint from one of the criminals who paid his bribe and was disappointed by the sentence reduction Judge Gibson had given him. So then he turned on Gibson. If Gibson had given him a better reduction, who knows? He might be still sitting on the federal bench instead of in a federal pen.

"Whether you have something illegal going on or just a string of cases being decided wrong by a small group of judges," Breedlove went on, "it's hard to say at this point. If you're going to make such grave allegations, you'd better be damn certain."

"Warren, you're right." But even as he said the words, Tim realized that he couldn't simply rest with his suspicions. He would have to keep investigating this—for his own sake, and for the sake of the dead Judge Rogers. "But if I do decide to pursue it, what should I do next?"

There was a long silence over the phone. "I guess you would have to talk to that sharp prosecutor from the Public Integrity Section at Justice. The one who handled the Gibson case. A good lawyer. I taught her at Columbia Law. In fact, she was there when you were. You must know her. Victoria Hauser."

"That's a good suggestion, Warren," Tim said. He didn't tell Breedlove whether or not he knew her, and he kept his voice steady. "Thanks for everything."

He hung up and stared out the window at more of those governmental buildings he had admired this morning for their sturdiness, their probity. He had not shared Rogers's checklist with the old man because he didn't want to risk distracting him from the analysis of the cases. Besides, at this stage, he didn't want to get his mentor involved in a possible connection to a murder case. For even as he had thought of Maxwell Rogers as he had talked to Breedlove, what had been a faint worry had fully blossomed into full suspicion in Tim's mind—that there might be more than case-fixing involved here. There may well be a possible connection between the checklist and Judge Rogers's murder.

Tim leaned back in his chair and placed the heels of his shoes on the corner of his desk. He closed his eyes and exhaled hard. Shit, he thought, he had so little to go on. Nothing conclusive. Maybe he should just forget the whole damn thing. He had a lot to lose. Christ, he was on a great court, and more importantly he had a real shot at the Supreme Court. The D.C. Circuit was a known breeding ground for U.S. Supreme Court justices. His court had produced Ginsberg, Thomas, Scalia, Burger, and a host of others over the years. And Winston had practically promised that he would suggest to the president that Tim be nominated for the Supreme Court if a vacancy occurred. Why was he risking all this to check out some possible connection between judges on his court and Draco? Maybe the Judge Rogers papers meant nothing. Maybe it wasn't even from Rogers. Just because it was taped under his desk drawer didn't mean that he wrote the damn checklist or made the list of cases.

And if he did pursue his suspicions, he would have to talk to Victoria Hauser. He cringed at the very idea. But Breedlove was right; Vicky was the perfect and logical prosecutor for him to see. Besides, he trusted her and knew from news reports on the Judge Gibson case that Vicky had done a super job. Funny, of all the lawyers in the Justice Department, and there must be at least five thousand, Breedlove had given him the name of probably the only one who might not take his call. Tim could still feel the sting of the cold wine she had flung in his face.

CHAPTER 11

"TIM, ARE YOU ON SOME KIND OF SUICIDE MISSION?"

Katy was stirring the boiling pasta. Tim sat at the island in the kitchen, perched on a tall stool and slumped forward, resting his elbows on the marble counter. He held a Corona long neck, rotating the bottle slowly.

Katy half turned and looked straight at him. "It sounds to me like you're about to risk not only your new judicial career, but the Supreme Court. And for what? Some unfounded suspicions about that creepy lawyer Leo Draco and some decisions on some silly cases that you and Judge Breedlove don't like? So what? So the XYZ corporation lost and the ABC corporation won." She turned back to stirring the pasta, but she wasn't through. "And the judges you think may be involved," she warned, "what if you're wrong? You'll be working with them for a long time. And you may end up destroying the reputations of some good people."

"Katy, I didn't ask for this problem. But now I can't avoid it."

"Yes, you can. Mind you own business. You know that with this president in office and with Harry's support, you could end up on the Supreme Court. That's your ultimate dream. Now you want to throw that away. And don't give me that West Point, it's-my-duty stuff. Why are you getting involved?"

"I don't know, Katy. I really don't know. I hear what you're saying, and it's good advice, it makes sense, but I can't just ignore this. I guess it's my nature."

Katy shook her head and spilled the pasta furiously into the colander. "All right, dinner's ready. Let's eat. But I've got to tell you, you are risking your future and I still don't understand why."

Tim woke up with a headache. He had not slept well. Katy's misgivings and his own second thoughts caused him to doubt the wisdom of reporting his suspicions. In his chambers that morning, he shut his door and studied the Rogers papers again. He considered several different courses of action. The easiest choice was to shred the papers and forget he found them. The toughest one, he decided, was to call Vicky Hauser. The stupidest was to show the papers to Harry Winston—as Judge Rogers might possibly have done. If Harry was part of a case-fixing plot, he would be alerted to the suspicion that the papers cast on him and Tim could wind up as dead as Maxwell Rogers.

Finally, at ten in the morning, Tim called the Justice Department and was told Victoria Hauser was in a meeting. When she didn't return his call by noon, Tim called again, this time politely emphasizing that this was an urgent, official matter; he was told she was still in a meeting. At two P.M., she still had not returned his call. Vicky obviously was avoiding him. Tim could understand, but still he was frustrated. He dialed Vicky's number and, when the same secretary answered, he said in a stern, chopped voice, "This is Federal Judge Quinn of the U.S. Court of Appeals calling on an official urgent matter. Please put Ms. Hauser on the line."

The secretary, after putting Tim on hold for a few moments, returned to the phone and said Ms. Hauser was out of the office. Tim gave his number again and said in no uncertain terms to immediately find her and tell her that a federal judge wanted to speak with her *or* her supervisor, as soon as possible, on official business.

Ten minutes later, Vicky Hauser called Tim's chambers. Her voice was frosty. "Judge Quinn, I understand you've been tossing your title around and that you want to speak with me."

Tim took a deep breath and steadied himself. "Vicky, I need to talk to you today. Can we meet?"

"We have nothing to talk about," Vicky quickly said.

"It is not about us. I may have another Judge Gibson case for you. Please meet me."

Tim heard silence on the other end of the line. Then Vicky spoke, sounding stunned, softer. "What do you mean, Tim? I don't understand."

"I can't talk over the phone. Can you be outside the Pennsylvania Avenue entrance to the FBI Building in twenty minutes? I'll pick you up. I'll be driving a silver Land Rover. Please."

There was another long pause. "Okay. I'll be there."

A half-hour later, Tim and Vicky were driving down Fourteenth Street, headed south toward Virginia. Vicky had tried to ask Tim what was going on as soon as she got into his car, but Tim said he wanted to show Vicky some papers before they talked. Vicky remained silent, staring straight ahead into the D.C. traffic. Tim didn't know what to say, so he kept an awkward silence as well.

Soon Tim pulled into the almost deserted parking lot of the Jefferson Memorial, which was closed for renovations. He had wanted a secluded spot to talk to Vicky. The incident at the Dubliner was still fresh in his mind.

"Vicky, I don't know where to begin. But first I want to say how sorry I am about things between us. I don't expect to ever be forgiven for what I did to you in New Orleans."

Vicky turned to face him in the front seat. "Don't worry, you won't be. Now, what did you mean by saying there was another Judge Gibson case?"

Tim's nerves felt charged with electricity. There was no turning back from what he was about to reveal to a federal prosecutor.

"This may be a Gibson-like thing. But before I start, the ground rules have to be that what I say will be just between you and me, at least for now. Do you agree?"

Vicky frowned. "No special deals. You got me here by saying you had something official. If you have something to say, it's on the record—or you can turn around and drive me back to Justice."

Vicky's words hit him like a slap. What did he expect? He was reporting a possible serious federal crime. Tim needed time to think, to shape further what he was going to do. He suggested that they get out and walk. The car was parked at the edge of the tidal basin, a body of water circled by D.C.'s famous cheery blossom trees.

Tim and Vicky started walking on the path next to the water. It was a warm day in May and a number of tourists slowly moved about the basin in two-person pedalboats rented by the hour. To the tourists, Tim and Vicky looked like two lovers strolling by the water, not a judge about to turn in one of his best friends and three of his fellow judges to a federal prosecutor.

"I think there may be something strange going on in our court," Tim hesitatingly started.

"That's nice, Tim, but 'strange' is not against the law. Get to the point. Do you have a dirty judge on your court?"

Tim stopped walking and looked Vicky in the eye. "I don't know. I do know there are cases on my court that are being won and shouldn't be won. There is a small firm here in D.C., Draco and Associates, and I think they may—and I emphasize the word 'may'—be involved in some sort of case-fixing deal in our court."

"Draco," Vicky said immediately. "Yes, I know him. He's a very smart lawyer with excellent credentials and that's a good firm. Especially on appeals before your court."

"Yeah, that's the problem—he's way *too* good. Over the past two years, he's won seven big cases, with lots of money involved. Cases that he would never be expected to win."

"So he's very good and he wins a lot of tough cases. So what?"

They started to walk again. Tim explained that it appeared that Draco in the last couple of years won seven cases that were impossible to win without someone having fixed the results. He went on to say that there were four judges on his court that he thought may be involved in helping Draco, either unwittingly or by design. Tim added that Judge Breedlove of the Second Circuit agreed with him that Draco's firm could never have won those seven cases without help from inside.

"Breedlove? The judge you clerked for after Columbia?"

"Yes, Warren Breedlove, whose seminar you took. He and I have been friends since I was in law school. We both think Draco has somehow fixed those cases. And—" Tim took another deep breath, because what he was about to say was the hardest part of all—"it looks like the late Judge Rogers may have seen the same trend before he died."

Vicky stopped so short she stumbled, turning to look at him directly. "What! How could you know *that?*" She couldn't contain her excited urgency. Tim took out of his suit coat four folded sheets of paper and handed them to Vicky. He told her they were copies of four sheets of paper found in Rogers's desk. He would give her the originals when they got back to the car. Then he went on to explain how he inherited Rogers's chambers and found the papers taped to the bottom of his desk drawer. "I don't know for sure, but I assume that Judge Rogers hid this list of cases and the checklist."

"So what is this? These three sheets just look like a list of cases heard by your court . . ."

"That's right, it is. But you will notice some of them are highlighted in yellow, with initials in the margin . . ."

Tim walked her through the papers and his suspicions. He also repeated the courthouse rumors he had heard from Judge Goldstein. Vicky was curious about the checklist. "Tim, if Rogers did make this checklist, then I understand the item about financial disclosure. The checklist points about talking to the chief judge and calling the FBI are self-explanatory. But what about this 'Call Yale' thing?"

"Well, I really don't know what it means. Chief Judge Winston is the only judge on our court that went to Yale, and maybe there is some kind of record up there . . . You know, I did handle his divorce ten years ago or so . . ."

"You did?" Vicky narrowed her eyes at him.

"Yeah, that's how we became friends and I became his lawyer for almost ten years. It was a simple uncontested divorce, very amicable; he was very generous to his wife in the settlement. I think that Camellia met him while he was at Yale Law. By the way, she was a big-time alcoholic at the time of the divorce. She's living down in Macon, Georgia. Maybe she could shed some light on the Yale thing, I don't know . . ."

Tim also told her of his detective work in checking the financial disclosure forms of the four judges. Vicky focused on the apparent financial connections that Judges Franklin, Janoff, and Bowen had with the chief judge. As they completed their tidal basin walk and had arrived back at the Land Rover, Vicky finally said, "Okay, Tim, I tentatively agree with you, this looks suspicious. What do you want me to do?"

Tim opened the car door and reached in to grab two large envelopes. He handed both to Vicky. "Here are two items that may tie the cases to Judge Rogers's death. In this envelope are the originals of the papers found in Rogers's desk. By the way, I have a copy of them. The second envelope contains the manila envelope and tape that my secretary and I found under the desk drawer. You can check the contents of both envelopes for fingerprints. My prints and those of my secretary, as well as Judge Rogers's will be in FBI records. Everyone at the court has a security clearance and has to be fingerprinted."

"Judge, you've become quite the detective," Vicky said dryly. "I'll have these run through FBI prints. What else do you suggest, Dick Tracy?"

"God damn it, Vicky. I'm not trying to do your job," Tim snapped.

Vicky almost smiled at him. "All right, don't be so touchy. What else do you think I should do?"

Tim outlined his rough plan of how the initial investigation should proceed. He wanted Vicky to first read the suspect seven cases and make up her own mind about them. Then he thought she should assign an FBI agent to investigate any possible connection of Draco and the four judges. He also thought someone should quietly check into the death of Judge Rogers. Vicky agreed, and then asked him if Camellia Winston should be interviewed; that was the most sensitive item. They decided an interview with her should be undertaken last, only if warranted by the results of the rest of the investigation.

Tim drove Vicky back to the Justice Department. Stopping at the side entrance, as she started to get out, Tim said, "Thank you for looking into this. One last thing and, I know this is a lot to ask—but can you do these things without opening an official file?"

Vicky started to interrupt him, but Tim plunged on. "If the

word ever got out that a new judge had instigated an investigation of other judges on his court—well, that would just destroy my judicial career. So can you keep this very, very quiet?"

Vicky hesitated. "First, I'll read those cases and look into the checklist. If everything you have told me is true, and I have no reason to doubt you, it could be a case-fixing scheme involving one or more judges. Or it could also just be good lawyering." She looked at him hard. "Your suspicions could be unfounded. You know how rumors get started in big organizations, and your court system is no different. This whole story could all be a function of skill, luck, envy, gossip, or who knows what?"

"Vicky, listen. I've considered those things, and I want you to know, this is not just my suspicion—Breedlove and Judge Goldstein agree. So counting me, that's three federal judges who suspect there's something strange going on. But you haven't answered my question. Can't you look into this without opening up an official file?"

"All right, Tim, for now I will try to keep this off the books. Quite frankly, after the prelim investigation, I don't expect to find anything the slightest bit illegal."

As Tim watched Vicky disappear into the Justice Department, he felt a huge twinge of guilt and anxiety—perhaps he should have been *completely* truthful with her and told her that Winston had already confessed to fixing cases for the president. If Winston and his "majority" were helping Draco, that was a crime. Surely helping the president win three cases in his court was equally a crime—obstruction of justice. And by keeping quiet about that, Quinn himself could be accused of aiding and abetting a criminal conspiracy. But he couldn't tell her now. Let her get down to the bottom of this Draco thing first. Then he would decide what to do about the White House arrangement. He rationalized it by the fact that when he looked at those three White House cases he saw no connection to Winston. In fact, of those cases that Winston mentioned as favors for the president, Winston hadn't even sat on any of them. *But* . . . at least two judges from his "majority" did.

The next morning, Vicky Hauser unlocked her office at the U.S. Department of Justice in Washington at 8 A.M., arriving as early as she did most mornings. When she graduated from Columbia Law School, she had spent several years with a Wall Street law firm, but still driven by idealism, she had given up the big money in New York and come to Washington to join the Public Integrity Section at Justice. That was twelve years ago. She had found her purpose in life. She prided herself on being both zealous and creative in her pursuit of corruption, and once she sensed the blood of guilt in her target, she showed no mercy. She had fostered a reputation as a relentless prosecutor, a woman you wouldn't want coming after you, especially if you were guilty.

Sitting down at her computer with a cup of coffee she had brewed herself, she began to follow up on the lead Tim had given her the afternoon before. He was such a bastard. He had no idea the problems that men caused women when they toyed with their hearts and their reputations. Sleeping with Tim in New Orleans had been a mistake, and a big one. Before that weekend, she hadn't seen Tim since they had been lovers at Columbia. Then, in New Orleans, in such a short time, he had blown those cool coals back to a hot flame. Too much alcohol had eased their unwise attempt to awaken passions from the past, but the feelings had been there in both of them. But it was she who had paid the price, not him, the married man. He had been such a shit! But what a sweet smile he had.

She brought up on the computer screen the seven listed cases, printed them out, and spent several hours intently focused on them. Before she started any investigation of some high-ranking federal judges, she had to be convinced personally that something was seriously wrong.

She ended her review of all seven cases just before lunch and sighed heavily. She hated to agree with Tim. Yet on the record, something was going on that smelled bad. She called up Bill Sharkey and asked him to come over from FBI Headquarters just across Pennsylvania Avenue from the Justice Department. Sharkey was one of the FBI agents she commonly used on investigations; he had just finished helping her put the assistant secretary for Commercial Affairs in the slammer for two years and she had been happy to write him a letter of commendation to the director of the FBI.

When Sharkey arrived, Vicky explained to him that she had a very sensitive investigation to discuss. The potential targets were a Washington lawyer and four federal judges on the U.S. Court of Appeals, all high-profile figures with a lot of juice around Washington. Another federal judge had reported the possible case-fixing scheme on his court. She didn't mention Tim by name. "There are some powerful indications of fraud on some cases. The whistleblower judge is scared, rightfully so," she told Sharkey. "He insists on no formal investigation at this stage."

Vicky slid across her desk a list of judges and the law firm to be investigated. Bill examined it, shook his head, and whistled. "Jesus, counselor! I've heard of all of these judges—Winston, Franklin, Bowen, and Janoff. And not opening a file on an investigation of sitting federal judges—I could get fired."

Vicky looked at him urgently. "Please, Bill, I gave my word that I would not open a file at this stage. I'll take responsibility for that. There seems to be something to the allegations. There may well be a case-fixing scheme at this court."

Bill exhaled hard. "Well, they can't fire me for following your orders, I guess, but I don't want to have to gag down early retirement if I can help it. I'll go along with you for a while, but as soon as we have something concrete, I'll have to open a file."

Vicky smiled. She now had landed a top investigator, one of the best she had ever worked with. "Here's your starting point. The whistle-blower judge I met with yesterday gave me some papers. These are the originals. He thinks they were hidden by the late Judge Rogers. Remember him?"

"Oh, yeah, the gay judge robbed and murdered over in the LBJ Park near the Pentagon, right? You think his death is tied into this?"

"I don't know," Vicky said, "but we sure in hell are going to find out."

"By the way, who is our whistle-blower?"

"Judge Tim Quinn."

Sharkey's face contorted in a grimace.

"Is there a problem?"

"There might be. You know some whistle-blowers are dirty themselves and run to rat out the others when they think the law is onto them?"

Vicky shook her head and said that that wasn't the case here since the cases under suspicion happened before Quinn got on the court and Quinn wasn't tied into the Draco firm in any way.

Still Vicky noticed Sharkey was troubled. "Out with it, Bill what's wrong?"

Sharkey was blunt. "Quinn is a dirtbag. He was the lawyer that sued the FBI to get Kathleen Falco rehired last year. Quinn filed suit and caused a shit storm over how the Bureau was treating female agents and eventually got a friend of mine at the Washington Field Office fired."

Vicky was silent, then softly said, "Bill, I remember the case. It seemed to me that the female agent was rehired for good reason and that her supervisor was sexually harassing her."

"Well . . . I guess you're right. My buddy did have wandering hands. But he was a great field agent and a good guy with a family. Now he's without a pension and working for some low-level security company in Virginia."

"Bill, can you put away your personal feelings for Quinn and do this case? Quinn is supposed to be the good guy here."

"Sure, counselor. I guess he was only doing his job. It's not like he's human; he's a lawyer."

Vicky smiled at the usual slam on lawyers and said, "Well, then let's do ours and see if we have some dirty judges."

CHAPTER 12

VICKY FACED FBI AGENT BILL SHARKEY ACROSS THE CONFERENCE table in Vicky's office. Sharkey was briefing her on some preliminary results on the Winston-Draco investigation. Vicky was taking notes on a yellow legal pad. Sharkey had been investigating the financial and other connections of Judges Franklin, Bowen, and Janoff with the chief judge.

"It appears that two of the judges, Franklin and Janoff, are receiving the maximum outside income they can earn as judges—twenty thousand dollars—and they're both earning it in the same place: Jefferson Law School here in D.C. They are getting this for teaching two seminars, one each semester. I checked around with some of the other law schools in the area, and the standard pay for seminars like this is two to three thousand dollars per semester, or no more than six thousand dollars per year." Sharkey raised his eyes from his notes to Vicky. "So it seems pretty suspicious to me that Franklin and Janoff would get such inflated salaries, which bring them right up to the maximum they are allowed to earn, for teaching two bullshit seminars. And when I went over to the law school and sniffed around a bit, I found out that Franklin's law clerks do most of the teaching for him, but Franklin is the one who gets paid. The clerks get zip. One more thing about Jefferson Law. I've confirmed that Chief Judge Winston has been on the Board of Trustees for nine years, *and* that Leo Draco is a major donor to Jefferson Law."

"What a coincidence," Vicky remarked. She gave Sharkey a wry smile. "How about Judge Rosemary Bowen's loan? Any info on that?"

Sharkey shuffled through his Bowen file and reported that the financing was actually a series of major loans from a small bank in Gardenia, Georgia. Judge Bowen had recently refinanced her house to just over three hundred thousand, and she rolled it over for the second time a few months ago. Each time she refinanced it, she got better terms, which now were as good as Sharkey had ever seen. "I should be so lucky with *my* mortgage," he said. "Her interest rate is just a hair above prime, with a six-month abatement on payments—in other words, an unbelievably sweet deal."

"What's the connection to Winston?" Vicky asked, massaging her forehead.

"Am I giving you a headache, counselor?"

"No, it's not you, Sharkey. Today's been headache heaven. But it's starting to go away. Just took some aspirin before you came in. You don't miss a thing, do you?"

"I try not to," Sharkey replied, smiling. He went on to explain that the connection between the Bowen loans and Winston was circumstantial at this point, but persuasive. The chief judge had grown up in Georgia near the small town where the bank was located; he is a major stockholder, and the president of the bank was a fellow fraternity brother of Winston's at Hobbes College in Georgia.

"So it seems that the chief judge got the bank he partially owns to arrange a very favorable loan for Judge Bowen. Nothing illegal, but that's a mighty big favor and trying to find out if there was any illegal quid pro quo would be tough."

"Right. One other thing, Vicky. Speaking of Hobbes College, Judge Janoff's only son is a student there, and he's attending on an academic scholarship."

"So what? He's obviously a smart kid," said Vicky. She was doing her job as a prosecutor to challenge her investigator on his results.

"Well, I've looked at his grades in high school and his disciplinary record, and there's no way he could have gotten into a school as prestigious and as selective as Hobbes without some grease being applied. And on an academic scholarship! No way, *not* without major grease!"

"So Winston's fingerprints are on Janoff also?"

Sharkey agreed. Winston was a big money donor at Hobbes and has been for years. Sharkey had found Winston's name in the lists of annual gifts over 100 K in the last five Hobbes annual reports. "Big donors have juice in any admissions office. It's a fact."

"Any way you can verify that Winston helped the kid get in?"

"No, and I don't think I should go down there and poke around the admissions office. That probably wouldn't go anywhere—and it would just set off too many alarm bells."

Vicky couldn't tell if her headache was worse or if she just had more to think about. "Okay. Anything else?"

"Well, I have found out some interesting things about the chief judge. Did you know that he and Draco were in the same class at Yale Law and that they were both on the *Yale Law Journal* together?"

"You're kidding."

"No, they were. And, get this, for their last two years at Yale Law, they shared a house off campus. I got that info from the Yale University housing records. It's a small two-bedroom house that is rented every year to Yale Law students. A very cozy arrangement."

"Yeah, and just think, the two of them can have little roommate reunions half a dozen times a year in appellate court. It's a wonder that Draco's adversaries haven't filed any motions to disqualify the chief judge when Draco appears before him."

Sharkey's eyes twinkled. "I actually checked that, and there haven't been any requests for disqualification ever on that basis. Obviously, it's not a widely known fact. But I have some other things on the chief judge. First of all, the guy is very wealthy. Old family money. His Georgetown place is owned free and clear, and he owns two family houses down in Macon, Georgia, one of them outside of town—a real antebellum plantation. The other is a big mansion in town. And they're both paid for, too. No mortgages at all. His ex-wife, Camellia, lives in the one in town, even though they've been apart for years. No children, but she gets an alimony check every month."

Vicky didn't even look up from the notes she was writing. "Bill, I've got a surprise for you. Guess who handled the divorce?"

"Draco?" Bill asked.

Vicky's head slowly rose and her eyes met the agent's. "No, Bill. It was our whistle-blower, Judge Timothy Quinn. That's how they met. When he was in private practice, Mr. Quinn, the attorney, did the divorce settlement for Judge Winston."

The FBI agent furrowed his brow. "Washington really is a small town."

Vicky could tell by Sharkey's reaction that he was hurt; a key piece of information had been left out of his initial briefing on the case. "By the way," she quickly added, "Quinn did disclose that to me at our initial meeting. I just forgot to relay it to you." Then she tried to put Sharkey back on track. "How much does the ex-wife get?"

Special Agent Sharkey put his game face back on as he relayed the facts of the alimony. Camellia had gotten payments of two thousand a month for the first six years after their divorce. But then, suddenly four years ago, Winston raised the amount to six thousand a month.

Vicky put her pen down and sat back, running her fingers through her long blond hair. "You mean he raised the amount voluntarily? *Without* a petition to or an order from a court? What ex-husband does that?"

"Yeah, that surprised me too. Why would he do that, especially after six years?"

Vicky shook her head and chewed on her pen. Sharkey had uncovered some potential conflicts of interest, but so far there was no hard evidence of any criminal activity that could be introduced at a trial to show case rigging or any other crime. The thing about the ex-wife intrigued her. Quinn had told her that Winston and Camellia were dating while he was at Yale Law School. Perhaps Mrs. Winston could help give more focus on the investigation. "Maybe I should go down to Macon and see Camellia Winston."

"Your call, counselor. Could be a good move. Sometimes ex-wives have axes to grind with their ex-husbands, and we may learn something from her."

"Anything else?"

Sharkey had found three sets of prints on the Judge Rogers papers, envelope, and the tape on the envelope found in Rogers's desk: those of Judge Quinn, Quinn's secretary, and Rogers himself. He also told Vicky that when he was double-checking the financial disclosures of the four judges over at the Administrative Office of the U.S. Courts, he asked for Judge Rogers's last three annual forms, hoping there would be a sample of his handwriting there. That long shot paid off because Rogers had filled all his forms out in longhand, so there were excellent baseline specimens of his handwriting. He had taken copies over to the documents section of the FBI lab, along with a copy of the checklist that Quinn found in Rogers's desk, and the people at the lab confirmed that the checklist was definitely in Judge Rogers's handwriting.

"Bottom line, Judge Rogers did write that checklist and it appears he was the one who put it under the drawer."

"Good. So we know now that Quinn's assumption that Rogers wrote the list was right. Anything else?"

"One last thing. There's an interesting sidetrack on the Rogers connection to this whole thing. But I want you to hear it from the source. He's waiting down the hall."

Sharkey explained that he had found the D.C. police detective who handled the Rogers murder investigation. "He's a street-savvy cop from the old school. You'll like him."

Soon Detective Turner joined them. Vicky could tell he was a tough cop who had seen it all, and wasn't fazed by dealing with the FBI. Sharkey had made it clear to him that this was an investigation off the books but hadn't told him what the case was about, beyond saying he wanted his take on the Rogers murder. "It's a closed case," Turner said. "Officially closed. But two things about it still bother me."

"What are those two things, detective?" Vicky asked.

"First, it was too convenient, too closed-loop." Turner told them he had been suspicious about the 911 call that led the police to the first body while it was still warm. Within hours, the second body was found and the case was solved.

"And what's the second thing?"

"The heroin. It was too pure. You don't see heroin like that on the street. It's like it came straight from the factory, unadulterated. And usually when you have an OD like that, other bodies start piling up in the hospitals. Nobody else died on heroin that pure. Not for years."

"So what do you conclude, Detective Turner?"

"I'd bet serious money that Rogers and the druggie who *officially* killed Rogers were both murdered."

Vicky felt chilled. "Can you prove that?"

"No, of course not."

"Do you have any leads?"

"Would I be talking to a prosecutor and an FBI gumshoe if I did?" Turner asked. He gathered up his trench coat and an old battered leather portfolio and stood up. "Good luck. And if you get any heat from the D.C. police department about nosing around on a closed case, well, tell them I came to you. I'm retiring in two months, so I'm bulletproof. Besides, my cracker supervisor pushed me to close the case too soon."

Vicky and Sharkey thanked Detective Turner and he left.

"Damn! Are we getting ourselves into a murder case here?" Vicky asked.

"I don't know, counselor," Sharkey said. "We may already be in one."

The next day Vicky made up her mind to see Camellia Winston in Macon, Georgia, since there were no other leads to follow. She called Tim Quinn and said that she agreed with his view that the seven cases were wrongly decided and that something strange was going on at the court. Then she told him of her plan to interview Winston's ex-wife.

"No, don't," Quinn said. "Please don't. You'll just get me in deep shit with Chief Judge Winston. This is escalating too fast. You're just supposed to investigate the cases and the conflicts with the judges."

"I'll investigate what I need to investigate, Judge," Vicky retorted. "But I'll interview her discreetly, I promise."

Seeing Vicky was set on this course, Tim warned, "As far as I know she still talks to Winston every week. They're practically as close as an old married couple."

Vicky could hear the anxiety in Tim's voice and she understood it. "Tim, do you want me to pursue this case or not?"

There was a brief pause on the end of the telephone line. Vicky didn't really doubt what his answer would be.

"See her during the morning, before lunch," Tim finally said. "She drinks. She'll be smashed by two P.M. Even Winston says that about her."

"Good idea, Tim. Thanks," Vicky said. "And I promise I'll be careful. For your sake. For everyone's."

Vicky was on a plane to Atlanta early the next morning. Sharkey had arranged for her plane to be met by a local FBI agent and for her to be driven to Macon. Soon the agent and Vicky were in a dark Crown Victoria sedan driving down a quiet, shaded street in a residential section of the old, aggressively Southern city. As the street numbers informed them they were nearing the Winston home, Vicky noted that the size of the houses was growing larger and the distance between them wider. Here the homes were well back from the sidewalk, sometimes hidden by large trees. When their car rolled to a stop at the curb in front of 1426 Oakview Drive, houses lined only one side of the street. On the opposite side, there were only trees. The agent informed her that this heavily wooded area was the border of a large nature preserve on the edge of the old part of town, where pre–Civil War merchants and bankers had erected their mansions.

Vicky was impressed. The lawn of the Winston home was carefully manicured, and twin flowering magnolia trees framed the large white house with tall black shutters. It was an antebellum Southern classic. Six large white pillars sheltered a brick verandah and supported a black wrought-iron balcony on the second floor. A hundred feet of weathered brick walkway led slightly uphill from the curb to the house. As Vicky approached the house alone, she felt as if she was walking up to the entrance of Tara.

She walked toward the front door, eerily aware of the midmorning silence of a hot day in the sleepy neighborhood that surrounded her. She rang the bell, which echoed through the house, and then heard the yapping of a small dog. Soon enough, the door swung open, and she found herself facing a heavyset black woman.

"May I help you?"

"Is Mrs. Winston in? I'd like to see her. I'm Vicky Hauser."

"I'll tell the missus that you are here."

A moment later, a frail pink face peeked around the door. Her voice was raspy. "Yes?"

"Are you Mrs. Winston?"

"Yes I am. And who are you, may I ask?"

"Yes, ma'am, I'm Vicky Hauser from the Justice Department in Washington, D.C. May I come in and speak to you for a moment?"

"Why . . . yes, yes, of course you may. Please come in."

The screen door swung open and Vicky stepped into the cool, dark interior. A miniature tan Yorkshire terrier was dancing nervously at the feet of Camellia Winston. Making not-quite-coherent but ladylike exclamations to her guest about the weather this time of year in Macon, Mrs. Winston led Vicky into a side parlor just off the high-ceilinged hallway at the bottom of a wide, sweeping staircase. The light was poor. Mrs. Winston smelled of alcohol and seemed a bit unsteady on her feet. She half stumbled on the dog, but she recovered before Vicky could extend her arm. They continued through the parlor, with its dark wood furniture, thick expensive carpets, and the large crystal chandelier hanging fifteen feet above their heads in dusty splendor, and went into the bright sunroom beyond. It was a beautiful room, Vicky thought, with sunlight streaming through louvered white shutters. The walls were pale yellow, and the long wooden blades of the ceiling fan barely stirred the air. Several large green palms grew from blue and white ceramic buckets along the wall, and the floor was marble, patterned in black-and-white diamonds. Mrs. Winston gestured toward a white wicker chair for Vicky, then took what was obviously her accustomed seat on a sofa across a glass-and-wicker coffee table. The Yorkie leaped into Mrs. Winston's lap and curled up against her.

Mrs. Winston began to stroke the dog. "This is Toby. He's the master of the house. Aren't you, Toby?" The dog responded with a high-pitched yap.

Vicky swallowed her preliminary sympathy for Mrs. Winston and put her briefcase on the floor next to her chair. She opened it and took out a legal pad and a pen. As Vicky looked up, she noted a half-full glass of white wine in front of Mrs. Winston on the coffee table, and smiled to herself. Harry Winston's ex-wife had started early. So much the better for Vicky's prospect of getting some good information that would fill in some of the blanks about the chief judge.

"May I offer you a glass of wine? I hate to drink alone . . ." Mrs. Winston began.

Good, Vicky thought. "Well, Mrs. Winston, if you don't mind, I would love a glass of wine."

"Wonderful, wonderful. Just help yourself from the tea cart over there. There's a wonderful bottle of Chablis open in the ice bucket, and glasses are on the shelf underneath."

"Why thank you, Mrs. Winston."

Vicky stood up and walked a few steps to the wheeled wicker tea cart. There was a large silver ice bucket containing two bottles of white wine; both had been uncorked. She continued talking as she got a glass for herself and filled it.

"Now, first of all, Mrs. Winston, let me explain why I am here. As I started to say, I am from the Justice Department in Washington,

D.C. I just want to ask you a few questions about your husband, Chief Judge Winston."

"Oh. Well, you know, we are divorced . . ."

"Yes, I know that. May I fill your glass?"

"Why, yes, please. Now, my husband, he's not in any trouble, is he?"

Vicky brought a wine bottle back with her and smoothly refilled Mrs. Winston's glass, returned the bottle to the tea cart, then sat back down in her chair opposite her hostess. It was time to lie. She felt bad about it, but she was doing it in the interests of justice. "Oh, no, Mrs. Winston. As a matter of fact, I am doing a preliminary background check on him for the possibility that he may be one of the candidates for the next vacancy on the United States Supreme Court." She winced inside even as she said the words.

"Oh. Why, that's wonderful! I didn't know. You understand, he never mentioned . . ."

"Yes, I know that, this is just deep-background for his possible appointment. It's very secret, but we need your help."

Mrs. Winston folded her hands in her lap, on top of her dog, and tried to look seriously focused. "All right, then, what are your questions?"

"I understand that you met the judge he was at Yale Law School?"

"Oh, yes, I had just graduated from Vassar, and I had taken a position as a buyer for the Jordan Marsh department store in New Haven."

"I see. Did you know another Yale student named Leo Draco?"

"Why yes, that was Harry's roommate, you know, and they were just the best of friends . . ."

"Okay, Mrs. Winston . . ."

"Please, you are such a nice young lady, please just call me by my first name, Camellia. That's what all my friends do."

"All right, Camellia . . ."

"Thank you, thank you." She abruptly got up and went over to the tea cart. "I was named after Camellia Straford, my great-grandmother, a lovely lady from Savannah." Camellia helped herself to the almost empty bottle and refilled her own glass. Then catching her mistake, she turned around. "Can I get some more wine for you? There is another opened bottle, honey."

"Yes, I think I will have a little more. This really is an excellent wine! I'll help myself."

As Mrs. Winston made her way back to the sofa, Vicky went over to get the new bottle of wine and brought it back to the table.

"I just love this wine. It's from the Tartan Vineyards in the Napa Valley of California. I buy it by the case. Now, where were we?" Camellia asked.

"Mrs. Winston, I mean, Camellia, we've gotten a lot of information about Chief Judge Winston, and he is a wonderful man; he would be a great presence on our highest court. But we need to make sure that the president"—Mrs. Winston's eyes widened—"knows everything he needs to know about the judge—including who his friends are. You understand. Now, it's important that we get all the details, so you would be doing him a great favor if you helped us resolve these issues. We are trying to help him out ahead of time, sort of clearing up whatever minefields might be out there. You understand."

Camellia suddenly looked confused and ashen, and Vicky couldn't tell if she had touched a nerve, or if it was just the alcohol.

"So tell me about Leo Draco."

Camellia touched her hair and smiled. "Oh, when we knew each other, back at Yale, he was a funny man, sometimes he could be the funniest man ever . . ." Then she stopped and her face turned serious. "But he did have a bad streak in him, and I believe he was a bad influence on Harry."

"How do you mean?"

"Well, for one thing, I guess it was the cheating. You said you know all about that, right?"

Vicky's heart jumped. "Oh, yes, we know all about it. Tell me your version."

"Well, there's really not that much to it. I know it's not a crime, Harry told me that. What I heard from Harry was that Leo had met this thirty-two-year-old woman, a fat girl, who ran the central copy center for the Yale Law School. Anyhow, when all the exams were written by the professors, they all had to be mimeographed at that one place, the copy center, and Leo, why, he seduced that woman within a month of getting to Yale, and he had her head all in a twitter for all three years. He kept promising to marry her, but as soon as he got his degree, why he just walked away. Went to Washington, D.C. I believe, and never looked back. Poor thing, she couldn't tell anybody, and she made a suicide attempt . . ."

"What do you mean? Did she give him advance copies of the exams?"

"Why, yes! She gave them advance copies of almost every exam they ever took at Yale. I mean, they were both plenty smart, but this way . . . they got good grades and made law journal without having to do much work at all. I told Harry it wasn't right, what they were doing, but he never paid any attention to me, and he just kept on going. He said that if he stopped or if he turned Leo in, why, he believed Leo would have actually killed him! Now I know that may sound wild to you, but I knew Leo well, and I'll tell you now, he was a cold, hard man, and I believe he was deep down evil inside. Sometimes, I was so dreadful scared of him myself . . . and I hope you never tell him what I just said."

Mrs. Winston was near tears, her chest twitching. The Yorkie leaped off her lap. Vicky, stunned by what she had heard, felt a stab of pity. "No, no, don't worry. It's such an old story, isn't it?" Vicky said. Mrs. Winston smiled unsteadily.

"Now, how about recently, have they been working together that you know?"

"Well, about five or so years ago, when Harry became chief judge, he came down here on some money business about a land purchase or something. That's when he told me that Leo and he were doing some business deals together, and he was going to raise my divorce allowance to six thousand dollars each month. Now, that goes a long way down here, especially since I don't pay any rent. I am taking care of Harry's family home, you see, and I do a good job, don't I?"

"You certainly do, Camellia."

"And it was so nice of Leo to help out Harry with his investments. He isn't the nicest man, but he can do nice things. I'm grateful to him." She nodded, as if to convince herself.

"Is there anything more you want to tell me?" Vicky asked gently.

"No, no, I don't think so. Well, there is one other thing, I don't know if it means anything, but, you know, when they were in law school, why, the second year, Leo, he went down to the Caribbean somewhere, and he opened up a bank account down there. You see, he just absolutely loved to gamble, and he was smart, so he won a lot, even going against the casinos and all, he still won. And then, of course, when he got into those big card games at Yale, usually he won big, and then he would send the money down to the Caribbean, he said to protect it, and not pay taxes and all. And I believe, from the way he and Harry used to talk, that Harry got into some kind of business with him, and they both had a lot more money down there."

Vicky was busy was taking notes. "Very interesting," she asked without looking up. "Do they both still have bank accounts in the Caribbean?"

"The bank? Why, yes. I sign the bank papers. That is one of my little jobs."

"Papers, what kind of papers?" Vicky's head had snapped up and she looked intently at Mrs. Winston.

Then she saw her sudden intense interest register in Camellia's brain and frighten her. Camellia stopped talking and went pale. It was clear she was thinking that she had volunteered too much information. "Wait a minute, now, Miss, ah, Miss . . ."

Vicky looked her square in the eye and smiled. The old lady had been drunk and relaxed; now she was clearly rattled and on alert. "My name is Vicky," she prompted, hoping to calm down the now wide-eyed Camellia.

"Uh, Vicky, yes . . . It's been so nice to spend some time with you. But I'm afraid I feel tired now. I must lie down. You must excuse me." Her Southern-belle smile flickered back on, more edgy than before. "Ah, now remember you said this was all confidential, and I hope that means you won't tell anybody what I said, right?"

"Absolutely, don't worry, this is all off the record."

"Good, good." Mrs. Winston struggled to her feet. "I would certainly hate to do anything that would hurt Harry's chances for the Supreme Court." Then she seemed to shake, to shudder a little. "I'll see you to the door. I don't mind telling you, I am still afraid of Leo. He is evil, plain evil."

Later that day, Camellia Winston woke up from her afternoon nap not only with her usual hangover but also with terrifying memories of having talked too much to a woman from Washington. She went to the bathroom to get some of the painkillers that the doctor had prescribed. The sunlight slanting through the bathroom window hurt her eyes. After she took the pills, she went back to sit on her bed. Camellia replayed the events of the morning as best as she could remember them. Then she walked to her dresser and took a worn slip of paper from beneath her jewelry box. There was a phone number on it and no name.

Camellia dialed the number. The call lasted for about five minutes, with the person on the other end doing much of the talking. After the call was over, Camellia was shaking. She went to her dresser and poured a large glass from a bottle of Absolut vodka she kept in her lingerie drawer. She drained the glass in two swallows and started to cry.

CHAPTER 13

WITH HER FINGERS MASSAGING HER FOREHEAD, VICKY LEANED over a yellow legal pad and focused intently on the phrasing of the words she had written in a rough draft of a legal brief. This morning she was deeply focused on drafting a brief opposing a defense attorney's slick effort to suppress a properly obtained confession in a bribery case, a case she wanted badly to win. She scratched out the sentence she had just written. She turned and started to leaf through one or two of the exhibits in the binder, then went back and wrote a new sentence, thinking of what she had learned long ago in college: The best writing is really rewriting.

A jackhammer from a few blocks away was rattling her office windows, but the intrusion didn't bother her. Ever since high school, she had been able to shut out the world around her and focus exclusively on the problem at hand. This ability had been a major asset when it came to taking tests; her high SAT and LSAT scores, added to her high grades, had given Vicky her pick of colleges and, later, law schools. When the phone rang, it startled her out of the bribery prosecution world, and she had trouble clearing her mind.

"Ms. Hauser, I have Special Agent Sharkey holding on line two."

Vicky pushed the button, her mind clicking into the case of Judge Winston and Leo Draco. "Hello, Bill. What's up?"

"Counselor, we have a problem. Something happened in Macon yesterday. Judge Winston's ex-wife was killed."

Vicky felt a chill. "My God! What happened?"

"The special agent who picked you up at the Macon airport told me Mrs. Winston was killed in a hit-and-run. Looks like a professional hit."

Vicky threw down the pencil she was holding. "Any witnesses?"

Sharkey said that there was one: the elderly woman next door who was on her front porch, watching Mrs. Winston walking her dog. She told the police that a big white SUV came speeding down the street, bounced up over the curb, hit Mrs. Winston from the rear, ran over her, chewed up the neighbor's lawn as it slid back into the street, and then was gone. The elderly lady immediately called 911 and then ran out to help Mrs. Winston. Mrs. Winston was in bad shape; the dog was not injured. She was pronounced dead at the scene. The neighbor told police it looked like there were two men in the front seat of the SUV, but the windows were dark-tinted glass, and all she saw were the outlines of torsos. It happened so fast that she didn't get a look at the plates.

"Jesus! Did they find the car, the white SUV?"

"Yeah, they think so, but it was only partially white when they found it—less than a half-mile away, behind a deserted warehouse and still burning. Apparently, the two guys who killed Mrs. Winston were pros. They didn't want to leave any fibers, prints, or any other evidence behind so they torched it—very professional. That SUV had been stolen from the Atlanta airport about five hours before the hit. Local police are running tests on the tire prints from the lawn, but they're almost positive that the burned-out car was the murder weapon."

Vicky was shaking her head. The thought that her visit had caused Camellia Winston's death started to register and she felt a wave of guilt. "Do we have anything on the killers?"

"Well, we have one slim lead. When they burned the car, the gas cap blew off and it was found a hundred feet away. There was one good thumbprint and two partial fingerprints on it. The local police found the car owner, and the prints don't belong to him. They could belong to one of the perps, because the owner said the car needed gas. He said it was running on fumes when he parked it in the Atlanta long-term lot. The police ran the prints through the National Crime Information Center database, but they came up with zip."

"Jesus! I wonder . . . a contract hit! Did I touch a nerve or something in Georgia, that Mrs. Winston would be murdered just to keep her quiet?" Vicky didn't want to believe it.

"Well, the timing is damn suspicious. Maybe there's an explanation that's not connected to your visit, but I sure as hell can't think of one now. If we're close to uncovering a major case-rigging scheme, there has to be quite a bit of money at risk, and jail time as well. We both know how desperate money and jail can make people."

"Bill, this is a much more serious matter than I ever dreamed possible," Vicky said somberly.

"Someone must have found out about your visit and decided to take her out. Alcoholics are weak links, and all of that."

Vicky thought for a few seconds, then asked Sharkey to come over so they could review the case and figure out where to go from here. Then she called Tim. "I need to see you right away," she told him. "There have been some important developments on the matter we discussed. Can you come to my office as soon as possible?"

"You mean . . . you mean right now?"

"Tim, it's important."

"Sure, I'll be right over. Vicky, you sound upset. Can't you tell me anything more over the phone right now?"

"No, I don't think that would be wise."

"Okay, I'm on my way."

When Tim left the courthouse, a young man in a dark suit began walking behind him. Every time he looked over his shoulder, the man was still there. Tim ducked into an office building one block from Justice and watched as the man walked by without even looking in Tim's direction, then disappeared down the street. Tim waited a few minutes and emerged onto Pennsylvania Avenue, saw nothing suspicious, and continued the short distance to Justice again. He was jumpy. Was the man really a tail? Or had his suspicions been stirred by the edge in Vicky's voice?

He walked into the Justice main security checkpoint and showed his federal judge credentials to a guard, who directed him around the metal detector. In his agitated state, Tim frowned at this courtesy, worried at the power his judge's credentials gave him. *Christ,* he thought, *I could be a terrorist with a fake ID on a suicide mission to take out the attorney general in his office.*

When he got to the Public Integrity Section, located in a cluster of offices at one corner of the massive Justice Department building, he glanced around him as he approached the door of Vicky's office. No one in the corridor recognized or even noticed him. Good, he thought. It would be tough to explain why a federal judge was visiting the section that prosecuted public corruption. He quickly knocked on the door bearing the number that Vicky had given him. Vicky's voice invited him to enter. As he stepped over the threshold of that office in the Justice Department, Tim had the feeling that he was passing a point of no return.

Inside were Vicky Hauser and a balding, sleepy-eyed man of medium height. Both of them stood up. "Judge, this is Special Agent Bill Sharkey of the FBI," Vicky said. "He's been working on the information you provided."

Tim immediately remembered the face of the FBI agent. He had questioned the agent about a year ago in a sexual harassment case he had handled pro-bono for his firm. He had won and made some enemies in the Bureau in doing it. Tim knew this was one of them. Not a happy thought when Tim was putting himself out on a limb, accusing fellow judges of possible crimes.

As soon as Judge Quinn sat down, Vicky sat across from him, her eyes grave. "I'll get right to the point. Something terrible has happened. Camellia Winston is dead. Hit-and-run. It appears to be murder."

Tim was stunned. He pressed his lips together, shaking his head, trying to clear his mind of the awful idea. "God, poor Camellia." Then Tim looked directly at Vicky. "How? Was this right after your visit?" He knew his words were clearly accusatory.

Vicky coldly returned his gaze. "Yes, Judge, it was right after my visit to her and may well be connected. The visit did give us some valuable information on Winston and Draco. I know you didn't want me to interview her, but it was required to further our investigation. Bill Sharkey will give you a rundown of the hit-and-run that killed Mrs. Winston."

Bill took over and walked Judge Quinn through the information he had received on the death of Mrs. Winston. Tim listened carefully, but everything Sharkey said sounded as implausible as a mobster movie. "It had all the markings of a contract hit," Sharkey concluded. "We do suspect that this death might be connected to the deaths of Judge Rogers and the druggie who killed him. The case-fixing scheme may be responsible for all three deaths, therefore Draco and Winston are prime suspects."

Tim shook his head. "No, I can't believe it."

"Believe it, Judge. The case-fixing is big bucks and a lot of jail time if they are caught. People are willing to kill here."

Tim turned to Vicky. His eyes were hard. "Why did you go down there?"

"Our investigation hit an impasse," Vicky said immediately. "Bill will explain later what he found out about the connections between the chief judge and the other three judges. And, as you know, some of the most carefully guarded secrets of a criminal suspect get blurted out by ex-wives, either through carelessness or vindictiveness. The interview with Mrs. Winston had to be done." Vicky paused and looked into Tim's eyes; he sensed she was seeking his understanding.

Tim nodded slowly. "Go ahead, Ms. Hauser."

Vicky related how she had talked her way into Camellia's mansion of a house, in which she lived rent-free, and how Winston's ex-wife had opened up to her. "By the way, even though it was morning, she was already drinking wine, apparently halfway through a bottle when I got there. You were right about her being an alcoholic." Vicky seemed less tense now that she had gotten into the story.

Tim nodded again. "Did you drink with her?"

"Yes I did, all the better to get her to talk."

"Probably a good move. What did you find out?"

"At first she was very talkative. She told me Winston and Draco were not only close at Yale Law School. They were roommates. And according to Mrs. Winston, they both did very well academically, even made law review, because they cheated all the way through law school."

This was too much for Tim. "Wait a minute. Almost all the exams in law school are essays. How could anyone possibly cheat their way through law school?"

"There was a way and Draco found it. He figured an ingenious way to cheat almost as soon as he got to Yale. It seems that he began sleeping with the woman who ran the copy center where all the tests were copied at Yale Law. Draco and Winston were able to get advance copies of almost all the tests they took at Yale."

"Really, that's amazing! No wonder they got good grades and made law review."

Vicky scanned her notes. "The two major things I learned from Mrs. Winston were that Draco and Winston had some sort of business relationship and bank accounts in the Caribbean. I couldn't get any details on either the business or the accounts. When I tried, she froze and ended the interview."

Tim was intrigued by this financial connection—an apparent violation of the strict ethical code governing judicial behavior. No judge should hear a case where he has a business relationship with one of the attorneys.

Vicky sighed. "I'm sorry about Mrs. Winston, but we had no idea that the visit would possibly lead to her death."

"The interview was the right decision, Vicky. You couldn't have known," Tim said thoughtfully.

When Sharkey's left eyebrow went up, Tim realized that he had erred in calling Vicky by her first name. Vicky caught it too; she quickly asked Bill to fill in the judge on the investigation so far. Bill outlined the suspicious incidents involving the four judges under investigation: the inflated fees paid to two of the judges for teaching courses at Jefferson Law School, the sweetheart loan to one judge, and the questionable admission to Hobbes College, complete with scholarship, given to a son of one of the judges. Sharkey mentioned that Winston was on the Board of Trustees at Jefferson Law, a major stockholder of the Georgia bank that had granted the loan, and a trustee and a major donor to Hobbes College. "Your Honor, we know that there were special favors received by these three judges, but all these acts are legal on their face."

Vicky leaned forward in her chair. "Judge, as I said before, the investigation has reached an impasse of sorts. We know that there was a pattern of wrongly decided cases and that there were some interesting favors given. We may suspect that a case-fixing scheme exists, but we don't know how it works." Her gaze, professional and appraising, fixed on his. "Judge, do you have any ideas?"

Tim leaned back in the sofa and rubbed his chin. This all felt so unreal, so unlikely. "Well, I've only been on the court for a few months, but I've sat on panels and worked with all three of these judges you suspect are involved on these cases—or all four, if we include the chief judge. I've eaten lunch with them, had coffee, laughed, complained, had the same sort of social interaction that you would expect from any group of professional peers. And I just can't believe these judges are being paid off—I can't believe these judges are selling their votes."

Bill Sharkey spoke up. "I don't think it's money driving the votes of Bowen, Franklin, and Janoff. I have carefully been over their Financial Disclosure forms, the bank accounts, and traceable assets of these judges, and unless there are some secret accounts, these judges all have relatively normal and modest net worths. I couldn't find any visible indication they are getting major money from anyone." He glanced at Vicky. "Now on Winston, his disclosure forms and his bank records showed no accounts in the Caribbean or in any other foreign location. But he's the only one of these four judges who seems to have any serious money, the only one you would call 'rich'. His income does show an increase since he became chief judge. Nothing to raise alarms, but his stocks and bonds have grown dramatically in the last few years, much more than the recent economy would justify. Either he's a very lucky investor or he's getting extra money from somewhere."

"Okay, Agent Sharkey," Tim said. "Let's put aside the money angle for now and concentrate on how a case-fixing scheme would work. If the chief wants to fix a given case of Draco's, he would need to guarantee a majority vote, which means he has to make sure that two out of the three judges on a panel would vote for Draco." Vicky started taking notes. "Now, the chief judge counts on his own vote, but he needs one more to make a majority. So he goes to selected judges, maybe to those who like him more because of favors he has done for them, and Winston merely asks them a week or so before the hearing how they'll vote in a Draco case that is set for oral argument. Hell, when the chief asked me how I was going to vote in a case before oral argument, I told him."

Vicky looked intrigued. "Your Honor, I may be wrong but I thought appellate judges weren't supposed to discuss or decide cases before the oral argument. Isn't that like prejudging a case, and an improper thing to do?"

It disconcerted Tim that Vicky kept calling him "Your Honor," but he tried to put that thought aside. "Well, technically, you're right. Judges are supposed to go into a case with an open mind—they're not supposed to discuss it ahead of time. But remember—" his eyes swept from Vicky to Sharkey—"the chief is an old friend who helped me get on the court. So when he came into my chambers and asked me how I would vote in a Draco case that was going to be heard on my first day on the bench, I told him." Tim shrugged. "I thought it was a little peculiar. But reflecting back on it, if the chief judge is doing that with these other three judges, I can see that he would know how another judge would vote before a case is argued. With that kind of advance knowledge, he could rearrange the panels so that Draco wins on big cases."

Sharkey seemed absorbed by the scenario Tim laid out. "Judge, maybe that's where the favors come in. The chief judge is arranging favorable loans, fat jobs with Jefferson Law School, helping Janoff 's son get into college—hell, there may be a lot more we don't even suspect, personal favors done by the chief for his favored judges!"

"Okay, the favors are important," Tim said, continuing the speculation. "They make those judges beholden to the chief judge. So let's get back to the mechanics—how does it work? Before a big Draco case, maybe the chief visits one of his favored judges. He begins with his own view of the case, and sees if they will agree with him. If they do, then he next has to set up a panel on which he and that other friendly judge will sit. It doesn't matter who the third judge is, because with the two votes he knows in advance, his and that of his 'friend,' the chief will be able to deliver a majority vote for Draco. Right?"

Vicky and Bill nodded. Tim went on. "Okay, then those three judges you've been looking at—Janoff, Franklin, and Bowen—are the ones Winston has done big favors for. As we've said, these favors are all quite legal, and you might say that given human nature, these judges are all obligated to the chief judge. So they would not object if the chief came in and asked for their views before they all heard an argument. And remember, at least two of them would fall in line with his views just because the chief, in their eyes, is a respected Yale Law, Rhodes Scholar judge renowned for his legal abilities."

Vicky seemed more intent on him than Tim had ever seen her before—at least since their ill-fated evening in New Orleans. "That's it, Your Honor! That must be how it works. The seven cases of Draco were all decided by the votes of the judges that were given favors by Winston."

"Good point. But remember this is just a theory. Let's assume the chief judge still has to rig the panels to make sure the right judges sit on the right panels for the targeted Draco cases. And it would only be a few panels that he needs to rig, so it shouldn't attract any attention. Once Winston knows which judge or judges he wants to sit on a Draco case—and remember, he doesn't want to sit on all the special Draco cases himself, because that would give away the game—well then, the whole scheme has to depend on the clerk of the court. Specifically it would depend on Winston and the clerk manipulating the panel selection for these special cases." This possibility bothered Tim a lot, because it would mean that the case-rigging was not just Winston's doing but required a larger conspiracy.

Vicky was curious. "Your Honor, aren't the court panels supposed to be randomly selected by computer?"

Tim had wondered that too. He told Vicky and Bill Sharkey that the chief judge might be able to change the panels. Right before the panel lists are published, the clerk of court, Mr. Nichols, has to bring them to the chief judge for his approval to finalize the assignments. This is normal and necessary because the chief judge is in charge of seeing that the assignments are properly made, insuring that all judges are receiving equal caseloads and that assignments are adjusted for vacation or health reasons. If Winston wanted to change assignments even at the last minute, the clerk would do it.

"Why?" Vicky asked.

"Simple. Nichols is deathly afraid of the chief judge. From what Loretta, my secretary, has told me, he'll do anything the chief asks, because he's terrified of losing his job, not to mention his annual twenty thousand dollar bonus. So with Nichols, Winston has a big carrot and a big stick."

"Sounds like the guy is in the chief's pocket," Sharkey commented.

"Yes, and I've been told that when Winston became the chief judge four years ago, he fired the clerk on his first day and brought in Nichols," Tim said. "I've heard he's gotten the maximum twenty thousand dollar bonus every year." He looked at them grimly. "Proving this whole scenario, however, would be tough. Where do we go from here?"

Vicky cleared her throat. First she looked at Sharkey. Then she stared directly at Tim. "We have a plan. But it's a little bit of a long shot. And it has some risk to it."

"What do you two have in mind?" Tim asked cautiously.

"Well, basically the usual way to crack a conspiracy like this is to get someone inside the conspiracy." Vicky paused to let that sink in. Tim felt suddenly very uncomfortable.

"Judge, you are an old friend of the chief judge," she continued, "and in fact, you told us that the first day you sat as a judge you sat on one of these Draco cases. The chief judge asked you in advance for your views on that Draco case, correct?"

"That's right," Tim said. He didn't like where this was going.

Vicky looked directly into Tim's eyes. "The next time he asks you in advance for your view on a Draco case, you could say that you think Draco should win. Maybe then he'll keep you on the panel hearing the Draco case and you can go along with Draco winning until the opinion is just about to be published. Then you can change your vote and see what happens. If the chief judge really needs your vote for a majority decision for Draco, he might try to pressure you to make sure Draco wins. Maybe at that stage we can get something incriminating on the chief judge."

Tim hated hearing this, but he steeled himself to let Vicky finish.

"Maybe he'll do something stupid, like offer you a bribe to switch your vote. If he does, and we can prove it, then we've got the chief judge on an obstruction of justice charge. And if we nail the chief judge, he might turn on Draco and then we can get Draco on the case-fixing, perhaps even on the murder of Camellia Winston, if Draco or Winston was involved." Vicky seemed to shudder a little at mentioning Camellia.

"Bottom line: You might be able to make the case for us from the inside." Then she raised her voice a little, as if to increase the urgency of what she said, and to clear it of her personal feelings about Tim. "What do you say, Judge, will you help?"

Tim's thoughts went back to Katy's warning that he would ruin his judicial future by getting involved with an internal investigation of his fellow judges. God, he should walk away from this whole mess. Let the goddamn FBI try some other way to crack this. He did enough bringing the case to them.

"No way. I'm not going to be an undercover informant! I'm a judge. I can't do it."

No one spoke for a very long moment. Then Vicky's gaze hardened. When she spoke, her voice was challenging. "Afraid to get on the front lines to do justice, Your Honor?"

That stung. A definite military jab. Vicky knew he had been in combat in Vietnam. Tim felt his face go red and his mouth tighten. Sharkey looked shocked that Vicky would talk to a federal judge in that tone. Tim saw him look sidelong at Vicky again; the agent had to know there was some history between the two of them.

Tim's thoughts churned. Vicky's comment had pierced him, dared him to act upon the values he had built his life around, as a ranger in Vietnam, an intelligence officer, a lawyer, and now as a judge. He had prided himself on being a stand-up guy in any situation, no matter how tough. Finally he spoke, in a low and even voice.

"I won't be an undercover FBI asset, *but* I'll let you know if Winston approaches me again on a Draco case. If that happens, we can play it from there."

Vicky and Bill looked at each other and Tim saw a tiny grin flash across her face.

"I'm impressed, Judge," Sharkey said. "Most judges I've known have been too cautious about their careers to stick their necks out. We appreciate it."

Tim was still thinking very hard. Although he said he wouldn't be an informant, he did want to know what was going on in his court. Maybe he could still plan some possible moves to get inside the conspiracy, if there was one. He took a quiet but deep breath.

"As a matter of fact, unless the aftermath of Camellia's death interferes, Winston and I will be spending a few days together at the end of next week at a criminal law conference in Quebec. I'll make sure he knows that I'm a team player and intend to rely on him for guidance on cases."

Tim saw Sharkey try to swallow his smile of approval. He got up to leave.

Vicky got up and moved toward him. "Your Honor, thank you. Let us know if anything comes up, but please be careful." She could not hide the fervor in her voice. "We'd hate to lose another federal judge." Tim went out the door of her office without looking back.

When Quinn got back to his chambers, he called Vicky.

"You know I questioned Sharkey as a witness in a rather unfriendly case against the FBI last year and got his friend fired from the FBI?"

"Yes, Sharkey told me that when he first got on the case. Sure, he's not a fan of yours; however, he's a professional and will do his job. Have any problems with that?" Vicky asked coldly.

Tim hesitated, then said, "Nope, if he's fair, that will do."

When Tim hung up, he thought: *Great investigation I started! Not exactly a dream team, both the prosecutor and the FBI agent hate me.* Thank God he didn't mention to Vicky that he knew about the special arrangement between the president and Winston. If he had, then he would be probably also a target of the investigation—as an accessory after the fact to an obstruction of justice conspiracy. Tim felt he had just started a dangerous game of Russian roulette. That night Tim began having nightmares of Vietnam. Something he hadn't had for years.

Camellia Winston's funeral was two days later in Macon. As Harry's colleague and onetime lawyer, and because her death had been so violent, abrupt, and suspicious, Tim felt impelled to go. He took an early morning flight from Reagan National to Atlanta and rented a car at the airport for the hour-long drive to Macon. Out of respect for Harry or because they knew Camellia during the twenty years she had lived with Harry in Georgetown, many of Winston's D.C. friends had made the trip, including Leo Draco, who stood next to Tim during the simple ceremony at the chapel in the Calvary Cemetery, an old graveyard on the outskirts of the city. Tim had tried hard not to look directly at Draco, worrying that his suspicions about the appellate lawyer would be revealed on his face.

The casket was open in the chapel, an old Georgia custom. At the end of the service before they closed the coffin, Harry Winston, with tears running down his face, gave Camellia a gentle kiss and put a yellow rose in her hands. Almost everyone in the packed chapel was touched. After the chapel service, there was a three-hundred-yard walk behind the hearse to the Winston mausoleum for the internment. A bagpiper led the procession.

Afterward, there was a well-attended reception in the Winston home in Macon. Harry Winston was red-eyed when Tim spoke words of condolence to him. Harry hugged Tim. "Thanks for coming," he said in a low, ragged voice. "You knew better than most people—that Camellia was a true Southern lady. I loved her. Eventually we realized that we just couldn't live together. The old story of the man in love with a mermaid. But to have her gone . . ." His voice went thick with grief.

Tim prided himself with judging the character and nature of

people he knew. Stepping back from Harry and watching him greet the mourners in the very parlor where Camellia had conducted her conversation with Vicky days before she died, Tim was certain that there was no way Harry Winston had had anything to do with the murder of his wife.

CHAPTER 14

TIM GOT OUT OF THE CAB IN FRONT OF THE GENERAL AVIAtion Terminal, an unimposing two-story concrete building at Reagan National used by the private and corporate jets. Walking through the double glass doors, he found himself suddenly immersed in luxury: thick carpets, warm recessed lighting, soft classical music. At the end of a self-service buffet table covered with platters of fruit and tea sandwiches, a bartender stood at a heavy dark wooden bar that could have been taken out of a top-grade English pub. To his right, leather chairs and couches were arranged around low glass coffee tables. This far surpassed any first-class airport lounge Tim had ever seen.

He sat down in a wing chair against the wall that gave him a clear view of the entrance—an old ranger habit. When the automatic doors hissed open, he looked up from his newspaper and saw Draco, then Winston walk through the door, followed by baggage carriers. *Jesus,* he thought, *if these guys really are involved in some kind of criminal conspiracy, traveling to the airport together—or anywhere, for that matter—would be about the most stupid thing they could do.*

"Tim!" Winston strode over as Tim folded the paper and rose to greet him. "Say hi to our tour director, Leo Draco. His car arrived just as I was coming in the door, so I waited for him."

Tim smiled to himself, relieved that Winston had a simple explanation for his arrival with Draco. He shook hands with Draco. "How are you, Leo? The chief judge and I certainly appreciate your arranging our transportation."

"Happy to help the cause of justice," Draco said.

"Well, the private jet does make the trip more pleasant," Tim said as the porters whisked away their baggage. "When do we leave?"

Leo and Harry shared a small laugh. "Judge, with a private jet, we leave whenever we want," Draco said. "That's one of the perks of traveling this way."

Soon the entire delegation of lawyers and judges had gathered, with Judge Tony Bandino of the U.S. District Court the last to arrive. When Winston asked him how he was doing, Bandino smiled a little grimly, Tim thought. "I was doing just great, Chief," he said, "until your court gave me another reversal the other day on a criminal case."

Winston laughed. "Now, don't take that personally, Tony. Our court calls them as we see them."

"I know, Chief, I'm just kidding," Bandino said. Tim wondered. "Well, I'm certainly looking forward to flying up to Canada in a corporate jet," Bandino continued.

Winston waved his arm toward Draco. "Leo here gets the credit for the jet. He's on the board of directors of the Free Enterprise Foundation—you know, one of the groups sponsoring this fine conference in Quebec City. Leo got them to provide one of their corporate jets free of charge, so we'll save the taxpayer and the bar association some change."

Draco made a small bow to the entire delegation. The foundation, he explained, sponsored several judicial conferences a year as part of its public service program. Tim wondered about how this worked, and whether Draco was telling the whole story. Access to a private jet was quite a perk.

The delegation went out the sole departure gate onto the tarmac, walking toward a line of five private jets. As they neared the planes, Tim saw they were headed for the largest aircraft, a white Gulfstream IV. A man in uniform hurried down the stairs to meet them. He held out his hand to Leo. "Mr. Draco, good to see you again, sir! The plane is ready, the baggage is stowed, and we'll be cleared to take off as soon as you're all seated."

Draco leaned forward and spoke in a low voice. "Did you put name cards on all the seats?" Tim heard him say.

"Yes sir, exactly as you directed."

"Good."

Leo turned to the group that had stopped behind him.

"Okay, gentlemen, let's board. You'll find name cards on the seats so you know where you're sitting. The plane we are flying today is configured for ten passengers. The other foundation jet, the same size as this one, is set up to seat eighteen passengers, so you can see that we got the more luxurious of the two." He smiled, clearly if casually proud of himself.

The chief clapped his hands and gave a thumbs up. "Bravo, Leo. We're in deep cotton. The U.S. delegation is going first-class!"

Tim mounted the stairs and stepped into the passenger cabin. Sunlight streamed through the large oval cabin windows, reflecting off pale walnut panels and softening the heavy leather curves of the interior. He found his name card on one of a trio of large leather captain's chairs around a large green marble table. Settling into his chair, he discovered that it swiveled. He spun it slowly, turning directly into Leo's smiling face.

"Pretty nice, eh?" asked Draco.

"You bet. Say, Leo, do you know how much one of these planes costs?"

Leo's smile broadened. "Well, I happen to know the answer to that. I did the foundation's contract to buy the plane. Normally you just buy a share in a plane like this, like a time-share condominium at the beach. You pay seven and a half million dollars up front to the corporation that actually owns, operates, and maintains airplanes like this. Then they'll bill you about thirty-nine thousand dollars a month, and every time you use the plane, you pay them three thousand dollars an hour. Then you can call up and get a plane to take you anywhere in the country with two hours' notice, and anywhere in the world with twelve hours' notice."

Tim's eyebrows arched. *Jesus,* he thought, *seven million up front and you still have to pay through the nose.* "Leo, who can afford prices like that?"

"Rock stars, foundations, corporations, and your usual upscale drug dealers," Draco said lightly. Winston, seated in the next captain's chair, chuckled. "Seriously, you'd be surprised how many individuals fly this way. And why not? A lot of very wealthy people and corporations in this country can write off travel as a tax deduction. Besides, there are no hassles, no nine-eleven security checkpoints. This is really just the ultimate first-class."

"Sir, do you want champagne like the other gentlemen?" asked a sultry voice.

Tim looked into the smiling face of the flight attendant, a truly stunning woman. "Uh . . . yes, I'd like that a lot."

"We have Krug, Cristal, and Dom Perignon. Which do you prefer?"

"Well, I . . . I guess Dom Perignon."

"Excellent, sir. I'll be right back."

Tim swiveled back to face Winston and Draco. Harry leaned forward.

"Pretty damned good service, right?"

"You bet, Chief. I could get used to this real easy."

Draco elegantly toasted to the success of the trip and to good camaraderie. Then the flight attendant politely took charge, reminding them to buckle in. The plane soon rocketed down the runway, roared into the sky, and headed north. During the trip, Tim chatted and laughed easily with the two men, even as he studied the easy warmth between Draco and Winston. *God,* he thought, *could they really be involved in fixing cases, and* murder?

Two vans met the Gulfstream IV jet at a general aviation section of the airport outside Quebec City, and whisked the U.S. delegation of judges and attorneys off to their hotel, the Chateau Frontenac. Perched on the crest of a hill in the heart of the old city, the Chateau Frontenac was a massive stone building that towered over the Saint Lawrence River two hundred feet below. It had originally served as a fortress for the early French settlers.

All the U.S. delegates except Draco had rooms on the third floor. Draco had a penthouse suite on the twelfth floor. The chief judge's room was right next to Tim's. Next to Tim's bed there was a small sitting area in a protruding turret of the castle-like hotel. It was well positioned for Tim's purposes; from the turret sitting area, he had a great view of the hotel entrance portico and the cobblestone plaza beyond. And since it was a corner room, the peephole in his door gave Tim an unobstructed view down the long carpeted hallway, all the way to the bank of elevators.

Tim attended a brief pre-conference meeting for the U.S. delegation in Draco's luxurious penthouse suite, then spent the afternoon reading over the conference materials and took a short nap before the welcoming dinner. He met Harry for a drink beforehand. The chief judge was at his most relaxed and talkative, and Tim felt more comfortable in his company than he ever had. As they laughed and chatted together, Tim began to have second thoughts about his suspicions. Harry just didn't seem like the type who would fix cases. But what about Maxwell Rogers's papers? They clearly pointed to some sort of involvement by Harry. Vicky and Bill Sharkey, the FBI agent, seem convinced that Harry was implicated in any case-fixing on the court. And Camellia Winston had been violently, murderously killed.

But in looking at the man across from him, Tim felt torn down the center. Here was a Rhodes Scholar, a Yale Law graduate, a federal Judge who had become the chief judge of the second highest court in the land, and a man already quite wealthy in his own right through inheritance—it just didn't make sense. Tim knew that Harry was so rich that it was unimaginable that he would fix cases for money. Could this be something else? What was it? Could Harry himself be coerced, a victim of blackmail that was forcing him to cooperate with Draco? Could it be some sort of drug thing? Was it a sexual scandal?

And he genuinely liked the man. Harry was clever and fun to be with. Tim was grateful to him; Winston had gone out of his way to help him get on the court. Tim owed him for that. He knew he had to adhere to his sense of duty; he could not let his friendship interfere with his judgment. Still, in his heart, Tim felt he was betraying Harry.

Tim knew that he already had crossed the Rubicon in taking those Rogers papers and his suspicions to Vicky. He had to continue to play this out, to see if Harry was as involved as Vicky and Sharkey suspected—and as Tim himself felt he had to believe.

He took a sip of bourbon and refocused on the charming man across the table from him.

As Tim and Harry were chatting about the conference, Dr. Helmut Kroneburg, the chief justice of the top court in Germany, the Constitutional Court, greeted Harry warmly and joined them, full of praise for Harry's lecture on legal ethics at last year's conference. Tim was taken aback. Here was the head of the entire German judiciary, apparently a long-standing friend of Harry's, publicly praising Winston's views on the very subject of the FBI investigation that featured him as its central suspect.

At the welcoming dinner, held in a private room in the hotel conference center, Tim noticed the plainclothes security personnel everywhere. There were two Royal Canadian Mounted Police officers at the entrance and another pair patrolled the surrounding corridors. A further security precaution was the lack of signs announcing the conference or its dinner. This many high-level judges congregated in one place made the event a prime terrorist target. Canada, as the host, wanted no incident to mar the conference. The subtle tension in the air made Tim feel even more uneasy.

At dinner, he sat next to Winston, full of second and third thoughts about Winston's culpability. The chief judge seemed to have close relationships with a number of judges from other nations, particularly the Canadian chief justice, who had spent a full ten minutes talking and laughing with Winston before they sat down to dinner. Two British trial judges from the Old Bailey, the central criminal court in London, came over to the table and embraced Winston. Why would Harry risk all this for a case-fixing scheme?

After the main course was served and eaten, Tim noticed Draco get up, nod to Winston, and leave the banquet room. Winston waited a few beats, and rose, telling Tim he was going to the rest room, then left by a different door. The thought raced through Tim's mind—should he follow? Tim had promised Vicky that he would keep his eyes open, so he got up, slipped into the hallway. He saw nobody there but the pair of roving RCMP officers. Tim asked the Mounties if they had seen anyone leave the dining room. The taller of the two said that two men just went into the rest room and pointed down the corridor. Tim headed for the men's room. At the door, he hesitated, inhaled a short breath, and pushed open the door.

Winston and Draco stood at opposite ends of the bathroom, talking. Their voices ceased as soon as Tim entered and they waited in awkward silence as Tim headed to a urinal. Tim's eyes met Draco's. Expressionless except for a slight grin, he nodded to Tim, then turned and left the men's room without a word. Winston, however, seemed rooted next to the towel dispenser, looking uncomfortable and shaken. Tim broke the silence.

"Harry, I see we both agree—it's best to hit the men's room before the speeches start."

Winston recovered nicely with the lead Tim had given him. "Damn right. An appellate judge should never miss an opportunity to relieve himself. No telling how long our Canadian host will go on. See you back in there, Tim."

Winston winked at Tim and left. Tim suspected this had not been a chance encounter for Winston and Draco. And why had the usually unflappable Harry lost his composure at the interruption?

After a mercifully short speech by the chief justice of the Canadian Supreme Court, Harry Winston went off to the hotel bar with the two judges from the Old Bailey. Tim begged off, saying that he needed to call Katy before it got too late. He walked down the long, dark-paneled hallway from the convention portion of the hotel toward the main lobby to the elevators. Just as the doors were starting to close, an attractive, very blond, thirtyish woman got in. She reached past Tim to punch in her floor and suddenly stopped when she saw the lighted button. "Oh, I see you've already pushed the third floor!" she said.

Tim smiled pleasantly. At the third floor, Tim let her exit first. He noticed that she was using Chanel No. 5, Katy's usual perfume. She was wearing an expensive, dark blue business suit that was short enough to show off her well-shaped legs.

Tim, with his long strides, quickly caught up with her and passed her at her door, as he proceeded to the end of the long corridor. He was almost at his door when he heard her call him. "Excuse me. Excuse me."

Tim turned to see her at her open door halfway down the corridor, motioning for him. Tim hesitated, then walked back to her. "I hate to bother you," she said as he got closer, "but could you do me a *big* favor and open the sliding glass door to my balcony? It seems to be stuck."

Tim said he would try and entered the room—a luxury suite, complete with a stone balcony overlooking the St. Lawrence River. The attractive woman gave Tim a warm smile. "I just love the view from the balcony," she told him. She explained that she owned a travel agency in Vancouver and that the hotel treated her to the best rooms because her agency sent the hotel a lot of business.

Tim gave the sliding glass door to the balcony a good pull, but it wouldn't open. Then he added more muscle and his weight. No luck. Then Tim examined the track the door slid on and saw that a wad of paper was jammed there. With his Swiss Army knife, Tim dug out the paper and opened the door, letting the cool evening air blow in from the stone balcony.

When Tim turned around he saw that the woman had removed her jacket, revealing a cream, short-sleeve sweater underneath and a gorgeous figure. "Thank you so much!" she said. "I'm Briget Dulay. Here's my card. Maybe you'll use my travel agency sometime. *Now*, I positively insist that you have a drink with me so I can properly thank you. What will you have?" She moved to the minibar and opened it, looking at him smiling.

Tim read the card and tucked it in his pocket. Was this really a good idea? But she seemed so grateful, and she was so attractive. "Really, fixing the door was no bother," he said. "By the way, I'm Tim Quinn, and I'm up here on business for a few days from the States." Tim offered his hand and she shook it. "Do you have cognac?" he asked.

"Sure do. Why don't you go out on the balcony and I'll fix us both a drink. There's a great view of the city and the river."

Tim hesitated, but then nodded and walked onto the stone terrace and took in the view of the glittering well-lit Quebec City shoreline and the river. Soon Briget slipped to his side. She put her drink on the stone railing and warmed Tim's balloon glass of cognac with both her hands. He took a sip as she pointed out the cross-river car ferry that was pulling away from the slip from the old section of the city below. The drink had a bitter taste to it, but was smooth because Briget had warmed it. "Quebec sure is a beautiful city," he remarked, trying to look at the view and not the woman.

"And a romantic one as well." She offered her glass for a toast.

Their glasses clinked and Tim took a deep pull of his drink. Then they both faced the river to quietly observe the river traffic. Briget slowly moved in to Tim's side, touching his arm. "Tim, I'm a little chilled. Could you hold me and keep me warm?"

Tim felt himself putting his arm around her. She cuddled up to him. She was warm and soft and smelled so familiar. Time seemed to slow down and Tim felt a little dizzy. He looked up and saw the beautiful half moon in the sky; the glare from the city couldn't mask the hundreds of stars. Tim was feeling strange. A very friendly, classy young woman was in his arms. A gorgeous woman he had met by chance. A fantasy for most men on a business trip to a foreign country.

Briget put down her glass and then Tim's. She looked up into

Tim's eyes and arched her neck back with her lips slightly parted, moving her head closer to his. She kissed him, at first softly, but then her tiny, firm tongue pushed expertly into his mouth. Soon they were pressing against each other. She moved one of her legs between his legs and he felt himself grow hard. The kiss ended when she suddenly pulled away, smiling, pulled her sweater over her head, and let it drop. She wore no bra and her nipples were dark and hard.

"Tim, let's go inside."

Tim was a little out of breath and his vision was blurry, but he could see that Briget was stunning. His thoughts were jumbled and random. *This thing just happened. I never tried to pick her up. I'm married. She is absolutely gorgeous.* But Tim started to pull back.

Briget, sensing his reluctance, smiled again, more playfully. "Judge, you don't have to worry about me. I'm a big girl. I find you attractive and just want to spend time with you. No commitments."

Judge! Tim's eyes widened. Alarm bells started ringing through the haze. "How . . . how did you know I was a judge?"

Briget faltered, and then her face flashed with irritation. "Well, the hotel said there was a judges' conference in the house. And I just assumed. Well, you look like a judge."

Tim, now on full alert, didn't buy this "look like a judge" thing. He had already started moving toward the door.

"Listen, Briget, I have to go," he said. "I have to leave. I'm sorry."

Briget made no sound and, her arms crossed over her breasts, did not follow him to the door.

Tim walked unsteadily down the corridor to his room, shaking his head to remain alert. He felt drunk. It wasn't a warm, happy drunk feeling. He went cold and clammy and almost fell against the hallway wall. God damn, she gave me a drug in the drink. He started to hurry.

He burst into his room and threw off his suit jacket and shirt. In the bathroom, he splashed some water on his face. Then he knelt in front of the toilet and put his index finger down his throat. At first all he could summon up were dry heaves, but then the dark brown bile came roaring up. Tim vomited until he was drained of energy. Then he stood and splashed more cold water on his face.

He was standing wobbly at the sink when he heard a door slam down the hall. He walked to his door, looked out the peephole, and saw Briget dragging a wheeled suitcase down the hall, headed hurriedly for the elevators. Tim felt lousy but he grabbed his shirt, put it on, snatched up his jacket and tie, and opened his door. Who was this Briget and why had she done this to him? He needed answers. The elevator's doors were closing as he came into the hall. With great effort, he broke into a run toward the elevators. When he got there, he saw that the elevator was going up, not down. She obviously had gotten on an up elevator by mistake in her hurry to leave. He watched as it stopped, only once, on the twelfth floor and then started down. Tim punched the down button. The elevator would now have to stop at his floor. He would pull her off and find out what was going on. He waited, panting, until the elevator dinged and the door slowly opened. Tim poised himself to grab her. But the elevator was empty.

Stunned, his vision still somewhat blurry and his head beginning to pound, he turned and headed back to his room. The run to the elevator had weakened him and he needed to think. At his room, he gulped four Anacin tablets and started sipping a Coke from the small refrigerator. He wasn't sure, but he thought some caffeine and sugar might help counter whatever drug she had slipped him. He sat on the bed and called Briget's room number. The phone rang until a computer voice said the room was not occupied. Tim hung up and started to think of what to do. Then he remembered that Leo Draco had a room on the twelfth floor.

After a half hour had passed, Tim felt strong enough to walk normally. He headed first to the twelfth floor. He had been in Draco's room that afternoon for the pre-conference meeting. The other three rooms on the floor were silent, and, when Tim put his ear to each door, he heard no noise from inside. When he edged toward Draco's room, he heard the sound of voices, all too muffled to make out. Tim didn't know what to do. Should he knock on the door to see if Briget was there? What if she wasn't? What would Draco think or say to others the next day? But what if she was inside—what would he do then? He decided to go to the front desk and check to see if Briget really was gone.

Downstairs, Tim asked for the night manager. He knew he had to play this very carefully. He identified himself to the manager only as a guest, flashing his electronic door card, and said he had left a business folder in the room of a colleague. Tim explained that he was having trouble with the room phone because there was no answer, and he needed the folder for an important morning meeting. Tim gave him Briget's room number. The manager was very helpful and checked his computer. "I'm sorry, sir, but that resident, Ms. Coffman from Washington, D.C., has just checked out."

"She has? Did you see her?"

"No, sir. She used the express checkout service from her room."

Tim was taken aback by the different name and the Washington reference, but recovered to ask if he could check the now-unoccupied room for his folder. With some hesitancy, the manager had a bellman take Tim up to the room. On the elevator to the third floor, Tim slipped the bellman a twenty dollar bill, which guaranteed him courteous treatment and no questions. Once inside, Tim had the run of the place while the bellman waited by the door. The suite looked as if it had never been occupied—except for the evidence of the two glasses he and Briget had used, and some disarray in the bathroom. In the bedroom, there was one odd thing that caught Tim's eye: The TV had been moved slightly to the side so someone could gain access to the TV's back cover. Tim looked. The cover's screws were loose, as if it had recently been removed.

He stared at the oddity and suddenly it came to him. From his years in intelligence work, he knew that a bedroom TV was the perfect place to hide a video recorder. TVs are normally positioned so you can watch television from the bed. And of course, it could work the other way around—a device in the TV could record whatever happened in the bed. God damn, Tim thought—this whole thing was a setup to get something on him.

Tim thanked the bellman for his trouble and returned to his room, where he called the number listed on the business card for Briget's travel agency in Vancouver. A computer voice said the phone was not in service. He sat on the bed, trying to make sense of what had happened. Definitely a setup, but he had dodged the bullet. Barely. Then he looked at his watch—11:30 P.M. He hoped Katy was still up. He had promised to call her. He punched in his calling card number. On the second ring, Katy's voice came on the line.

"Katy, just got back to my room," he said, his voice hurried but thick. "Long dinner, lots of speeches. Sorry I didn't call sooner, but I got tied up. How are you?"

"Just fine. You sound strange. Is everything all right?"

"Yes, I'm fine. It's just been a long day and I'm bushed."

Katy went on talking for a while about her day; for Tim, her warm, slightly accented voice was a balm. After he told her he loved her and hung up, he showered and tried to fall asleep. It took a long time.

All through the next day's meetings Tim felt the effects of the drug, his head splitting and his body queasy, but he forced himself to converse with some respected judges he had not met before, and he eyed Harry Winston, utterly at home among the world's judiciary.

That night, Tim joined Harry and two Hong Kong High Court justices for dinner at a nearby French restaurant.

The Hong Kong judges were fascinating. Although both were educated at top schools in England—one at the London School of Economics and one at Brasenose College, Oxford—they represented the two faces of present-day Hong Kong. One was Chinese, newly appointed to the bench by Beijing after China took over the city and its surrounding territory in 1997; the other, English, had been appointed years ago by the queen. With expert questions, Harry Winston explored the history of the Hong Kong legal system and got the judges to let their guards down about its future.

Okay, he thought, maybe Winston was too talented and important to be party to a case-fixing scheme—and too moral to murder his own wife. But not so for Leo Draco. Maybe with the help of women like Briget, he was the mastermind of a blackmail scheme targeting judges to win cases. Tim himself had most likely come close to being the star in a porn film last night.

The dinner ended a little before eleven o'clock. Winston, over protests, picked up the check, and the four judges walked back to the hotel amid rumblings of thunder. Tim smelled the rain in the air and saw lightning in the clouds across the river. Tim and Harry rode up on the elevator together and walked to their adjacent rooms, saying their good nights at the doorway.

Tim started to read a novel he had brought along. At around 11:30, he heard Winston's door slam. Curious, he went to the peephole and saw the chief judge strolling toward the elevators, wearing a khaki trench coat and carrying a black-and-gold umbrella that obviously belonged to the hotel, as a standard amenity. It was pouring outside. Where was Winston going?

Tim went to his small turret sitting room, turning off the lights to get a better view of the hotel's entrance. After several minutes he saw Winston emerge from under the overhanging hotel-entrance portico, the rain hammering at his umbrella. At this time of night, all the stores near the hotel were closed, and the widely spaced streetlights left pockets of darkness between them. Tim watched as Winston crossed the small plaza in front of the hotel and took a left, then began walking downhill along a narrow, winding street toward the riverfront below.

As Winston disappeared from sight, Tim saw movement at the hotel entrance. Leo Draco, with his distinctive white hair, was stepping into the rain under an umbrella, hurrying down the same residential street Winston had taken.

Tim had to follow them. Ignoring the umbrella in his closet, Tim pulled on a dark blue running jacket as he raced out of his room to the emergency stairs, which led directly out a fire door into the plaza. He jogged across the plaza and down the street after Winston and Draco. Finally he saw them farther down the block, walking under a single umbrella.

Although the distance and the noise of the rain kept the conversation from Tim's ears, he could tell the two men were arguing heatedly. Tim used the doorways and front yards of some of the homes as cover, tailing the two men from a hundred feet, moving quickly under the streetlamps and pausing in the darkness between them. The rain covered the sound of his movement and made him less visible.

Tim was behind a large tree near a sidewalk bus shelter, with Winston and Draco about seventy-five feet ahead of him, when suddenly both men stopped dead. Then they turned and started to walk back uphill toward him. Tim started to panic. They were coming back up the street toward the tree he was hiding behind. A bright halogen streetlight illuminated the street-corner bus shelter just behind him. If he moved from the tree, they would surely see him. Three feet to his right were the dense hedges of a residential front yard, a wrought-iron fence lining the sidewalk. If he could just get into that yard, he might be able to hide. But when he peeked from his vantage point, he could see that Winston and Draco were looking directly up the sidewalk as they walked uphill toward him. Tim was frozen in place. His mind was racing.

Just then, a car sped around the corner behind Draco and Winston, its tires squealing, and the pair jumped, turning to look toward the car. Tim dived into the yard through the gate. He rolled to his left under the hedge and crawled next to the wrought-iron fence, pulling leaves over his body for concealment. He grabbed a clump of mud and smeared it on his face and hands. Skills from his ambush patrols in Vietnam kicked into operation.

Leo, with Harry at his side under the umbrella, was approaching Tim's location. The rain had started to increase. Tim saw them huddle into the bus shelter. "Let's stop a while here until the rain lets up a bit," he heard Harry say. Winston sat down heavily on a plastic bench, put his elbows on his knees, leaned forward, and began to run his fingers through his short gray hair. Leo collapsed the umbrella and shook it. Gusts of rain swept over the shelter, pounding the plastic roof. Leo was sitting at the end of the bench and started to talk. Lying down in his hiding place under the hedges a little more than six feet away from them, Tim could make out most of what they were saying despite the sound of the rain and wind.

"Harry, forget Camellia for now. We can get into that later. Right now, we have some major problems on the front burner."

"I can't forget."

"Well, if you're upset about people dying, then worry about yourself. General Morenta has threatened to have us both killed."

"What?" Tim could hear the shock in Winston's voice. Tim's mind was processing the information. What where they talking about? Who was this General what's-his-name? Then he heard Draco clearly speak.

"I saw him last week, at the prison. He's being held in maximum security, but that didn't stop him from threatening me."

Harry turned and faced Draco. "Leo, what the hell are you talking about?"

"Okay. As you remember, the retainer fee was five million with a bonus of five million if we get him out of jail and on a plane back to Colombia. We've already got the five million retainer in the offshore account."

"But why did he threaten you?"

"He said he knows why I win so much at your court—that we've got one or more of the judges in our pockets . . ."

Just then a car drove down the street and Tim was unable to hear the rest of what Draco said. After the auto passed, Winston was speaking.

"Hell no. I've assigned myself to that panel, but I'm having some problems putting together a sure second vote. All I really need is one other judge who'll agree to hold with me that the immunity grant controls this case. But I've got some problems. First off, we can't use Janoff—he disqualified himself immediately when the appeal was filed in our court, something about him being a consultant to the State Department when they were formulating the policies that eventually led to 'Plan Colombia.' I can't use Bowen because she's in the middle of chemotherapy. She won't be sitting on the bench again for at least two months. Maybe I can use Franklin . . . Street drugs . . ." The rain and wind picked up and made it hard for Tim to hear.

Then Tim heard snatches of the conversation: ". . . maybe I'll ask Quinn . . . golfing at . . . this Saturday."

When he heard his name, Tim felt a chill that had nothing to do with the rain and wind. He strained to hear. Then another car drove by. Moments later, Tim peered up to see Draco shaking his head. "This can't wait two months. Morenta wants out of jail, like *yesterday!* What are you going to do?"

The wind kicked up violently and the rain drummed on the roof of the bus shelter. It was several minutes before the rain began to abate and Tim could hear anything but fragments of Winston's voice. Finally, he heard the words, "Fucking right. We're in a hell of a mess."

Draco stood up. "Looks like we can start back to the hotel."

A serious-faced Winston got up from the bench and joined Draco as they walked up the street toward the Chateau Frontenac.

Tim remained in his hiding position for a good five minutes and then crawled out from the hedges and the pile of leaves. He stood up and stretched to get his circulation going. He was cold, wet, and muddy, but now he knew the truth. His friend Harry was a crook.

CHAPTER 15

THE PHONE RANG AT 6:15 A.M. AT VICKY HAUSER'S APARTMENT in the Dupont Circle area of Washington. Vicky was already up and reading the *Washington Post* as she ate her breakfast, but still she was surprised at such an early call. It was Tim, calling from a pay phone at his hotel in Canada with the news that he had spent the last part of his evening tailing Winston and Draco in the rain. He told her the specifics of their meeting and what snatches of conversation he had heard.

Vicky was stunned and pleased with the results. But still she was angry that Quinn would take such a risk. "God damn it, Tim. You're not twenty-five years old and in the rangers anymore. What were you thinking? These are dangerous men. What if they saw you?"

"Listen, I followed my instincts, and now we *know* that Winston and Draco are about to fix the General Morenta case, which is coming up for oral argument soon in our court. And Morenta's threat makes it a must-win for Draco."

Vicky, of course, knew about the high-profile Morenta case. General Jose Morenta was the former head of Colombia's military and was reputed to be a major drug dealer. He had traveled to the United States under a diplomatic passport in order to get his cancer treated at Johns Hopkins Medical Center in Baltimore. However, Morenta was arrested by some DEA agents on orders from the ambitious U.S. attorney in Washington, D.C., and charged with conspiracy related to drug smuggling. The arrest, with the resulting protest by the Colombian government on diplomatic grounds, had led the nightly news and been featured on newspapers' front pages. The actual trial in U.S. District Court in D.C. had been ferociously covered by all the major networks and was televised live by Court TV.

Vicky was aware that the appeal had some merit. The Colombian minister of justice had given General Morenta complete immunity for his help in "Plan Colombia," the big anti-drug effort the country had made two years earlier. The Colombian Supreme Court ratified the immunity agreement, and the present Colombian government formally transmitted it to the District Court during Morenta's trial. However, the trial judge kept out the immunity papers, very likely making a reversible error for the appeal. The issue had been recognized even by the U.S. State Department, which took the extraordinary step of filing an *amicus* brief urging the court to dismiss the case based on diplomatic immunity. Vicky knew that this case was a possible winner for Draco even if Winston didn't stack the panel of judges that would be picked to hear the case.

Tim sounded hurried; he told her there was a conference breakfast starting soon. He did briefly tell Vicky about the attempt to drug him and to possibly set him up with a hooker. As he painfully relayed the information, Vicky had to steel herself; she knew the trouble that Tim had gotten into in a hotel room once before, with her. The resonance now was at once perverse and personal. She wondered what he wasn't telling her—had he been attracted to the woman, maybe even been on the verge of falling for her—and Vicky wondered if the discomfort in his voice was because he now felt unfaithful not just to his wife but also to her.

Vicky agreed with Tim that the effort to trap Tim made sense if sexual blackmail was being used by Draco to get the judges to cooperate in the case-fixing operation. Maybe this was the first move to get Tim inside the conspiracy? Still, this activity made Vicky very worried about his safety. "You're taking too many chances in this damn investigation," she told him. "When do you get back from Quebec? We have to meet. We need to set some limits on the investigation."

"I'm just taking opportunities as I see them. On meeting, that's a good idea. The conference is over after lunch today and we should be back to D.C. by four. We shouldn't meet at your office," Tim said. "I can't come back from a trip with Draco and head directly to the Justice Department. Why don't we meet at the elephant display in the center foyer of the Smithsonian Museum of Natural History? The museum is right across from the Justice Department and a ten-minute walk from the courthouse. Can you make it there at five o'clock?"

"Okay, the elephant at the Smithsonian at five."

After she hung up, Vicky tried to concentrate on the paper, but her mind kept going back to the startling news she had just heard from Tim. Winston and Draco were going to try to fix the *Morenta* case. It would be the biggest conspiracy against justice that had ever been launched from within the judiciary. That fact awed and worried her.

An hour later, as she unlocked her office door at Justice, her mind was still working on the Morenta matter. Preoccupied, she dumped her purse on her desk, turned on her computer, and headed next door to make coffee. Soon she came back to her office with her morning ration of caffeine, and put in her password and entered the Department of Justice computer e-mail system.

The first thing that popped up was a new message notification. It was from FBI Agent Sharkey and time-noted at 6:10 A.M. that morning. All it said was "CALL ME!"

Vicky immediately had two thoughts. First, everyone seems to be up early today, first Tim, and now Bill. Second, Sharkey was his usual laconic self. She called him right away.

"Well, counselor," he said, "I need to bring you up to speed on two major developments in that unofficial case we're *not* working on together." Vicky told him to come over right away; she had news too. When Sharkey arrived half an hour later, she briefed him on what Tim had discovered. He was properly impressed. Then he pulled out a pocket notepad.

"Well . . . I've done some *unofficial* . . ." Bill looked directly into her eyes. ". . . and believe me, I have been like a ghost. No one at the Bureau knows I'm working on this case, and I mean no one."

Vicky nodded in appreciation.

"Some interesting phone calls were made right after you visited Mrs. Winston. The detective in Macon has been very forthcoming. He told me that the phone records of the judge's ex-wife showed that a call was made from her phone to the chambers of Chief Judge Winston the afternoon of your visit to see her. Then, as we know, two days later, she's murdered."

"Definitely suspicious. But, by itself, it doesn't prove anything."

Bill agreed, and then he told Vicky that he also paid a visit to one of his friends that worked the night shift at the main telephone company for the District. She let him peek at the phone records from the chief judge's chambers. A call had been made to an unlisted phone number at Draco and Associates *ten minutes* after that call from Macon to Winston's chambers.

"Damn. My visit to Macon. That afternoon Mrs. Winston calls the chief judge, he then calls Draco, and, two days later, she's dead from a hit-and-run, a contract hit."

"That's it in a nutshell, counselor. But still we've got some big questions. Like, did Mrs. Winston tell the chief judge of your visit? And, more importantly, did the call from Winston's chambers trigger a series of events that led to Camellia's murder? But the calls are damn interesting, aren't they?"

"Yes, they are." Vicky thought in silence. "You said you had two developments."

Bill flipped a few pages in his notebook. "It may sound disconnected but it's about the Judge Rogers murder. Remember when we talked to Turner, the D.C. police detective in charge of the Rogers investigation? He told us the drug overdose death of Rogers's killer was suspicious, even though he signed off as primary investigator and closed the case."

"Right."

"Well, I just went over and visited with Turner again. We both looked at the Rogers file and something jumped out at us. Remember the dirtbag they found dead of an overdose in his apartment, who the police eventually said had killed Rogers?"

"Sure, Ben something, I think." Vicky shrugged.

"And guess who was Ben Warren's lawyer on the male prostitution and murder charges that were dismissed for lack of evidence a year before Ben had his fatal heroin overdose?"

Vicky saw a big grin on Sharkey's face. She shook her head. It couldn't be. "No!"

Bill smiled as he tennis-balled the reply back at her.

"Yes!"

"Not Draco?" she asked.

"None other. Mr. Leo Draco of Draco and Associates. Ben Warren was Draco's court-appointed client. Draco was appointed by the D.C. Superior Court."

"Damn! So there is a definite connection of Draco to Rogers's murder!"

"Absolutely, a definite connection. However, it's far from solid proof, counselor. It's interesting that Draco is connected to three supposedly unrelated deaths. Ben, one of Draco's clients, kills Judge Rogers, then Ben dies of a suspicious overdose. Then the curious fact that both Winston and Draco are possibly connected to Camellia's death via the timing of phone calls."

"Jesus! From case fixing to multiple murders by a chief judge and his Yale roommate. . . . I need to tell Judge Quinn. But Bill, still not a word to anyone, okay?"

"Okay, counselor, but we're approaching a limit. Pretty soon I'm going to have to tell my supervisor about this and enter it as an official investigation, or I could lose my job."

Walking from the bright street into the dark Smithsonian, Vicky was briefly blinded. Her eyes soon grew accustomed to the light, and then she saw Tim standing next to the huge stuffed African elephant dominating the central foyer. As she came closer, he saw her and nodded his head, signaling her to follow him down one of the hallways. She noted they were entering a series of alcoves, each displaying stuffed arctic animals arrayed behind Plexiglas in their native scenery. Tim stepped into one of the alcoves and turned toward Vicky. The exhibit was one of arctic wolves slaughtering a seal. Tim leaned around the corner of the alcove and checked the corridor. There was no one else in either direction. If someone entered the exhibit hallway, there was no clear line of sight to him or her, but they could easily hear anyone approaching.

"Okay, this looks good, Vicky. I told you the important things about Canada this morning. By the way, I'm sorry I woke you."

Vicky frowned. "I was up already."

Tim sensed she was on edge. "What's up? Has something happened?"

Vicky regretted snapping at Tim and softened her voice and attitude. "The stakes seem to be going up," she said. "Special Agent Sharkey just came to see me with some things in our 'off-the-record' investigation. First of all, on Camellia's death, we've got some more information."

Vicky went on to explain the curious coincidence of phone calls surrounding Camellia Winston's death. Tim shook his head. "No. I can't believe that Winston had any role in Camellia's death. In his own way, he loved her. But what's your take?"

"I don't know. Maybe Winston was an unwitting accomplice. He may have told Draco about the visit, not knowing that Draco would have her murdered as a weak link or as a damaging source of information," Vicky said. This was hard to talk about—she still felt guilty that her visit had resulted in the death of a sad, innocent woman.

She went on to explain the very curious connection Sharkey had found between Draco and Ben, the young man who killed Judge Rogers.

Tim was stunned. Vicky knew he had just seen the situation in an entirely different context. "Jesus Christ! Draco is connected to three deaths?"

"Yes. This is getting dangerous for you, Tim. And the next step may put you in deeper."

Tim pressed his lips together, nodded his head. "Okay. What's the next step?"

"Up to now you've been, more or less, watching from the sidelines and, I admit, you've come up with some good stuff. But now you might have to become live bait to trap Winston. Got the balls for it?" Vicky smiled as she laid forth the challenge.

Tim stroked his chin with the fingers of his right hand. Then he dropped his hand and smiled back, staring directly into Vicky's eyes.

"You would know. But I started this, and I intend to see it through to the end. I'm now a player, not a watcher. Let's roll."

Vicky shook her head, grinning.

"What about you, Vicky? Any regrets getting involved with this?" Tim added with feeling. She appreciated that he could tell this was a risky case for her. Winston and Draco were powerful men with friends in the White House and in the Justice Department. And he knew well how much Vicky was risking in keeping this investigation off the books for now.

"No," Vicky said somberly. "This is my job. I get the bad guys and put them away." They were talking about her vocation now. She knew she would be a prosecutor for the rest of her life.

"Okay," Tim said, with fresh resolution. "Let me give you an update on things from my end." Vicky took a small notepad from her purse and wrote as Tim talked, recounting in greater detail the specifics of his trip to Quebec, his ease and camaraderie with Winston, and then finally the strange rainy meeting between Draco and Winston. When he got to the fragments of conversations he had overheard at the bus shelter in Canada, both Tim and Vicky agreed it was significant that Arnie Janoff and Rosemary Bowen were not going to be used for the *Morenta* case. If Winston needed to pick a judge to make a majority for Draco, it would have to be Franklin or perhaps Tim. The golf reference with regard to Tim seemed an odd comment to Vicky.

"By the way," Tim added, "on the golf thing, on the flight home Winston *did* ask me to join him and Franklin to play golf tomorrow. A banker friend of his is coming to town from Georgia. They needed a fourth. I think Winston might use the occasion to approach me for my advance views on the *Morenta* case."

Tim went on, with obvious and physical discomfort, to relate in detail what had happened with Briget, the drugging seductress. Vicky wondered again how far Tim went with Briget. "That incident was obviously a blackmail attempt," she said when he finished. "Do you think that's how Draco gets Winston and the other judges to participate?"

"Maybe blackmail was used by Draco to hook Winston, but on the other three judges I don't think they are being blackmailed." Tim then explained that he had been observing and working with the three judges who seemed to be cooperating with the chief judge on the Draco cases. In his view, Franklin, Bowen, and Janoff were being used unwittingly by the master puppeteer—the chief judge. The reason that Winston could manipulate each judge so easily was clear to Tim—Franklin was a political hack who became a federal judge due of connections rather than competence. Tim could only guess at the massive inferiority complex he must have, not only because he went to a low-ranking law school, but also because Franklin probably realized that he just wasn't very smart. Tim had observed that most of the time he didn't even seem to grasp many of the issues argued before him. Tim speculated that Franklin usually depended on the chief judge as a rock to cling to in a river of tough legal cases. In conferences, he almost always followed the lead of the chief judge in deciding a case. On key cases, like those involving Draco's law firm, Tim was almost certain that Winston prepped Franklin before oral argument on which way to vote. Winston could rely on

Franklin in everything but drug cases. Most lawyers knew Franklin was death on drugs because his sister had been a junkie and died in a crack house in L.A. Franklin wasn't ashamed about it and often mentioned it in speeches on drug prevention. Otherwise, for Winston, having Franklin on a panel was like having a vote in his pocket.

"Amazing how one judge can control another judge like that," Vicky remarked. "What about Bowen?"

Judge Bowen, according to Tim, was considered by most lawyers and judges as a bright woman. But when you got her out of her narrow specialty of tax law—and there weren't many tax cases on Tim's court—then she seemed to lose her confidence, and tended to rely heavily on the chief judge for direction. Tim thought that for her, Winston functioned more as a mentor—Bowen was very impressed by the fact that he was a Rhodes Scholar and on the law review at Yale. She almost always deferred to his intellect and long experience on the bench, and this was especially true as she struggled with the treatment for her cancer. Winston could usually count on her vote if he put any pressure on her at all, even as little as announcing how he was going to vote on a case.

"Tim, you're confirming my worst cynicism, and that's scary," Vicky said. "Do courts really have judges who decide cases like that?"

"Vicky, the judicial branch is the most secretive arm of our government. People just don't have any idea what goes on unless they see it from the inside. It's been a major revelation to me in just the few months I've been on the bench. It's frightening how votes are given out and how cases are decided sometimes by relationships between two judges. Some judges vote just to go along and get along. Friendship on the bench sometimes means that one judge may give his vote to another judge just so he won't offend him." Tim stopped briefly, leaned out into the corridor, and looked in both directions to make sure they were alone. Then he continued, "Now, remember, Vicky, we're talking about a minority here. Most judges are pretty damned independent. But not ones like Bowen and Franklin."

"What about Judge Janoff?"

Tim admitted that, at first, Janoff had seemed somewhat of a puzzle to him. But after looking at his voting record and hearing him discuss a few cases, Tim found that he was the simplest of all to understand—Janoff just plainly *hated* the government. Tim classified him as a pure example of an agenda judge. Any chance he got, he would vote against the federal government, whether in a civil or a criminal case. His past as a public defender, coupled with his resentment of the federal government, especially its mismanagement of medical research, had resulted in making him a bitter enemy of the state. Tim had heard him declaim about how proper management of federal medical research might have saved his wife's life. If Winston was somehow able to control the panel membership for cases, and Draco was representing someone challenging the authority of the federal government, then all Winston needed to do was see that Janoff sat on that panel to win the case for Draco.

Vicky turned so that Quinn had to look directly into her eyes. "You have *got* to get assigned that Morenta case. If you do, you will be inside the conspiracy."

"Winston might select me for the Morenta panel. With the pressure on him to fix it right away, he'll either pick Franklin or me to sit with him. He can't use Janoff or Bowen and Franklin's a poor choice because *Morenta* is a drug case."

Tim paused and looked at Vicky. She saw him tighten his lips while nodding his head. As she studied him, Vicky got the impression that the judge was wrestling with a big decision here.

Finally he said, "Well, if he picks me, I'll be inside and then we'll nail him somehow. Maybe tomorrow when we play golf, he'll ask me to sit on the *Morenta* case."

Vicky smiled. "Well, you always said you wanted to be a player. Here's your chance."

CHAPTER 16

ALTHOUGH HIS CONFIDENT FACE GAVE NOTHING AWAY, CHIEF Judge Winston was in a serious and contemplative mood as he drove his black Cadillac Deville along River Road into the Maryland countryside that Saturday. This was going to be a very big day for Draco and himself. The threat from General Morenta had definitely raised the stakes. Today Winston had to find a safe vote for Morenta's case.

Beside Winston sat Carl Franklin, blathering on about his passion, his one and only hobby—golf.

They would be golfing with Tim Quinn and Earl Traymont, the president of Georgia Bank. A very close friend of Harry's since their fraternity days at Hobbes College, he was in town for a few days on business with the Federal Reserve. When Winston invited them, he told Tim and Franklin that he had put together this little outing as a treat for his visiting classmate, but the chief judge's agenda involved more than hitting a little white ball. Although Winston was a natural athlete, he merely used golf as a pleasant place to do business. To Winston and a kindred cynic, Will Rogers, golf was a good walk spoiled.

Soon the big black sedan turned into the private lane leading to the Congressional Country Club in one of the more affluent suburbs just outside of the District of Columbia. Winston had been a member of this old prestigious club ever since he came to Washington over two decades ago. Arching over the driveway were chestnut oaks planted before the Civil War, shading the car's climb up the gentle hill to the main clubhouse. Winston pulled up to the main portico, pushed the button that released his trunk lid, then stepped out onto the pavement. A teenager in a blue polo shirt and tan Bermuda shorts stepped up and took his proffered key, while another boy in a matching uniform unloaded the two golf bags from the trunk, securing them to the back of the first electric golf cart in a long line next to the club's entrance.

"Why, thank you, son." Winston turned to Judge Carl Franklin who had stepped out of the other side of the car. "Carl, I suppose we can hit some balls on the driving range for a while. We've got another hour before we're supposed to tee off. I told Tim and Earl Traymont that we would meet them on the driving range before tee time."

Carl wiped the sticky summer sweat from his neck. "Sounds good. Man, it's hot, isn't it?"

Winston smiled and shook his head. "Carl, this is nothing. Maryland here is supposed to be part of the South, but you haven't felt heat until you come to Georgia in August."

Warming up on the driving range, both Winston and Franklin were hitting their drives in fairly consistent straight lines and getting respectable distance. After Carl hit a long one, Winston said, "Good shot, my friend." He rested the heels of both palms on the top of his club. "Carl, it seems I'm having some trouble putting together a panel for this *Morenta* thing coming up. You know, the one that looks like the judge in the court below screwed up by not letting in the immunity documents from the Colombia government. How would you feel about sitting with me and Judge Forrester on that panel?"

Carl eyed his ball on the tee. "I'll sit if you want me to, Chief. Personally, I think that if the judge below did anything wrong, it was to give that crook too lenient a sentence. I would have hammered that drug killer with mandatory life, no parole."

"Now, now. If there was a trial error, our court may have to reverse it, no matter what the crime."

Carl stood up and looked right at Harry. "Not on this one. Sorry, Chief. You know how much I respect your opinion on things, but drug dealing . . . Well, I just think of my dead baby sister. Just imagine if the crack that killed her was shipped up here by that motherfucker Morenta." Franklin swung at the ball and crushed it. Over 220 yards. Best shot all morning. He smiled. "See that baby fly! Just shows you that anger can give you strength."

Winston gave Franklin a false smile and bent to tee up a ball. He wasn't concentrating on his shot, and his head came up too soon as he swung his titanium driver. With a sharp whoosh, he topped the ball and it bounced weakly down the range. Winston pressed his lips together and shook his head. *Focus,* he told himself. God damn it, Franklin definitely was out for the *Morenta* case. Maybe Quinn would help him on this one.

When Tim Quinn and Earl Traymont—small, white-haired, portly—walked up to Winston and Franklin on the range, the chief boomed a warm greeting. "Earl! Tim! Ready for golf on the best course in Washington? Take some practice swings. Here, use the rest of my bucket of balls."

Earl Traymont and Winston exchanged some gossip about Georgia and Hobbes College as Tim and Earl hit some practice drives. As the foursome prepared to drive the two carts to the first tee, Winston said, "Tim, why don't you come on over here in my cart and ride with me today." Tim paused for a moment, then smiled and climbed in with Harry.

While they were waiting to tee off at the first hole, Winston put his arm around Tim's shoulders and started guiding him apart from Franklin and Traymont, announcing to the other men that he and Tim had to attend to some court business. When they were out of hearing distance, Winston got right to the point and asked Tim about the *Morenta* case. First, he told Tim that he thought the trial judge had committed reversible error in not admitting the documents pertaining to the immunity the Colombian government had given to Morenta. "What do you say, Tim boy? Do I have it right?"

Tim hesitated, just a beat. "You know, Harry, I have to say I agree with you completely. I think we have to reverse Morenta's conviction—obviously, the trial judge should have dismissed the criminal case on the basis of immunity."

Winston broke into a broad smile. He patted Tim on the back. "I always said you were a smart fellow, Tim. We see eye to eye. I'm going to put you on the panel. Is that okay with you?"

"Whatever you want, Chief," Tim said agreeably. "Now can we play some golf?"

Winston wanted to raise his fists over his head like a prizefighter. His and Draco's problem was now solved. With Tim, he had the vital second vote to make sure the *Morenta* case was reversed. It didn't matter how the third member of the panel, Judge Forrester, voted. Winston had two votes. Majority wins.

The group soon got to tee off and Winston started enjoying the day. On one of the greens, Traymont casually let slip out to the group that he had personally arranged some very nice refinancing for Judge Rosemary Bowen's home. He offered to do the same for Tim and Franklin. "Any friend of Harry's is a friend of mine,"

Traymont said, relishing his favor-offering. "Let me know if you decide to refinance." Traymont handed his card to Tim and Carl.

After eighteen holes, the four men had a drink in the club bar overlooking the eighteenth hole. The little party broke up when Tim offered to give Traymont a ride back to his hotel. Then Winston and Franklin went downstairs to the locker room to shower and change. When they were dressed, the chief judge said to Franklin, "Carl, I don't think we should allow this wonderful day to end just yet." He suggested that Franklin call his wife and tell her that he had been invited to go to an important bar meeting with the chief judge this evening and that it won't be over until late. "If you can get away, we can go down to the Chesapeake Club in Georgetown again. You can be my guest for dinner and some special relaxation."

Franklin's eyes widened and he nearly licked his lips in anticipatory pleasure. "Great, Chief. I'll just call Susan. Can I borrow your cell phone?"

As they raced down the four-lane divided highway of River Road, heading toward Georgetown, the heavy Cadillac sped through two traffic lights just as they were turning red. After the second one Carl could not contain himself. "Damn, Chief, you really cut it close! Don't you worry about getting a ticket?"

Winston turned to Carl and grinned craftily. His eyes flicked to the rearview mirror, checking to see if a police car followed them as they flew down the road. Then he pulled a small leather packet from the left inside breast pocket of his blazer and extended it to Carl. It was a three-by-five-inch black leather badge case. On the outside, embossed in bright gold, was the Great Seal of the United States, an eagle with wings open, its claws holding arrows on one side and an olive branch in the other. Printed below the eagle were the words UNITED STATES COURTS in gold lettering.

"Carl, as you know, this is our federal judge credential case."

Winston flipped it open with his thumb. "Now, on the bottom half, as you can see, behind the plastic window, is my photo ID that says FEDERAL JUDGE in bold letters. At the top, where normally there is nothing, I have inserted my Georgia driver's license. So when I get stopped—and it has happened a few times—why, I just give the officer the credential case with my license next to my judge's ID. The trooper just smiles and waves me on. I haven't had a ticket since I became a judge."

Carl looked surprised and thrilled. "Sounds like a plan to me! I guess from now on, that's what I'll do. Damn clever, Chief."

Within a few minutes, the Cadillac rolled slowly down a quiet cobblestoned street, just off the busy thoroughfare of Wisconsin Avenue in the wealthiest part of Georgetown. A soft rain was starting to come down. Evening had fallen and the street was only partially illuminated by the quaint gas fixtures atop wrought-iron lampposts.

The Chesapeake Club had been established in this neighborhood just after World War II, before zoning had become restrictive. Three adjoining townhouses had been gutted and joined, a fact not noticeable to passersby. It was probably the most exclusive in-town club in Washington, with prohibitively expensive dues and a membership list firmly capped at one hundred. One distinctive aspect of the club, and one reason for its enduring popularity, was that members were free to make use of it anonymously. As long as the bills were paid, false names could protect members' identity. Winston had a secret membership in the name of a "Mister Longstreet," a name he selected to honor one of his heroes, Confederate General James Longstreet. The general's grave was near Macon. Harry admired Longstreet's loyalty to General Lee, which was summed up in a simple phrase on his grave: "With Lee from

Manassas to Appomattox." To Winston, loyalty was one of the highest virtues.

Use of the club facilities required reservations, and certain members had more priority than others. The name of Longstreet was near the top on the list, due in part to Winston's habit of giving one-hundred-dollar tips to the staff and a generous yearly cash bonus to the manager.

As Winston's car pulled up, he left the key in the ignition, then he got out and smiled at the valet. A young man in a discreet blazer and tie appeared from the club's reception room, and a valet took the member's car and whisked it off to a secure parking garage nearby. "Good evening, Mister Longstreet. Do you have any luggage or other items we can handle for you?"

"No, no, I'm just here for dinner with my friend here."

"Very good, sir."

As Winston and Carl walked up the wide steps, the door opened and the club manager, wearing a tuxedo, escorted them in. "Good evening, Mister Longstreet. Your two guests have already arrived and are awaiting you in the Green suite on the third floor. As you requested, I have had three iced bottles of Krug champagne and a cold buffet placed in that suite, and I trust everything will be satisfactory. If you need anything more, of course . . ."

Winston nodded, then walked down the familiar hall with Carl in his wake. They entered an elevator and rode up in silence, with Carl marveling at the elevator's mirrors and intricately carved gilt ceiling. As they stepped off on the third floor, they heard smothered laughter coming from the Green suite. As Winston unlocked the door, two women came rushing forward, arms open, exclaiming their greeting. Harry recognized the first woman, a well-endowed brunette named Brandy who had hosted him at two previous such soirees. He hugged her tight as she shivered, her hands running almost feverishly over his back. These girls were worth the thousand dollars a night he paid their discreet escort service. He liked Brandy and had slipped her an extra three hundred the last time. He suspected her warmth and enthusiasm was a function of the money, but you never know . . . maybe she really was fascinated, as she had several times told him, by the clout he had—apparent simply from his membership in this club. Power, as Henry Kissinger had said, is the strongest aphrodisiac. Maybe she really liked him, but in the end, what did it matter? She really knew how to please a man.

"Why, Brandy, it's so nice to see you again. And who is this beautiful friend of yours?"

"Mister Longstreet, this is Cindy. We're in modeling school together."

"Well, Cindy, it is a true pleasure to meet such a beautiful young lady. This here is my friend, Richard Pendergast. Now, before we go any further, I must say it's been a long day. And Richard and I are both very thirsty. Shall we have a cold glass of champagne?"

Harry turned and watched as this new girl, Cindy, put her arms around Carl, then kissed him, full on the lips. He smiled. Obviously, Cindy well knew the terms of her job. He winked at Brandy, then wrapped one arm around her slim waist and moved toward the champagne and elegant cold buffet awaiting them.

An hour later, Harry was lying on his back, flushed and naked under the sheets in one of the bedrooms. Brandy's superb body was twisted across his, and he could feel her heartbeat in time with his own. Intimacy with a young, lean woman always made him feel decades younger.

Suddenly, Brandy bolted up into a sitting position, her large breasts swinging up off his belly. "Oh, I almost forgot! My supervisor gave me an envelope and said it was for the four of us to use tonight. He said it was a bonus for good customers."

"He did? Where is it, dahlin'?"

"Just a minute, I'll get it."

Brandy scrambled out of bed and knelt over her big purse. He gazed at her tight, rounded butt-cheeks and felt aroused again. Then she held up a light brown envelope and came leaping back into bed, a blur of jiggling pink flesh and brown hair. Winston ripped open the thick envelope and withdrew four small, clear, plastic vials filled with white powder. He examined them in the light, smiled, and handed all of them to Brandy. "Brandy, dahlin', why I do believe this is some first-class cocaine, right?"

She nodded. "That's what he said, and he told me we should all have a good time."

"Well, I tell you what. Why don't you keep two of them? All I need are champagne and you. But take the other two next door to Cindy and my friend and tell them to enjoy! Okay?"

"Sure! I'll be right back." Brandy pulled on her silk robe.

Two hours later, Harry and Carl walked Brandy and Cindy down to the elevator. As they went out the front door, Harry palmed three one-hundred-dollar bills into each woman's hands as he leaned over and bussed their cheeks in a fatherly way. "There's some cab fare for you, girls, and maybe we'll see each other again next time we're in town, hear?"

The valet had Harry's car waiting. Harry briefly thought of the risks of climbing behind the wheel in an over-policed area like Georgetown, but felt there would be no problem in his driving. He had had what, two, no, three glasses of champagne, but over a three-hour period, and he had eaten well from the buffet. He was fine to drive. He also felt flushed and pleasurably exhausted. It never ceased to amaze him how a young, eager, tight-bodied woman could reinvigorate him, *thrill* him. He checked his watch. It wasn't even ten-thirty, and he would have Carl back home in Rockville, Maryland, by eleven.

When Winston pulled into the driveway of Franklin's home, Carl got his golf clubs out of the trunk. "Chief, I just can't tell you how much fun I had today," Carl said, his face still red with excitement. "And how grateful I am to you for your tremendous generosity. What a great golf match, and—"

"We sure did have some fun, Carl."

Carl looked up to see if his wife was at the front door. She wasn't. He leaned closer to Winston and whispered, "And Chief, that dinner at your club, the Chesapeake Club, that was just unbelievable."

Winston looked at Franklin with great seriousness. "Well, Carl, I'm a lucky man. My ancestors were good to my family, and I don't depend on my salary." He sighed. "And you also know that I'm all alone in life, and it's good, once in a while, to go out with one of my close men friends—and you are one of my closest, most trusted friends, Carl—and do *man* things together, if you understand my drift . . ."

Carl smiled, happy as a boy admitted to his big brother's treehouse. "Thanks, Chief. You should know that I consider you one of my closest friends also." He chuckled. "And I guess it is good to go every once in a while and do our man things."

Before Harry pulled away, he paused and waved his arm out the open window, raising his voice for the benefit of Carl's wife. "Carl, thanks again for all your support at that bar meeting. Say hi to Susan for me. See you at work on Monday!"

As the chief judge pulled into his Georgetown driveway, he pushed the remote button on his visor and waited while the garage door cranked up. Tired but satisfied, he closed the door behind him, punched in the security code, and climbed up the staircase into his townhouse. He flipped through the mail that the maid had stacked on the kitchen counter, then poured a small snifter of Blue Label

Martel cognac. He slipped his feet out of his shoes and into his comfortable old slippers, and took his first sip. Excellent.

He padded down the hall to his study and flipped on the CD player. The soft chords of a Brahms concerto echoed off the book-lined walls. Ever since his days at Hobbes College, he had always valued books more than any other possessions, and he prided himself in straining the wisdom from them and applying it to his own life. He took another sip. Yes, it had been a good day. Most importantly, he had lined up the *Morenta* case as he had said he would for Draco.

He mused on the cocaine he had been offered at the Chesapeake Club. Obviously a special perk for very good customers. Would the escort-service owner be shocked to learn he had given coke to two federal judges? It proved that his cover as Mr. Longstreet really was working. Had Carl taken the cocaine Winston had sent him? It didn't matter. What mattered was that Winston was consolidating the loyalty of the other judges to him. Franklin, Janoff, Bowen, and now Quinn. Winston had done big favors for all, and he was reminded of an old German proverb he had first heard at Yale Law: "Whose bread I eat, his song I will sing."

Winston took another sip. Tim Quinn really had come through for him. Tim was a good man. It didn't matter whether he was going along with him because he believed the immunity argument or because Tim owed him as a friend. In Washington, the reason why a favor was done was of no consequence. What counted was doing the favor when you're asked.

Now his court was safe, and his court was everything to him. Nothing beyond beckoned him. He knew that, as much as he had desired it all his life, he could no longer realistically aspire to be appointed to the United States Supreme Court. After all, even Oliver Wendell Holmes, appointed to the Supreme Court at the age of sixty, had been sharply criticized as being too old for such a key post. Winston, already approaching seventy with far too much velocity, had long accepted that his post as the chief judge of the second most powerful court in the land, was the summit of his career. The power of the Washington game was what he loved the most about his court. He was a very powerful man in a very powerful city.

His majority could sing sweetly, very sweetly indeed. A happy prospect, especially now when his and Draco's lives were at stake.

CHAPTER 17

THE MONDAY MORNING AFTER THE SATURDAY GOLF OUTING, Judge Tim Quinn was in his chambers going over the bench memos for the four cases he would be sitting on that day. Tim had debated calling Vicky Hauser over the weekend to tell her that he might be sitting on the General Morenta case with the chief judge. But he had decided to wait to see if he really would be assigned to that panel. Maybe Winston had second thoughts about him and would use Carl Franklin for the *Morenta* case. At the golf outing, Franklin had seemed as loyal and attentive to Winston as a Labrador. Rather than risk assigning the seemingly agreeable Tim to the case, Winston might still go with Franklin. But thanks to one of today's cases, Tim had a plan that might cement Winston's opinion of his reliability and help insure his placement on the *Morenta* panel.

Tim would hear today's cases with Chief Judge Winston and Judge Judith Bickel. Although he had been on panels with Judge Bickel before and had spent a little time chatting with her, he felt he really didn't know her very well. Courthouse gossip classified her as a liberal judge. Courteous but aloof, tall and big-boned, she wore her gray hair short and, from a distance in the courtroom, it was hard to tell she was a woman, except for the frilly lace collars that she wore outside her black judge's robe. The lace collar was her trademark. At court functions, she was accompanied by her life partner, a small, pretty, blond woman very near Bickel's own age, which Tim guessed to be in the late forties. Tim admired her independence and the forthright way she conducted herself in the conferences with him and the other judges.

Tim gave the day's case materials to Loretta to put on the bench and headed for the robing room. He might not endear himself to Judge Bickel today, but he had a bigger goal in mind.

By just after two in the afternoon, Tim, Winston, and Bickel were alone in a conference room on the sixth floor, deciding the fourth and last case they had heard that day, *Renay Fredericks v. The District of Columbia Housing Authority*. The first three cases decided in the conference had been routine, and the three judges easily reached consensus; the votes had been three to zero right down the line. But this fourth case was going to be difficult because their questions during the oral argument had revealed a pronounced split in views between Judge Bickel and the chief judge. Quinn knew this case was his opportunity to earn some points with Winston and maybe nail his placement on the panel to hear Draco's vital case with General Morenta.

The case was interesting and unusual. A woman who was a welfare recipient living in subsidized housing had brought a civil lawsuit for money damages against the Housing Authority of the District of Columbia. The complaint alleged that her constitutional right of privacy was infringed by loud music from other apartments that she could hear through her apartment's thin walls. Since the apartment, with its substandard walls, was provided to her by the city Housing Authority, she claimed that the city owed her money damages. This unique "noise pollution" case had been dismissed by the U.S. District Court below. Its decision stated that her delay in reporting this condition after taking possession of the apartment precluded her recovering any money from the city. The Washington ACLU office, a premiere supporter of civil rights, had stepped in and filed the appeal. The ACLU presented a challenging legal argument that the city had, by construction of such thin walls, violated its own building code, and thus was liable for money damages.

Judge Bickel, the known liberal on the panel, had been very receptive to the ACLU's argument. Tim knew that the ACLU was using this as a test case in an attempt to expand the rights of welfare recipients. He had researched the law in this area before the case was argued and couldn't find any decision where a court had granted money damages for a noise nuisance like this—especially when the plaintiff herself had not complained for more than six months after moving in. Tim had made up his mind after reading his bench memo the day before that he would vote against the ACLU's position. He was reluctant to expand welfare rights based on a test case like this. But he had kept that conclusion to himself and made sure that his brief questions were neutral in tone—setting himself up as the swing vote in the eyes of Bickel and the chief judge. Tim was aware that Winston hated the ACLU and would almost certainly reject their position here. If Tim could curry favor with the chief judge, it might aid his goal of getting inside the case-fixing ring.

"Well, on this last case, here," the chief judge began, "I see this woman as just looking out to rip off more money from the government. My Lord, she's already getting a good deal, paying only fifty dollars a month for a two-bedroom apartment, and now she wants the city to pay her more money because she can hear loud music through the walls. I think she is way out of line. No doubt about it—I think we should uphold the District Court. This is just a welfare queen looking for a windfall she doesn't deserve anyway. I vote to affirm the District Court in this case. As far as the constitutional claim of the ACLU, I am reminded of Supreme Court Justice Charles Evans Hughes, who said, 'The Constitution governs our land, but the Constitution is what we judges say it is,' and I say this woman shouldn't get a nickel."

Judge Bickel frowned. Tim could see that she was quite upset and ready to challenge Winston. "But Chief Judge, there is a far bigger right involved here," she said. "Whether she is on welfare or not—that's not the issue. The point is that a person has a right to enjoy peace and quiet in his or her own home. And since the city built the apartment building in violation of its own building code, the city is responsible for her being subjected to unbearable noise in that home and the city should pay." Judge Bickel carefully went through her theory that the Constitution guaranteed people a right to the quiet enjoyment of their own homes, even if that home was government-owned housing.

Winston's face went cold and glassy as Bickel spoke. After she was finished, he turned to Tim, his lips pressed together in irritation at Judge Bickel. Tim felt that Winston's look was an unspoken request for Tim's support. Then Winston smiled and softly said, "Tim, how do *you* feel? You seem to be the swing vote here."

Tim glanced down, adjusted the papers in his case file, and looked over his notes from the oral argument, pausing to raise the suspense and make Winston even more relieved when Tim came out on his side. Then Tim looked directly at Winston and said, "Well, I think Judith is right when she says that the welfare aspect of this case is not relevant. It doesn't matter whether she is rich or poor. To me, the issue is not so much the right to privacy. The key to this case, I think, is that this woman knew the condition of the apartment and the thin nature of the walls when she moved in. But she didn't say anything about this noise nuisance for over six months, and therefore I have to go with you, Chief Judge." He saw Winston trying to hide his triumphant smile. "I would hold that she has waived her right to complain about this noise nuisance at this stage, and that we should affirm the District Court's dismissal of this case based on the theory of waiver. I might add that I could find no precedent in any jurisdiction where a city has had to pay money damages for a noise nuisance like this in subsidized housing. It would be a dangerous precedent, I think, if housing authorities across the country suddenly had to worry about suits like this. We shouldn't go the ACLU's way on this case."

The chief judge nodded his head vigorously, grinning unabashedly. "Tim boy, I think you've got a good handle on this case. Judith, what do you think of our waiver position, the one Tim and I are taking on this case?"

Bickel looked grim. "Well, I'm sorry to disagree with you two on this, but I still have a different view. I think this is a very important right-of-privacy case, and I plan to write a dissent along the lines of the ACLU's position in their brief."

"All right, Judith, that's your prerogative to write a dissent. Tim, would you like to write up the opinion for the majority in this case?"

"I'd be happy to, Chief."

Winston sat back happy, as if he had just finished a satisfying dinner. "Good, I assign this case to you to write the majority opinion. Well that's it. Thank you. Judith and Tim, that finishes our day. I believe we did some good work today."

Judge Judith Bickel abruptly stood up, scooped up her files, and left the conference room without a further word.

As the door closed behind her, the chief judge leaned over to Tim and spoke in a low tone. "Tim, I really do appreciate your support on that last case. I guess you know how I am about the damned ACLU. I try not to get emotional and show it in court, but you seem to get the picture that the fuzzy-headed liberals are trying to milk the government with these test welfare cases. I applaud the clever waiver argument you figured out to get the right result in this case."

"Well, thank you, Chief. I don't much care for the ACLU either . . ." Tim winked and continued. "And on cases like this, I'll try to give you all the support I can and follow your lead."

An hour after Tim had returned to his desk, Mr. Nichols, the clerk of court, appeared in Tim's chambers. Nichols got right to the point. "Judge Quinn, there has been a computer error, and you will be sitting with the chief judge and Judge Forester next week on *United States v. General Morenta.* All the briefs and other papers will be delivered to your chambers by nine A.M. tomorrow morning."

Tim tried to hide his elation. He was sitting on a Draco case, and the most murderously significant of all of them. The chief judge had come through with the proposed assignment, as he had promised on the golf course. By reflex, Tim asked, "What was the computer error?"

Nichols instantly grew evasive. "Uh, sometimes the random case selection software doubles assignments. And uh . . ."

Tim realized he shouldn't be too inquisitive. Obviously, Nichols was covering for Winston's role in selecting Tim as a panel member on this special case. "Well, thank you for catching the mistake, Mr. Nichols," he said blandly. How interesting that the clerk of court would lie to him about the reason for the assignment. With his power as chief judge, all his colleagues on the court recognized that Winston could override the "random" assignment software process on any particular case for good reasons like sickness or a conflict of interest. Yet here was a cover-up on the real reason—that Winston wanted Quinn to be the second vote to win the case for Draco.

Nichols gratefully hurried out. Tim got up and closed the door behind the clerk, then went back to his desk and dialed Vicky from his cell phone. He smiled with satisfaction as he punched in her telephone number. "Vicky, Tim," he said as soon as she picked up. "We've got to meet right away. Something just happened."

"Are you in danger, Tim?" Vicky sounded worried

"No, no, nothing like that. We've just gotten an important break. You need to know about it and we can't talk on the phone. Can you met me in the same place in half an hour?"

"At the elephant?"

"Right."

"Half an hour, see you there."

When he hung up, Tim sat down in his chair and thought about what he was getting into. A Chinese warning came into his thoughts: Watch what you wish for—you may get it.

CHAPTER 18

TIM STARTED WALKING THE FEW BLOCKS FROM THE COURT-house to the Smithsonian Museum of Natural History on Constitution Avenue. He was excited now, and scared. Tim truly believed that, with the assignment to the *Morenta* case, Winston unknowingly had just invited him inside the conspiracy.

He hated what he had been required to do. Christ! He had gotten assigned to *Morenta* only because he lied to Winston. Tim had falsely promised his vote in advance to Winston on the golf course. It was a vote he didn't believe in. But he had to promise Winston that false vote in an attempt to get close enough to obtain some evidence against Winston. If he had told Winston how he really wanted to vote, he never would have been assigned to the case.

His true feelings on the *Morenta* case were that he would never let that drug-dealing General Morenta out of jail on some bullshit immunity agreement that was probably bought with drug cartel money. But since Tim thought Winston was going to fix the case for Draco, he was ready to give Winston the one vote he needed.

And Winston would certainly need Tim's vote. The other judge on the panel was Judge William Forrester, who was very independent and most likely would never be party to giving a vote to the chief judge. Judge Forrester was very cool, if not cold, toward the chief judge, and he rarely showed any deference at all beyond normal civility. No, Forrester was definitely not a member of the chief judge's little *majority*. So that meant Winston had to count on Tim.

Second thoughts flooded his mind. Was the chief judge really a crook? *Absolutely yes* was the answer. Although there was no direct evidence, Tim was convinced by the string of circumstantial evidence. First, the list made by Judge Rogers, followed by the murder of both Rogers and his killer, a former client of Draco. Then there was the visit of Vicky to Winston's ex-wife in Macon, her phone call to Winston, and Winston's call to Draco—and Camellia's murder by hit men. Then the incriminating meeting on the rainy night in Quebec. No, Winston was a part of this. All the evidence showed that he was dirty. Tim couldn't allow himself to be taken in by friendship. That Southern charm was just another mask.

Agitated and edgy, he walked faster and faster, his anger brimming over. He was tired. Tim hadn't been sleeping well the past few nights, troubled by nightmares from Vietnam. The pressure was tremendous. The court, his court, was being used by Winston to get votes for Draco . . . and the president. Yes, Tim felt a little guilty about what he had just done to get in close to Winston. But there were three murders connected to Winston and Draco—Judge Rogers, the druggie who killed Rogers, and Winston's ex-wife—and if Winston and Draco were responsible for them, then they had to be stopped immediately. In this case, the end justified the means.

Tim had to accept that the undercover role he was playing was dangerous—the three murders meant someone was dealing death to protect the case-fixing fraud in Tim's own court, the court on which he sat as a sworn federal judge. Suddenly, fear flooded him. He had put himself and possibly his family in a very precarious position. Lying to the chief judge about the pending case of General Morenta was an ethical Rubicon he had crossed when the chief judge approached him on the golf course. He could be dead professionally if he was wrong. But if he was right, he could still end up as dead as Judge Rogers.

He tried to concentrate on what he was going to say to Vicky, but the anger kept building, growing into a quiet rage, controlled but lethal.

As he strode down Constitution Avenue toward the museum, he tried to calm himself, but his heart was pumping hard, and he found himself breathing through his mouth. He felt a strange high, a feeling both light and tense. And suddenly he was, once again, superconscious of everything around him. The hairs on the back of his neck stirred in the light breeze. He felt the cracks of the sidewalk under his shoe, saw colors flash from across the street, and found himself snapping his head in every direction. He was on full alert.

Take it easy, he told himself. *Everything's under control.*

It was one of those hot, muggy Washington summer days, where the oppression of the weather hovering over an area that had once been a swamp drove human beings to distraction. The heat. Tim felt it, carried it, waded through it. He took his suit jacket off and slung it over his shoulder.

As he approached Pennsylvania Avenue, he was faintly aware that a construction crew was working somewhere off to the right. The smell of fresh tar bit his nostrils, and then he walked through a cloud of diesel fumes discharged by a large metro bus churning away from the curb. The thumping of a generator at the construction site became louder as he approached it, and more irregular metallic banging and whacking hurt his ears. A jackhammer kicked in on his left, and the pavement shuddered from it ever so slightly as he walked. He was caught by its thudding, M-60 machine-gun rhythm, and by the booming, the shaking, the harsh but familiar smells, the heat.

He was plunged back into the terror-filled days of his youth.

He was again an American infantry platoon leader in Vietnam, in that sun-splashed jungle on a day thirty, thirty-five years ago. He didn't even have to close his eyes for the moment to swallow him completely.

He was with his platoon, moving down that muddy trail. The raised fists rippled back, and everyone froze. He had stopped breathing as he slowly rotated his head to the left and saw movement through the brush: five, six men, who could only be North Vietnamese soldiers moving almost parallel to their own trail. Up front, one of his M-60 machine guns opened up, the dull thumping like a bass drum underscoring the screaming bursts of rifle fire from his men, slashing out and chewing the thick brush on their left.

Then they were running, down the small depression, and now they were among the enemy. Six, seven, eight enemy soldiers down, dead, or dying, their bodies crumpled and ripped open. Blood splashed everywhere, bright and shiny on the green jungle leaves. He pointed to muzzle flashes on his right front, directing the rage of his men toward the NVA survivors who were still trying to return fire. The arteries in his neck gorged with blood as he roared: "KILL THEM! KILL THEM!"

Then a new sound ripped into the noise of the firefight. *A fucking zipper.*

The NVA were waiting and sprung the trap—they had a ZPU-1 gun up the hill. The heavy machine gun was firing six hundred rounds a minute, big rounds, 14.5 mm rods of steel chopping through bamboo, small trees bursting into splinters, shredded leaves flying like confetti.

Tim saw nothing but the dirt an inch away. When he looked up and forward, he saw a green wall, a wall that shook violently whenever the zipper raked his position. Tim held his M-16 up over his head and emptied a magazine uphill toward the heavy machine gun, then tossed both his smoke grenades to his front. His thoughts were surprisingly rational. *We can't stay here. We all will die here.* Then he shouted, "Cover fire, right front. Move back to the ridge at six o'clock. . . . Move, Move!"

Soon his platoon was back over the protective small hump of ground and out of the killing zone. He was still shaking as he called in artillery and gun ships on the zipper machine-gun position. He sucked on his canteen and breathed heavily. The head count came up from his platoon sergeant—three missing. *God, I've got to go back out there. I've got to . . . got to . . .*

Beads of sweat stood out on Tim's forehead, but it wasn't from the Washington sun.

He stopped, leaned against a tree, and tried to calm his nerves. His heart was still pounding. His mouth bone-dry. *Not so fast,* he thought, *I'm not in Vietnam. Deep breath now, I'm in Washington, D.C. The war is over. Everything is under control.*

He walked more slowly now, then up the steps of the Smithsonian. As he entered the cool interior of the tall marble building, he felt the heat and the rage ease out of him. But the episode had scared him. He never wanted to be that way again. Never.

He stopped and looked around, then saw Vicky by the elephant in the center of the immense domed entrance foyer. She had not noticed him yet, so he paused to breathe deep and slow his pulse. Okay, time to tuck Lieutenant Quinn and his jungle memories back in their box and bury it deep. *I am safely back from Vietnam, I am Federal Judge Quinn, I am meeting with a Justice Department prosecutor, and we are going to devise a way to trap a crooked judge who quite probably helped to murder three people.* The notion didn't comfort him. Nor did knowing that his only weapon in this battle would be a cool, legal mind.

Tim went over to a water fountain at the edge of the rotunda. After a long drink, he looked up and saw Vicky watching him. He nodded to her. She nodded back and smiled, then started toward him. He was still sweating, so he loosened his tie and unbuttoned his collar button. He saw concern on her face as she approached.

"You look pale. Are you okay, Tim?"

"I'm fine. Let's go into the alcoves."

"No, you're not fine. Your shirt is soaking wet. What's wrong?"

"Nothing. I got ambushed on the way over by some nasty memories. It's all right now."

"God, Tim, you're still having those flashbacks, aren't you?"

Tim tried to smile. "Now and then."

"You just had one, didn't you? The stress is triggering it."

Tim looked down at his shoes.

"Poor Tim." She touched his forearm.

He pulled his arm away violently. The rage surged back. "Yeah, poor Tim is fucking up his judicial career. God damn it, Vicky. Can't you and the fucking FBI nail Winston by yourselves? Why do I have to do this, wear the Judas shirt?" He caught his breath. "Christ. Let's go over to the alcoves where we can talk."

Vicky looked taken aback, but she was quiet. She just walked with him across the foyer and started down a long hallway lined with glass-enclosed wildlife displays. They passed the arctic wolves; the woolly mammoth display where they had stopped before was only three or four alcoves ahead on the left. With each step, Tim became calmer. As he walked with her next to him, he felt regret for taking out his inner conflicts on her. It wasn't her fault. It was him. The stress of being solo in an undercover investigation was a wake-up call for his ghosts from Vietnam.

"Sorry for the blow-up, Vicky," he said finally. "It's gone now. I haven't been sleeping well. But I'm okay. I can do this thing. I'm in it with you. I won't let you down."

Now they had arrived at the woolly mammoth display and they turned in to it and stopped.

"It's all right," Vicky said. "I know you're feeling that you're out there alone. And we are asking you to risk a lot."

Tim made no response. It was time to change the subject. "I think this is a safe meeting place for us. The museum is near both our offices; we're able to talk privately without being seen or heard. From now on, if we need to meet during the day, this will be our set meeting place, at the woolly mammoth display. Either of us can just say 'usual place,' and that will be here, okay?"

Vicky looked at him hard. "I hope it is healthy that you have such an ability to compartmentalize."

"What?"

"You were in Vietnam five minutes ago. Now you're here, and you're focused."

Tim looked at her, not knowing whether he was embarrassed for himself or grateful to her. "Well, we've got work to do. You think it's good to make this our meeting place?"

"Okay, Tim, that's fine," Vicky said, nodding.

"Oh, and another thing. About telephones. After my time in the intelligence community, I know too much to trust telephones, especially now." Tim looked around the corner of the alcove in both directions. No one was in the corridor.

"I guess you're right," Vicky said. "Phones aren't really secure, so if one of us has important information, face-to-face is best. And you're right, this is a good place. Even directional microphones couldn't be used here easily. But what happens if we need to meet and the museum is closed?"

"The outdoor entrance to the metro on the Mall."

"Okay. Now why am I here?" asked Vicky.

"I think I'm on—and maybe inside—one of Draco's fixed cases."

Vicky's face registered shock. Then she broke into a tentative smile.

Tim told her how Winston had approached him on the golf course to get his advance views on the *General Jose Morenta* case. Tim explained how he had heartily agreed with Winston's hint that the case should be reversed on the immunity argument. Along with the vehement agreement he had given Winston on another case just this afternoon, it was enough for Winston to assign him to the panel. Tim told Vicky that Nichols had assigned him to the *Morenta* panel just an hour earlier. Vicky agreed that Tim's role on the panel would be pivotal. Judge Forrester, a former prosecutor who was known to be tough on drug dealers, would never vote to release Morenta. "Good job!" she said. "You're where we want you to be."

"There's more. I'm worried that I may have an ethical problem."

Vicky shrugged. "What's the problem? You're on the inside of one of Winston's little *majorities*. That's great for us. You've landed in a position where we can get some incriminating evidence on both Winston and Draco. Don't get cold feet on me now."

Stung, Tim felt a fresh bolt of anger. "God damn it, Vicky. I am a fucking judge. I may just have breached judicial ethics for you by falsely promising a vote on a real case. Hell, if this investigation goes south or gets leaked to the press, I probably could even be accused of committing a crime."

"Tim, you're working for the Justice Department as a confidential informant," Vicky retorted. "You're trying to get evidence on a case-fixing scheme. I'm not asking you to violate judicial ethics. All you have to do is play along with Winston on this case and see where it gets us." She smiled at him reassuringly, but her expression faltered when she met Tim's grim eyes. "When it comes time to release the opinion to the public, you merely disqualify yourself, and the case will have to be reassigned and reargued before another panel. The end of catching a crooked judge justifies the means you're using to do it."

"All right," Tim said. "But I'm very uncomfortable playing this game with a real case, especially with one as high-profile as Morenta's. I may already have tainted this case by giving Winston false advance notice of my vote. So you and I and the FBI are *required* to find a way to prevent this case from becoming final."

"Don't worry, Tim, I assure you, we will. Let's not forget that this is the break we've been waiting for. A 'special' Draco case they appear to be trying to fix, you're on the panel, and they need your vote. We're in a good position."

"Okay, Vicky, we'll play this out as far as we can," Tim said with resignation.

Vicky looked hesitant.

"You've got something on your mind," Tim said. "What is it?"

Vicky regarded him a little warily.

"Since this case is now going critical, I can't go any further without opening a formal file, both in my office and over at the FBI."

"Vicky—"

"Bill Sharkey has to open a file now, and notify his supervisor, but I'll ask him to keep this on a need-to-know basis, briefing the minimum amount of people. His supervisor, given the sensitive nature of the target, will probably have to bring it all the way up to the deputy director of the FBI. And I have to do more or less the same thing in Justice. I'll have to brief the assistant attorney general in charge of the Criminal Division, and eventually, I may have to brief the attorney general himself. But I will promise you, Tim"—Vicky's voice grew firmer and more urgent—"that I will work to impress on everyone the need to keep this case under wraps for as long as we can."

Vicky hesitated and added, "By the way, Sharkey is on your team now as a fan. He was impressed with your military recon at the bus stop in Canada."

Tim gave a grim smile and nodded, still reluctant. "I guess I have to thank you both for keeping it a 'ghost' case up to now. But the press better not hear about it—this is a small town."

"You don't have to warn me about that. Look what happened with ABSCAM." In that investigation several decades earlier, most of the prosecutors working the case thought that the FBI could have easily nailed a dozen more senators and congressmen if the operation hadn't been blown so early by the press.

"Thanks for the reassurance," Tim muttered.

"Well, this is hardball, Tim. I'll use the same tight reporting procedures that I used in the Judge Gibson case. Nobody knew about that until Bill Sharkey and I took him down. The case stays in my office safe, there are no computer reports, and I brief the Justice Department principals orally—which means I tell only the head of the Criminal Division and the attorney general in person. No assistants involved. Besides me, Tim, only two people in Justice will know about this case."

Vicky leaned into him, her eyes softer. "Tim, please, please be careful. This is a dangerous operation. People have died here. Judge Rogers and Mrs. Winston"—Vicky shuddered at the mention of her name, and Tim could tell how much her role in Camellia's fate still haunted her. "Winston is very smart, and very slick, and so is Draco. Harry may talk slow and get you to relax and feel he's just a good old boy, but he's not. He and Draco, if cornered, will have you killed without a second thought."

"Vicky, I know that. And yes, I'm afraid," Tim said. "But fear is good sometimes. In Vietnam, I was scared all the time, *literally all the time,* and more than once I think that helped keep me and my men from dying in an ambush."

"And this time it's you who gets to spring the ambush," Vicky said. She kept her eyes steady on Tim, knowing the power of her words.

Vicky had already thought through how they would trap Winston and Draco. She told Tim that the investigation now required her to apply for judicial wiretaps on Winston, Draco, and the clerk of the court, and so she asked Tim if he could come back to her office to have him execute an affidavit describing the evidence and his observations to date. Affidavits from Tim and Bill Sharkey would be necessary to get court-ordered wiretaps. Tim knew it was a reasonable step now that things were moving quickly. He didn't want to go to her office, but he had no real choice.

"Why don't you go first and I'll meet you at your office?" Tim told her. "I don't want to be seen walking into Justice with you. And let's agree now to meet here again next Tuesday immediately after the *Morenta* case hearing. I should be free about four-thirty, because we'll probably wrap up our conference for *Morenta* and the other cases we hear that day by four o'clock. So we meet here at four-thirty, unless I call you and cancel. Okay?"

"That's fine. Remember to try to cut phone calls down to a minimum, in case Draco has your phone bugged."

"Vicky, he can't get a wiretap on my phone in the federal courthouse."

Vicky smiled grimly. "If Draco can kill people without a trace and has the chief judge of your court in his pocket, then he can bug your courthouse phone." She took out a card from her wallet with only a phone number written on it. "That's for my beeper. To cancel our meeting, just enter the numbers one one one. Otherwise, the meeting is on for four-thirty."

"Okay. Now you head out first. I'll meet you in your office to sign the wiretap affidavit in ten minutes," Tim said, looking up for the first time at the huge mammoth looming up behind him, like the image of fear itself.

Tim was frightened. His mind was racing forward—maybe he should have told Vicky about the White House connection with Winston just now. Things were moving too fast. This whole investigation was like a sinking ship that may drag him under with Winston and Draco.

CHAPTER 19

"ARE YOU *SERIOUS?* ARE YOU REALLY ASKING FOR . . . FOR A wiretap on the chief judge of the U.S. Court of Appeals?" asked Judge Goldstein.

Vicky and FBI Special Agent Bill Sharkey were in the chambers of U.S. District Judge Goldstein on the third floor of the federal courthouse. Goldstein was the duty federal judge that week for authorizing wiretaps in the District of Columbia. A short, solid man known as a level-headed judge but vain enough to comb long white strands of his hair over his bald spot, he peered intently over his wire-rimmed reading glasses at Vicky and the FBI agent, sizing them up.

"Yes, Your Honor, we're very serious," Vicky answered. "If you finish reading the attached affidavits, you'll see that there is adequate probable cause to believe that the chief judge is involved with the Draco law firm in case-fixing at that court. In addition, there are some disturbing connections between the case-fixing scheme and the deaths of three people, including Judge Rogers."

"All right, counselor," Goldstein replied, sounding either impressed or dubious—Vicky couldn't be sure. "Let me finish reading the request."

Long minutes passed in silence as the judge slowly completed his examination of the motion papers and the attached affidavits of Judge Quinn and Agent Sharkey. Then he dropped the papers on his desk and looked directly at Vicky. She was surprised to see that he was no longer quite so stern looking. Was that a smile on the face of the notoriously serious Judge Goldstein? Then his face grew grave.

"Well, counselor, I must say, for the last several years, several judges on this court have thought that something strange was going on at the Court of Appeals above us. Your papers and the evidence you refer to in them are very serious. . . . No, they're shocking. Shocking, but convincing, so I *am* going to authorize some of these wiretaps you request—and with some restrictions. I personally don't care for the chief judge, and he's certainly not a popular man down here in the district court. But before reading these papers, I never suspected he was involved in such outrageous criminal activity. Our system of justice requires that I do my duty and authorize the wiretaps against Judge Winston and Mr. Draco. I must say that I do so with some relish."

Vicky exhaled in relief.

The judge had more to say. "You have not demonstrated to me, however, that the clerk is a knowing participant in criminal activity, and therefore, I will deny the wiretap on him. I authorize full wiretap coverage for Winston's residence, but not full-time on the three phone lines in his chambers. You are authorized to tap them only when the chief judge is physically present in his chambers. On Draco, full wiretap coverage on his home is authorized. But in his office, you can tap only his private phone line, the one that is mentioned in the affidavit of Agent Sharkey. None of the other phone lines into the law firm can be tapped." Goldstein gazed at her firmly. "There would be too many problems in the way of potential attorney-client privilege problems there, and you haven't met your burden of proof in that area. Do you have any questions?"

"No, Your Honor. Thank you for your time."

Goldstein allowed himself another slight smile. "Good hunting, Ms. Hauser. In light of the sensitivity of this investigation, I am sealing this entire file. Don't make me regret authorizing these wiretaps. If you are wrong, Chief Judge Winston is reputed to have a long memory, and that means for both of us." The smile vanished.

Ever since he returned to his chambers from his rendezvous with Vicky, Tim had been thinking furiously about the *Morenta* case. He even had one of his law clerks do a supplemental memo on the merits of the case. It was clear that Draco was cleverly advancing the immunity theory in an international criminal case, similar to the one that had been used in the Pinochet case in England, when the former Chilean dictator had resisted extradition to stand trial for crimes while he was in office. But the closer Tim looked, the more he believed that Draco should lose his challenge on the immunity argument. Tim also thought Judge Forrester would almost certainly reject Draco's theory.

A respected "law and order" judge, Forrester had an impressive background. After graduating from law school at Georgetown, Forrester did a stint in the U.S. Attorney's Office in D.C. as a prosecutor. Later he had been very successful with a large firm, specializing in white-collar crime until he was selected to be the assistant attorney general of the Criminal Division at the Justice Department. From Justice, Forrester had been nominated to be a judge on this court. All indications from Forrester's background pointed to a vote against Morenta. The case would almost certainly be a two-to-one decision, one way or the other. With the stakes so murderously high for Winston, Tim hoped only that Judge Forrester would not be buffaloed by the chief judge into a three-to-nothing stampede. If the case came down to a two-to-one vote, then Vicky and he had devised a bluff with which to trap Winston. But it was a long shot.

The morning of General Morenta's appeal, the courthouse was surrounded with TV vans and mobile antennas. Extra U.S. marshals had been put on the entrances for crowd and press control. Tim was tense as he drove into the court's underground parking lot. This would be a long, tough, dangerous day.

The gavel banged, and the crowded courtroom rose as the three judges, Winston, Forrester, and Quinn, came into the courtroom and took their seats on the bench. The first three cases went by quickly and with little drama. Then the chief judge called a fifteen-minute recess so the media and interested spectators could be settled before they heard the *Morenta* case. The three judges knew it would be standing-room only. They had already voted to deny motions for in-court television coverage from all the major networks.

"All rise."

Tim entered the chamber and looked out uneasily at the packed courtroom. Morenta's case had caused a feeding frenzy in the press, and various reporters from the national and international media were there in full force.

As the loser in the court below, General Morenta was the appellant, and Draco, as his lawyer, got to speak first. He was eloquent and passionate about his client and the unjust way in which the diplomatic and transactional immunity extended by a sovereign nation to one of its citizens had been ignored in the district court trial. Neither Quinn nor Winston had any questions for Draco, but Judge Forrester frequently interrupted him, querying the validity of the immunity given to General Morenta. From the nature of the questions Forrester asked, and the tone of voice in which he asked them, it was easy for even the most casual of observers to predict how Forrester would vote: He was clearly against Morenta's appeal position.

The assistant U.S. attorney followed Draco with a tight, succinct argument countering Draco and declaring that the immunity was a sham and should never be recognized in a U.S. courtroom. Moreover, she hammered home parts of the trial record indicating that, although General Morenta had never previously come to the United States before this visit for medical reasons, his drug organization in Colombia had been clearly "present" in this country by orchestrating the movement of massive illegal drug shipments into the United States.

None of the judges asked the assistant U.S. attorney any questions. Tim was purposefully silent during the oral argument. The action he planned would wait until the important stage of the case conference that would follow. He felt his foot tapping beneath the table and had trouble stopping it. His heart pumped hard.

In the conference room, following the *Morenta* case, the three judges removed their robes and took a brief break. Within a few minutes, all three were reassembled around the large rectangular conference table, and they quickly sped through the first three cases, voting in each case three to zero. Tim forced himself to keep his breathing deep and even, working hard to seem casual and relaxed as the three men did the serious work of adjudication. The last case was *Morenta,* and Winston opened the discussion by going to the heart of Draco's argument, forcefully stating his view that the immunity given Morenta clearly should have been honored by the district court. He was not about to let Forrester take command of the debate. He seemed as suave and cool as ever, but Tim could see the chief judge's fists clenching involuntarily, as Tim tried to listen without betraying any emotion.

Forrester didn't hesitate to disagree with Winston—vehemently. "Chief, you can't be serious about that. Why, it's obvious that immunity agreements of foreign countries should not be controlling U.S. courts, especially with a trial record like this one, which shows some actual contacts between Morenta's organization in Colombia and drug dealers here in the United States."

Winston gave him a tight smile. "Bill, now I see where you are coming from. But you're getting a little bit too tied up in the drug-dealing portion of that trial record, and you're missing the big picture. I'm not saying this-here general is a good man. As a matter of fact, he's probably the corrupt man that the newspapers all say he is. Nevertheless, he gets cancer, his country gives him diplomatic and transactional immunity so he can come up here and get treated at Johns Hopkins Hospital." Winston's voice began to get higher, more strident than Tim had ever heard it, his Southern accent fraying. "Then some overzealous and publicity-seeking young female U.S. attorney indicts him for crimes he allegedly committed in Colombia. Alleged crimes that are clearly covered by these immunity agreements. So now we have to look at this as a purely legal case. Accordingly, the trial judge in the court below erred by not admitting those immunity agreements into evidence. He should have dismissed the case based on reciprocal immunity between nations."

Judge Forrester scowled. "Damn it, Chief Judge, there's plenty of evidence in the trial record to prove that those immunity agreements were bought and paid for by this *drug lord*. Hell, we just can't give any validity to government documents coming from Colombia. Drug money buys both judges and government officials down there! Remember, there's testimony in the record on that issue which supports the trial judge's decision to exclude the immunity agreements."

Winston glanced at Tim, as if to say, *rescue me*, and then turned back to Forrester. "Now, Judge Forrester, the proof in the record is far from being clear on this. I don't see that the immunity has been fraudulently procured, so our country must honor these agreements on their face as a matter of reciprocity. And that's what I intend to do." His eyes swept back to Tim. "What do you think, Tim?" Winston's face was tense with anticipation.

This was the first move in the plan Tim had formulated with Vicky. It was important that he play his role well here. He steadied his breathing.

"Well, Chief, this is a rather unique case, and perhaps a legal matter of first impression. It's also a close case, but I am prepared to go along with you on this. I vote to reverse the district court and to dismiss the conviction of General Morenta."

Judge Forrester's face billowed into shock and outrage. "Wait a minute! We need to discuss this! There are plenty of facts in the trial record indicating that those immunity agreements are invalid on their face! You two are turning this case on its head! You are ignoring facts in the record!"

Winston suddenly was his usual, courtly self—and he put Forrester in his place. "Now Judge Forrester, there's no need to get so worked up here. You feel one way; Judge Quinn and I feel another. We ought to be able to disagree without being disagreeable. Let's vote. I vote in favor of reversal, and Judge Quinn, how do you vote?"

"Chief, I also vote to reverse this case."

"Good. Judge Forrester, how do you vote, sir?"

"Chief, this is . . ." Forrester was sputtering in outrage. "This vote is peremptory. I don't believe this . . . the district court judge properly refused to admit the immunity agreements on solid grounds. I insist on further debate before we vote."

Winston grinned pleasantly. "Well, I don't believe there is any need for that—the votes are in. Tim, do you think we need further discussion on this case?"

"No, Chief Judge, I'm satisfied," Tim said as amiably as he could manage.

"Well, then, that settles it. The vote is two to reverse and one to affirm. Judge Forrester, are you planning on writing a dissent?"

"I most certainly will, Chief Judge Winston—your position is dead wrong! Reversing this case will let free a dangerous and guilty man." Forrester seemed stunned at the prospect.

"Well, that's your view and you are entitled to it. You go ahead and write your dissent. I assign this case to Judge Quinn to prepare the majority opinion. Is that satisfactory to you, Judge Quinn?"

"Yes. I'll be happy to draft the majority opinion."

"Well then, okay. I guess that concludes today's business. Good afternoon, gentlemen."

The chief judge got up from the table and swept out of the conference room without another word to Tim and Judge Forrester. Tim got to his feet and began assembling his papers. He turned to go.

"Judge Quinn."

Judge Forrester's voice made him look up.

"Tim, I was surprised at you on the *Morenta* case and, I must say, I am quite disappointed," Forrester said, looking directly into Tim's eyes. He shook his head. "You know we should have had more discussion on this. And you're a former prosecutor! I don't understand . . ."

Tim looked down, picked up his papers, and turned to leave, carefully avoiding Forrester's gaze. He knew he had to hurry—he had only fifteen minutes to make his meeting with Vicky. However, Forrester's words stung him.

CHAPTER 20

AT 4:35 P.M., TIM TOOK THE STEPS TWO AT A TIME INSIDE THE Smithsonian Museum of Natural History, a few minutes late for his meeting with Vicky. He passed the elephant on his right as he angled left through the main rotunda toward the corridor of the prehistoric mammals section. School was out and Washington was flooded with tourists, so the museum rotunda was crowded as he made his way to the hallway where he would meet Vicky. He walked quickly down the display-lined, narrow, winding hallway, then saw the shimmer of Vicky's blond hair in front of the skeleton of the woolly mammoth. He stopped and looked behind him, then walked past her twenty or thirty feet. Not a soul around. He came back to Vicky's alcove and joined her, going all the way in and turning his back to the display so that he could hear and see anyone approaching from either direction. He spoke in a low voice, his eyes continually sweeping right and left.

"Okay, Vicky. We just finished hearing the *Morenta* case, and at conference, the vote was two to one—just as we'd hoped. Judge

Forrester, the third judge on the panel, was really angry. He's going to file a strong dissent. Just before I left the conference room, he told me he was both surprised and disappointed by my vote." Tim could not hide the frustration in his voice.

Vicky regarded him with determination. "I'm sorry about Forrester, but your vote on *Morenta* is our ticket to the evidence we need against Winston and Draco—if we play it right. And because the vote is two to one, we've now got a chance to nail Winston. Are you ready to go through with the rest of the plan?"

Tim grimaced. The stratagem he and Vicky had agreed upon last week still made him uncomfortable. First, he had gotten himself assigned to a case that was literally do-or-die for Winston and Draco. Morenta was facing a mandatory sentence of thirty years on his conviction—really a life sentence for a sixty-five-year-old man with colon cancer—and there was no doubt he would put out a murder contract on both Draco and Winston if Draco failed to get the general out of jail. Then Tim had given Winston the second vote he needed to reverse. The third part of the plan lay ahead. Since all votes at conference were not binding, Tim could switch sides when he wrote up the draft decision. This might force Winston to show his hand and possibly incriminate himself and Draco by attempting to pressure or bribe Tim. Tim would have to tape the meeting with Chief Judge Winston to get irrefutable evidence of an attempted bribe or obstruction of justice charge. Vicky would need more evidence for a conviction than one judge's word against another's. Tim thought it was a good plan, but, like all plans, it depended on proper execution.

"Tim, what's the timing for your next move?" Vicky asked.

"I think I'll be ready by next Wednesday to circulate the draft opinion to Winston and also to Forrester showing that I switched my vote—I am now voting *against* Morenta and in effect to keep him in jail."

Vicky frowned. “Won’t they just kill you once you’ve switched your vote?”

Tim smiled grimly. “No, I don’t think so. The risk is too great. If I die before the opinion is released to the public, the rules of the court would require the case to be reargued before three different judges. And Winston certainly doesn’t want that to happen.”

Vicky still looked troubled. Tim could tell that she was pained by the risks he was taking. “How do you see this vote-switch scenario playing out?”

“After Winston becomes a minority of one, he’ll have to try right away either to bribe me or threaten me to get me to switch my vote back. Just so he says it on tape—and I’ve got to get him to implicate Draco too.” It would be tricky to get such an offer on tape, but then they would have a tight federal obstruction of justice or bribery case against Winston. If Winston made incriminating statements implicating Draco, then they would have them both—case closed.

“I want you to be very careful, every second,” Vicky said. Her voice softened and nearly trembled. “Your life means more to me than making this case.”

Tim smiled. “Don’t worry, Vick, I’ll be careful. We’ve got to take this chance to get to the endgame. I’m sure this will work. Winston will believe I want in on the money deal. One thing a crooked judge will always believe is that other judges can be bought too.”

Vicky smiled at this truism. A liar always thinks everybody is lying and a thief’s biggest fear is that someone will steal from him.

“Bill Sharkey has gotten the wire for you,” Vicky said. “Are you still okay with that?”

Tim scowled. “So this is where I become the ‘rat judge.’ Yeah, I’ll wear the wire, but let’s make sure it’s a God damned good one. Winston is shrewd as hell, and if I’m the one that has to bring up the notion of a bribe, he may suspect I'm wired. So we can't have any bulges or static noises. What's the state of the art for the FBI these days?"

"You'll have the 'Ear Link 250', the latest gear from the FBI. The mike is micro-technology and it's concealed inside a chunky gold cuff link. It really is unbelievable. The wireless power pack for it is separate, disguised as a box of matches you can put in your pocket. I've arranged to set up the remote tape recorder in a room we commandeered from the U.S. Probation Office on the third floor of the courthouse. This device is really top of the line and impressive, very dependable."

"Good, good."

"What will you do if Winston doesn't come right out and offer you a bribe?"

"I'll have to hint to him that my vote can be bought. And if he still balks, I may come out and tell him that I have a list of his fixed cases over the last few years and a detailed memo that Judge Rogers left in his desk, a memo that describes everything he suspected or found out about the case-fixing system. And I'll tell him that I want in or else I'll turn the Rogers memo and list over to the Justice Department."

Vicky's eyes popped wide and her mouth opened. She was stunned. "Tim, do you—"

There were voices behind them, and Tim quickly touched his finger to his lips. Vicky froze.

Ten feet behind her, a woman and two pre-school girls appeared in the corridor, talking and laughing as they walked by. Tim and Vicky were silent until they moved some fifty feet farther down the corridor and turned a corner. Tim nodded all-clear to her, and Vicky exploded.

"Jesus, I don't believe this! You have a *memo* from Rogers describing this scheme?"

Tim smiled and shook his head. "Of course not. All I have is the list of cases that I gave you. I'll be bluffing, but Winston won't know that."

He still saw that the tension in Vicky's face had not faded. "What if Winston asks to see the nonexistent memo?"

"I'll tell him he can't see it. I'll tell him what's in it and that he can have a copy when I get my money. I'll also say the original memo will always be in a safe place as insurance for me."

"Do you think you'll be able to bluff him like that? I mean, they've already probably killed three people—what will keep them from killing you too?"

Tim shrugged. "Nothing. Except I'll tell Winston that if I suddenly die, I've arranged for the memo will be sent to the Justice Department and the *Washington Post*."

Vicky sighed, still edgy about the risks involved. She asked Tim to again run through how judges can switch their votes after the conference. Tim told her that it was rare, but sometimes the judge assigned to write the opinion will review the record and come to a different conclusion. He then will send the other two judges a draft opinion that comes to a different result than that reached in the conference. Ordinarily, judges stand behind their vote in conference, but the rules were clear that the votes were only tentative. So in theory, an opinion could swing back and forth several times before the final decision is released.

"How much will you ask for the payoff?"

"Morenta's supposedly worth two billion dollars, right? In Quebec, the fee arrangement I heard was five million retainer, with a five million bonus. So would two hundred thousand be a credible amount they won't haggle over? What do you think?" Tim asked Vicky.

"It's good. Not too little for you to sell your vote, but not too greedy. Now what's the timing on this again? When will you confront Winston?"

"I'll review my notes over the weekend and then start to write up the draft opinion Monday. By Wednesday I should have a good draft to circulate to Winston and Forrester. I expect Winston will blow up immediately and have me down in his office for a 'come to Jesus' meeting—and that's when I'll try to trap him, or at least set the trap."

"I'd better have the FBI technical people come over to my office now and set you up with the Ear Link apparatus."

"Okay, let's roll." Tim was pumped and ready for the last phase; he had set his reservations aside.

Vicky called Sharkey on her cell phone and Sharkey promised to have the tech team in Vicky's office in ten minutes.

"All right, Ms. prosecutor. You go first and I'll see you over there in ten minutes."

The next Monday, Tim reviewed his notes and the case file from the *Morenta* case oral argument once again and started working on his draft opinion, his bombshell to the chief judge. By Tuesday morning, he was satisfied with it and gave it to his law clerk Dorothy to add some case citations Tim thought necessary. Tim reminded the clerk not to mention to anyone, not even the other two law clerks in chambers, that he was switching his vote. Dorothy, excited to be selected to work on such an important opinion, worked through the lunch hour, and by the end of the day she gave Tim the finished product. Tim reviewed the opinion and smiled as he read. It had become a well-crafted, resounding defeat for Morenta. At six-thirty P.M., Tim threw the draft opinion into his briefcase and headed for his car in the underground parking lot. The chief judge would receive a tremendous shock tomorrow.

After dinner that night, Tim had a long talk with Katy. As he briefed her on what he was doing, her face grew strained and angry. Tim was intentionally wrecking his judicial career, she warned him. "No judge is going to trust you after this. After you've been an undercover informant for the FBI."

Tim spread his hands palms upward before her. "Honey, I have to pursue this. I couldn't live with myself if I didn't go through with this."

"Can't that Vicky person find someone else to do her dirty work for her?" Katy demanded.

Tim tensed. Did Katy suspect something was going on between him and Vicky? All he told Katy was that he had known Vicky slightly at Columbia Law. But he knew that all women have a built-in radar system to seek out relationships between their men and other women, and Katy's radar was keener than most. Katy didn't pursue the matter, but as they went to bed that night she was both frosty and resigned. Tim slept fitfully. Tomorrow was the day of the big game. He would either break this case wide open or possibly destroy himself and his career.

The next morning, his new gold cuff links feeling heavy at his wrists, he had Loretta hand-carry copies of the draft *Morenta* opinion to the chambers of Chief Judge Winston and Judge Forrester. He hadn't finished his first cup of coffee before Winston was on the phone.

"Judge Quinn, I just read the draft opinion in the *Morenta* case. I don't understand what the hell is going on! Why did you change your conference vote?" The chief 's voice was high, demanding, cold.

Tim took a deep breath. "Well, Chief Judge, I reviewed the record and the briefs, and I had some second thoughts. I eventually decided to change my vote from reversing the case to affirming it. Judge

Forrester has already called me and said he's very pleased with the switch and is ready to sign up for my draft opinion as it is now written."

The additional lie about Forrester would put more pressure on Winston. There was a long, uncomfortable silence on the telephone. Then: "Tim boy, I need to talk to you about that case right away," Winston said, his tone strained and urgent. "Can you come to my chambers?"

"Well, I'm in the middle of something right now," Tim lied, then added, "I could come over in half an hour. How would that be?"

"That will be fine, Judge Quinn," the chief said icily. "I'll be expecting you in a half hour."

It sounded to Tim as if Winston slammed down the phone, and he frowned. Well, he had known this was coming and that it was going to be a tough confrontation. He stood up and stretched. Winston was angry, very angry. Tim had anticipated that reaction, and moreover he wanted it. He would use Winston's anger to his own advantage as much as possible. The previous night, he had game-planned the whole showdown, and he knew what he would say and do. He had decided to wait at least a half hour after Winston's inevitable call before going to see him. He had correctly anticipated that Winston would not come to see him, but rather would summon Tim to the chief judge's own turf. Tim wanted to make an angry man angrier, because he knew that angry men make mistakes. Now the tough part for Tim was to calm himself before the meeting. In order to succeed today, he had to be cool, collected, and focused.

He turned his desk radio on, and soft classical music filled the room. Then he picked up his phone and dialed Vicky's beeper. Once the voice message came on, he punched in a coded number. This number would inform Vicky and the FBI agents in the listening room on the third floor of the courthouse that Winston had called and that they should start monitoring transmissions from the Ear Link device. That done, he sat down on his sofa and paged through a *Time* magazine. With just a few minutes left in the half hour, he stood, checked his cuff link with the tiny mike, then took the Ear Link wireless relay box out of his pocket and activated it as he had been instructed. He picked up the *Morenta* case file from his desk and headed for the door. With any luck, Winston would be in a killer rage by now.

When he entered the chief judge's chambers, the head secretary immediately motioned him into the chief 's inner office.

Tim appeared in the doorway. "You wanted to see me, Chief Judge?"

Winston walked past him in silence and shut the door behind him. As he came back, he looked up into Tim's eyes, and his face was red with anger. He took a chair and waved Tim to another directly facing his.

"Sit down, Judge Quinn. Now . . ."

Winston's neck veins were standing out, and his hands trembled ever so slightly as he stroked his chin with the fingers of his right hand. Then he turned to face Tim. His voice was low and quiet. "Why . . . why did you change your vote on the *Morenta* case, Tim?"

"Well, like I said, Chief, I rethought my position, and now I think Morenta's conviction should be affirmed. The record shows that immunity agreement really is bogus."

"We went all through that at conference, Tim, and you sided with me . . ."

"I know, I know."

Winton stared at him. "Is . . . is there something else going on here, Tim?"

Tim held Winston's stare, but kept his voice casual. "Chief, what difference does this case make to you? Why is the *Morenta* case so important to you?"

Winston sat back in his chair and smiled. *Here comes the charm,* Tim thought.

"Tim, listen," Winston began. "You're a new judge here, and a smart one. I've always liked you and thought you have a lot of promise as a judge. But on cases like this, a judge has to be able to see the big picture, to be able to make decisions that sometimes affect our nation's relations with other nations." Winston sounded as if he was instructing a slightly slow student at one of his legal seminars. "This case is a big one—and really, at its core, just about diplomatic reciprocity. Basically our country has to accept as valid these legal documents from other countries, or they won't accept ours! It is as simple as that." Winston shrugged. "Christ, unless we let Morenta go, our diplomats will face a tough time in Colombia." He smiled, more widely this time. "Now why don't you just follow my lead on this one? Hell, my Rhodes thesis at Oxford was about reciprocity between nations, so trust me on this one, Tim. The right decision for this court is to let Morenta go. Our country wins and our court helps out the State Department on a very politically sensitive case."

Tim was ready with his retort. "Chief, the State Department never had the balls to put an affidavit in the record of this case. So there is no official State Department position in this case. Furthermore, the record shows repeatedly hints that the immunity agreement was bought with drug money."

"Damn it, Judge Quinn, do I have to spell it out? The president called me on this case. He wants us to let the general go back to Colombia."

"Bullshit, Harry. Don't give me that president-secret-call shit. The president's Justice Department brought this case. Do you think that the U.S. attorney would have arrested Morenta without White House approval?"

Winston's face visibly tightened and reddened even more.

Without saying a word, he got up and walked to one of his windows that overlooked Constitution Avenue. He stared out for twenty seconds and then, without turning, spoke in a low voice.

"Tim, we go back a long way. You handled my divorce, and we've been friends ever since. You've been to my home for dinner, and I've eaten in your home with you and Katy. I even know your children."

He turned and faced Tim.

"And we've been more than friends, Tim. I've helped you over the years. Hell, if it weren't for me, you wouldn't be a judge on this court!" His face abruptly filled with fury. "I made you a judge and you owe me!" Then he smiled tightly. "Now I understand your legal position on this case, and I respect it. But this case is very important to me, so I am now asking you as a favor to go back to your chambers and rewrite this opinion so that it comes out the way we initially decided it in conference. I am calling in a chit on this one, and I expect you to deliver."

Tim stood up and looked Winston squarely in the eye.

"Harry, I'm disappointed that you would ask me to change my vote on a case based on our friendship. That's a separate matter. You're right, I do owe you, and I am grateful for all you have done to help me. But I'm not going to change my vote on this case just because we're friends."

Winston glared at him. "What if I threatened to tell Katy about your little affair?"

The threat struck Tim like a lightning bolt. His brain almost seized up. He had foolishly not anticipated this—he realized he had blocked out the fact that he had told Winston about his secret affair with Vicky Hauser when he sought the chief's advice during the FBI background check before his Senate confirmation. *God, what a nightmare! And I'm wearing an FBI wire*. Christ, thank God he never mentioned Vicky's name. Tim steeled himself and lied as calmly as he could. "Katy already knows. It surfaced during the Senate investigation and I told her then."

Winston's shoulders sagged. It looked as if the chief believed him, and Tim silently exhaled in relief. Winston walked slowly to the sofa and sat down heavily. Without a word, he leaned forward and covered his face with his hands. Visions of Quebec flashed through Tim's mind; he knew what the chief judge was thinking. Draco's warnings about the deadly Colombians were haunting Winston. Tim could only guess how desperate Winston was right now. The chief would probably do anything to get Tim to change his mind. This was no longer just about money. For Winston, the vote had become a matter of survival.

A long minute of silence passed. Finally, Winston stood up and returned to the chair facing Tim's. As he sat, he began to speak again, this time in a soft voice tinged with defeat. "Tim, I can't tell you the reason, but this decision has to go my way this time. I am begging you. Please give me your vote. I will do anything for your vote on this one case. I will give you anything. Tell me what I can do for you, please."

Tim paused as if to consider this for a moment. "Well, if it really means that much to you, there may be a way for us to change the opinion back and release Morenta."

"What do you mean?" There was hope in his voice.

Tim met Winston's eyes again. "This may surprise you, but there have been some rumors in the courthouse that your Yale Law School roommate Draco wins a lot of big money cases in this court that he shouldn't win, and that you orchestrate these wins for him."

Tim thought he saw Winston flinch.

"I . . . I don't know what you're talking about."

"Come on, Harry. When I first moved into my chambers, Judge Rogers's old chambers, I found an interesting set of papers inside an envelope that was taped to the bottom of one of the drawers in Rogers's desk. When I opened it and read it, I found that it was a very detailed memo together with an attached list of cases heard by this court over the last two years. Nine cases were highlighted, all involving big money." Winton made no move and betrayed no expression. "Leo Draco, according to Judge Rogers, was the attorney whose firm represented one of the parties in all nine cases. Remarkably enough, Chief, he won seven of them. In all seven of these cases, and I have reviewed them in detail after reading the memo, Draco's clients should have been losers, not winners."

Winston narrowed his eyes, but remained silent. Tim continued in a low but firm voice. "The Judge Rogers memo went on to summarize in detail the case-fixing scheme you're running in this court with Draco's law firm and the supportive, deciding votes that you got from Judges Bowen, Janoff, and Franklin."

Tim kept his voice conversational. "The memo goes on to describe special favors you have given to your little 'majority,' like the great low-interest loan to Bowen, and the no-show, high-paying teaching jobs for Franklin and Janoff, and even the special assist you gave Janoff 's son to get him into Hobbes College . . . with a nice financial package." Tim raised his eyebrows in a gesture of frankness. "To me, it looks like you've done very well in arranging a cooperative majority on this court that can, on call, serve your personal interests, and certainly those of Mr. Draco. Rogers saw it, and now I see it." Tim leaned forward in his chair. "But the bottom line is, maybe you can do something for me that would get you my vote on the *Morenta* case."

Winston's mouth had fallen half-open. His color changed from red to white as the blood drained from his head. He closed his mouth and stared at Quinn silently, thinking very hard. Slowly he stood and spoke in a loud, deliberate, but unnatural voice. "Judge Quinn, that is a crazy and false idea!"

Then, without another word, Chief Judge Winston crossed the room to his desk, where he pressed a button on what appeared to be a tiny radio, one small enough to fit into a suit pocket. An immediate high-pitched hum filled the room. Quinn was perplexed at first. Then, thanks to his years in the intelligence community, he realized what was happening, but he stalled for time to react by feigning ignorance.

"Harry, what's going on? What's that sound?"

Winston smiled his Cheshire cat smile, his confidence somewhat restored. "Son, I didn't serve four years as chairman of the Technology Committee of the Judicial Conference for nothing! That little device that looks like a radio is really a white-noise producer."

"What is white noise?" Tim asked. He already knew the answer—and his chances of getting evidence on Winston were plummeting. *God damn, this ruins everything!*

"Well, Tim, let's just say that if either one of us is wearing some kind of recording device, a tape recorder of some sort, after I press that button, white noise fills this room. Why, with that device on, no tape recorder in the world can pick up anything either one of us says, or anything else, for that matter. It's sort of a frequency blocker for human voices—like a reverse dog whistle we humans can't hear, but that cancels out our voice frequency on any recording device."

"You don't think I'm wearing a tape recorder, do you?"

"Now it doesn't matter whether you are or you are not. No tape recorder would work anyway with the white noise running." Winston gave him a tight grin. "I'm a careful man, a belt-and-suspenders man. Now then, what is this you are saying about how I am, what, fixing cases? That's the craziest thing I ever heard!"

"Let's not play games," Tim shot back. "I've read those nine cases myself, and there is no question but that you threw seven of them, you and your colleague of the moment, either Franklin,

Bowen, or Janoff." Tim was trying to pile it on, to regain some momentum. "I've seen how you do that by getting advance notice of how a judge will rule. I even went along with you—pretending to give you my vote on the *Morenta* case before oral argument. I know what's going on. And I figure you and Draco are going to get some very good money for helping our friend General Morenta," Tim concluded.

"You're just bluffing. And I'm beginning to get angry. You've got some goddamn nerve, coming into my chambers and accusing me!"

"Oh, I'm bluffing? Okay, look at this."

Tim stood up and strode to a bookcase, pulling out a bound volume of the *Federal Reporter 3rd* that recorded this court's most recent cases. He quickly flipped through the pages and found the case he wanted, then turned and showed it to Winston.

"There, Chief, *United States v. Jameson*, that's one of the cases you fixed, a majority of you and Judge Janoff. The attorney representing the appellant Jameson was Leo Draco himself. Surprised? If you take this decision to ten law professors, all ten will say it was decided wrong, that there *was* adequate legal probable cause for the search warrant you and Janoff threw out. Read the dissent by Senior Judge Harley; he shows how you and Janoff reached a completely wrong decision in that case. The bottom line is that you're throwing cases here, Harry, and you're throwing them for Draco's law firm. Judge Rogers knew about it, and now I know about it—and I want some money for my vote on *Morenta*."

Winston angrily thrust the book away. But Tim could see that this attack had knocked the wind out of him. "What have you got in mind?" Winston asked warily.

Tim fervently hoped that this exchange was being intelligibly taped, but even if it wasn't he had to plunge ahead; he had gone too far into the plan not to complete it, and maybe there was some other way he would be able to nail Harry based on what he was about to do now.

"Well, I know you're a fair and generous man," Tim began. "I expect you'll treat me right. Morenta is a multi-billionaire, and I'm sure he will pay dearly to get out of prison and back home to Colombia. I expect you and Draco will get a figure in the millions, but I'm not greedy. Let's just say you give me two hundred thousand dollars and the *Morenta* decision will come out the way you want."

Winston studied Tim for a few seconds, then rubbed his face. "Well, your accusations and this whole turn of events have taken me by surprise. Things are moving fast, here, I . . . I will have to think about things."

Tim took a step closer to the other man, deliberately crowding him . . . pushing him. "Come on, just pay me the money and you've got what you want. By the way, remember I have that Rogers memo, which really reveals the whole scheme in great detail. And if anything happens to me, copies are ready to go to Justice and to the *Washington Post.* That's just an insurance policy for my continued excellent state of health." Tim smiled.

"Tim, you are a real surprise! I had no idea about this side of you when I took you into this court!" Winston exclaimed. "You were my friend, and now you're standing here blackmailing me!"

Tim pressed on. "It's simple: Either pay me or lose the *Morenta* case. The choice is yours."

"I . . . I don't know what to say . . . Let me think for a minute . . ."

Winston stood and walked behind his desk, then sat in his black leather judge's chair. He swiveled to one side and looked up into the corner of the wall and the ceiling. He was still and silent for a long moment. Eventually, he looked back down and slowly rotated his chair until he faced Tim. First he looked stern, and then a crafty smile slowly spread across his face. Winston looked oddly contented. The hum from the white-noise transmitter was still background music to the meeting. Then he opened his mouth.

"Tim, you are a very clever and dangerous man. Welcome to my little *majority*."

Tim smiled in relief. Apparently, he had won with a very long shot. Then Harry leaned forward and spoke in a hushed voice. "Now on this money thing, Tim, I will have to talk to someone, and I will let you know. Meanwhile, why don't you rewrite that opinion to favor of General Morenta?"

"Chief Judge, this is strictly business to me. When I get the money, I will withdraw this draft opinion and release a new one, which will allow Morenta's release. I'll start the rewrite tomorrow to show my good faith."

Winston managed a small grin and nodded.

Tim left Winston's chambers a shaken man. The chief judge had come close to winning when he brought up Tim's affair with Vicky. Tim had pulled off the biggest bluff of his life by saying Katy knew. As he walked back to his chambers, he played out scenarios of how Katy might find out about his adultery. When he arrived at his chambers, Vicky and Bill were waiting for him. They must have run up from the third floor, Tim guessed. He led them into his inner office and closed his door.

"How did I do, guys?"

Both looked glum, and Sharkey answered. "We didn't get anything incriminating on Winston. Listen."

Sharkey flipped on a small tape recorder. Sure enough, as Tim listened, the tape turned out to have only recorded the first half of the Winston-Quinn conversation. None of Winston's words on tape were incriminating in any way. Halfway through the tape, all audible conversation ended, and the only noise recorded was a high-pitched hum. After Tim explained that Winston had turned on the white-noise device, Sharkey said he would give the tape to the FBI lab, but Tim knew it didn't look good. He had seen the results of such devices before. There was no way a conversation could be recorded within twenty feet of such a device. And sure enough, within two hours the FBI lab confirmed that from the point where the hum started, there was nothing else audible recorded on the tape. Just the hum.

CHAPTER 21

VICKY'S JUSTICE DEPARTMENT PHONE RANG. A NAMELESS FBI agent spoke. "Ms. Hauser, this is listening post Blue. There has been an interesting intercept on our wiretap. It appears to be a conversation between both targets. I'll start a chain of custody on the original tape and make a copy to be sent over to you right away."

"Thanks. I'll be waiting." Vicky checked her wiretap operation sheet, which showed the location of the three active FBI listening posts for this operation. LP Blue was based in a van set up outside of the federal courthouse, targeting calls to and from Chief Judge Winston's chambers.

Vicky clicked the call off, then punched in Bill Sharkey's number at the FBI's office across Pennsylvania Avenue. "Bill, we've got an intercept. They're sending me the tape—why don't you come over to my office and we'll listen to it together?"

"I'll be right over. Are you going to have Judge Quinn come over too?"

"Good idea," Vicky said. "He is an insider on this, and he may be able to explain the intercept."

One hour later, Sharkey turned the tape machine on, and he and Tim and Vicky all listened intently to the wiretap intercept of the conversation between Winston and Draco. The FBI trace of the call had identified the incoming call as a cell phone number registered in Draco's name. Winston's Southern accent was unmistakable. So was Leo Draco's brisk drone.

"Leo? Where the hell are you?" Winston began. "And why didn't you answer your God damn beeper sooner?"

"Calm down, Harry. I forgot to turn it on until just fifteen minutes ago. I'm on my yacht in the Chesapeake Bay with some important clients. So what's the emergency? By the way, I'm on a cell phone, so don't be too specific."

"I understand," Winston said. "Here's the emergency. We've got some problems with our new member. Big problems. We have got to meet as soon as possible."

"Shit. I had a feeling that guy was going to cause problems! Should I contact that security firm in London to take care of him?"

Tim and Vicky exchanged glances.

"No, Leo. Don't do *anything* before our meeting! Don't call London! But make no mistake about it, this is a true emergency—we must meet *soon!* When can you get back here?"

"Look, I'm down here with the CEO of a big meat processing corporation. His general counsel and his current outside counsel are here also. They're on a break in the middle of a long trial that they think they're almost certainly going to lose. The CEO obviously doesn't like the situation so he just contacted me and is paying me some big money to tell the trial team how to build some appealable errors into the trial before it ends."

Tim scowled at this, one of Draco's smaller attempts to grease the wheels of justice.

"They've already paid me a big retainer for this meeting, and we'll be going late into this evening. In fact, we'll be spending the night on the boat—all four staterooms are full. Can't this wait?"

"No, it can't wait." The chief judge now sounded more urgent than angry. "We are in a very high-risk situation. We have to meet!"

"All right! I'll be bringing the yacht up the Potomac tomorrow for the Fourth of July celebration on Friday. I'm going to host a party again this year to watch the fireworks display. We can meet tomorrow, late afternoon or early evening—depends on when we dock. You just tell me where and when."

"Okay, let's do this. We'll meet in the Hirschorn Sculpture Garden, tomorrow, six P.M. Can you make it?"

"Sure, I'll make it. We meet tomorrow at the Hirschorn Sculpture Garden, six o'clock. I'll be there."

"And as a precaution, the next time you call me, go ashore and use a fucking pay phone!" Winston said and hung up.

Now that the tape ended, Sharkey reached over and turned off the recorder. Tim looked at Vicky, who was taking furious notes, and then at Sharkey. "What was the time of this call?" he asked.

"Three-fifteen this afternoon," Sharkey replied.

"Well, that was after my confrontation with Winston this morning. Winston seems to have taken the bait and involved Draco. This proves our theory that Winston's in bed with Draco on this, but it doesn't give us any incriminating evidence. Maybe we can get some evidence at his meeting with Draco. I'm sure topic A will be me and my two-hundred-thousand-dollar bribe."

Vicky was excited. "Judge, you seem to have gotten us inside the conspiracy. But you've got to remember whom we're dealing with here. This meeting could also be to decide where and when they're going to kill you. That reference to a security company in London means they've got a hit man just a telephone call away. Probably the same people who murdered Mrs. Winston."

"Right," said Sharkey. "A professional hit from outside the country. That might explain the untraceable fingerprints from the gas cap on the hit car. Our fingerprint database covers just U.S. files, not English files."

"I just don't want to put Judge Quinn in further jeopardy," Vicky said. She glanced at Tim, then back at Sharkey.

Tim wasn't shaken by Draco's willingness to take him out. "Yeah, but they're not stupid enough to kill me before the *Morenta* opinion is out. Bill, at this meeting tomorrow—it's vital that the FBI get complete surveillance at the meeting to record everything they say. No white-noise machines, no inaudible whispers. Can you do it?"

Sharkey nodded. "Don't worry, Judge, I'll lay on some good coverage for that meeting at the Hirschorn."

"Like what?" Vicky asked.

"First of all, I know the place," Sharkey said. "It's an outdoor two-level garden next to the Hirschorn Museum on the Mall. But I have to check out the meeting site personally before I give you our exact coverage plan. I'll go over there right now with a couple of people from the tech division, see what we'll need."

"Sounds good to me," Tim said. "Bill, could I get a duplicate copy of that tape right away? I want to play it for a friend of mine in the intelligence community, maybe he could offer some suggestions . . ."

Vicky winced. "Whoa! Your Honor, I don't mind having Bill give you a duplicate—after all, you're the one most at risk right now. But please, no outside help! Why don't we just leave it to the FBI? They're very, very good. Please don't interfere with this investigation by dragging in some intelligence agency that could only screw this up."

Vicky's jaw was set, but Tim would not back down. "Listen, Ms. Hauser, you're in charge of this investigation, and I will not interfere with it. But I do insist that I get a copy of the tape, and that you understand I'm going to share it with a high-level intelligence agent. He won't interfere, but he may be able to help us with some suggestions."

Vicky glared at him, then sighed. "All right. Bill, get Judge Quinn a copy right away, and then make sure the FBI chain-of-custody record for the original tape shows that Judge Quinn received a copy of this working duplicate per my authorization."

Tim thanked Vicky but then asked, "Mind if I tag along with Bill to see the setup for the surveillance?"

Vicky rolled her eyes upward and nodded. "Okay, you earned the right."

Agent Bill Sharkey, Judge Quinn, and two FBI technicians walked around the Hirschorn Sculpture Garden, on the Mall side of the museum, a lushly planted area below ground level but open to the sky. Large sculptures were scattered on manicured patches of lawn intersected by winding gravel paths. The garden was divided into somewhat of a maze with ten-foot walls, affording multiple places where people could meet in relative privacy.

Tim could tell by the FBI agent's severe expression that Sharkey felt under pressure. This meeting could be the make-or-break factor for the criminal case against Winston and Draco. This surveillance operation needed to produce incriminating statements between these two, some direct evidence that Vicky could take into a court of law to support all the circumstantial evidence they had gathered about the case-fixing conspiracy. But obtaining that evidence was going to be extremely problematic in this environment. The garden was a difficult surveillance site, with two hundred square feet of nooks and crannies, half of it at street level and half below.

Knowing that any battlefield is controlled by the high ground, Tim looked up to see if there was a prominent overlook area to base the surveillance. Then he saw it. A long concrete balcony near the top of the Hirschorn Museum itself. It faced the garden from a height of fifty feet—a perfect lookout for the meeting. Tim casually pointed this out to Bill, who immediately saw the advantages of the position. "Thanks, Judge. That looks like the perfect crow's nest, doesn't it?" He called both techies over and told them to check out the balcony as a possible control center for the operation and also as a platform for a closed-circuit TV camera and some directional microphones.

Ten minutes later, as Tim and Bill explored the garden's various rendezvous sites, the techies came out of the museum's north door and found them. "The balcony is perfect," said the lead techie, whose name was Gordon. "We'll mount our major equipment up there. The elevation is nice—great view. I'll get some construction apparatus up there by tomorrow morning to hide the gear. We'll make it look like the balcony is under repair. Now let's go over this again. What specific coverage will you need?"

"We need total audio and visual coverage of two guys meeting in this garden, tomorrow evening around six o'clock," Sharkey told them. "We don't know where specifically, just somewhere inside the garden, so we've got to have flexible coverage."

Gordon frowned. "Okay, well, this is a tough area, because it's open air and there are a lot of walls creating dead spots for fixed coverage. And to compound the problem, it may be crowded because this is the Fourth of July weekend. So we'll probably use three directional microphones and video cameras with remote controls. We'll have to put two of the video packages into trees, and we'll use a big MEN AT WORK canopy on that balcony to conceal the third surveillance package and the control module. I assume that's where you'll run the show from, right?"

"Right. I'll be up there."

"Okay. But Agent Sharkey," Gordon went on, "there are some

areas I don't like at all. Like that little boxed-off section on the northwest corner of the garden. Those walls have to be ten or so feet high, and there's only one way in, so I think one of our modules has to be in a tree covering that. Then the one on the balcony will cover the low area by the reflecting pool, but they won't meet there."

"Why not?" Tim asked.

The techie shrugged. "It's too open and not much privacy, and there will probably be loads of tourists there near the pool, a natural focal point of the garden. I'd bet money on it."

Bill still looked concerned. "Yeah, but there are other areas, like that long ramp down from the Mall, and under those trees at the edge of the garden on the northeast side. How can you get coverage there?"

"Well, that's where we'll put the third package. Plus, we'll have two roving crews that will have cameras and microphones inside tote bags or briefcases, and then we'll have a lip reader from the local college for the deaf who may be able to pick up conversation and dictate it into a recorder."

Tim was impressed. He glanced over at Sharkey, who had a small smile on his face. "Okay, you guys sound like you've got a pretty thorough coverage plan," he said. "I like it. Let's make sure that the entire surveillance team is in my office at the Bureau for a final briefing at three P.M."

Tim kept silent but was studying the area intently and made notes in a small notebook.

"Roger that, we'll be there," Gordon said. "Just for your info, on the fixed camera packages, it's best for us to install these things when no one's around, so we'll probably get over here tonight around two A.M. to do that. We should have this place wired and ready to roll before dawn. One last thing—my team needs to get several photos of the two subjects well ahead of time, so everybody knows the targets. Can you take care of that for us?"

"Absolutely," Sharkey replied. "Come to my office with me and I'll give you whatever photos you need right now."

Tim left as the FBI people made their final technical plans. For the first time since Winston had flipped the switch on his white-noise machine, he felt hopeful that Vicky was right and that they would nail Winston and Draco—ideally before they came after him or his family.

At six-thirty A.M. on Thursday, July 3, dawn was just breaking as Tim's silver Land Rover entered the huge expanse of concrete that made up the South Parking Lot at the Pentagon. It was already about a quarter full. Tim stayed on the outer-perimeter road of the lot, and drove to the southernmost end, then backed into a space with his rear bumper touching the shrubs that edged the parking lot. He waited silently, watching the steady stream of cars pour into the lot before him. The closest cars were still more than a hundred yards away, but he knew that, within an hour or so, the entire lot would be full. As the cars filled in the spaces, a black Crown Victoria broke the pattern and kept coming his way. As it approached, he counted four short antennas on the top and trunk. The big car flashed its headlights twice as it approached Tim's SUV, then pulled into the space next to him. As Tim waited, the driver's door of the Crown Vic opened, and a tall, lean man with a "high-and-tight" marine haircut stepped out. Tim opened his door and got out. "Hello, Tony," he said.

Tony said nothing as he opened his arms. The two men hugged hard then broke away.

"Damn, it's good to see you again, Tim," he said. "I must say that after so long, I was really surprised to get your call."

"I know. This is important, Tony, and I know this is a big favor. Thanks for coming."

"Hey, you've been there for me before. Besides, this is an interesting situation, a challenge."

"Thanks, Tony. This means a lot to me."

"Tim, did you tell anybody where you were going today?"

"I told my chambers that I would be unavailable to anybody. Only Katy knows I'm going somewhere with you."

"Does she know where we're going?"

"No, and she knew better than to ask."

"Good. Let's get started. Just one thing first." He reached inside the Crown Vic, then came back and handed Tim a five-by-eight-inch blue plastic placard. It was an official Pentagon parking permit.

"Damn, you spooks cover all the bases, don't you?"

"Just figured you might not want your car towed while we're on our little field trip. Security is pretty tight around the Pentagon these days. Just put it on your dashboard, and then we'll go."

They drove north up the George Washington Parkway, then turned onto U.S. 495, the Washington Beltway, and crossed the Potomac River, into Maryland. After a few miles, they took the main branch to the left onto Interstate 270 north and entered the Maryland countryside. Within half an hour, they were driving through the rolling Catoctin Mountains. Soon, they turned onto a state highway, and then passed the U.S. Army post, Fort Ritchie. They followed signs for Camp David as the mountain road grew steeper and the woods grew thicker. They took the second Camp David exit, and followed a narrow, winding road deeper into the forest. Suddenly, they entered a clearing, and stopped at a concrete guardhouse protecting a closed gate. As far as Tim could see in either direction, there was a double chain-link fence topped with razor wire. A black steel plate ten feet wide and an inch thick rose some three feet vertically out of the roadway to block the road through the gate.

Two armed marine guards approached the car as Tony pulled out his identification and rolled down the window. Tim handed his federal judge ID credentials to Tony, who showed both to one of the guards. After the marine had checked both their names off the list on his clipboard, he saluted Tony. Then he asked him to pop the trunk. Meanwhile, the other marine used a long pole with a small mirror on the end to examine the undercarriage of their sedan. Once the Crown Vic had been inspected to the satisfaction of the marines, one of them disappeared into the guardhouse. Soon the steel plate whirred softly as it sank into its sheath in the roadway, the gate swung open, and Tony proceeded slowly forward into the compound. To their right, a large antenna farm and several huge satellite dishes were enclosed by another chain-link fence with razor wire on top. They drove on through the woods.

Today's meeting between Winston and Draco was extremely important, and Tim was determined to give Vicky some further backup. He thought of the old saying—there are three kinds of people in the world. Those who make things happen, those who watch things happen, and those who wonder what happened. Tim Quinn was determined to be in the first category.

It was twenty minutes before two in the afternoon of July 3. Vicky was finishing a carryout salad at her desk, getting mentally ready for the crucial meeting that evening at six o'clock. She managed her nervousness by planning her supervision of the FBI surveillance station. So many things could go wrong. The Winston-Draco case was at a crucial stage.

Sharkey telephoned. "I just got two calls," he told her. "The first was from the courthouse. An agent just told me that the chief judge has exited the south entrance of the courthouse and is headed for the Mall on foot. Our agent is following him. The second call was from the surveillance team staking out Draco's boat slip at the marina. They reported that his yacht arrived half an hour ago. Draco and two men in suits, who looked like bodyguards, just got off and were picked up by a black Lincoln Town Car. Vicky, I'm pretty sure the meeting is going down now, four hours early. Maybe they changed the time last night."

Vicky was stunned. "God damn it! Bill, can you get the roving teams over there right now?"

"I've already called and they're on the way. All except the lip reader—they're scrambling to get her over there. But don't worry. We're covered. The fixed camera packages in the trees and on the balcony have been ready since dawn."

"Jesus, Bill, I hope we can make it." Vicky was already gathering her notebook and purse.

"So do I, and we still don't know if this is a false alarm or not, but we're hustling to get full surveillance up."

"Okay, I'll meet you in the control section at the Hirschorn balcony ASAP."

The black Lincoln smoothly rolled to a stop at the curb of the street on the eastern side of the Hirschorn Museum. Two tall, bulky men in dark blue suits got out. Each had short, military-looking haircuts, and as they exited, they both pulled flesh-colored elastic coils tipped by ear plugs out of their collars and placed them securely in their ears. They looked exactly like government security agents, right down to the official-looking gold pins they both wore in their suit lapel buttonholes. Then the silver-haired Draco alighted from the Town Car, wearing an elegantly tailored dark suit and carrying a thin briefcase. He was as tall as his bodyguards, but thinner, and with his erect patrician profile, he could easily have been selected by a Hollywood casting agent to play a secretary of state or an ambassador. His quick, purposeful walk only added to his aura. The two big bodyguards preceded him, clearing a path through pedestrians on the Mall. One of the roving FBI teams, posing as husband-and-wife tourists, had just arrived on station. They recognized Draco, and swung into line fifty feet behind him.

The Draco entourage walked north a few hundred feet, then turned west and entered the sculpture garden, walking down a long ramp. As they reached the bottom, they turned to the left and descended a narrow set of concrete stairs to the lowest level of the sculpture garden, a large area with a thirty-foot-long rectangular reflecting pool in the center and twelve-foot-high masonry walls. Harry Winston was sitting on a bench beside the pool with his back to a wall. One of Draco's bodyguards stopped at the top of the stairs, let Draco pass, then turned around, spread his feet, and crossed his arms in front of his chest, effectively blocking access to the stairs.

There were only five tourists in this lower section of the garden, and the second Draco bodyguard walked down the stairs in front of Draco and politely asked these tourists to leave. Apparently assuming that the security man was an official government agent, all five tourists obediently ascended the other mirroring set of stairs on the opposite side of the reflecting pool. Then the Draco security man stood guard at the top of this second set of stairs. Draco and Winston now had the lower level of the garden to themselves. The two security men had sealed off their meeting place.

An FBI team posing as a tourist couple tried to follow Draco down the steps. The burly bodyguard guarding the top of the stairs politely but firmly blocked their passage. "I'm sorry, sir, ma'am, but this area will be off-limits for a few minutes. Please enjoy the rest of the garden."

"But we want to see the reflecting pool . . ."

"I'm sorry, I'm afraid this area is temporarily off-limits to visitors, but it will only be for a few minutes. Please, the rest of the garden is lovely, we will let you in here in just a short time." The security man gave them a hard smile.

The team backed off, not wanting to tip their hand to Draco and Winston. The female agent moved only a short distance away to where the video camera and microphone in her tote bag could pick up a long-distance shot of the meeting. They stood quietly in front of a stone sculpture, pretending to study it, while the woman tried to keep the tote bag pointed just so to catch images of the meeting as it began.

From the control center on the balcony, the directional microphones were picking up sounds of the meeting. As Draco sat down on the wrought-iron bench next to the chief judge, Winston spoke first.

"Hello, Leo."

The closed-circuit TV on the balcony was the only camera that had a direct shot of the two men meeting in the lower-level garden. Vicky and Sharkey had joined the techies running the control center and both clearly saw on the TV monitors the action of Draco turning to Winston and putting his finger over his lips in a signal for silence. Then Draco opened his slim leather briefcase, and pulled out a light gray pad of paper. He took a pen out of his shirt pocket and began to write. After he had finished a few lines, he passed the pad to Winston.

Winston frowned, shaking his head, and said, "Leo. I can't read it. I don't have my glasses."

Leo replied, "Don't worry. I'll write big," and took the pad back to write again.

Vicky was still breathing hard as she watched two monitors. Both showed Draco and Winston. One view from the balcony was a straight-on shot; the other, from an angle, was from the tote bag of the closest roving team. Vicky was confused.

"What's going on? Where's the audio? Why can't we hear them speak?"

Bill looked up at her. His face was glum as he explained.

"We've got a great picture from the surveillance package on the balcony, and one of our roving teams has a good distance shot. But the pictures are all we've got—because they're not talking."

"What?"

"They're not talking. Beyond what you heard, they haven't said a word. They're writing things down on a pad of paper and passing it back and forth." He shook his head. "We can't see what they're writing. There's no zoom on the camera that's covering that spot; besides the angle's no good to see the face of the pad. Damn slick, these two! This meeting is going to all be on a pad of paper. There's nothing we can do.'

"Jesus H. Christ!" Vicky swore to no one in particular. Then she had an idea and announced, "Not if I can help it!"

She pulled her cell phone out of her purse and called the U.S. attorney for the District of Columbia. When he came on the line, she briefed him quickly on the situation—that two suspects under surveillance in a major case were writing on a pad of paper instead of speaking. Then she asked him to personally go to Judge Goldstein, who knew of the investigation and had authorized the wiretaps, and ask for an emergency search warrant for Draco's notepad. She gave him her cell phone number and asked him to call her as soon as the search warrant was authorized. Then she turned back to the live video of the meeting going on near the reflecting pool in the sculpture garden.

Meanwhile Draco and Winston were still communicating by the use of the pad. Draco looked angry this time, as he handed the pad to Winston. Winston wrote back quickly. And so the meeting progressed. Vicky kept looking at her watch and wondering whether the search warrant would arrive in time to save the day. She told Bill to position two agents by Draco's car and two agents by one of the stairs leading to the lower garden. She would order them to seize the pad from Draco once the search warrant came through. Nervously Vicky watched the TV monitors of the silent meeting. She just had to get that pad. Until the search warrant was issued, she was confined to watching the crucial piece of evidence pass back and forth, out of her reach.

Just then a sudden shriek and a whoosh behind the two men snapped their heads around and up. A star cluster skyrocket burst a hundred feet above the garden, and for the first time since the initial greeting, both Draco and Winston broke the silence between them as they looked straight up. Vicky and Bill heard quite clearly on the audio monitors what they said.

"Holy shit . . ."

"Damn! What was . . . oh, look, it's just a fireworks thing," Winston reassured Draco, pointing to the trail of smoke.

"Oh yeah, tomorrow is the Fourth of July. That must be some kids celebrating early, that's all."

After that interruption with the fireworks, Draco wrote one more time on the pad and handed it to Winston, who read it, then violently shook his head as he wrote and then gave it to Draco.

Winston stood and started to walk away from Draco, who was still sitting on the bench staring at the note. After a few steps, the chief judge stopped on the gravel path next to the garden pool and spoke. His voice on the monitor was low, sad, and flat.

"Good-bye, Leo. It's over." His face was grave.

Draco said nothing and sat for a full minute, watching Winston's figure ascend the steps and leave the garden. Then he stood up, stepped over to the reflecting pool, and dropped the entire pad into the water. Vicky gasped and leaped out of her chair, as if she could grab it from him at this distance. Bill and everyone else in the control room was transfixed in shock. Vicky watched as the paper touched the water and started dissolving, swiftly turning into a milky slush. Within seconds, only the bare outline of the edges of the pages could still be seen, but then even that portion disappeared.

Draco turned and walked toward one of the stairs leading out of the reflecting pool area. The two bodyguards joined him and walked on either side of him toward his waiting car. Winston, by this time, was halfway across the central grass area of the Mall, walking slowly toward the federal courthouse.

In the control room inside the Hirschorn, Vicky and Bill stared blankly at each other, dejected, crushed, as Draco and Winston disappeared from the TV monitors.

Vicky turned to Bill. "Christ! They wrote on water-soluble paper, just like the illegal gambling houses and bookmakers do when they expect a police raid and have to dispose of evidence quickly."

Vicky's cell phone rang. She pulled it out of her purse and answered. She listened for about thirty seconds, then spoke. "Well, thanks anyway, I appreciate the effort, but it's all academic now. The evidence has been destroyed."

"Who was that?" Bill asked as she clicked off the phone.

"The U.S. attorney. We got the warrant. But we don't have anything to seize, or, for that matter, any evidence of any crime, do we?"

Bill shrugged. "We've got pictures of a federal judge meeting a prominent member of the bar in a public garden. The only voice we heard was their shocked cries when that kid fired off that damned skyrocket. Other than that, we've got nothing. We were just outsmarted."

Vicky wouldn't give up. "Wait a minute, Bill. Judge Quinn has offered to change his vote for money. We can still get them for bribery if they actually pay him money, can't we?"

"Yes, counselor, we can, but *only* if we can trace the money. After today's show, I somehow don't think that these two are going to make any mistakes. They're too slick. I just don't think they're going to provide us with evidence that will enable us to prove a bribery count—or anything else, for that matter."

Vicky returned to her office, and as soon as she was settled, picked up the phone to pass the unfortunate news about the meeting to Tim. She hated having to tell him that they had been thwarted again. And she was more worried than ever about Tim's safety. She punched in his office number, and Loretta answered. "Judge Quinn's chambers."

"Good afternoon, this is Ms. Hauser from the Justice Department. Is Judge Quinn available?"

"I'm sorry, Ms. Hauser, but Judge Quinn did not come in today, and he told us he would be unreachable by anyone before this evening. We do expect him back in chambers on the fifth of July, however. Is there any message you would like to leave for him?"

Vicky didn't like how this sounded. "Not reachable by anyone? Actually, this is pretty important, and I am sure he would want to talk to me . . ."

"I'm sorry, Ms. Hauser, he was quite specific, he told me he was taking a short trip out of town today and that he would not be available to anyone. He even said he was going to turn his cell phone off. But if you want to leave a message on his voice mail, he told me he would check that this evening."

"Well, I don't want to leave . . . Wait, yes—please put me on his voice mail. I'll leave my cell and home numbers for him."

After she hung up, Vicky was overwhelmed with worry. How could her star witness disappear like this? He was in the middle of a big criminal undercover operation. Hell, he might wind up the target of a contract hit. What was going on?

That evening when Tim retrieved his SUV from the Pentagon parking lot, it was almost eight o'clock. He sat in his car and checked his chambers' voice mail with his cell phone. The first two were routine calls that could wait until tomorrow. But the third message was one from Vicky. The time identifier on the voice mail put the call just after the Hirschorn meeting. Tim cursed himself for not calling Vicky earlier, but he had been busy all day. More importantly, he didn't want to have to face Vicky's questions about why he was taking a trip out of town on the day that the investigation of Winston and Draco climaxed.

Tim immediately called Vicky at her home. When she answered, she told him how poorly their surveillance of Draco and Winston had gone. Tim had never heard her so discouraged. This was understandable. Vicky was the lead prosecutor of a stalled investigation. Her main lead failed to produce expected evidence.

"Basically we came up with a dry hole. Nothing we heard could be considered incriminating by any spin we could put on it."

"Sorry, Vick. But don't worry—we still have a great shot at some evidence if Winston offers me the two hundred thousand I asked for. I'll wear the Ear Link recorder anytime I'm near Winston. I'm sure that's where we'll nail him."

Vicky sighed. "That's my Tim—always positive, even in the worst of times." Then she suddenly added, "That's the thing I miss about you the most. I . . . I mean . . . Nevermind me, I'm just rambling. It's been a long day."

Tim was surprised at her sudden vulnerability and sought unsuccessfully to find the right words to respond. The conversation had just turned very awkward—for both of them—so he quickly ended the call.

After he hung up, Tim stayed in the parking lot and thought about Katy, his wife and true love. God, he did love her, even more now that she was struggling with Parkinson's. She needed him and he would always be there for her. But then his mind returned to Vicky, the first woman he had ever loved. Tim usually never liked to think about the past and roads not taken, but as he sat in the parking lot, he wondered if a man could have two true loves in his life.

CHAPTER 22

THE FOLLOWING WEEK WAS COURT WEEK, AND FOR THREE days, Tim heard nothing from Winston. Then at 9:55 A.M. Thursday, Tim was robed and in the conference room behind the courtroom, talking with the other two judges on that morning's panel. Just as the three judges were about to enter the courtroom, the door opened from the judges' corridor and the chief judge poked his head in. "Hi, y'all," Winston said. "Tim, could I see you for a minute before you go on the bench?"

Slightly startled, Tim turned toward Winston, while the other two judges nodded and smiled warmly at the chief judge. The chief judge motioned Tim out into the corridor, then bent his head over and leaned conspiratorially close to him, whispering, "Tim, I know you wouldn't wear a wire into court—there's too big a chance of feedback from the microphones up on the bench. And besides being a careful man, I am carrying my white-noise producer." Winston patted his suit coat pocket and smiled.

Tim heard the familiar hum and was speechless.

Winston kept whispering quickly. "There's two hundred thousand dollars' worth of casino chips at the cashier's cage of the Shamrock Casino in Antigua, and they're waiting to be picked up by someone named Mr. Diamond. *That's you, Tim.*" Winston almost smiled. " 'But don't worry, they also have your picture, so you just show up there and get your money, no questions asked. You can play the chips on the tables, or you can cash them in right away, I don't care. But the chips are ready right now"—Winston beamed—"and now I expect the *Morenta* case to be changed back to the result we voted in conference, say within two weeks. Okay?"

Tim was stunned. The time and place of the money offer had caught him by surprise. And Winston was right; Tim wasn't wearing a wire. Even though he had on the Ear Link cuff links, he had purposely left the power pack back in his chambers because he had anticipated just what Winston was counting on—that the electrical feedback from the power pack might be picked up by the powerful audio speaker system used in the courtroom. The bribe offer Tim had hoped for had just been made, but with no tape recording to prove it. It would be just Quinn's word against that of the chief judge, with no corroborating evidence. Very clever.

Tim kept his cool and allowed himself to look pleased. "Okay, Harry. Shamrock Casino in Antigua, Mr. Diamond, right?"

"Tim, you *are* a fast learner." Winston did not smile.

After the conference following the last case that day, Tim went back to his chambers and beeped Vicky with a coded message, setting up a meeting in thirty minutes at the usual place: the skeleton of the woolly mammoth. He returned a few calls from the messages left by his secretary, but then had to leave for the museum several blocks away. On every step of the short walk, his intelligence instincts were on full alert, looking about to make sure he wasn't being followed. As a precaution, he expertly took a detour through the nearby National Archives Building, getting lost in the crush of tourists, to lose any possible tail.

Vicky was waiting for him when he arrived. Calming himself down, Tim outlined to her the surprise meeting the chief judge had engineered. Again they had been outwitted. "Damn it, Vicky," he said. "I knew he was going to come back to me soon on the money I asked for, so I wore those cuff links every day in hopes of taping him. But with that damn white-noise device, even if I had the wire turned on, we'd still have come up blank. Winston seems invincible to taping."

Vicky bit her lip and thought for a moment. "The missed opportunity can't be helped. Let's talk about the bribe. This money pickup procedure is very smart. Neither Draco nor Winston would be touching the bribe money directly when it gets to you, and I'd bet that the purchase of the chips at the casino can't be traced to either Draco or Winston. Casinos in foreign countries, especially in tax havens like Antigua, are black holes for tracing funds. But still we've got to play this hand out as far as we can. Today's Thursday. Can you go to Antigua tomorrow?"

"Sure, I guess so," Tim said. "Today's the last court day this week."

"Good, I'll try to get a FBI Lear jet scheduled to take you and Bill down and back. At least that way the trip will be less of a hassle for you both. I'm sure I can justify requesting the use of a Bureau jet in this significant case."

"Antigua! You're going to Antigua tomorrow with the FBI?" Katy exclaimed.

Tim had relayed the latest development in the investigation to his wife when he got home that evening, and Katy was pacing the living room, furious and extremely anxious. "Don't go! Harry Winston and this man Draco are dangerous. You've said they've killed people—three people! I am scared, Tim—very scared. You can't go!"

Katy had started to tear up and Tim saw that her hands were shaking. *God,* he thought *I'm hurting her. She has enough to worry about without having me risk my life—and her happiness—with heroics for the FBI. When will I start putting Katy first?*

He pulled her into his arms and felt her quiet, convulsive weeping. He held her tight for a while, wordlessly, then whispered in her ear, "Baby, I'll be careful. But I have to go. I'm in too deep to pull out now. I want us to be safe too. And for that, our best chance is to go forward and get the evidence to put them away so they won't hurt us or anyone else." Katy kept crying. "Please trust me on this. I love you more than life and will always take care of you. I've got to do this."

He held her until she stopped shaking, petting her hair with his hands. Finally they broke their embrace. "I love you, Tim," Katy said, with the tears still wet on her face. "I trust you," she added and managed a weak smile.

Early the next morning, Bill Sharkey and Tim were alone in the passenger compartment of a seven-passenger Lear jet streaking at forty-two thousand feet above the Caribbean to the small island of Antigua. The unmarked jet was one of several operated by the Federal Bureau of Investigation. Both the pilot and copilot were special agents from the Bureau's aviation division. Today the plane was flying under the cover of one of the FBI front corporations, the Midas Trading Company. Its flight plan listed the transport of two company executives for a day business visit. Bill had the necessary documents for the immigration and customs officials of Antigua, including a fake passport for Tim if he needed it. Bill had found out from the FBI intelligence division that passengers of luxury jets were rarely asked for papers when they landed in Antigua. It was a very friendly country, especially if you were rich.

"Judge," Sharkey said, "I think it is best you make the pickup alone. These places have cameras all over. And don't expect to get much from questions at the casino. The Shamrock is owned by wise guys in the New York area."

"Can I use some of the money to try to buy some answers?"

"Sure, why not? It's not our money. But don't go overboard. Although anything you get at the casino is going directly to the U.S. Treasury as seized contraband, I still have to write up and file a form three-zero-two, reporting this trip and accounting for all the money to the brass."

"Well, don't expect any receipts from the folks I give money to," Tim said. "I want to see how far I can go up the food chain."

Sharkey smiled. "Judge, You're a real optimist and a high roller. Why don't you knock yourself out up to five thousand? I'll have trouble justifying any payout above that. I will say I'm not hopeful about our uncovering any evidence incriminating Winston or Draco, but we have to go through all the motions." Bill told Quinn that an advance team of agents had flown to Antigua the previous night to arrange logistics and, if necessary, to provide armed backup for this mission. One member of the FBI advance team would meet the plane and drop Tim off at the casino, picking him up an hour later at the front entrance. For security purposes, there would be an armed undercover agent in the casino watching over him. Tim wished Katy could hear that. While Tim was at the casino, Bill would be meeting with a high-ranking FBI informant on the local police force, to see if he could help trace any of the payoff money back to Winston or Draco.

Forty minutes after landing, Tim was walking up to the front entrance of the Shamrock Casino. Coming from the hot, bright, midday sun into the cool, windowless interior of the casino was like entering a subterranean cave. Tim took a moment to adjust his eyes to the artificial lighting and then threaded his way to the cashiers' cage. Although the casino was packed, there was no line for the one cashier on duty, a middle-aged, portly black man with sleepy eyes. When Tim identified himself as Mr. Diamond, the cashier's eyes popped open wide and he immediately straightened up to full alert. He took a photo out of a drawer behind him and studied it, looking Tim up and down. Then he broke into a smile.

"Ah yes. Mr. Diamond, we have been expecting you. Let me get your chips. Enjoy playing, and anything you drink or eat is on the house," the man said in a pleasant island accent. He quickly counted out an impressive stack of gambling chips.

"Unfortunately my trip to your island has been cut short. Can I cash the chips in now?" Tim looked again into the man's sleepy eyes and pushed the stack of chips back to him.

"Certainly, whatever you wish. How would you like it?"

"In hundreds, and keep a thousand for a tip."

"Hey, man. Very generous. Thank you." The cashier now had a broad toothy grin and was nodding in glee.

"One thing I would like to know," Tim said in a low voice that made the cashier lean toward him.

"What's that?"

"Who's my Santa?"

The cashier recoiled as if a snake bit him. He nervously looked around.

"Hey, man," he said in a low voice. "Some advice for you. Don't go around asking questions here. Word on you came from the Big Apple. That's all I can say. Take your money and leave. Tony Soprano is not just on HBO. No questions, man, *please*."

Tim nodded and waited as the cashier counted out his money and put it in a canvas tote bag with a green shamrock on it. One hundred and ninety-nine thousand dollars. Tim thanked him and, keeping a tight grip on the bag, had a Corona and played the quarter slots until the hour was up. He lost over thirty dollars of his own money before the car came for him. It was clear that at the Shamrock, the house always wins.

The FBI agent dropped Tim off at the airport and told him to meet Sharkey at a sixties-style diner in the airport complex. Sharkey was waiting at the diner entrance beside a cardboard cutout of Elvis.

"Judge, let's have a bite before we take off. The plane is being refueled."

Tim took the lead into the dining area and picked a table next to the jukebox, where they would have less chance of being overheard.

"Nice choice of tables, Judge. Still feel we're in enemy territory?" Sharkey asked.

"Doesn't hurt to be careful. How did you make out at the police department?"

Sharkey shrugged. "About as I expected. We got nada. The casino's heavy-duty connection to the mob in New York means that the local police are either bought off or afraid."

Tim's face sagged. "I struck out too. But it only cost you a grand."

"It's only money," Bill said, grinning.

At the table, Tim tried to use his cell phone to call his office, but it didn't work in this exotic locale. After they ordered, Tim left to use one of the restaurant's pay phones to check in with his chambers.

He had received one interesting phone message.

When Tim got back to the table, he asked Bill, "Your first-class jet have a phone?"

"Sure, we have everything except booze. The director goes only so far."

"Great, I have a call to make and I'd feel safer making it from an FBI phone."

On the plane, Tim made the return call to his friend from the Pentagon parking lot, Tony Lombardi—the general counsel of the National Reconnaissance Office. Right at the start of the conversation, Tim told Lombardi he was talking on a nonsecure phone from a plane headed for Washington and would be landing in a couple of hours.

Lombardi paused, and then talked in the clipped, vague manner of one who knew this telephone conversation could be intercepted or taped. "Tim, I've got something for you," he said. "An interesting intercept from yesterday's sweeps. I can have the transcript delivered to you by courier. Where should it be delivered?"

"To my home in Alexandria, I should be there by seven." Then Tim exhaled and asked, "Is it good news?"

"No, sorry. The event we thought they might try has actually been scheduled. Not right away. The full picture is in the package you'll receive. Come see me Monday and we can discuss some options."

Tim put down the phone, shaken. He got up and started toward the front of the jet to get a bottle of water from a small refrigerator. When he returned to his seat, Tim could see Bill was studying him. Sharkey leaned across the aisle and asked softly, "Judge, I don't mean to intrude, but it sounds like you had some bad news. If you want to talk about it, I'm a good listener. By the way, I think you are doing a good job on this case." Bill paused and added, "And I want you to know that the female agent case you handled is water under the bridge. My buddy was a serial groper and a jerk. He deserved what he got."

Tim nodded. He felt now he could trust Sharkey. Moreover, the news he just received made it necessary to share some information with Vicky and Sharkey. So Tim related to Bill a selected portion of the parallel investigation he had started with his old friends in the intelligence community, specifically Tony Lombardi at the National Reconnaissance Office, the highly classified intelligence agency that collected data, photos, and audio intercepts from a network of spy satellites. Its clients were the White House, the CIA, NSA, military intelligence agencies, and other spy agencies of the American government. Tim had been the NRO's general counsel for five years and remained close to the organization.

At first Bill Sharkey clearly was shocked and irritated that the judge would pull such a freelance stunt on a pending investigation, and he tried to interrupt several times as Tim outlined what he had done. But when Tim told him of the precautions he had taken, Sharkey began to nod. "Okay, I see what you're up to," he said. "And I agree—such a small, internal investigation, one that uses data pulled from satellite intelligence files, isn't such a bad idea. And it's low risk to us, I guess," he said. "What did the NRO guy just tell you?"

"There's been an intercept. Lombardi didn't give me the info because I was on an unsecure phone, but I'll have it tonight and share it with you tomorrow."

Tim didn't tell Bill that the intercept was definitely bad news. He needed time to digest it. And to devise countermeasures.

"Okay," Sharkey concluded. "Whatever you and the NRO have going, it better give us a lead we can use—because this investigation is at a stone wall right now."

As they walked across the tarmac to the General Aviation Terminal at Reagan National Airport, Tim saw Vicky and waved. When they got close enough to speak, Tim got right to the point. "We struck out. I got the money without a hitch in the casino," he told her. "But the money had been laundered, very clean, not traceable. Bill spent some time with the Antiguan authorities, but we ended up with zip."

Bill nodded. "A real dead end. There's no way we could trace that money."

Vicky sighed. "After all this work, we still have nothing. And as far as the bribe offer goes, all we have is two federal judges, each one swearing the other is a liar and a crook."

Tim had never heard her so dejected. Her face was drawn and her eyes were tearing up as the three of them walked across the tarmac. "Listen, it's not all over yet," Tim said. He decided he would let her know about the NRO side of the investigation. "We've got quite a bit of circumstantial evidence. Yeah, I know that none of it proves anything right now. But on the plane, I was telling Bill one of my intelligence friends has gotten something from a recent telephone intercept. It pertains to Draco and Winston. Bill can brief you on it. I've got to run; the intercept package is being delivered to my home this evening."

Vicky was visibly confused and Tim saw the anger start to rise on her face. She started to argue but Bill interrupted her. "Don't worry, I'll fill you in on it during our ride back to Justice."

Tim turned toward the parking lot and his car. "Can the three of us meet in your office, Vicky, tomorrow, Saturday morning, let's say at ten o'clock? We can go over the new information then."

Vicky looked at him with frustration, hope, and something else in her eyes—relief, concern? She looked at Bill, who nodded. "Okay, we'll see you then."

It was a little after seven when Tim got home to a fierce hug from Katy. The package wasn't there. Katy told him there were no messages. Tim gave Katy a rundown of the trip to Antigua. She was worried, preoccupied by the fact that the bribe had been paid in gambling chips. "It's just so eerie," she said. "It's so *underworld.*" During dinner they had a long, tense discussions about the fallout and the consequences of the Winston investigation; Katy urged him to wrap up his part in it as soon as he could. "You've done more than enough. Leave the heavy lifting to the professionals," she told him in a hard voice. "You're a judge, not a G-man."

"I want this over as much as you do," Tim said. "But I've got to follow through. We have no choice."

Katy rose and swept silently into the kitchen.

It was nearly eight o'clock, and still no package from Tony Lombardi. Tim was having a tough time waiting for the delivery of what he suspected was news that only put him—and Katy—even more at risk.

The NRO messenger arrived twenty minutes later with a sealed envelope, explaining that the message declassification procedure had taken longer than expected. When the messenger left, Tim ripped the envelope open and read the single sheet of paper inside. He read it again and stared at it, thinking for several minutes. Then he handed it to Katy. Bad news had arrived at the Quinn home.

CHAPTER 23

THE NEXT MORNING WAS SATURDAY. AT 10 A.M. SHARP, TIM pulled his Land Rover into a visitor slot in the parking area of the inner courtyard of the massive Justice Department. Soon he was at Vicky's door and started speaking to Vicky and Bill as soon as he entered the room. "Well, it looks like our friend Leo has put a contract out on me. He has actually done it. Here, look at this." From his briefcase, he pulled out a long sheet of paper.

The three bent heads over Vicky's conference table so they could all view it. The sheet had computer-generated numbers and abbreviations in a block at the top, obviously identification markers, but the main body of the sheet contained legible text in type. Tim pointed out the header of the paper, which read: "This is a transcript of a transatlantic phone call made two days ago by Mr. Leo Draco (a U.S. national) to a phone number listed in London, England."

"How did you get this?" Vicky asked.

"A listening satellite intercepted it, and the NRO gave me this copy last night. Take a look at the conversation under the header." Vicky pulled her hair from her face and, along with Sharkey, bent to read it.

"GOOD AFTERNOON, RAM SECURITY. HOW MAY I HELP YOU?"

"HELLO, THIS IS ACCOUNT NUMBER 6871. PLEASE CONNECT ME TO THE OPERATIONS DEPARTMENT." (This has been identified as the voice of Leo Draco, a U.S. National.)

"OPERATIONS HERE."

"THIS IS ACCOUNT NUMBER 6871, CALLING UNSECURE." (Draco voice)

"WHAT IS YOUR COLOR CODE"

"MY COLOR CODE IS RED BLACK GREEN." (Draco voice)

"CONFIRMED. HOW MAY I HELP YOU?"

"PLEASE PULL UP MY LAST SERVICE TRANSACTION."(Draco voice)

"ONE MOMENT PLEASE . . . YES, I HAVE IT. A FULL CLEANING JOB IN MACON, GEORGIA, USA."

"THAT IS CORRECT. NOW I NEED ANOTHER FULL CLEANING JOB, THIS ONE IN WASHINGTON, D.C. THE CARPET IS TO DISAPPEAR, NO TRACE. (Draco voice)

"NAME OF AND ADDRESS OF CLEANING JOB AND TIME FRAME, PLEASE."

"TIMOTHY J. QUINN, GOVERNMENT OFFICIAL, HOME IS 428

KNIGHT STREET, ALEXANDRIA, VIRGINIA. NEED CLEANING COMPLETED ON AUGUST 2, NOT SOONER OR LATER THAN THAT DATE." (Draco voice)

"VERY GOOD, 6871. WE SHOULD BE ABLE TO GIVE YOU A FULL CLEANING ON AUGUST 2ND. NO CARPET IS TO REMAIN. SAME PRICE SCHEDULE AS IN GEORGIA. DO YOU WANT THE SAME BILLING SYSTEM AS YOU USED FOR GEORGIA?"

"THAT'S SATISFACTORY. (Draco voice)

"VERY GOOD SIR."

Vicky looked up, shocked. "Tim . . . I mean Judge . . . Draco has taken a murder contract out on your life, just like he did for Mrs. Winston! That 'Georgia cleaning job' was the hit on her! God, what can we do?" She turned to Sharkey. "Bill, we have to locate this firm and neutralize the threat!"

"Easier said than done," Tim remarked dryly.

"Yeah, it's going to be tough," Bill said in a low voice. "First I'll get in touch with our FBI legal attaché office at the U.S. Embassy in London to have them contact Scotland Yard. Maybe the Yard can get us some info on this security firm. Maybe they can turn this off somehow. Let's see . . . London is five hours ahead of us, so it's after three in the afternoon there. Although it's on the weekend, I can probably get through to the office duty officer because the FBI phones are manned twenty-four hours a day. By the way, I know the head of that FBI office. He's sharp and very plugged-in with Scotland Yard." Bill thought a bit more and added, looking at Judge Quinn, "Judge, I think we should alert the U.S. marshals and get a protective detail for you."

Tim had already thought about this. "No, Bill. Thanks anyway, but that move would blow the investigation for sure. If you request a security detail for me, the head marshal of the court will inform Winston, since he's the chief judge. Then Winston and Draco will know something has leaked and they might just run. They could hightail it to Rio or somewhere else in South America where we'd have trouble extraditing them. Remember that Draco has two private jets and an oceangoing one hundred and fifty-foot yacht at his command."

"But Tim, at any time you could be—" Vicky started.

"The murder threat isn't an option, at least for now," Tim said. "I've been paid two hundred thousand dollars to reverse my vote, and they won't kill me before I write the *Morenta* opinion. That opinion will keep me alive until—" Tim hesitated "—until we can arrest them," he said firmly. "But it sure would make me happy if the FBI in London figure out a way to turn this off."

To buttress his own resolve, and to keep from worrying Vicky too much, Tim had made a show of disregarding the danger he faced, but he was worried. It was a mistake to underestimate your enemies—sometimes a fatal mistake. Draco was involved in three murders already and wouldn't hesitate to kill again. The *Morenta* opinion would, probably, keep him alive for now. He also knew, however, that once a contract hit is put in motion, it was going to be hard to stop—even if the FBI arrested Draco and Winston.

"Judge," Bill asked, looking up from the transcript, "how did you get this? And can we use it for evidence? Is it legally admissible?"

"Yes, it's admissible. And here's how we got it." Tim outlined the process that started when he and Tony Lombardi had met on the day of the Hirschorn meeting. Lombardi had offered to request authorization to use one of the surveillance satellites for an audio expansion of the existing wiretaps on Draco, who was linked by circumstantial evidence to three murders. Lombardi got the authorization from the director of the NRO to order the intercept, but the NRO still needed a judicial authorization to legally conduct the intercept. So Lombardi sent one of his NRO attorneys over to ask Judge Goldstein for an expansion of the existing wiretap authorization. Tim revealed that he gave Lombardi a further affidavit with his knowledge of the case-fixing conspiracy. The NRO attorney used Tim's affidavit to convince Judge Goldstein that there was sufficient probable cause to authorize a two-week National Security interception of any phone calls made by Draco. A satellite picked up this transatlantic call the next day. The transcript of it was delivered to Tim last night.

Bill looked puzzled. "Your Honor, how in the hell could a satellite sort out the thousands and thousands of phone calls each day and find the ones made by Draco?"

"Well, remember before the Hirschorn meeting, I asked Ms. Hauser for a duplicate of that first tape between Draco and Winston," Tim said.

"Right . . ."

"I wanted my NRO friends to have the voice print of Draco from that tape. Once the NRO had the voice print, they arranged to feed the print into the computers that control the listening devices on the satellites on station over the East Coast and the Atlantic. Then the downlink computers sorted out all conversations with Draco's voiceprint. This incriminating transcript is the product of that search."

Bill whistled. "Amazing, Judge. Thank you. Now, how can us ordinary FBI gumshoes investigate Ram Security? Maybe we can use this Ram company to get some evidence against Draco. But first we have to stop this hit on you. I'll get the FBI office at the embassy to do a complete check on Ram Security."

"Bill, I probably don't need to say this," Vicky added, "but just so there's no slipup, be sure to tell the FBI to walk softly with Scotland Yard. We don't want to spook Ram Security. That wouldn't be good for anybody." Her eyes met Tim's. "Try to get a client list and a past history of the firm's business if you can. We need to figure out some leverage against them to stop the hit."

"Thanks, guys," Tim said. "I really would like to survive long enough to testify."

Once Sharkey left, Vicky just gazed at Tim for a long moment and then finally spoke.

"I should never have let you go inside the Winston scheme. We have to get you protection."

"No, absolutely not."

"Tim, I'm scared for you."

"Protection isn't necessary. Really. And it's counterproductive. I've got more than two weeks until the contract is scheduled. Ram Security's hit man—or hit team—remember, there were two people in the SUV that killed Mrs. Winston—will probably put surveillance on me a week or so before the hit. They'll follow me, to develop patterns and to make a decision where and when to 'do' me. We can talk about protection next week if we don't turn off the contract before then."

"How are *we* going to do that?" Vicky asked.

"I've given this matter a lot of thought since last night. The prospect of being murdered in two weeks has a way of focusing your attention. I have a plan."

"This better be good, or I'm going to have a FBI team shadowing you night and day," Vicky muttered.

"First thing Monday, I'm going to the court and run a little test on Winston to see if he is really in the dark about this Draco contract. My gut tells me that Winston would not have anything to do with murder—at least not until after it happens, as with Camellia. But I'm not sure. Knowing if Winston is involved with the hit contract may give us a little edge with Ram Security and Draco."

Vicky nodded. "How are you going to test him?"

Tim would simply request Winston for more time to prepare the *Morenta* opinion—he would ask for a time past the deadly timeline of the second of August that Draco gave Ram Security. If the chief judge agreed to it, then they would know that Draco was alone on the hit contract. If Winston refused and demanded that the opinion be done right away, then Winston was probably in on the hit.

Tim also told Vicky that, after he saw the chief judge, he would go to the NRO complex to talk to Tony Lombardi. The NRO and other agencies in the intelligence community had a lot of information in their databases. Lombardi had already started a NRO declassification action on some data that may be incriminating evidence on Draco and Winston for the case-fixing scheme.

"What? The NRO might be able to give us evidence on the case-fixing?" Vicky was surprised.

Damn. Tim realized that he had strayed into forbidden territory, referring to an operation that the NRO had conducted for the Hirschorn meeting that had not yet been declassified. And the NRO might never allow the information to be made public. Tim mentally kicked himself; he had just made a major mistake mentioning possible evidence to a federal prosecutor with subpoena power. The last thing Tim wanted was a tug of war over evidence between the Justice Department and his old agency, the NRO.

"Well, it is probably nothing," he said, trying to cover up his mistake. "The NRO was just doing me a small favor to use their assets to try to find some information that we could use. You realize that anything they find most likely will be highly classified and the declassification process may be difficult. Some things can't be declassified, because the release of information would compromise sources and methods of the NRO. So I wouldn't count on anything for sure from the NRO."

"Not even for an investigation into corruption and murder on one of America's highest courts?" Vicky's voice was hard.

"No," Tim said flatly. He hoped Vicky wouldn't pursue the fact that Tim had been using his intelligence friends to undertake a major operation on Winston and Draco. The results, although known to Tim, were in the delicate process of being declassified, a process the NRO could halt at any time. To the U.S. intelligence community, protecting national security counted more there than the prosecution of a criminal bribery case. "I think Lombardi can help us out in dealing with Ram," he said, hoping to distract her from further inquiry into what the NRO was up to. He told her they had started a close scrub on the security firm ever since the intercept. By now Lombardi should have a full background check on the security firm.

When Tim got up to go, Vicky came around from her desk and hugged him. Tim kissed her gently on her forehead and smiled gamely.

"Don't worry, baby," he said. "I've been in tougher spots. Remember, I've always said that people are born either smart, handsome, or lucky. I've always been strong on luck."

Tim turned and left.

The rest of the weekend was tense at the Quinn home. Monday morning at nine o'clock, Tim went straight to Winston's chambers. The chief judge was in and surprised to see Tim. After the door closed, Tim refused Winston's offer of a seat. "Harry, this won't take long. I've been thinking that we should not rush the *Morenta* opinion too much. Our normal delay from oral argument until we issue an opinion is right around sixty days. Why don't I take my time writing the opinion and wait until mid-August to circulate the final draft to you and Judge Forrester? That would be more in line with a normal processing time for the *Morenta* case. So, how about August fifteenth?"

Winston thought for a few moments. "Good idea, Tim. You're a smart cookie. We wouldn't want to do anything unusual on the *Morenta* case. Around the fifteenth of August would be just fine."

Now it was clear to Tim—Harry Winston had no knowledge that Tim was supposed to be murdered on August 2. Draco *was* operating solo on the contract. Tim left the chief judge and went to his own chambers, grabbing his briefcase and car keys. He told Loretta that he had an appointment in Virginia and could be reached only on his cell phone. He took the judges' elevator to the underground parking lot, in a hurry to get to the NRO headquarters near Dulles Airport.

As Tim's Land Rover pulled out of the underground parking lot at the courthouse, two men were watching it from a white van with a large dish antenna on top of it. The van was parked in an area known as Monica Beach, where media vehicles were allowed to park during courthouse legal proceedings ever since the Clinton scandal years.

Both sides of the van sported a large magnetic label with the name of a fictitious TV station. Inside, a bulky white man, with a shaved head and a scar that dominated his face, stared at a laptop displaying a bright dot moving on a screen with grids that represented the streets of Washington, D.C. In the driver's seat was a large black man who wore his hair in long cornrows. "Go on, Number Two," the white man said in a Cockney accent. "Start following him, but stay back at least a block until we get some cars between us." The van started to shadow Tim's car as the Brit penciled the time and direction in a notebook. Soon the van and the Land Rover were driving west on the George Washington Parkway, following the twist and turns of the Potomac River alongside it.

"Bloody good job this tracking beeper is doing. So you had no trouble putting it on the judge's car?"

"Piece of cake. A *brother* can go anywhere in a federal building in D.C. dressed in a janitor uniform. Almost all the guards in the courthouse are black."

The van did not need to have a visual on Tim's car so it remained at least three hundred feet back. This was easy. "Wonder where the judge is headed?" Cornrows said.

"He can go to the goddamn grocery store if he wants. Just so we know his routine."

By now Judge Quinn's Land Rover was on the Dulles Airport Toll Road, nearing the turnoff for the NRO Headquarters. The van was in a lazy tail, almost five hundred feet behind. When the judge's car went through the exit tollbooth, Cornrows closed the distance to a good visual tail. Not far from the tollbooth, when the SUV passed a sign for the National Reconnaissance Office Headquarters, the car's right blinker went on.

"What's this? The guy's headed into the NRO complex!" Cornrows peered forward.

"Don't sweat it, mate," the Brit said. "I've read his background. The judge was a spook here for over five years. Probably going back to see his spy pals for lunch. Go past the entrance and double back on the other side of the road, over by that petrol station. We'll wait for him there."

"I don't like this assignment," Cornrows muttered. "This motherfucker is too connected."

. . .

According to Lombardi's contacts at the CIA, Ram Security was a London-based, full-service security and consulting firm. Offering a wide variety of services—corporate security reviews, bodyguard service, anti-terrorist training for corporate executives, business intelligence-gathering, and other consulting services—it was a private CIA for the rich and powerful. Their client list included major global corporations, wealthy individuals, and, on occasion, special contract work for governments throughout the world. A large percentage of the employees in its operations were ex-military.

According to CIA intelligence, Ram Security's largest client was the British government. The NRO people verified the CIA's information through direct contacts at the British Secret Intelligence Service, known as "MI6," which also added the fact that Ram Securities has been involved peripherally in a number of Third World revolutions and assassinations over the last decade. It was also clear that Ram was a valuable outside asset of British Intelligence, tied financially and philosophically to MI6.

Another important fact, from Tim's perspective, was that the director of the NRO was a good friend of the head of British Intelligence, Sir Richard Thornton. Tim immediately asked to see the NRO director. Lombardi made a call to verify that his boss was in and available, then led Tim down the executive hallway to the director's office. Tim and Lombardi had a long talk with the director who, at the end, agreed to call Sir Richard the next morning in an effort to stop the execution of the contract. Tim immediately breathed a little easier. It was good that all these high-level intelligence people knew each other. But Tim was not going to rely on phone chats among bureaucrats to insure his safety. "I want to go to London myself and talk to Richard Thornton," Tim told Lombardi and the NRO director. "Can you arrange a meeting for me?"

The director cleared his throat. "Judge Quinn, I can assure you that—"

"If MI6 has the power to stop the contract with Ram Security, I don't want to rely just on a phone call."

"Judge Quinn—"

"Sir, my life and the safety of my family is on the line. I'd like to go to see Sir Richard personally to get his help to end this contract."

The director stared at Tim a moment. "I can arrange that," he said.

"See if you can make it for tomorrow. I'm leaving for London tonight," Tim added.

Within half an hour Lombardi's efficient staff had booked Tim's air tickets and hotel. Then Tim called Vicky to tell her, asking her to go to the fifth-floor Justice Department Command Center so they could talk on a secure phone. Within ten minutes, Tim called her back at the command center, using Lombardi's STU-3 secure phone, which scrambled the call so no intercept was possible. Tim told Vicky he was headed to London to meet with MI6, and gave her his contact numbers. Then, almost as an afterthought, he asked her to have Bill Sharkey electronically send the thumbprint and two partials from the Georgia hit-and-run of Mrs. Winston to Scotland Yard, so British law enforcement could perform an immediate match run in the English criminal and military fingerprint databases. If Ram was involved in the hit on Mrs. Winston, maybe the prints recovered from the SUV gas cap would get a match in the British system.

"I'm glad you're doing this," Vicky said softly. "I'll sleep better tonight."

"So will I," Tim said, winking at Tony. "If Lombardi gets me a first-class upgrade on the flight."

Tim next had to safeguard his family. He had to get Katy out of their house while he was in England. Ram would most likely monitor the Quinn house for some time before they moved to kill Tim. The place was no longer safe. Lombardi arranged for Katy to stay at a CIA safe house in Virginia until Tim returned. Now Tim would have to tell her what he had done—which was the hardest thing he had to do all day.

He telephoned her, resolving to sound cheerful and in charge. "Hi, baby. I'm out with Tony. Like we talked about last night, we both might have to take a little trip. Tony will help us."

"Oh no, Tim. This is a nightmare!"

"Baby, you know we can't talk now. I'll be home in thirty minutes. I'll explain everything. I love you." Tim looked bleakly at Lombardi after he finished the call.

Lombardi nodded. "Don't worry, Tim. I'll take care of her while you're gone." He walked Tim to his car in the underground NRO parking lot. Of all the federal agencies, the NRO knew the value of covered parking lots. During debriefings, defectors from the Soviet Union had told the CIA that the Kremlin could anticipate imminent U.S. military activity through Russian satellite intelligence showing the occupancy rate of the two main Pentagon parking lots during the weekends. Another indicator was the upswing in Domino's pizza deliveries to the Pentagon.

At his car, Tim stopped and abruptly hugged Lombardi. "Buddy, I'll never forget your help on this. In prosperity, a guy learns who his enemies are. In adversity, he finds out his true friends. Thanks for everything, Tony." Tony nodded gravely.

What a roller-coaster, Tim thought to himself as he drove down the George Washington Parkway toward his home in Alexandria. Friday night he found out he was at the top of a one-man death list, and tonight he was flying to London to meet with the head of MI6, somebody possibly powerful enough to erase the hit.

When he pulled into the garage of their town house, Katy was at the door of the garage, her eyes reddened, her trembling hands more visible. Tim hugged her and kissed her hard. With his arm around her, they went up to the living room, where he explained what was going on and what would happen that night.

Katy started to shake more and wept.

Tim held her and rocked her back and forth. "Baby, don't cry. I'm going to solve this whole thing, maybe in the next day or two over in London. Then I'll be back."

"I can't live without you," Katy choked out. "Please find a way out for us." Her tears nearly swallowed her words.

"Come on, honey, let's give the kids a call," Tim urged her. The more they could both take command of the situation, the less anxious they would be. "We can't get too detailed on the phone, but we have to warn them not to come home or call us, until this thing blows over," Tim said. "It's possible to back-trace calls and I don't know when the Ram Security firm will be putting our house and phones under surveillance."

Katy's tears swelled at that prospect. But soon she collected herself. "You make the calls alone," she told him. "I don't want to cry again talking to them." She swallowed twice. "I guess I have to go pack, don't I?"

Tim telephoned both their children, Anne in New York City and Paul in Chicago, telling them in vague terms that he and Katy would not be reachable for a few days due to a security exercise at the court, and giving them specific instructions not to visit or call home until he contacted them and said the exercise was over. The children were both concerned—and suspicious—but trusted their father when he assured them that everything was okay.

Then Sharkey called from his cell phone, en route to Tim's home. "I have a package to deliver to you," he said. Thank God Vicky wasn't coming as well, Tim thought as he hung up. It would be uncomfortable and perhaps dangerous to let Katy meet Vicky. He had slept with both women; he had loved both. And Katy, with her keen ability to read people—and her unsurpassed ability to read him—might pick up on his feelings for Vicky. This was no time for a summit meeting between the two women. He wondered what Bill was hand delivering.

Katy was still upstairs packing when Sharkey arrived. Tim took him into the large family room and briefed him on the day's developments. Sharkey handed him a photo and a sheet of biographical data. "Courtesy of the Scotland Yard military database. The picture is of Allen Canby. His prints were on the gas cap in Macon."

Tim studied the photo—a straight-on shot of a face with a shaven head, probably a copy of a picture from the English passport files. The man had closely set eyes and a long scar running top to bottom on his right cheek. The photo projected strength and cruelty.

"He's a retired sergeant major from the British Special Air Services Regiment," Sharkey said. "Now he works for Ram Security in their London main office."

"So it appears that Mrs. Winston was killed by an operative of Ram, an ex-SAS boy," Tim mused.

"Looks that way, Judge. I'll have the FBI start a possible extradition file on Canby here. But I thought you might need this information to take with you. Good idea to go to England to try to stop the contract at its source."

"It beats waiting for Allen Canby and his mates to knock on my door."

"Your Honor, I'd do the same thing. By the way, the head of the FBI office in the U.S. Embassy in London has been instructed to arrange any backup support you need. Including twenty-four-seven security."

Tim kept his eyes on the photo of Allen Canby. "Thanks, Bill.

I'll be in touch with you and Ms. Hauser as soon as I can. Who knows? Maybe I'll bring back some solid evidence to nail Draco for the hit on Mrs. Winston."

"Here comes trouble!" announced Cornrows as he slid down in the driver's seat. The van was parked three houses down from Judge Quinn's house. A black Chevy Suburban with crash bumpers and a top-rack of blue, red, and white lights silently advertised to Cornrows that a U.S. government official vehicle was passing the van.

Gone from the Brit's white van was the fake satellite dish. The "news station" labels for the side panels had been replaced by magnetic labels with the name OLD DOMINION PLUMBERS—24 HOUR SERVICE. A plumber's van parked in a residential neighborhood would blend in easily.

"Got it," said the Brit from the back of the van. "Looks like another government visitor for the Quinn's." The Brit was seated in a swivel chair in the back of the van, studying the Quinn home with an assortment of devices. He adjusted his night-vision goggles so he could see clearly the two men in suits going up to the Quinns' front door. A third man, a driver, stayed in the vehicle. The Brit switched to a Nikon camera and took several low-light pictures of the arrival scene. A close-up shot of the back of the large SUV revealed the suspected U.S. government license plate. There had been another government visitor an hour after the van had trailed Quinn home from the NRO headquarters that afternoon—a middle-aged, balding man, driving a dark blue Ford Crown Vic with three small antennas on the trunk lid. In the detailed log they were keeping on the activities of Judge Quinn, Cornrows and the Brit had guessed that the visitor was from the FBI. The man stayed thirty minutes and then left.

Ten minutes after the arrival of the Suburban, Quinn and

his wife emerged from the front door with the two visitors.

"Bloody hell, they are carrying suitcases. The Quinns are leaving! Bugger me!" roared the Brit.

"Mother fuck. If we follow them, they'll spot us in this fucking plumber's truck."

"Start up and get ready to move," the Brit ordered. "We'll do a shadow until we can make a rolling trace on the SUV."

The Chevy Suburban moved down the street toward busy King Street. The van expertly drove slowly without lights until the Suburban turned the corner; then it shot forward and put its lights on. The shadow had started. The large Chevy soon was on the George Washington Parkway heading west. The van was three cars behind.

From the rear of the van, the Brit shouted, "I'm going to nail their ass with a sticky tracker. Stand ready. When I say so, start to pass them. Then lean on your horn and swerve toward them. Don't hit them—I just want the horn to hide the noise of the paintball hitting their bumper."

The Brit took out a paintball gun from a storage trunk. He pried open a paintball, filled with a sticky, colorless gum-like substance, and inserted an electronic bug inside. Then he closed it up. This was going to be a "rolling trace" operation. A paintball is shot at a moving vehicle; the ball breaks on contact, allowing the electronic tracking device to stick to the vehicle. The Brit knew that the rolling trace was their only chance to track the SUV containing the Quinns. A white van would be spotted too easily in a long shadowing operation.

The Brit moved to the back of the van and opened the tinted window on the right rear of the van. With the Brit in position, Cornrows made the honking swerve toward the Chevy Suburban just after they passed Reagan National Airport. The paintball shot was perfect—just under the left rear light above the bumper. After it swerved, the white van put on its emergency blinkers and fell back and stopped by the side of the road to give the impression it had engine trouble.

"Yes!" the Brit yelled. "It worked. We've got a strong track of the SUV."

"You're *the man!* Good job."

Soon the van started trailing the Suburban again, this time from beyond visual range, homing in on the strong signal coming from the bug stuck to the SUV's rear. After forty-five minutes, the laptop showed the SUV stopped on a residential street in Clifton, Virginia, a development of new homes south of Dulles Airport. The van drove to within a block of the signal and the Brit got out, holding his night-vision goggles. He jogged down the street to a position in a clump of bushes, where he could observe the Chevy Suburban parked in the driveway of one of the homes. After twenty minutes of waiting, the Brit saw Judge Quinn appear inside the front door of the house and kiss his wife. As the judge pulled off in the Chevy, the Brit saw another female move to stand next to Quinn's wife in the doorway of the house. The Brit hurried back to the van and the electronic chase began again.

Brit and Cornrows soon realized the SUV was headed to Dulles Airport. When the large Chevy got on the Dulles Airport access road, Cornrows pulled the van to within visual observation. At the airport, the SUV stopped in front of the United Airlines entrance on the departure level. Quinn got out, accompanied by a man in a suit. The Brit exited the van, ordering Cornrows to wait for him in the nearby hourly parking lot.

He watched as Quinn checked in at the United Airlines counter, then examined the departure board. Only one more United flight that day—the 11:30 P.M. nonstop to London Heathrow Airport. The Brit watched the judge disappear through the security checkpoint. Quinn was alone now. The man who came with Quinn into the airport wasn't traveling with him. The Brit was truly puzzled. Quinn's wife appeared to be in government protective custody at what might be a CIA or FBI safe house, and the judge was headed to London alone. Something was wrong. The Brit called Cornrows on his cell phone.

CHAPTER 24

WHEN THE DOORS SHUT ON THE 747, TIM WAS PLEASED TO see the flight was far from full. No one was seated next to him. He took three Sominex sleeping pills as the plane was rolling down the runway and put the DO NOT DISTURB sticker on the top of his seat. By the time the 747 reached thirty-five thousand feet, he was asleep.

When the plane was one hour into the seven-hour flight, he was roused by one of the flight attendants. "Judge Quinn, I am sorry to wake you," she said, "but the captain would like to see you on the flight deck."

Tim rubbed his face and tried to clear his brain. *Had something happened to Katy?* He woke to full consciousness and followed the flight attendant to the front of the plane where the pilot waited outside the cabin door.

"Judge Quinn?" the pilot queried. "Could you please show me some ID?"

Tim reached into his pocket and produced his federal judge credentials. "What is this all about, Captain?"

"We received a priority message for you from Dulles control for immediate delivery to you." The pilot handed Tim a sheet of paper. Tim read it.

> JUDGE QUINN, TRACKING DEVICE FOUND ON TRANSPORT CAR. HAVE MOVED YOUR WIFE TO NEW SECURE LOCATION. SAME CONTACT NUMBER APPLIES. ASSUME OPPOSITION KNOWS YOUR ITINERARY. I HAVE TRANSMITTED NEW PRECAUTION REQUIREMENTS TO U.S. EMBASSY (LONDON). LOMBARDI

Tim thanked the pilot and made his way back to his seat, disturbed and angry. So Ram Security had followed him, first to the CIA safe house, then to the airport. They obviously knew he was headed to London. He *had* to turn off this contract. Tim ordered a Jack Daniels and coke and started watching the movie playing in the seatback monitor in front of him. Sleep was hopeless, he thought, even with an in-flight movie worse than the usual, but he underestimated the effects of the Sominex, the Jack, and the intense exhaustion of the past two days. Four hours later, he was awakened for breakfast, and shortly thereafter the plane began its descent. When the plane's wheels made touchdown on the wet tarmac of the runway of Heathrow Airport outside of London, it was a little after ten in the morning. As the plane approached the gate, he heard the rain hammering the skin of the airplane on a gray English morning. Somewhere out there in the weather, he reminded himself, was the boss of the men hired to kill him.

Awaiting him in the jetway were two crew-cut men in civilian clothes, along with a uniformed British policeman. "Welcome to England, Judge Quinn," said the taller of the two men. "I'm Gunnery Sergeant Reavie and this is Lance Corporal Armstrong. We're from the Embassy Marine security detail and assigned to you during your stay in London. Also this is our British escort, Constable Woolscot of the Heathrow Airport Police." The policeman nodded genially. "Do you have any checked bags, sir?"

Tim said that he only had his carry-on, and Reavie nodded and opened a door in the jetway that led outside to metal stairs. Waiting at the foot of the stairs was a black BMW 750il sedan. Accompanied by his welcoming committee, Tim descended and got in the waiting car. Reavie explained that Tim was being given high security access to the country following a request from the American ambassador. This was reassuring.

The BMW sped off to a VIP lounge where Tim's passport was stamped by a British immigration official. Soon Tim was back in the rear seat of the BMW 750 sedan next to Reavie, with Lance Corporal Armstrong riding shotgun in the front. The car sped through an airport service gate without stopping. Tim noticed the heavy weight of the vehicle as they made a sharp turn onto the M4 expressway headed to London. He noticed the thickness of the window glass and realized that they were in an armored car. Tony Lombardi and Bill Sharkey had gotten through to the right people. Tim thought about Katy and hoped that she was as safe as he seemed to be.

On the way into central London, Reavie, the senior of the two marines, briefed Tim, telling him he was to be guarded by a two-man security detail at all times while he was in London. Reavie and Armstrong were the day shift. The embassy had gotten permission for the security team to carry firearms—highly unusual in England with its strict gun laws. Obviously the U.S. Embassy and the British Home Office, the central coordinator of law enforcement in England, took the threat against Tim seriously.

Lombardi had arranged for Tim to use a false name to check into the London Marriott in Grosvenor Square, just one block down from the U.S. Embassy. Hotel reception gave him a message from the FBI office in the embassy telling him that the MI6 head had agreed to meet him. A driver from MI6 would pick him up at the hotel at six-thirty that evening.

This was welcome news. Tim would have time to rest. Armstrong would be stationed just outside his room and Gunnery Sergeant Reavie would take a position in the lobby.

In his room, Tim called the contact number Lombardi gave him and talked to Katy. "I feel safe, I guess," she said. "I really do." But her voice belied her words. "Are you safe too?"

"You should see the guys guarding me," Tim told her. "I feel like James Bond."

The hotel room telephone rang at five P.M. to wake him. Tim showered, dressed, and went downstairs with Corporal Armstrong to the hotel restaurant for a Coke and a club sandwich. Reavie joined them there, and they talked over the safest way to move from the hotel to MI6 headquarters. Tim decided to ride with the M16 driver. To do otherwise might seem a snub to the head of MI6. Reavie, however, would ride with Tim and Armstrong would follow with the embassy BMW.

At six-thirty P.M., Tim and the two marines met the MI6 driver, who led them out front to a black Bentley. Soon, the Bentley and the BMW were inching through London rush-hour traffic, headed for the British government office complex at Vauxhall Cross on the south bank of the Thames.

Tim was familiar with M16's history from his work with the NRO. Britain's Secret Intelligence Service had been founded in 1909 and functioned in happy anonymity until the 1960s, when Ian Fleming's James Bond novels glamorized it. MI6 was an elite agency devoted to intelligence gathering, counterintelligence, combating terrorism, and preventing the spread of nuclear, chemical, and biological weapons. The agency had more than its share of time-honored traditions; for example, the head of MI6 was historically referred to as "C" of the Secret Service. This was done initially for security reasons, to protect the real name of the head, since only in recent years had the name of MI6's chief been public record. In another tradition, the MI6 chief wrote his memos to the prime minister in green ink and signed them with only the initial "C." In his Bond novels, Fleming, a former member of M16, remained loyal to the Secret Service by using the letter "M" to designate the head of the British Secret Service. Now, as the car arrived at the headquarters of the real life "C," Tim was more than a little intimidated. This was, literally, a do-or-die meeting. Could he convince such a man that his life was worth the risk of saving?

Sir Richard Thornton was only the twelfth person to be "C." As Tim was shown into his office, the man rose from behind his immense desk, came around, and warmly greeted him, shaking his hand and patting his shoulder, then guided him to a side cluster of armchairs and a sofa around a coffee table. They sat down, and Tim noticed that a tea service and cups were awaiting them. Tim felt reassured—unless all this courtesy was merely British manners at work, the prelude to a polite brush-off.

"Judge Quinn," Sir Richard began, "let me say right away that I was most distressed to learn that Ram Security was involved in a contract on your life. We've taken this matter quite seriously. The message from your government and the intercept itself, as you can well imagine, caused quite a stir in our intelligence community. The fact that Ram Security had taken on a contract to eliminate a sitting federal judge in the U.S.—why, I was just astounded!"

Tim smiled. "Thank you, Sir Richard. I was pretty astounded to be targeted. I hope you can help me put a full stop to the contract Mr. Draco made with Ram Security."

Thornton leaned forward and nodded. "I cannot imagine how one must feel to be targeted in a matter like this! Ram Security, of course, is one of the outside private firms that we use quite regularly, and I was really quite stunned to learn of this. This morning, I immediately called in the CEO of the firm, Colonel Fitzhugh Parker, and gave him a proper dressing down. Parker has assured me that the contract most definitely will *not* be implemented. Ram Security will not do anything to harm you."

A tremendous wave of relief hit Tim. Thank God! Sir Richard saw the effect of his words in Tim's eyes and smiled. "My dear Judge Quinn, did you have any doubts that MI6 would let such a contract proceed?"

Tim was too choked up to speak. Sir Richard continued. "I assume you don't mind that I took the liberty of insisting, for the time being, that Colonel Parker maintain the appearances that the contract is still operational. We wouldn't want Mr. Draco hiring other killers just yet, would we?"

"No, sir. Thank you for thinking of that."

Sir Richard reached for the pot of tea and began pouring. "I don't mind telling you, Judge Quinn, this whole affair could have ended up a genuine disaster, not just for you, but for both our governments. Imagine the headlines in the *Daily Mail*: 'Yank Judge Killed for Cash by MI6 Undercover Firm!' No, no, we can't have any of that! Milk?" he asked, handing Tim the cup.

"No, thank you."

"You can be assured that your life is no longer in any danger from Ram Security, and that this firm will be under intensive oversight for all of their future operations." Thornton sat back with his own cup of tea and smiled.

"Well, thank you again, Sir Richard. This has been an enormous strain on my family, and they will be relieved to know that the danger has passed."

His life now saved—or so it seemed, unless Ram turned rogue on MI6, or the people who had tailed him from Alexandria somehow had their own plans—Tim now had to press for the favor Vicky had asked him to pursue. He was reluctant, but he had to do all he could for Vicky and the investigation.

"Sir Richard, there is another reason for my trip. An FBI agent and a prosecutor from the U.S. Justice Department are conducting a criminal investigation involving the man who retained Ram Security on this contract, an American attorney named Leo Draco. I am working closely with them, and we would appreciate your help in getting Ram Security to provide information on Mr. Draco."

Sir Richard shifted slightly in his chair and Tim knew he had ventured into an uncomfortable area. "I'm not sure how much I can do on that point," he mused. "These are delicate matters. Ram Security and my directorate are somewhat intertwined, I'm afraid, and this covert relationship can never be made public." He smiled faintly. "Hmmm—a member of the judiciary entangled in a criminal investigation. Tell me more."

As they sipped their tea, Tim briefed an attentive Sir Richard on the inquiry into Winston and Draco. "What I need, Sir Richard," he finished, "is some hard evidence to incriminate Draco. Ram Security might also be able to fill in some blanks around the deaths of Judge Rogers and Mrs. Winston."

Thornton looked grim. "So one judge has already died," he said.

"Yes, sir."

"And a judge's former wife?"

"Yes, Sir Richard. What can you tell me about Ram Security?"

"Quite a bit, actually."

Ram Security was a rather unique company that was used by his organization for some sensitive intelligence jobs that needed to be done discreetly without leaving behind the fingerprints of the British government. Sir Richard hinted that Ram was particularly good at military and surveillance work close to the edge of permissible governmental action. Its founder and current head, Fitzhugh

Parker, was a retired army colonel and a friend of his, both socially and professionally.

"What can you tell me about Colonel Parker?"

Sir Richard frowned. "Fitz is somewhat of a contradiction, I suppose. He comes from an old, well-established, and financially secure family, and is very well educated—a graduate of Harrow, Cambridge, and Sandhurst. A lot of tradition, stability, if you see what I mean." He frowned again. "However, his army career allowed him to develop a bit of a wild streak. He started with the Coldstream Guards, but ended up with SAS, and he was damned good at it, too—rose to be executive officer of the regiment. He has served in Northern Ireland, Rhodesia, and the Sudan, and he got the Military Medal for leading the SAS team that took down the Iranian Embassy hostage situation in London some years back. Perhaps you remember it."

"Yes, I remember," Tim said. The siege had occurred while he was at the NRO, and all his colleagues had admired how the SAS acquitted itself. "Will the colonel help in my government's effort to gather evidence on Draco?"

Sir Richard was direct. "I would think he would rather not meet you. I would imagine that it would be somewhat awkward for him, meeting the man he has targeted to be killed. But I shall ask him to do so as a special favor. You must remember, he inhabits a very special 'black world,' and information doesn't flow out of there very easily at all."

Abruptly Thornton chuckled. "But he may see it my way. Now then, you're staying at the Marriott? False name as well, clever! I'll try to set up a meeting for you at my club, which Fitz also belongs to, the Greenham Club. It's on Pall Mall close to your hotel. I'll call him and give him a little nudge. I'll have the answer sent to your hotel. Is there anything else I can do for you?"

"Actually, Sir Richard, your putting a stop to the contract has me in your debt forever. The meeting with Colonel Parker is the only other thing I ask. And for that I thank you in advance."

"You're quite welcome. Now, do try some of these biscuits. They're quite nice with tea."

As soon as Tim returned to the Marriott, he called Katy with the good news that they were no longer targeted for murder. She began crying in relief, but agreed that she should stay where she was until Tim was certain the hit order had been lifted.

Later that evening, a private messenger, after being patted down by Corporal Armstrong, delivered a sealed envelope to Tim's room. Tim opened it.

> COLONEL PARKER WILL MEET WITH JUDGE QUINN ALONE IN THE SECOND-FLOOR LIBRARY OF THE GREENHAM CLUB, 29 PALL MALL, FOUR P.M. SHARP TOMORROW.

At three-fifty in the afternoon the next day, the BMW pulled into the circular gravel driveway of the massive, four-story stone building whose only outside marking was a large brass plate bearing the numerals 29. No name or any other indication of the club's presence marked the granite exterior. The Greenham was one of the oldest and most prestigious clubs in London, and the standard waiting list for membership was four years. Both bloodlines and money counted for admission.

Before Tim got out of the BMW, Gunnery Sergeant Reavie said to him, "Sir, I wish one of us could come to the meeting with you."

"Gunny, we've been over this. The message said 'alone' and that's how we'll play it. You and Armstrong wait down the street. If I need you, I'll call you on the cell phone."

Reavie gravely handed Tim a 9mm Berretta pistol.

Tim knew that carrying this firearm was a breach of the

permission received from the British government and protested. "If I use this, you'll get in trouble."

The gunnery sergeant said, "Sir, if you *have* to use it, we're all in trouble anyway."

Tim nodded, checked the weapon to see if it had a round in the chamber, and stuck it in the waistband of his suit pants near the small of his back. Then he got out of the car and saluted the two marines as they moved off down Pall Mall.

Tim walked up to the massive oak doors and entered the club. He identified himself to the porter who sat at a desk immediately inside the entrance door and was told that Colonel Parker was waiting for him in the library upstairs. He was directed to the central hall; from there he was to go up to the balcony where someone would meet him. Tim proceeded from the porter's desk down a dark wood-paneled hallway to the center atrium. Not a person seemed to be in the building, and there was no sound at all. When he got to the marble center hall, he could see a wide stone staircase on the opposite side, leading to a large balcony. Suspended forty feet above the floor of the atrium was a huge stained-glass skylight. Tim looked around. The club seemed eerily deserted. He felt a bolt of his old combat anxiety, and his body reflexively tensed for ambush.

A figure stepped out from behind one of the columns ringing the second-story balcony. The man moved to the top of the staircase and stood there silently. Tim could see him clearly now—a fit but bulky man in a black suit, with a shaved head and a wicked scar on his cheek. *God,* he thought, *it's Allen Canby*. Tim had stared at that picture too many times since Sharkey had given it to him not to recognize the man. He froze.

"Judge Quinn, please come up," boomed the Cockney voice from the top of the stairs.

Tim hesitated. Damn, this could be a setup? Was he brought here to be killed?

He wouldn't know unless he went up the stairs. He climbed up the stairs.

As soon as he reached the top, the man with the shaved head eyed him up and down, as if measuring him for his casket. Then he silently motioned with his hand for Tim to follow him.

They walked around the balcony that overlooked the center hall, along a row of dark portraits of long-dead men, some in suits, some in uniform, some in royal robes. Tim purposely kept several paces behind the man and close to the wall. He unconsciously checked the gun he was carrying by patting it under his suit jacket. The brass railings on the balcony looked very low and Tim didn't want to be the victim of an "accidental fall" into the marble floor of the empty atrium.

They continued to a carpeted side hallway and, at the end, Tim's guide opened a tall mahogany door and held it for him.

Tim passed his guide and entered the large library. It smelled of mildewed books. Inside he stopped and looked around. It was a large, high-ceilinged room, littered with easy chairs, the walls lined by tall, full bookcases. Crystal chandeliers hung from the ceiling, and reading lights stood by each chair, only a few of them turned on.

The room was deserted except for a man sitting in one of two leather wing chairs next to a glass door that led out onto a stone balcony. The man put down his newspaper and stood up. Tim began to move toward him, and heard the door close behind him. He turned around to see that the man with the shaved head had left. A quick glance around the room reassured Tim that the two of them were alone.

The man waiting across the room was a few inches taller than

Tim, and stood ramrod erect, his shoulders back, his heavy jaw prominent, wearing a well-tailored pinstriped navy suit. His gray hair was clipped short in a military cut.

Tim extended his hand as he approached. "Thanks for meeting with me, Colonel Parker."

Parker's silent handshake was very strong. Tim reciprocated and added pressure to his grip. A test of strength between old soldiers, between a U.S. ranger and a British SAS man.

Suddenly, Parker's face broke into a wide smile. "You're a quality chap, Judge. And you obviously have some friends in my government."

"Yes, well, I am grateful to them and to you for voiding Mr. Draco's contract."

"Not at all. Sir Richard is a much bigger customer than Mr. Draco, and business is business."

Tim held Parker's gaze. "I just want to get something clear up front. Does my family have anything to worry about from your people? Has anything been set in motion?"

Parker seemed amused. "No, not now, most certainly not. There was a prelim recon done on you, merely tracking your movements, but that and the fulfillment of our contract has been terminated. You have nothing to worry about from our firm. I think Sir Richard told you that, as far as Mr. Draco is concerned, he'll continue to believe that his contract will be carried out on the second of August. So I will state the obvious: You had better neutralize Mr. Draco before then."

"Colonel, that brings us to why I need to see you. The United States Justice Department is about to arrest Draco for complicity in a judicial corruption case. A conviction on that case will most likely put Draco in prison. However, the U.S. Justice Department and I would very much like to put Mr. Draco away for a far longer time. But to do that, we need some hard evidence on him regarding the three murders we suspect he ordered, possibly through your firm."

Parker gave Tim an opaque look, sat back down in his chair, and gestured for Tim to sit next to him. He was silent for several moments, then sighed slightly. "Judge Quinn, I have had some discussions with my solicitors about what I can and cannot discuss with you and under what circumstances. I'm sure you noticed that you were not searched for a recording device before you came in here. That was not a mistake, as it was not necessary. Don't you agree that recording devices have become almost too sophisticated these days?" Parker paused.

Tim could see the question was not one that called for him to answer specifically, so he didn't say anything; he just nodded. He was observing Parker closely, trying to get a feel for where this was leading.

"Well, I do as well," Parker continued. "Sometimes they can be too sophisticated to detect easily, so I have come up with a simple solution to assure myself that my private conversations remain *private*." His face suddenly lightened. "Well now, we do have an excellent steam room in this club, and I suggest we adjourn there to continue this discussion about Draco, when we're both *au naturel*."

Tim grinned. "Colonel, I'm impressed with your creativity. You seem to be a very careful man, and I don't mind at all. Lead the way."

In the men's dressing room, Parker saw the Berreta as Tim undressed and smiled. "You are a most unusual judge."

Tim smiled back. "That's what my wife tells me."

The high-security, unrecordable steam room session lasted over thirty minutes. Parker filled Tim in on the connection between Ram Securities and Draco and answered almost all of Tim's questions. Tim was impressed with Parker's straight talk and affability.

They dressed and moved to the main bar upstairs, where they

swapped stories about their common military experiences. Both men were, at the core, just soldiers. They had attended their countries' military academies (West Point and Sandhurst), had served in elite units (Rangers and SAS), and had seen combat (Vietnam and, for Parker, trouble spots of England around the world—Sudan, Rhodesia, and Northern Ireland).

Tim had to remind himself that one major factor separated him from the colonel: Fitz Parker was a hired killer.

The men's business concluded, the conversation turned to their families and continued over cognac until Tim started feeling jet lag and said he had to go.

He used his cell phone to call his marine security detail, and soon the BMW pulled into the club driveway, right behind Parker's large Mercedes. In the driveway, Tim turned from the car door to say a final good-bye to Colonel Parker—and standing next to him was the man with the shaved head and the scar on his face.

Parker had a sly smirk. "My driver has recently been on a holiday to the States and just got back to London this morning," he said. Tim knew the man was Canby, the killer of Camellia Winston, even before Parker introduced him.

CHAPTER 25

"WHERE ARE YOU HIDING MY WIFE?" TIM ASKED.

It was the day after the meeting with Colonel Parker at the Greenham Club. Tim was talking to Tony Lombardi on an unsecure cell phone, sitting in the backseat of the armored embassy BMW, headed toward Heathrow. His plane was leaving in two hours for Washington.

Tim had called Lombardi at the National Reconnaissance Office to see if someone from his office could meet his plane to take him to the CIA safe house where Katy was staying.

"I'll meet the plane personally and bring you to Katy," Tony said.

Then he relayed a development at the NRO.

Tim was stunned.

"You got the okay on releasing the video! The whole thing?" Tim exclaimed.

"Yep, you can have the whole enchilada on VHS," Tony replied.

Tim felt incredible relief. "Jesus, that's great, Tony. I know you must have had to break your back to do it. But now we've got solid evidence on both D and W." Tim's mind raced—Draco and Winston were now practically walking indictments.

When Tim hung up from the phone call, he was smiling broadly. His mission to London, up to this point, had been both a success and a failure. He had succeeded in stopping the Draco hit contract with Ram Security, but he had failed to gain any solid evidence against Draco or Winston from Ram Security or the British government. The investigation here was still a dry hole—but in the U.S. they had struck oil.

At the Greenham Club, Colonel Parker had made it clear that Draco was guilty of murder, having ordered Ram Security to plan and oversee three killings—the murders of Judge Rogers and the druggie who killed him, and the hit-and-run of Camellia Winston—but Tim was denied any proof that could be used in court. Everything that Parker had revealed to Tim was pure hearsay, inadmissible in a court of law. It didn't matter that Parker and his firm possessed the direct evidence that Draco had hired Ram Security to kill these three people and that this evidence alone would be sufficient to convict Draco of conspiracy and murder.

Tim had been told that the British government would never let the Ram evidence be introduced in any court proceeding. Moreover, neither Colonel Parker nor any of the Ram operatives involved in the three murders could ever be extradited to the United States: The British government would go to the highest level to block it. The British government would never let any of Parker's people be subject to questioning by publicity-prone American defense attorneys hired by Draco to defend him in a murder trial. Tim knew well that MI6 would not jeopardize the people who did their dirty work.

So Parker had been ordered by Sir Richard to give Tim the full story, but provide no admissible evidence to Judge Quinn. If knowing what happened would help Quinn analyze evidence already in the possession of the Justice Department, then that would be fine. If the U.S. Justice Department needed any cooperation beyond that, they could forget it.

But now Tim could nail Draco and Winston without Ram—thanks to his own intelligence connections. When Tim's plane landed in Washington, Tony would meet him and give him strong, incriminating evidence against both Winston and Draco on the case-fixing scheme, bribery, and conspiracy to commit murder. Vicky would be happy she had what she needed for an indictment—but Tim could still be devastated.

The prosecution of Winston might well destroy his marriage. Winston once had threatened to expose Tim's adultery. Tim had bluffed his way out of that past threat, but now, if Winston were arrested, he or his attorney would most likely reveal this secret—that the main witness had committed adultery with the prosecutor. This was, to put it mildly, a major conflict of interest. An unscrupulous defense attorney could use such a sensational fact, either in the press or in court, to damage or destroy the prosecution's case.

Tim could feel his guts twist at the dilemma that now loomed before him. During the seven-plus hour flight to Washington, he replayed the various scenarios before him. The last thing he wanted to do was to hurt Katy. But the more he thought about it, he realized that hurting her was inevitable. All he could choose was how much he hurt her. But what a choice for someone he loved, someone who was fighting a terrible disease. Toward the end of the flight, he made his decision.

Tony Lombardi was waiting for him as he cleared U.S. Customs at Dulles. As they walked to Tony's sedan, Tim filled in him in on his adventure in London. Once they were in the car, Tony handed him a thick package.

"Here is your copy of what I was able to get declassified. The video is dynamite. I'll keep the original video with a chain of custody form in my safe until you tell me to release them to the Justice Department."

Tim opened the package and fingered the videocassette. "You do good work. Now I want my wife back. Where is she?"

"You'll be surprised," Tony said as he put the car in gear.

The big Ford Crown Vic exited the Dulles access road onto the Washington Beltway and then proceeded north to Bethesda, Maryland. Soon the car was approaching a military complex dominated by a tall central tower. As they pulled into a security checkpoint, Tim whistled. "No way. The CIA safe house is in the Bethesda Naval Hospital?"

"You got it. After that first house was compromised, we decided to get creative. Katy is in a distinguished visitor suite on the top floor with round-the-clock security from the Agency."

When she saw him, Katy ran down the hall to him like a young girl and threw her arms around him. Tim felt stabbed in his heart by love, relief, and guilt. His eyes welled up and he could feel Katy's tears on his neck. "God, baby, it's so good to hold you," he managed. "Everything went well in London. Like I said on the phone, we have nothing to fear." Those last words felt more hopeful than true.

Tony Lombardi gave Tim and Katy a ride home to Alexandria, with Katy chattering in nervous happiness the whole way home, even joking about the hospital food. Once they closed the door behind them, Tim opened a bottle of wine and Katy heated a microwave pizza. Dinner was simple, their conversation blessedly ordinary. But Tim had trouble eating. After dinner, he called Anne in New York and Paul in Chicago, telling them that the court security exercise was over and that both he and Katy were back at home. Then Tim took Katy into the den, where he told her about the events of his London trip, from his meeting with the head of MI6 to the naked session in the steam room of the Greenham Club.

"So Draco is responsible for three murders?" Katy was shocked to hear that a prominent D.C. lawyer they knew socially could have someone killed.

"Yes. It's amazing that he would go to such extremes to cover up the arrangement he had with Winston. But he did."

Then Tim told her the good news of the declassified intelligence evidence from Lombardi. "That's it!" Katy exclaimed. "The smoking gun! I'm so glad. This has been a nightmare and now it's over." She sighed and leaned back, bothered by the import of what she heard, but relieved.

Tim looked at her sadly. His hands were shaking. "Honey, I'm afraid it's not really over for us." Katy's eyes rose to meet his. "I have something to tell you. Something I should have told you long ago."

Tim began by laying out the problem in cooler, legal terms—that he had a conflict of interest that was sure to come out when Winston was indicted, and it was a conflict that he didn't want Katy to read about in the newspapers. He took a deep breath and wished with all his heart he didn't have to say what he was about to say.

"I had a sexual encounter with the prosecutor—six years ago, in New Orleans one night. I am sorry. I am so sorry."

Katy went white.

"You've heard me mention her. Vicky Hauser." Katy had known Tim had lived with Vicky in law school, but the two women had never met, and Katy had been ostentatiously uninterested in her. Now he told her about running into Vicky years later at the New Orleans convention, and how he had made a huge, one-time mistake with her. He did not excuse himself by saying he had been drinking heavily that night. He told her how he had put the night behind him, that it hadn't changed his love for her, but that he had told Winston about it, afraid that it would come out during the investigation of him for the judgeship. Later, once Winston stirred Tim's suspicions, he had no choice but to go to the one person who could bring Winston down, Justice Department Prosecutor Vicky Hauser. "But there is just one important fact here for us," Tim concluded. "I betrayed you."

Katy seemed to be in shock. She was pale and had no facial expression; her hands and head started to shake slightly but uncontrollably.

"I love you so much," Tim said, near tears. "I apologize from the bottom of my heart."

"Is she pretty?" Katy almost whispered.

They say people say very strange things in times of severe stress, but to Tim this wasn't so strange. It seemed to reflect the essence in the betrayal of a spouse who deeply loved her mate and felt her own attractiveness for him was fading, with age and illness. God, that realization ripped Tim. He loved her now more than ever. She was so wrong about the reason. He moved toward her. He wanted to comfort her. He wanted her to feel his love.

But now she was sobbing. When she sensed him moving closer, she said, "Don't come near me!"

Then she turned and ran upstairs to their bedroom. Tim let her be alone for a few minutes. He poured himself another glass of wine and sat alone in the den. Later he went to the door of the bedroom and softly knocked.

"Baby, please let me in. I need to hold you."

"Stay away. You've done enough!"

Tim tried the doorknob. It was locked. He went downstairs to the den and stared dully at the wall. After a long while, he fell asleep on the leather sofa. His dreams were wild and terrifying. The sun coming through the den window woke him very early. He went upstairs to check on Katy. The door to the bedroom was open. She was gone.

Tim sleepwalked into the kitchen to make coffee, and there he found it: A note from Katy. She said she was going to New York to spend some time with Anne. Jesus, what did he expect? That she would instantly forgive him? No, Katy was a proud woman, a woman whose whole life revolved around her husband. She loved and trusted him completely. That was why Tim's betrayal was such an earthquake for her. She had to escape somewhere. Tim was glad she had chosen to go to one of the children, because Katy needed to be with someone now, someone she trusted and who could help her make sense of what had happened.

Tim made bacon and eggs. He needed fuel; it was already a rough day and it would become even rougher. He needed to compartmentalize and focus on the next step of his plan. He understood that Katy needed time away from him. He would win Katy back, but not today.

Today he was to finish enacting the plan he had devised on the long plane ride from England. The first part of it had been the toughest—telling Katy about his adultery. It had to be done. He was sure that his infidelity would inevitably leak from any prosecution of Winston. He had withheld this secret from her for years; she had deserved to hear the truth from his lips, as tough as it had been to tell her and for her to hear.

The second part of his plan was to confront Winston with the NRO tape and convince him that the game was over. Using the shock of seeing the video with the strong incriminating evidence on it against him and Draco, Tim thought he had a chance to pressure Winston to cut a deal giving up Draco and obtaining evidence for the three murders. The killings were the only part of the criminal scheme where, so far, the prosecution lacked hard evidence. More than ever, he wanted to destroy Draco, the man who had ordered him and his family killed.

The third part of Tim's plan was the closing act that he would play in the investigation. And by far the easiest—Tim needed to turn over and explain to Vicky and Bill the NRO evidence he now possessed.

In the hauntingly empty bedroom, he dressed quickly and headed to the courthouse to face Chief Judge Winston. During the drive into D.C., Tim rehearsed how he would break Winston into turning on Draco. Basically, he would let the tape do the reasoning for him. Winston was a smart man. Once he saw the enhanced images of his fateful meeting with Draco, captured vividly on the video from the NRO spy satellite, Winston would realize that he was caught and had no way out. Then Tim, his former lawyer, would suggest that Winston cut a deal with the Justice Department to corral Draco and minimize his own prison exposure. It wouldn't take a Rhodes scholar to figure out that cooperation with Justice was the best option.

Soon Tim pulled into the underground parking lot of the U.S. Courthouse. He went directly to his chambers to check on his messages. One pink call slip jumped out at him—a call from the head of Ram Security, Col. Fitzhugh Parker. *Jesus, what does he want?* Immediately, he punched in the London cell phone of Parker. Parker answered on the second ring.

"Judge, Mister D just moved the contract date from August 2 to the last week in August," Parker told him. "I just wanted you to know you have more time. More importantly, Mister D apparently still trusts us to solve his problems."

"Thanks for the update, Fitz. I hope I won't need the time. I'm working to take him off the street shortly."

When he hung up, Tim nodded to himself. So Winston had apparently told Draco about Tim's idea to slow down the publishing date of the *Morenta* opinion until mid-August, and Draco had adjusted his timetable accordingly. As Tim expected, Draco needed the *Morenta* decision to be made final before Tim disappeared. The *Morenta* opinion was still keeping Tim alive. The moving of the date also showed him that the conspiracy was alive and working. Now it was time for Tim to put an end to the Winston-Draco alliance. It was almost a cliché that crooks usually turned on each other if given the right incentive. Hoping the cliché held true, Tim took the NRO tape and headed for Winston's chambers. It was make-or-break time.

What had made Winston do it, Tim wondered as he walked down the judges' corridor. Why had he betrayed the office? Most judges were frightened of making the smallest breach of law or ethics. Yet Harry Winston had committed treason regarding his judicial duties. His crime went to the core of the judicial process—instead of being impartial in his judgment, he was apparently selling his vote. Was it the arrogance that came with a brilliant mind and the best schools, or the basic drive of most criminals, greed? Either way, he was a crook.

The secretary motioned him into the chief's inner office. When he got into the room with Winston, Tim closed the door and kept his breathing as even as he could. Winston remained seated behind his big desk, watching Tim warily and smiling more out of habit than friendship. The friendship between them was gone, replaced by need: Winston needed Tim to make the *Morenta* opinion go his way.

"Good morning, Tim. What's on your mind?"

"Got time to see a little movie? You're one of the stars."

"What the hell do you mean?" Winston's phony smile twisted into a scowl.

Tim went to Winston's television. He put the NRO tape in the VCR and pressed play. Curiosity made Harry Winston rise from his chair and come over to the TV, which filled with silent images.

He stood transfixed by the show unraveling on the TV monitor.

The tape ran for over fifteen minutes. Neither Tim nor Harry spoke. Harry watched the TV and Tim watched Harry.

At the end of the tape, Winston returned to his desk and sat down heavily in his high-back leather chair. Tim went over to the VCR and removed the tape, sticking it in his suit pocket.

"Where did you get this?" Winston asked.

"Does it matter, Harry?"

"No, no, I guess it doesn't," came the flat, tired reply. Winston rubbed his face with both hands and shook his head. Tim was expecting Harry to put on his white-noise machine. But Harry didn't. He met Tim's eyes. "You're working with the Justice Department. You set me up on the *Morenta* case, asking for a payoff. Am I right?"

"Yes, Harry. You're right. This is a government spy-satellite video that will be turned over to Justice this afternoon. I delayed the delivery to Justice to give you a chance to give up Leo Draco. It will go better if you cooperate. As a friend, I wanted to give you an opportunity to get a deal."

Winston looked sadly at Tim. "*As a friend,*" he said. "A strange choice of words for you in this situation. So you want me to make a deal?"

"Harry, there is no other way out. I know you. You weren't in on the murders. Rogers, Camellia. That's not you. Give up Leo and it will go much better for you. They need your testimony on Leo and the murders."

Winston's eyes glazed over. He was deep in thought. Then he reached into his desk and to Tim's shock, pulled out a Glock 9mm pistol. Tim started toward him, but Winston cocked the gun, putting a round in the chamber. The metallic noise of chambering a round sounded very loud to Tim. All his senses were at maximum level.

"Harry, this is not a good idea," he said softly. "There are copies of this tape. This won't help your situation." He had survived Draco's hit, but now—

"Tim, you're wrong," Harry said, with what seemed an eerie serenity. "This is the answer. I am on top now and I will be there forever. I can't go to prison. I'm the chief judge." Winston smiled, cradling the gun. "Christ, just last week, I entertained Lord Morton, the chief justice of England in my home. No, no, Harry Winston will not be disgraced. He will never, never go to prison."

Tim realized that Winston was going to kill himself. Tim slowly approached the desk, inching closer to Harry, and said, "Now, there's no need for this. I'll talk to Justice and get them to give you a good deal. There will be no prison for you."

"You West Pointers never were good liars. Of course there will be prison," Harry replied, waving the gun at Tim. "Stay away or I'll shoot you first."

Tim stopped moving forward and put his hands out to his side, palms outward. "Come on, Harry. Don't do this!"

"Get out of here, Tim! I want to be alone!" Winston screamed.

The waving gun and the sheer velocity of Winston's cry made Tim back out of the room and shut the door.

Winston's secretary looked fearfully at Tim. "Call the marshal!" Tim ordered. Then he ran across the hallway and into the darkened, vacant courtroom. He fumbled in the dark on the bench for the "panic button"—the security device in every federal courtroom, a silent alarm that alerts a U.S. marshal SWAT team that there is a dangerous threat in the courtroom. Maybe the police response team could talk Winston out of taking his own life. His fingers found the button. He pressed it. He heard a shot.

Tim dashed back into Harry's office. The chief judge was slouched in his desk chair, below a spray of red blood on the wall. He had put the gun in his mouth and shot himself in his brilliant legal brain.

. . .

That afternoon, still shaken from the day's double blows—Katy's departure, Winston's suicide—Tim sat in Vicky's office as she and Bill Sharkey listened intently to his narration of the events that led to the suicide of Chief Judge Winston that morning. It helped calm him to tell them sequentially of his trip to England, the denial of evidence by British Intelligence, then this receipt of NRO evidence from Tony Lombardi and the last event, Winston's taking of his own life.

Winston's death had solved the last remaining problem for Tim. Now there was no need to tell anyone about Winston's secret connection with the White House. Telling Vicky would lead to one of those political investigations that went nowhere anyway. Getting any incriminating evidence on a sitting president with Winston dead would be next to impossible and could lead to an indictment of Tim for keeping silent about it. Only the side players suffered in Watergate, Iran-Contra, and Whitewater—the presidents all walked. Let that "arrangement" be buried with the chief judge as well, thought Tim.

"I still can't believe he killed himself," Vicky was saying. "The Hirschorn meeting produced nothing incriminating. Neither did our tape of the meeting."

Tim ended his reflections on Winston's death. Then he responded to Vicky with a smile. "You don't have a tape *anything* like this one."

He went over to the combination TV and VCR on the side table and inserted the tape that had killed a man.

The video started with an overhead view of the Mall in Washington, D.C. Slowly the image zoomed in on the Hirschorn Sculpture Garden.

"Okay," Tim began, "this is an airborne videotape of activity on the Mall in the vicinity of the Hirschorn Museum, taken from a *satellite.*" He reached for the remote. "It was a little after one in the afternoon on the third of July when the bird arrived on station over Washington. I'll fast-forward until a little after two P.M. That's when the action starts to get interesting."

Vicky shook her head slightly. "Judge, a satellite . . . and how were you able to get this surveillance going at two o'clock, four hours earlier than we anticipated?"

"Pure luck, Vicky. The satellite bird was in an orbit over China when we were able to get permission to move its orbit to cover the meeting in Washington. It arrived on a station over D.C. at about one P.M. and was going to be out of range at about seven that night. My intelligence friends did get caught a little flat-footed by the early meeting, because we also had planned to have audio coverage of the meet from a Sparrow Hawk acoustical drone flown out of Davidson Airfield at Fort Belvoir, Virginia. When the meeting started so early, although we were okay with the video from the satellite, we couldn't get the audio drone launched in time. But at least we have pictures, and it turns out that pictures were all we needed. Damned clever of Winston and Draco to pass notes."

"A drone?" Bill asked. "What would that do?"

"Basically, operating by remote control from four thousand feet, a drone is an unmanned twelve-foot airplane that can collect all sounds coming from an area two hundred yards square. Digital computers can sift out and enhance individual voices, so you get a reasonably clear audio of all conversations in that area. But we missed that opportunity—sorry, Bill. Let's watch the video."

The tape continued rolling, and Bill began shaking his head as he stared intently at the TV screen. "I'm completely amazed. That's got to be Winston sitting against the wall on the bench, and here comes Draco. Yeah, here is where the bodyguards shoo the tourists out of the lower level of the garden, then Draco sits down and pulls out a pad of paper. And you can actually . . . *Wow.*"

"This is really something, isn't it?" Tim said. "Keep watching. There's a further zoom."

Bill's eyebrows arched in surprise. "Jesus H. Christ, you zoomed in to the point where you can actually read the writing! Look at what Draco just wrote on the pad!"

On the screen they could clearly read the words: "NO TALKING—WE WILL USE THIS PAD."

I don't believe this!" Vicky said, amazed.

"Now watch what they write." Tim adjusted the VCR to slow down the speed.

The room was silent for a few minutes as the tape continued. After the pad had been passed between Draco and Winston a few times, Bill Sharkey started making furious notes, but Vicky just stared at the TV screen with her mouth slightly open. "Look," Tim said, "you can actually see the words, like right here. I'm going to freeze this frame." Tim punched a button on the remote and the video stopped. "Look at that. Think that sentence will play well with a grand jury?"

It was like reading the tag line on a commercial: "QUINN SAID HE WANTS $200,000 TO CHANGE HIS VOTE BACK TO FREE MORENTA—CAN WE GIVE HIM $200,000 WITH NO TRACE BACK TO US?"

"Let me roll it forward a few more frames here, to get the answer to that question."

The video read, "YES, WE CAN PAY HIM $200,000—I'LL HAVE TO THINK ABOUT HOW WE WILL GET IT TO HIM."

"How's that?" Tim asked. "Evidence of conspiracy, bribery of a federal official, and obstruction of justice, all in one neat package."

"Tim, this is just fantastic!" Vicky cried.

"I know. But there's more. Look what was just written."

It was the final, fatal blow: "I'LL HAVE QUINN KILLED BY LONDON AS SOON AS MORENTA OPINION IS IN."

"That's conspiracy to murder a United States judge, 18 USC section 115, twenty years imprisonment on that count alone for Draco," Tim said, with relish. "Also by using Ram Security, that makes it solicitation to commit a crime of violence against a federal official—twenty more years under 18 USC section 373. . . . Wait. Look here! Winston tries to stop him."

"NO MORE KILLING," read the screen.

"Winston tried to save my life," Tim said. He felt an odd bolt of gratitude to this man who had so corrupted the system and who had been, in part, responsible for three deaths.

"Your Honor, the tape is great!" Bill said. "But we just see the tops of their heads. We know who they are because we were at the Hirschorn, but how can we identify them in the tape?"

"Just wait, that's coming up. Remember the point in the meeting when a kid on the Mall fired a sky rocket and they both looked up?"

"Yeah, sure."

"Well, that wasn't a kid. It was a member of a team from the National Reconnaissance Office. Here it comes, watch—Draco and Winston looking up into the camera, plain as day! No doubt about who was passing the notes, is there?" There was Draco on the left and Chief Judge Winston on the right, big as life.

Vicky was grinning by the time the tape ended. "Okay, we've got incriminating statements on paying a bribe to a federal judge. Tim, you and Bill can testify about the collection of the bribe itself in Antigua. We have statements that will put Draco away for obstruction of justice in fixing the *Morenta* case. Also we have Draco admitting to put a murder contract on Judge Quinn. Great evidence on all these charges. Now tell me exactly how you got this tape."

Tim took a deep breath. "The videotape came from a film strip recorded by a National Reconnaissance Office satellite, four hundred miles above Washington, D.C. I told you I had some friends from my days in the intelligence community. Well, when I explained to Tony Lombardi, the general counsel at the NRO, the gravity of this investigation, he got permission to divert one of their satellite assets to give us surveillance coverage of the Mall during the day of the meeting. Remember when I couldn't be reached that day? Well, I was at an NRO ground station near Camp David, watching the whole meeting between Winston and Draco live on a TV monitor."

"Camp David? Is the NRO a part of the presidential compound?"

"No, but they use Camp David as cover for their ground station next to it. A hilltop full of antennas and satellite dishes doesn't look out of place next to a presidential compound. There's an old saying that the best place to hide a pile of sand is on a beach."

"I would have lost a lot less sleep if I knew you were doing this," Vicky said, with a hint of prosecutorial reprimand.

"I'm sorry I couldn't tell you guys about this sooner, but declassification of NRO surveillance film takes a long time. It's also a very sensitive process. I wasn't really sure we could actually get this whole operation declassified until yesterday."

"It's the Mall and the Hirschorn Garden," Vicky said. "Why would they be classified in the first place?"

"Anything taken from above that reveals the operations and capabilities of the NRO's satellites is automatically classified. But since this case was about high-level judicial corruption, I got them to make an exception. And Bill, don't worry about using these in a criminal prosecution. The chain of custody for the tape has been properly preserved, and there will be no problem on the admissibility of this evidence. An official from the NRO will verify the evidence."

Bill smiled and shook his head. "Well, I was sure the case was in the toilet. Winston and Draco were winning every round. But you are like the Lone Ranger who comes to save the day."

"Thanks, Bill." Tim grinned. "But it's the NRO that should get the credit."

"Amazing that a spy satellite could be that precise," Vicky said. "It's one thing to be able to find an enemy's nuclear weapons' facility from space—but to be able to read handwriting . . ." Vicky nodded in professional admiration.

Knowing that Vicky would have to explain the evidence before a grand jury, Tim quickly briefed her and Bill on the NRO, which operated all U.S. overhead surveillance from space. Up until recently, even the existence of the NRO had been a dark secret; nobody in the intelligence community was even allowed to say the initials, NRO, without breaking the National Security Act. The existence of the NRO had been highly classified since the agency was founded in 1959, following the Russians' success with their Sputnik. The NRO remained in the deep black world until 1992, when it was finally declassified. Although the NRO still performed highly classified operations for the intelligence community, the organization was out in the open now. It was even listed in the Virginia phone book and has its own Web site.

"Bill, we've been very lucky," Vicky said. "Winston has closed the file on himself, but with this video we can nail Draco, at the very minimum, on conspiracy to murder a federal official, bribery, and obstruction of justice felony counts. The murders are more problematic. We just don't have the evidence to convict Draco. And Winston had nothing to do with it?" Vicky asked.

"That's right. According to Ram Security, Draco had directly ordered and paid for all the murders. But we can't use in court anything I learned from Colonel Parker in the steam room."

"That must have been some meeting," Vicky blurted out. "I only wish I could have been in the steam room with you." As soon as she said it, she blushed.

Tim joked. "It was a real show-and-tell session. He hid nothing from me."

Vicky and Bill laughed. Then she said, "The video alone gives us tremendous visual evidence. It will be very convincing before a jury if Draco doesn't plea bargain. I guess Bill and I will get started with the memorandum of prosecution and drawing up the charges."

Tim realized that he was just a prosecution witness now. "Okay, this is where I should leave," he said. "I don't want to be caught up in the Justice Department's decision on prosecuting Draco, so I'd better not get involved any further. That would complicate your case unnecessarily. But before I leave, I wonder if I could talk to you alone, Ms. Hauser?"

Bill Sharkey stood up. "I'd better put a shadow surveillance team on Draco. So we know where to find him once we get the arrest warrant."

He left. Alone in the room, Tim pressed his lips tight together and rubbed his eyes with his fingers, speaking without looking at Vicky. "There's a possible landmine in prosecuting Draco."

Vicky frowned. "What kind of landmine?"

"Draco *may* be aware of the conflict of interest I have as the main prosecution witness." Tim continued, looking intently at Vicky. "Winston knew I had an affair with you. He knew that we slept together in New Orleans and he *may* have told Draco."

Vicky inhaled sharply. "Oh, God! If Draco knows that, his defense lawyer will have a field day at trial. What a conflict of interest!"

"Yeah. The chief government witness literally in bed with the prosecution."

Vicky flinched at the words. "How did Winston find out?"

"I made a mistake," Tim said. "I confided it to him during a strategy session before my Senate confirmation hearing. He was acting as my mentor, giving me advice on potential problems that could come up." He met her eyes at last. "I'm so sorry, Vicky. I know this may hurt the case if it goes to trial. And I know it hurts you—again."

"A lot more than the case is at risk here," Vicky said, with a strange edge in her voice.

"What else is at risk?" Tim demanded.

Then she told him her secret—the New Orleans incident *had* been reported by someone during the FBI background check for Tim's judgeship. That night, someone at the ABA Convention obviously had seen them dancing intimately or going to her room—some incident or moment that suggested the two of them were having an affair—and ultimately reported it to the FBI during its required check of a potential judge's background. Two FBI agents had interviewed her about it. She lied to them, denying that there was an affair. Then again right before his confirmation hearing, an aggressive Senate investigator from the Judiciary Committee called her up with the same questions on New Orleans. She lied to him also. Her face was pale and grave as she told him what had happened.

Tim sat back, absorbing the news. Vicky Hauser had committed *perjury* so he could get the judgeship. Now there was a risk not only that Vicky's case would be hurt, but also that her job and possibly her freedom was at stake if this came out. Tim felt the awful predicament grip him like a vise and squeeze air out of his chest. He worked to breathe through it, searching for a solution. "Vicky, there is a big chance that Winston never told Draco about the conflict. Remember, Draco and Winston *never* expected to be caught. Besides, even if Draco was told, that will only become a card to play at trial where my credibility is at stake on the witness stand. This case will never go to trial. Draco will take a plea. Christ, even Winston saw the evidence was unshakable. That's why he committed suicide."

"Maybe you're right, Tim," Vicky said, her voice uncertain. "The evidence is strong. And since this case is about corruption at a federal court, everybody—from the attorney general and the chief justice of the Supreme Court on down—will want a swift resolution with a guilty plea."

"Everything is going to be all right, Vicky," Tim said urgently. "Draco will plead guilty. He's not stupid."

"Let's hope you're right." Vicky stood up, looking a little frightened.

Tim wanted to give her strength for the difficult job ahead of her. He reached out and impulsively hugged her. When they broke apart, the look in her eyes told him he had done just the right thing.

CHAPTER 26

THAT AFTERNOON, NEWS OF CHIEF JUDGE WINSTON'S DEATH swept through Washington like brushfire. Leaks from the courthouse confirmed that it was a suicide. Although no news story had linked Judge Quinn to the incident, Vicky knew it was only a matter of time before reports would mention that Tim Quinn was the last person to see Winston alive. This made the danger of flight by Draco a very real possibility. Accordingly, Vicky made sure that the prosecution memorandum she prepared, to authorize the arrest and prosecution of Draco, would be handled on an expedited basis. By five P.M., the attorney general of the United States had authorized the prosecution. By 5:30, Vicky was standing alongside Bill Sharkey in front of a U.S. magistrate judge at the Federal Courthouse seeking an arrest warrant, and concluding her petition: "Therefore, Your Honor, the United States, in light of the considerable wealth and access of Mr. Leo Draco to an oceangoing yacht and to charter aircraft, request that an immediate arrest warrant be issued."

The judge didn't hesitate. "Your papers seem to be in order, Ms. Hauser. Therefore the arrest warrant is hereby issued. All papers are sealed until further order of this court."

Outside the courtroom, Sharkey made a call on his cell phone as Vicky listened. Within minutes, Leo Draco was arrested by the FBI at his home—he had been off all day and had just gotten back from the golf course. According to the arresting officers, he seemed absolutely stunned, which pleased Vicky: On the golf course all day with clients, amazingly he had not heard that his friend Harry Winston was dead by his own hand. Instead of being transported to the federal lockup for processing, Draco was taken to the conference room of the attorney general at the Department of Justice on Constitution Avenue. From the start, this case was going to get special treatment.

"What the hell is going on? I want an attorney," growled Draco when Vicky and Sharkey entered the conference room.

Vicky and Bill Sharkey let him call a lawyer. Leaving Draco guarded by two FBI agents, Vicky went into the nearby office of Attorney General Taggert. The attorney general had asked for her to see him before she questioned Draco. As she was waiting to see the AG, she asked Sharkey to call Judge Quinn and fill him in on developments. Sharkey went outside in the marble corridor to use his cell phone.

Soon she was called in to the attorney general's private office. There were only two people in the room—the AG and a man she immediately recognized.

"Mr. Attorney General, Draco has lawyered up. He called Bruce Gallios. Gallios will be here shortly." Vickey was nervous as she reported the status.

"Gallios is sharp. Good choice. Draco should have counsel now. Ms. Hauser, I want you to meet Bill Monroe, the president's counsel.

The White House is very interested in this case. Now please fill in Mr. Monroe on the strength of the case."

Vicky, a little shaken by the White House involvement, quickly went through the case from the initial suspicions of Judge Quinn through the arrest of Draco.

Most of the questions from the White House counsel centered on the scope of the case-fixing scheme.

"How widespread was this case-fixing? . . . Were there any other cases involved besides these seven cases of Draco? . . . Does Judge Quinn think Winston was fixing any cases for anybody else beside Draco? . . ."

Monroe's pointed questions made Vicky think perhaps the White House had information about other instances of case-fixing on the court.

No, impossible! Vicky thought. This was just a Winston-Draco operation. There was no other lead she missed. She had the entire case of corruption on the U.S. Court of Appeals cooling his heels waiting for his lawyer.

Once the briefing of the White House counsel finished, the attorney general got right to the point.

"Ms. Hauser, the corruption of the U.S. Court of Appeals has put an unwelcome spotlight on the fairness of the federal judiciary. Mr. Monroe and I want you to conclude this matter as soon as possible. Get a plea agreement from Mr. Draco now. Do whatever it takes."

Meanwhile, Judge Quinn was in his kitchen, staring at the unfinished Domino's pizza and fingering the long neck of his Corona. Christ! The news from Sharkey shocked him. Things were moving very fast. Draco's in the fucking conference room of the attorney general! How much higher profile can this case get? What was going to be revealed by Draco now that he is cornered? Trading information was a common tool to get a good deal with the prosecutors.

Tim had deep concerns that two facts may be revealed as Draco fought hard in a plea-bargain negotiation. Both could provide some advantage for Draco.

And both would definitely hurt Tim . . . and Vicky.

If Draco revealed Tim's adultery with Vicky—that would be a conflict of interest for the prosecutor and a short-term advantage for Draco, since Vicky would have to be replaced by another prosecutor. However it would be a disaster for Tim and Vicky. Tim's marriage would suffer a major embarrassment, but, more importantly, it could lead to a perjury charge for Vicky who had lied about her affair with Tim during the investigation for Tim's judgeship.

The second secret was that Tim had prior knowledge about Chief Judge Winston's fixing of three cases for the president . . . and Tim kept silent about it. Tim's keeping quiet about Winston's White House case-fixing made Tim a criminal—an accessory after the fact. Winston, by confessing to Tim, cleverly made him a part of the crime. If Draco knew about this, he could possibly put pressure on the Justice Department and the White House to get a more favorable plea bargain because this information would damage the prosecution's key witness—Tim.

So obviously there were two big questions in Tim's mind: Did Winston tell Draco about these secrets? . . . and would Draco tell the Justice Department as he fought for a deal?

Tim was certain that the events unfolding at Justice would reveal the answers to these questions, but all he could do was to wait. Things seemed out of control to Tim.

As she waited for Draco's attorney to come to the Justice Department, Vicky thought about the stakes with regard to Draco's possible knowledge of the adultery—a big conflict of interest since Tim was the key witness against Draco. Tim had told her that Winston knew about the adultery. She wondered if Winston had told Draco. If he had, Draco was sure to use it in the plea negotiation that was about to happen.

Things got moving when Draco's attorney, Bruce Gallios, a flamboyant and highly qualified defense attorney, arrived at Justice. Draco was given a short time to confer with him and then Vicky and Sharkey entered the wood-paneled conference room. Vicky and Sharkey sat across the conference table from Draco and his attorney.

"Mr. Draco and Mr. Gallios, I'm Victoria Hauser, chief of the Public Integrity Section, and this is Special Agent Sharkey of the FBI. We have some information that perhaps you may need to assess the situation. After you digest the information, you may want to open plea negotiations. If so, tonight would be the time. Tomorrow I plan to present this evidence I am about to show you to the grand jury."

Draco, reinforced by the arrival of his attorney, now reasserted his predictable arrogance. "What possible evidence could you have? These charges are outrageous. I have instructed my attorney to charge you personally with false arrest. I am a former deputy solicitor general and a former president of the D.C. bar."

Besides his bluster and pompous attitude, Draco seemed to have no recognition or knowledge of Vicky, beyond her role as the lead Justice Department prosecutor. This was encouraging to Vicky and relieved her somewhat. Perhaps Winston hadn't told Draco about Tim and her? Still it was very early in the meeting. A good attorney would wait for all the cards to be on the table before he played a hole card.

Gallios wisely saw this as an unusual opportunity to view the government's case.

"Leo, why don't we listen to what Ms. Hauser has to say?"

Vicky continued, "Mr. Draco, we are aware of your standing in the bar. That is one of the reasons why you were not taken to the lockup and processed in normal fashion. Moreover, we are here in the AG's conference room because of your status." Vicky was starting to play to his ego. The stick would come soon enough. The strong evidence would devastate him more if it was preceded by deference.

"Mr. Draco, no doubt you have heard that Chief Judge Winston took his own life this morning. He committed suicide right after he viewed a video that I will allow you to see shortly."

Then Vicky proceeded to tell him in detail the charges and the evidence he was facing. Hearing her relate the specifics and particulars of the charges, naming times, places, and the undercover work done by Judge Quinn had a physical effect on Draco. His face turned as white as his hair. His eyes glazed over. Literally, Vicky's presentation took the fight out of the renowned appellate lawyer. Both Draco and Gallios remained silent, contesting nothing. Vicky pressed on.

"Mr. Draco, after I'm finished, you and your attorney can stay in this room and use the combo TV/VCR here to view the NRO videotape of your meeting with Chief Judge Winston in the Hirschorn Garden. It is very damaging as you shall see." She looked directly into the man's now glassy blue eyes and added, "You can also have access to a copy of the transcript of the intercepted telephone call you made to Ram Security Company in London setting up the murder contract on Judge Quinn."

Vicky was even able to use Winston's death to her advantage.

"One more thing—Judge Quinn was with the chief judge right before he committed suicide and Winston confessed to Quinn about your role in fixing cases. Now Judge Quinn has yet to furnish a written statement of the incriminating admissions that Winston made about you, but I think you have enough to tentatively assess the very strong case against you."

When she said that Winston had incriminated him in statements to Judge Quinn, Vicky was lying to put further pressure on Draco. Vicky inwardly winced at her false statement, but it was accepted practice for the police to lie to a criminal to get a confession. The attorney general had told Vicky to push hard to trigger a Draco plea bargain and she was doing it. Besides, her mentioning of a Quinn statement as key evidence would force an early disclosure of whether Draco was aware of the conflict of interest involving Tim Quinn and herself. It was better for the case to explode in her face now rather than later.

"This is the video you'll want to see and here is the transcript of the intercepted call to London. Just let the agent outside the door know when you want to talk again. Gentlemen, I hope we can come to an understanding tonight. I'll have sandwiches and soft drinks sent in shortly."

Then Vicky and Sharkey left to report back to the attorney general. When they got back to the AG's outer office, it was starting to fill up. Word of Winston's death and Draco's arrest was everywhere, and the United States attorney for Washington, D.C., the White House deputy counsel, and the head of the Administrative Office of the U.S. Courts were among various high-ranking Justice officials milling about the reception area of the attorney general. As soon as the AG's personal secretary saw her, Vicky was told to go into the inner office where she found the White House counsel and the attorney general sitting around a round conference table eating from a tray of sandwiches and fruit.

"Ms. Hauser, please sit down and have a bit to eat."

Vicky was too nervous to eat. Her career in Justice might possibly be destroyed that night if Draco emerged from his video viewing to declare that the lead prosecutor had a conflict of interest with the lead witness against him.

Monroe was very interested in how things were going. "Did Mr. Draco give you an idea that he would fight a plea at this time?"

"Mr. Monroe, it is too early to tell. Gallios had his client in the listen mode. Then I gave them the hard evidence. I figured I'd let the evidence do the convincing on cutting a deal now. I think we should give them some time to review the evidence and to make some decisions about a plea."

"Ms. Hauser, the White House is very interested to learn if this case-fixing was just confined to these few cases with Draco."

"Now, now, Bill. All that will be looked into by Ms. Hauser. She knows what she is doing. She is the one who handled the Judge Gibson bribery case a few years ago. I agree with her approach. Let's just see how Draco reacts to the evidence against him."

Then the AG turned to Vicky and said, "Cut a deal with Draco tonight. Don't try for a home run. Just get a deal we can call respectable and live with. And forget about evidence on the murders. The White House just checked again with the ambassador from England—*no* evidence will be coming from Ram Security . . . ever. That simplifies your dealings—the prosecutors from Georgia, Virginia, and the District of Columbia are not going to be players because murder as a state crime was their only entry into this card game."

"Yes, sir. I'll do my best."

Then Vicky excused herself to go to confer with Sharkey and plan strategy for further discussions with Draco and his attorney. Vicky had negotiated a number of plea bargains, but none had so much riding on it.

By eight P.M., Vicky was sure her "shock and awe" attempt at a plea bargain was doomed. But at a little after eight, Draco's attorney sent word that he wanted to talk.

When Vicky and Bill arrived, Gallios got right to the point.

"What's on the table?"

The negotiations then proceeded. By midnight, both sides had agreed on a deal and the formal papers were signed. Draco would plead guilty to seven felony counts of obstruction of justice, one count of bribery, and one count of conspiracy to murder a United States judge. In order to help restore public confidence in the federal court system, Draco's attorney agreed, after the plea was formally accepted in court, to issue a statement for public release, outlining the limited scope of the case-fixing scheme and identifying the seven already completed cases that were tainted by the scheme. In an obvious concession, Draco agreed to withdraw from the *General Morenta* case immediately. That case also was tainted and would be assigned to another court for a new appeal. He also agreed to resign from the bars of the District of Columbia, New York, and Massachusetts, the only three jurisdictions where he was qualified to practice law. Furthermore, Draco's plea agreement provided that he would pay a fine of $2.4 million. Vicky thought this low figure was probably a fraction of what Draco and Winston made on the scheme, but there was absolutely no proof in this area and Draco wisely was silent about this aspect.

Not surprisingly, the biggest hang-up in the negotiations was the jail time—Vicky and Draco's lawyer fought over the provision for a prison term. Vicky's hand in the negotiation, however, was weakened because the attorney general had given her orders to "cut a deal with Draco tonight." Vicky eventually agreed to the proposal that Draco would serve eight years, with no parole, in a federal prison farm—one of the facilities nicknamed "Club Fed." Vicky was disappointed in the length and site of his imprisonment. This was a huge concession to Draco—he was facing over seventy-five years of possible imprisonment under the federal sentencing guidelines. But in spite of the strength of the prosecution case, she had to accede to pressure from the AG and the White House to wrap up this case tonight.

All in all, Draco had gotten a very good deal. In spite of her disappointment on the terms of the plea, Vicky was secretly overjoyed that no mention had been made of the conflict of interest of the main prosecution witness, Judge Quinn. Justice had been done, she believed, and the secret was safe.

As soon as the plea-bargain meeting broke around one A.M, Vicky slipped away and made a short call to Tim at his home, waking him.

"I'm sorry to call so late, but I wanted to tell you it's over. Draco just signed a plea agreement. It's not great, but he'll get eight years, no parole." She took a breath and added the personal aspect for both of them. "No mention of the conflict came out."

"That's great, Vicky. Really great! Congratulations. You did a very good job on this case," Tim said.

"Did Draco mention any other cases that Winston had fixed . . . that is, besides the seven and the *Morenta* case?"

This question shocked Vicky, because it mirrored the strange concern of the White House counsel in the case. Vicky could tell the importance of the question in Tim's voice.

"No other cases came out in the negotiations. Were there other cases?"

"No. No. Just checking. Great work, Vick." Tim's relief was apparent by his tone.

"Well, I have a few things left to do. I just wanted you to know how things came out. Good night, Tim."

"Thanks for the call . . . and thanks for everything, Vicky. Good night."

Vicky was still confused. *Had she and Sharkey missed other cases?*

After Vicky's call, Tim laid awake thinking. Winston obviously never told Draco about his affair with Vicky. Katy's humiliation about the adultery had been private; perhaps now it would remain so. And more importantly, Vicky's lying to the FBI about the affair would now never come out.

Vicky's answer about whether Winston had fixed other cases was a huge, private relief to Tim. That revelation would have ruined Tim's career and possibly put him in jail. So Winston had kept Tim's knowledge about the "special favors" done for the president to himself and didn't tell Draco. *Thank you, Chief Judge, for that!*

Tim couldn't sleep. He was wired so he went downstairs and made a Jack Daniels on the rocks. Then he sat in the den, trying to get used to the idea that the investigation had finally ended—that Winston was dead and Draco captured. The case had changed his whole life in a big way. Katy had left him. When he had called Anne's apartment in New York tonight, Anne told him that Katy didn't want to speak to him, but Anne herself had talked to him. So had Paul who had flown out from Chicago. The children were pulling together to help their mom.

Tim told Anne and Paul, in general terms, why their mother had left him. Confessing his infidelity to his children was tough, but necessary. They deserved to know why their parents' marriage had suddenly ripped apart. They had listened, their responses cool, but they had not hung up on him. That was all he could hope for now, with his children and his wife—that they could still all communicate, and that he and Katy could talk their way through the trauma Tim had caused.

Why the hell had he ever wanted to be a judge? His life as a partner at Wellington & Stone had been perfect. He had been happy;

he didn't need the judgeship. Was it his pride or vanity that had led him to seek the prestigious position? Whatever his motive, the decision was in the past. He was a judge who had risked his life to protect the integrity of his court, and for now at least, he would remain a judge. But more important, he needed to win Katy back and to take care of her. She was his whole life. Now that he lost her, he realized this truth.

The next day there was a closed-door session where Draco pled guilty in the Federal Courthouse in D.C. Judge Murphy was the U.S. District Court judge assigned to Draco's criminal case. Vicky Hauser represented the government. Draco's attorney was Bruce Gallios. The judge's responsibility was to take Draco's plea and, normally at a later date, enter a sentence according to the plea-bargain agreement. However, today was far from normal. The judge would sentence Draco immediately after the guilty plea was entered. The White House wanted this case closed ASAP.

"Mr. Draco, under the terms of the agreement, do you realize that you may be sentenced up to eight years in prison?" said Judge Murphy in a question that was a necessary ingredient of any plea hearing.

"Yes, Your Honor. I understand," replied Leo Draco, a false frown of unhappiness and remorse on his face.

Inside Draco was celebrating his own cleverness. *I'll never serve over two years, Your fucking Honor!*

Last night after the shock of Harry's death and the shame of his arrest had worn off, Draco's legendary brilliance took control. Yes, that damn NRO satellite and the incriminating telephone call to Ram Security had boxed him in. He couldn't win at trial. The evidence was too strong and had the optics that would have guaranteed that any jury would have convicted him. Draco had no choice, but to plea guilty and to cut the best deal possible.

During the negotiations, it was all Leo Draco could do to restrain himself from yelling across the table at that prosecutor. *You bitch, you've been fucking Judge Quinn, your star witness! How dare you prosecute me!* But Leo wisely kept his tongue in check. Exposing the conflict of interest would only have triggered a temporary delay and gotten another prosecutor assigned. Moreover, when Draco was being led into Attorney General Taggert's conference room last night, he saw Bill Monroe, the White House counsel hurrying into Taggert's office. The White House was understandably exercising damage control in person. Yes, the time to get a sweet deal was last night with Monroe prodding Taggert to close the deal and end this politically sensitive case. Of course, Draco knew about Quinn's conflict of interest, but exposing it would only have delayed the inevitable—a guilty plea.

Harry Winston always had shared *everything* with Leo Draco, including the Quinn affair and the three special cases Harry had fixed using his "majority" for the president.

Harry, in a stroke of luck and foresight, had managed to tape a phone call from Bill Monroe. The phone call where White House Counsel Monroe—on behalf of the president of the United States—had asked Harry to insure that the Iranian terrorist came out according to the president's wishes. And Harry delivered a majority for the president on that case.

Draco, now in the midst of his troubles, was comforted by the fact that he had White House Counsel Monroe on tape asking that Harry fix a case. Priceless! The tape was in one of the joint safety deposit boxes Harry and Draco shared in Antigua.

That tape was Leo's future ticket out of prison in less than two years—the time left on the president's second term.

Draco was planning to get a "Clinton"—a last-minute pardon by the departing president. The president was sure to give the pardon because of the tape. About three months before the end of the president's second term, Draco would hire a politically savvy attorney who would approach the White House counsel, Bill Monroe—and the pardon was as good as done.

Yes, Draco had no problem in the guilty-plea hearing today. Within two years, he would be out of Club Fed and working hard to spend the $28 million Harry and he had socked away in the banks of Antigua. Draco could easily do two years at Club Fed. The payoff was waiting for him—two years at fourteen million dollars a year! Not bad work if you can get it.

CHAPTER 27

THE COURTHOUSE WAS A WILD PLACE WHEN TIM ARRIVED the next morning, with the surrounding streets overrun with media vehicles. Winston's suicide paired with Draco's guilty plea that day was big news. Draco's sentencing took place immediately after the plea, a break in the usual practice. The suicide of Winston had also caused a strange twist of power at the Court of Appeals. With an irony sometimes imbedded in the operation of the U.S. government and its unthinking laws, in the event of a vacancy, the position of chief judge on the U.S. Court of Appeals for the D.C. Circuit was, by law, to be filled by the next most senior judge. That was Carl Franklin, who was probably also the most incompetent. Therefore, the moment Winston died, Carl Franklin became the chief judge.

With corruption in the U.S. Court of Appeals as the day's leading story, Franklin was under pressure to repair his court. That morning, Tim heard that Franklin was called up to the Supreme Court for a two-hour meeting with the chief justice. That afternoon, Tim and all the judges of the U.S. Court of Appeals for the D.C. Circuit were summoned to a five P.M. meeting with the new chief judge.

When Tim walked into the judges' conference room a little after five, the other judges all stared at him. Their oral greetings were frosty. Franklin, his face quivering with importance and probably fear, called the meeting to order and announced that there were three items of business. First, all judges were asked to sign an order vacating all seven of the cases that were tainted by the Draco-Winston scheme. Franklin told the judges that the chief justice had strongly suggested this action as one of the steps to help restore public confidence in the federal court system. The order was passed around and signed by all judges with no dissents. When Franklin was handed the signed order, he announced, "I will request in writing that the chief justice assign judges from other courts of appeals to hear these seven cases."

He went on to announce that Mr. Nichols, the clerk of court, had been fired by the chief justice, acting in his capacity as the supervising justice for the D.C. Circuit. Tim thought that this was an unusual action and wondered why Franklin hadn't fired Nichols himself. Then he remembered that Nichols was a good friend of Winston's, and Franklin was devoted to Winston.

The third item was a proposal from Franklin that there be a formal chief judge installation ceremony that Friday, two days hence. Franklin said that such an event was needed to help reinforce the standing of the court after much of its luster had been besmirched by the Draco scandal. "I think it will be a day of healing for the court and the D.C. bar," he said. Later, he would make a "State of the Court" address to the bar in an attempt to put the scandal in the past.

No one voiced any opposition to this proposed event, but Tim thought that this was a bad idea. He raised his hand and spoke out. "Chief Judge, I've been around D.C. for a while and I believe that